UNBREAKABLE STORM

UNBREAKABLE STORM

THE DARKEST STORM - BOOK 2

PATRICK DUGAN

Charlotte, NC

FALSTAFF
BOOKS
WWW.FALSTAFFBOOKS.COM

To my Booger Bear (Emerson) Miss you every day RIP 2/2006 – 8/2017

1

I t'd been a week since Powell murdered Wendi, and the Reclaimers were showing the episode again since "technical difficulties" ended the broadcast the previous week. They made a huge deal of the rebroadcast, which landed on the anniversary of the Dark Brigade attacks, or the Darkest Storm, as most people called it. I would give anything in the world to not see this again, and the worst part is that it was all my fault.

It also was my seventeenth birthday.

We had returned to Castle, the safe house we'd inhabited since we couldn't return to Redemption. Instead of cake and balloons, we watched Wendi's death in Hi-Def. Mom attempted to turn off the TV multiple times. Dad sat in silence next to me, a scowl entrenched on his face. Marcel stood in the doorway, his face ashen with grief. Abby sprawled on the recliner; her hair kept her face hidden. No one spoke as the fight progressed.

I saw parts of the fight I hadn't witnessed in the heat of battle. Abby snarled as she saw herself get knocked down and beaten by the troops we fought. I was glad to see her anger hadn't translated into her growing as her Gift kicked in. Jon dropped three of them before a guard's baton struck him in the head; Powell knocked Dad to the ground as I attacked.

The glee showing on Powell's face as he unloaded into me changed to shock when I blew him across the arena.

My stomach tightened, the bile strong in the back of my throat. I closed my eyes, even though I felt it was disrespectful to Wendi's memory to not watch her sacrifice her life to save my mom. I heard Mom's gentle sobs as they crashed against the mental walls I'd built against crying. I forced my eyes open to watch.

When I walked away from Powell's limp form, the camera focus shifted to the gun as he raised it. The shot flew past me and headed toward Mom as she hung by her arms. A blur entered the screen as Wendi sped to get Mom out of danger. Blood plumed from her as the slug struck her in the side of the head; she'd never seen the bullet coming for her. Her beautiful blond hair, now dark red with blood, flowed away from her as she spun out of control. Mom cried openly as she watched Wendi's lifeless form tumble. The numbness prevented the pain from getting to me. It bounced off my detachment like a rubber ball hitting a steel shield. I stared at the scene, aware of my mom clutching my hand and Dad putting his arm around my shoulders in a show of support. We were comrades now. Blood had been spilled by all to win our freedom at the cost of Wendi's life, but emotions would have to wait.

The camera moved to a wide view of the arena. The film betrayed what I knew to be true. On TV, Powell regained his feet, retrieved his rifle and proceeded to kill my mother, father, Abby, and Jon. For some reason, I stood frozen in the middle of the floor, immobile as my enemy executed my friends and family. When Powell finished, the camera zoomed in as he turned toward me, rage contorting his face. "Executioner, you will pay for your crimes with your life!"

I cringed inside at the stupid name with which the Reclaimers had dubbed me. Given everything that had happened, a stupid nickname seemed the lamest thing to get upset over, but it ate away at me. Saturday Night Showdown was all a game to them, and the Gifted paid the price for losing. I felt my mental shield slip as the emotions hit me.

On screen, Powell pulled a long-bladed dagger with his uninjured hand, the remains of his left arm swung like a broken clock pendulum. "Prepare to die!" he screamed, spittle flying from his mouth.

"Bring it on!" The voice didn't belong to me, being much higher than mine; the scene flickered slightly.

Marcel snickered, rubbing the sparse stubble which acted as his goatee. Given his lack of showering lately, he smelled more like a goat. "Amateurs. They didn't align the edges of your face correctly before they overlaid the actor. Not to mention the guy is at least thirty pounds heavier than you."

"And probably twice as hot," Abby chipped in.

I shot them a quick smirk. Marcel was a constant in my life; his humor always pulled me out of bad spots. Abby melded with us as if she'd always been here. None of us had been at Castle long. Dresden had been compromised when Jon turned rogue, so now we lived in Castle, an old Infinity Guards hideout in the Appalachian Mountains west of Charlotte, North Carolina.

My 'twin' ran into battle with Powell. They traded blows. Powell's ruined arm erupted as lightning struck it. He rained down blow after blow which staggered "me." In reality, it would have energized me. I would have blown him to smithereens with all the power I'd built up. I almost laughed.

Knocked to the ground, Powell raised his arm in triumph. "This is for all of you that lost family to these abominations!" he roared in time with the crowd as they surged to their feet, whipped to a frenzy by the bloodshed.

"I'll see you in Hell, Executioner!" he screamed. He grabbed me by the hair and used the knife to cut my head off. The blood sprayed every-where, bathing him in a robe of gore.

"Oh my God, they really killed him," Marcel said, before running for the bathroom, his hands holding the vomit as it spewed from his mouth. Mom jumped up to help him; his heaving and crying echoed through the complex's living area.

"Probably some criminal," Abby said, her voice thick and low. She perched on the edge of her seat like a predator about to strike. Ever since the fight, she'd been full of pent-up aggression. Dad assured us it would pass; it was her reaction both to losing Wendi's death and Jon's leaving the group. He said some people withdrew into themselves after their first fight. Abby descended into a murderous rage.

On the TV, Powell threw my dismembered head, causing it to skid and bounce to land face first in front of the camera. Desmond Roberts' voice overlaid the screaming crowds.

3

"Folks, I know you waited an extra week, but what a fight. This will go down as one of the greatest fights, even greater than the Dominion Gauntlet. Five Discordants dead along with a known sympathizer."

Imagine that; my mom supported her husband and son. Who would have guessed? The more I watched, the angrier I got. The scene switched to a slow motion of Wendi's death. I couldn't take it anymore. The energy sprang to life with my anger, flowing like magma through my bloodstream. The surge increased tenfold as I concentrated it into a tight sphere in the center of my chest. The heat felt as if it would scorch me where I stood, which would be a proper punishment for killing Wendi, but no such luck. As I prepared to release the built-up energy into the TV, it snapped off. Dad held the remote up like some religious artifact in an attempt to calm me.

"Tommy, take it downstairs to the gym, but stay out of the combat rooms," he said in his quiet but commanding way. Dad was Cyclone Ranger, one of the world's strongest, and most hated, Gifted. Clad in a ratty NYU sweatshirt and a pair of oversized sweatpants, he didn't look the part. "I'm going to check to see how Marcel is doing." The man could give stealth lessons to cats with how quietly he moved.

I headed to the gym to release the pent-up energy, but Abby blocked my way. She snarled as she said, "I'll go with you, I need to hit someone."

She stormed away from me, red and black hair splaying out behind her like a Valkyrie's cloak. What she meant to say was, *I need to hit you.* Abby and Wendi had gotten close, and we all knew I was responsible for Powell killing her. Being pounded by Abby wouldn't be enough punishment for what I had done, but it was a start.

She stopped in the stairwell doorway. "You coming? Oh, and if you wear your inhibitor cuff, I'll make you eat it."

I realized too late I had been holding the cuff on my wrist. To an outsider, it looked like a watch, but it allowed me to turn off my gifts when needed, like at boxing practice. Not much use firing off lightning bolts at your sparring partner. I broke the seal and shoved it in my pocket. The energy still swirled like a hurricane in my chest. I'd have to hold back; I didn't want to hurt Abby. She was one of the few friends I had left. Maybe I'd switch on the inhibitor and let her end me.

I followed her down two flights of stairs and out into the workout rooms. Every sort of exercise equipment known to man was here:

barbells, weight machines, rowers, and treadmills large enough for an elephant to use stood around the room, grouped by the exercise type. At the far end, rock climbing walls and a full obstacle course had been installed. I couldn't identify what a third of these machines even did.

Abby emerged from the locker rooms at the back of the gym. I passed her as she started warming up on the parkour course. It amazed me to watch her workout, her speed and agility surpassed everyone on our team. Jon could keep up with her, but he'd abandoned us after his twin Wendi's death. I jogged into the locker room and jumped into my combat suit, but left the helmet sitting on the shelf. Mom would have a fit if she found out I'd gone without a helmet, but nothing could hurt me, at least not much. Being able to absorb energy had its perks as well as its costs.

I walked out to sit on a stack of weights only Titan could lift while waiting for Abby to finish the course. She could leap twenty feet at a time, swing around on the bars like an Olympic gymnast, and power through the larger obstacles without breaking a sweat. The longer she left her cuff off, the stronger she grew. I'd noticed she wore her inhibitor constantly now, with the exception of training time. She landed with a dull thud after back-flipping off the last wall.

I entered the training room, Abby close behind me. In all reality, you could probably test a nuclear bomb in here and maybe scratch the paint. Dad didn't know I'd seen him unleash enough lightning down here, after Wendi's funeral, to destroy a city block. With the amount of power at his command, he could level buildings. No damage remained to mark his fury, except the cracked, bleeding burns covering his arms.

The room only had one door. The Air-Lock back in Redemption could have been a screen door here. Marcel had just about wet himself as he examined the technology involved in making the training room. He explained it, but all I heard was like blah, blah, Carbinium enriched tubes, blah, blah, repulsor ray, blah, blah, blah. Twenty minutes in, he realized I wasn't listening and gave up. I got the point: nothing could penetrate the walls here.

Once inside, Abby pressed the button; the door slid quickly out of sight as the room sunk deeper into the mountain "You ready, Ward? I'll take it easy on you since you're the birthday boy." She cracked her knuckles, grinning at me.

"Screw you; I'm ready for your worst. I'll try not to mess up your hair."

She scoffed. "I've had the cuff off longer this time. You won't touch me, Sparky." She stretched her arms out wide, rolling her neck back and forth to limber herself up. "You need to stick your finger in a light socket before we start?"

"Funny." I pulled deep from the well I kept stored within me. I'd never get caught out of juice, like with Powell. I had found I acted like a battery as long as I didn't use the cuff. Once the inhibitor turned on, no juice for me. Luckily, it came back once the cuff turned off.

"Take your best shot, low voltage." She squatted awaiting my opening shot. I started small, knowing she'd move before it got close to hitting her. She rolled left and came back up in the same position.

"That was weak. You take it easy on me, and I'll kick your balls in."

While she couldn't do any lasting damage with my body absorbing the force of her blows as energy, it would still hurt like hell.

The next shot streaked directly at her. The thick bolt would have rattled her teeth had it hit. She laughed as she easily avoided the shot but hadn't seen the second blast, thin as a laser beam, which ricocheted off the wall, hitting her fully in the ribs. With a whoosh of exhaled breath, she landed hard on the floor but managed to get to her feet somehow.

"Now that's more like it," she snarled. "I like to play rough."

I opened up with a set of short bursts that she avoided like a running back through the secondary. The last blast flew below her as she somersaulted over it. Both her feet, clad in her normal steel-toed boots, struck square on my chest. Pain burst like water through a broken dam; even with my powers, I'd have a bruise for a week. Her strike would have knocked anyone else out, but my body absorbed the energy, saving me from a few broken ribs. There are benefits to having Gifts, for sure.

Instead of mimicking the roll Abby does, I flopped. As hard as I practiced, the backward roll eluded me. Her boot missed my head by a millimeter or so as I scuttled away from her. She pursued, low to the ground, fists ready to strike. I punched a blast of energy at her head, hoping if not to hit her, at least distract her, to let me regain my feet. Abby hit like a Mack truck on steroids.

My shot hit her square in the face. Her head cracked back, and I heard an audible crunch. Blood flowed from her nose, down her face. "Abby, are you all right?" I ran to help her up.

As I approached, she reverse-rolled to her feet and launched in one smooth movement. Her fist hit me under the chin. I tasted blood from where I bit my tongue in the process. I collapsed under her weight. She straddled over me, raining punches on my arms and face.

I raised my arms to protect my head. "Abby, what are you doing? I give up."

"Of course, you give up!" she screamed, froth splattering as she spoke. "You always give up, and people die, right? You never give up!"

A loud horn blared, and blue lights flickered on. Someone had triggered the inhibitor override. Abby kept punching. "You never give up, NEVER! You fucking could have killed Powell, but you quit!"

Blood flowed from my face as the pummeling continued. Even without her Gift, Abby was strong as an ox.

Hands grabbed Abby and pulled her off me. Dad wrestled to hold her as she lashed out with both feet and words. I couldn't understand what she was saying, though I wasn't sure if it was from my head spinning or her shouting incoherently.

"Enough!" Dad bellowed as he continued to pull Abby away from me. "You are not using your Gifts to fight. You'll both wear your cuffs from now on, or I'll lock you in the holding cells. Understand?"

"Yes," I said wiping the blood from my face. More replaced it, but I deserved what I got.

Abby pushed Dad out of the way and left the room. He watched her go, shaking his head as if trying to figure out what to do with her. He turned back to me.

"We are having a meeting upstairs about this," he said and followed after Abby.

Great. All I needed was a lecture on top of my injuries. I'm sure the injuries would be shorter lived.

2

I stalled the inevitable by heading to the locker room. After I stripped off my combat suit, the mirror confirmed what I had already known. Bruises covered my arms and torso, blood dripped from my nose, and my mouth had swollen up from the beating I had taken. My dark brown hair currently had a red tinge to it from splattered blood and a gash in my scalp. With the dampening unit on, my body would heal at the same rate as a Norm.

I threw on clothes and tied my shoes, stopping to replace the tissues shoved in my nose as the blood soaked through them again. I guessed I'd be a vampire's snack with all the blood dripping out of me.

I stomped up the stairs. The sooner this ended, the sooner I'd be able to heal. Healing the injuries would be easy, the wounds from the words would take a lot longer. The sad part: I agreed with Abby. I'd stopped fighting; I let Powell kill Wendi, and if not her, my mom. I thought I had been merciful, but the cost of mercy had been much steeper than I'd ever imagined.

As I entered the second floor of Castle, I slowly surveyed the area. All the levels were circular, having been built in an old missile silo. A huge kitchen dominated with an enormous stove and three refrigerators. A sink I could bathe in took up the far end of the space. The main table sat adjacent to the kitchen area, could seat twenty, but four of the chairs could hold three people easily. A birthday cake sat in the middle of the table, untouched. The other side of the circle contained a living room, media room, and a couple of meeting rooms.

I crossed over to the living room with its huge couches and armchairs. Mom and Dad sat with Abby. It was nice to see the scorch mark on her chin. At least she'd felt some effects of the fight. I sat across from them, waiting for the lecture. The worst part was that they were right. Fighting with our Gifts could have gotten someone seriously injured.

Dad cleared his throat. "I'm not used to being a parent, for obvious reasons. I'm more accustomed to combat teams than teenagers, but things have to change around here." He paused as Mom nodded her support. "What you two did was stupid but understandable. Teams fight, but it's why you're fighting that is the problem. Frankly, go ahead and kick the shit out of each other about who ate the last bagel, but not over who's responsible for Wendi's death."

Neither of us said anything, though if the furniture burst into flames from the heat seething between us, I wouldn't have been surprised.

"Any time you two want to pull your heads out of your asses, I'm ready," Dad said, clearly pissed off by the stalemate. "We aren't leaving until you two clear the air."

"I didn't do anything."

Abby's head shot up. "Definitely your style. Stand by and watch while innocent people get killed. You could have ended Powell, but no, you went soft."

"What?" My voice was a lot louder than I'd intended. I could feel the heat rising as my anger flared to life again. "So, you want me to be the Executioner? Is that it? I have more blood on my hands than I can ever wash off." My fist slammed against my leg. "I didn't know Powell had a pistol."

Abby's face twisted with rage. "It didn't matter. You kill them before they murder the people you love. You're just like the villagers, stand aside and let the Reclaimers do their job. Screw it. When we play, it's to win. Not until you don't feel like fighting anymore. How many more people I love have to die before you understand?"

I stood and moved, heading out of the room. She had no right, and I didn't have to put up with her mouth. That first day I should have told

Mr. Tyler to forget it. An arm pulled me around. "Just like you Ward, walk away from a fight."

I slapped her arm away, hard. "I'm sorry about your parents, but I didn't kill them. I know it's my fault Wendi is dead."

"Tommy, it's not..." Mom started to rise before Dad pushed her gently back to her seat.

"I killed Ryder and Clint. I killed Reclaimers in the Megadrome. Everywhere I go, I leave dead bodies behind. If your parents hadn't betrayed you-"

I didn't get to finish as Abby's fist slammed into my mouth. I fell flat on the floor, blood from my mouth joining with my bleeding nose from earlier.

"Don't you talk about my parents!" Her eyes burned with rage, saliva dripping from her open mouth.

"Why not?" Marcel's voice came from across the space as he entered the room. "You're sure fast enough to blame everyone else for their screw-ups. Why didn't you save your parents?" Abby whirled on him. To his credit, he didn't flinch much.

"Easy for you hiding behind your laptop."

"Yes, it is. Just like it's easy to blame Tommy for Wendi when you were out cold on the Megadrome floor. Maybe if you'd fought better, she wouldn't have needed to rescue Mom. Or maybe it would have been better if Mom died instead. You're used to it, right?"

I'm not sure which of us Marcel shocked the most. My bet was on himself.

"I should kill you," Abby said in a low growl of a voice. "I'm done with you both."

I got to my feet. "Now who's walking away? You accuse me of quitting, and then you give up."

She stopped dead in her tracks. Her head bowed, tears hitting the floor in front of her. "I should have hit you harder."

I snorted, spraying blood in the process. "If you had, I'd be missing a head."

"Wouldn't change much. It's empty anyway." Marcel grinned at me although his eyes didn't reflect it. "Wendi's death is on me. If I'd been able to hack the systems like we planned, you wouldn't have had to fight."

Abby shook her head. "No. It's nobody's fault except the Protectorate for keeping us chained." She wiped at her eyes with the heel of her hands. "I didn't fight when they killed my parents."

I stepped over, placing my hand on her shoulder. "You were a kid."

"I could have fought." She faced me. "You didn't kill Wendi. I know it. I'm so angry, and sitting here isn't solving anything. We need to fight the Reclaimers and force them to free us."

"No," Dad said, taking control of the situation. "We don't make any moves against the Protectorate or the Reclaimers. No running off to rescue Waxenby, either. We got away, and, for now, I mark that as a win."

Abby sighed. "What a surprise."

Dad held up his hands. "I see you aren't happy with the safe plan. There are only four of us with Gifts, and Marcel can't fight."

Marcel crossed his arms, his face darkening. "I can't punch people, but I can fight. I think I've found a way to drop the dampener at the Protectorate holding sites. The Gifted can break out and be free."

Dad took his turn being shocked. "Marcel, there are hardened criminals in those facilities along with crime fighters and others who got swept up by the Reclaimers."

"So, you're the only one who gets to be free?" Marcel asked. I'd never heard such a belligerent tone come out of him before today. Marcel had changed since we left Redemption. "Wendi died freeing you. This way no one else has to die."

"Marcel, you are..." Dad started, but Mom squeezed his upper arm, and he stopped.

Mom moved to stand in front of Marcel. "I agree, the Gifted have been unlawfully imprisoned, and we will address the issue."

Marcel lit up like he had won the battle. But I knew he would be losing the war. Mom's superpower was lawyering.

"But to let out people like the Grim Reaper, who use their powers to murder and rob, wouldn't be right either. We have to plan on how to do this."

And the war ended with a harrumph.

Leave it to Abby to launch a new offensive.

"We can't just sit here and hide. The Reclaimers are killing more than the Gifted ever did," Abby said. She leaned forward, body tensing like she would pummel Mom into submission.

"The Gifted destroyed half the world," I mumbled.

Abby's eyes bored into my skull. "Whose side are you on, Ward?"

I glanced at Mom for support and got nothing more than a slight grin. I'd jumped into this on my own. "Having a Gift doesn't make you a saint, just like being a Norm doesn't make you Brunner. I want to free everyone and end the Protectorate, but we need to be careful. I don't want any more blood on my hands."

"Ward, you are..."

"Enough," Dad said sternly. "We aren't headed down this path now. We are talking about a plan for today. I've asked Blaze to train with us. I don't know if we will have to fight, but better safe than sorry."

"Are we just leaving Waxenby to die then?" Abby asked pointedly. Her anger bubbled under a calm surface, for now.

Mom cleared her throat, stopping Dad's angry retort. She answered. "No, we are going to keep searching for him. Everyone is upset and tired. Let's get you three some food and let you heal up."

Dad pulled the training room remote from his pocket, looking embarrassed. "Sorry, guys. I should have turned off the dampening field."

A trickle of power returned as the field released my Gift. I'd used most of my charge fighting with Abby. I followed along to the kitchen. Marcel tossed me a bottle of Mountain Dew before taking his. Opening it slowly, I only lost a little from the shaken bottle.

Before Marcel could reach back into the fridge, Mom motioned to him. "Hands?"

"Oh, yeah." He went over to wash in the sink.

Dad handed me a towel to clean up my face. "Are we all good?" He caught my eye.

"We're good."

Marcel and Abby agreed as Mom put out sandwich makings for us. Everyone grabbed plates and filled them before sitting around the large dining table. The room grew quiet as we devoured the food.

"I have something to talk about," Abby said around bites of food. "Can we enforce a daily shower rule for the boys?"

Marcel gasped. "I just showered."

"Yeah, but it took you barfing before you did." Abby tore another piece off her sandwich. "We've been here a week, and I don't think you've showered once."

I laughed.

Mom arched her eyebrows at me. "You haven't been much better."

"Oh. I've had other things on my mind."

She nodded sagely. "I understand."

Marcel rubbed the stubble on his chin. "I probably should shape up my goatee as well."

That got everyone laughing.

Mom lit the candles on the cake as they sang a halfhearted version of *Happy Birthday*. This was the first birthday I'd ever spent with my dad. The double chocolate cake tasted amazing, but I ate it mechanically. Celebrating today felt wrong. At least Mom had agreed to no presents, but she refused to let my birthday pass without a cake.

Dad caught my eye. "Tommy, I'll need you to go get Blaze. Use the doorbell and wait with Alyx, if you don't mind."

"Sure thing, Dad." I shot him a silent thank you, glad for the excuse to be away from any more reminders of my old life.

Mom glanced at Marcel, noticing the stains on his shirt and the mass of hair shooting in every direction. "Maybe you've got time to clean up before Blaze gets here?"

He grimaced. "Affirmative, Mom."

Dad stood, reaching his hand out to Abby. "How about a bit of sparring, partner?"

She grinned. After saving her in the Gauntlet, Abby borderline worshiped Dad. "Let's go. I'll take it easy on you."

Dad laughed. "You will? How kind of you."

"Well, you saw what I did to your double, right?" She asked, playing up the innocent act.

I left to get my backpack. We'd avoided a nuclear meltdown over freeing the Gifted. I wondered how long it would be before it went supernova.

3

My backpack sat at the end of my bed. The room was larger than the room I had at Dresden. A queen bed took up the middle of the room, flanked by matching black nightstands. Nothing in this room, besides my backpack, belonged to me. Since I'd fled Redemption, all my worldly belongings stayed in my pack.

The fight with Abby had taken a toll on my stored energy. Dad had given me a black box to shock my finger when I inserted it into the hole. Pulling it from the zippered pocket, I stared at it for a second before pushing my index finger in and receiving a jolt of energy. The skin burned every time I had to use it—another cost of using my Gift. I put the box back where it belonged.

I hoisted the bag over my shoulder, pulling the door closed behind me after leaving the room. Marcel headed toward me, carrying his ever-present tablet. His face lit up as I stopped in front of him.

"Bruh, you need to see this. I built a virus capable of breaking all the collars in Redemption. Once someone clicks on it, the collars will fail."

I shook my head. "Marcel, Dad already said we aren't breaking everyone free." I hated playing bad cop with Marcel. He'd been my best friend since we landed in Redemption. "I've got to go get Blaze."

Marcel's face screwed up in a grimace. "More combat training. I'm still sore from the summer." He groaned loudly. "After a summer of bruises and pulled muscles, all I could do was hit Turk with a chair."

Leave it to Marcel to complain about training. "It won't be too bad. No collar means more healing, less pain." He must be upset; he didn't rub it in that he'd had to knock out Turk to keep him from beating the snot out of me.

"Maybe for you, Bruh." He glanced up and down the hall. "I think we should release the kids in Redemption."

"You heard Dad. What do you think would happen if collars started falling off during school? The guards would kill them all. Are you willing to accept that responsibility?"

Marcel shook his great shaggy head. "The collars stay in place. With the dampener off, their powers would have a chance to form. We got lucky you freed us. Don't those kids deserve a power-up, or is it just game over for them?"

I sighed. "Man, the first kid who used a power would get everyone killed. You know it. If one collar can fail, then the guards would assume they all failed. At best, the kids would be taken to the Block; the worst, genocide."

Marcel glared at me. "Abby is right. Whose side are you on?"

I put my hand on his shoulder. For the first time in my life, I stood as tall as him. "Marcel, I want to free them, but we have to be smart. Some kid farts a toxic cloud on accident, and the guards will start shooting."

His shoulders slumped. I could see the defeat and frustration in his eyes. "I just want to help. I'm useless here."

"No freaking way," I said with a laugh. "We'd be living under an overpass, eating out of the trash without you. Instead of unleashing the virus, could you track down where Waxenby is? He needs to be our highest priority."

He gave me a sly look. "I thought your dad said no."

I shrugged. "He said we couldn't rescue him, not a word about searching for him."

Marcel's smile beamed. "Having a lawyer for our mom comes in handy. I'll find him if I have to stuff a tracker up Grim Reaper's ass."

I laughed. "Make it so, Number One!"

Marcel walked away chuckling. I watched him go, thinking about how useless I'd felt trying to rescue Dad and how badly that experience sucked. Things should be different, but it didn't change anything. I readjusted my backpack and headed to the doorbell.

Alyx had left the magical doorbell. According to him, it created a vortex connected between two points, regardless of distance. Unlike the portal that moved you directly from one place to another, the doorbell's endpoints were fixed and didn't require Alyx to be present. At first, Dad had refused since anybody could use it, but Alyx tinkered for a while, and now only the five of us could activate it.

I pushed the button and stepped back. The wall swelled out then appeared to be pulled in, revealing a blue-purple maelstrom. Lights flashed within it, strokes of magical energy coalescing and dispersing around the edges. It reminded me of a kaleidoscopic Pink Floyd video Mom had shown me as a kid.

The light-show raged before me as I pulled the second strap of my backpack on. When stepping through a portal, a faint shimmering of energy tingled across my skin. This vortex felt more like skydiving, and if you let go of your stuff, it might not get there; Alyx didn't know where the missing things went. I honestly didn't care and didn't want to find out.

I drew a deep breath and stepped into the Technicolor swirl. My stomach dropped like I rode on the world's tallest roller coaster. I concentrated on keeping my lunch and three slices of birthday cake down as I tumbled through the magic realm. Faces flickered into view, only to be swept away by the storm of lights. Faint sounds reached my ears as I plunged through the whirlpool.

Finally, a glowing, golden door appeared before me in the distance. I knew the trip took seconds to complete, but time held no meaning here. The door grew larger and more distinct as I closed on it. A door knocker affixed under a stained-glass window depicted the Death Star firing its weapon. Leave it to Alyx to design a geeky door.

"Thomas," A strong female voice said just over my shoulder. I would have jumped if I could have, but that's hard to accomplish while floating. Peering around, I didn't see anyone. I felt a sharp tug on my arm, but then I passed through the door and into Alyx's hideout.

I fell hard on the floor, reeling from a bout of vertigo. The room tilted at odd angles trying to throw me off the tiles, but I held on like a rodeo star. A minute or so later, the nausea subsided, and I began to return to normal. The portals were the limos of magical transportation verses the Vespa that the doorbell was. Abby and Marcel had thrown up during their trips here, which made me the logical choice for these missions.

After the fight with the Reclaimers, we had stopped here. It belonged to Alyx's parents, and we used it as a safe house from time to time. Fortunately for us, Jon didn't know where it was. The room had been emptied down to the terra cotta tiles and paneled walls that bore the outlines of removed pictures. Mementos of Alyx's old life had been shed like a snake's skin.

The last of the nausea fled as I stood up. I heard steps upstairs, so I figured Blaze would be waiting for me. I'm not sure why he needed an escort, but here I was. Frankly, after the argument with Abby, I needed the break. I took the stairs up, opening the door into the living room. Alyx sat in a brown wing-backed chair and stared into the fireplace. There was an assortment of similar chairs arranged in a circle; a large, circular, mahogany coffee table anchored the chairs in orbit around it.

"Alyx?"

He didn't respond. I glanced around, but I didn't see Gladiator either. I stepped to his side. His mouth moved, but no sound came out. His eyes had a white cast to them. I had seen him raving mad at times as well as comatose, but this was something very different. Placing my hand on his shoulder, I gave him a gentle shake, but he kept mumbling. Blaze or Gladiator would know what to do. I took a seat in a blue and silver leather chair, which sat to my right, then put my backpack on the floor and leaned back to wait for help.

"Oh, hey Tommy," Alyx said, jolting me awake. I hadn't realized I'd drifted off. "Sorry, Warlock business. Blaze hasn't gotten here yet?"

I wiped the sleep from my eyes with the back of my hands. "I don't think so."

Alyx grinned. "Conference call with the Warlock council. Not very exciting, but usually people don't fall asleep during them."

I shook my head. Alyx the jokester, at least when he had control of himself. Gladiator had said Alyx had been much better since leaving the Zoo. "Well, next time I'll listen in."

Alyx barked a laugh. "That would be priceless! An uninitiated at a council meeting. Maya would fall off her high councilor throne."

I had no idea who Maya was, but Alyx laughed, so it must be funny.

"When is Blaze supposed to be here? Dad sent me to bring him back. Are you going to portal us?"

"Afraid not. I'm headed out. We've seen a couple odd occurrences up in the North Western Region of the South American Zone. I'm about to go check things out."

I paused. My thoughts had been on this question since the finale of Saturday Night Showdown. I decided to take my shot. "Alyx, can I ask you something?"

Alyx's facial expression changed. A sharpness I'd never seen before flickered in his eyes. "Sure."

I steeled myself. "You can do magic; would it be possible to bring Wendi back?" My eyes hit the floor; I knew I shouldn't have asked, but I had to know. My last-ditch effort to save her.

"Oh, Tommy," Alyx said, his voice soft. "I wouldn't if I could. There are good reasons it is forbidden. Even if it worked, she wouldn't be Wendi any more, just a pale imitation."

My head snapped up. "If she would be alive, I'd take it. It's my fault she died. Can you use me to bring her back fully?"

Alyx's eyes bored into me. My friend had vanished and left the Warlock in his stead. "Tommy, Wendi freely made her sacrifice. Would you bring her back to a life of misery and pain? Did you love her so little?"

My face flushed. "No, I miss her so much."

Alyx stood up, which shocked me since he's missing both legs below the knees, walked over, and knelt before me. I could see the faint outline of legs shimmering in place of the missing ones. "Tommy, Wendi loved you more than anything, but she's gone. Bringing her back would be cruel. I've lost a lot of people I loved, and I know how it leaves a hole in your heart. The good news is you won't hurt forever. I promise."

Tears ran down my cheeks. I'd convinced myself that Alyx, with his strange magical powers, would be able to reverse time or summon her from the dead. My final ray of hope vanished like a ring in a magician's hand. I nodded to Alyx; words failed me.

"Blaze will be here soon. Will you be alright?"

I glanced up; concern etched his face. I'd only known Alyx a short time, but we'd been through a lot together, which meant more than he'd ever know.

I swallowed the lump in my throat. "Thanks, Alyx. I'll be fine."

He smiled at me. "Tommy, you will be. I've got to go see what is happening on Victoria Island."

I grinned, trying to push away the pain. "Hmmm, December in Canada? My guess is snow. You might want to take a coat."

He rolled his eyes at me. In a deep, powerful voice, he exclaimed. "I AM ALYX THE SUMMONER! NEITHER SNOW, NOR SLEET, NOR DARK OF NIGHT WILL STOP ME!"

I laughed. "So, you're a mailman?" Sometimes being forced to watch old television shows paid off.

"Foolish mortal, begone!" He turned, muttered a few words, and the portal appeared. Snow flew through on a frigid blast of air. A blue glow emanated from him as he strode through on magical legs.

"Hey, close the door, we aren't heating the outdoors," I called after him. He turned and winked as the portal collapsed, leaving melting snowflakes on the living room floor. I stepped into the kitchen to get a paper towel. I didn't want the puddles to ruin the floor. Spending most of my life in the far north had taught me about snow melting on wood floors.

I threw out the trash and took a Mountain Dew from the fridge before grabbing my backpack and flopping on the couch. I retrieved my book, opened it to the bookmark, and started to read. Marcel and I both read a lot of science fiction and fantasy. Those books allowed us to escape into worlds where the good guys usually won the day. I'd been on a fantasy kick lately, devouring the Wheel of Time saga with delight. I found it strange, after reading so many novels about wizards and warriors, that I now knew a real-life pair. My life had taken a turn into the peculiar for sure.

An hour or so later, the front door opened. I heard the sound of crickets greeting the starry night even from where I sat. I put my bookmark in, quickly storing the book away in my backpack. Gladiator's booming voice reassured me as I strolled down the hall. He wore jeans and a baby blue buttoned short-sleeve shirt. His biceps stretched the fabric, like if he flexed, those sleeves would tear. On the other hand, Blaze held a duffel bag and wore a bright Hawaiian shirt and cargo shorts with sandals, looking completely at home.

"Thomas!" Gladiator said, pulling me into a bear hug. I groaned as his massive arms crushed me. "An unexpected gift is your visit."

"Hey, guys. Dad sent me to bring Blaze back."

Blaze came over and gave me a less painful hug. It had been a few months since I'd seen him; the same smile lit up his face, but he appeared tired.

"Is everything okay?" I asked.

"Of course, dude," Blaze said, moving the duffel bag to the living room. "It was a long trip, and I'm tired. We had to make sure we weren't followed. The Protectorate is riding a bad wave."

Being around Gladiator and Alyx made things a little better, but having Blaze here was like a security blanket for me.

I hesitated, wanting to ask what had happened at the school, but not positive I wanted an answer. "Is it bad at the school?"

Blaze shrugged. "Well, not as bad as it could have been. Kids who lived at home were kept at the Institute's dorms, but after yesterday, they relented. Guards surround the school, and no one is allowed in without a pass. Fortunately, the Protectorate has to be careful the secret of your survival doesn't leak, so the Reclaimers aren't going nuts punishing anyone."

Things could have been much worse. I'd worried they would be sending kids to the Block or executing teachers, like what happened with Mr. Taylor. I didn't want my actions to hurt the other kids at school.

Blaze and Gladiator discussed a few details about covering Blaze's tracks, with some remembrances from their Stryke Force days thrown in. With any luck, Blaze would drop off everyone's radar, and he could stay with us. They hugged, and then we grabbed our bags and walked downstairs to use the doorbell. I pushed the button, and the wall pulsed before opening into the vortex.

I turned to Blaze. "Make sure you hold on to your bag. Marcel lost a laptop the first trip through."

Blaze slid his arms through the duffel's straps, wearing it like a backpack. "Looks like the first step is a doozy."

I grimaced. "I hope you didn't just eat. You'll step out through the gold door at the end. It doesn't take long."

Blaze gave Gladiator a salute, fist over heart, and stepped into the vortex. He appeared to fall away from us as we watched. I said my good-byes to Gladiator, earning another rib-cracking hug in the process, before stepping into the vortex.

The world spun, and everything I thought I knew was about to change.

4

I realized something had gone wrong as soon as I stepped through the entry. The blue/purple vortex which usually greeted me had been replaced with angry, red bolts of energy which cascaded around me, soundless in their fury.

Nothing else moved. Every other time, I'd float through the maelstrom until the door appeared on Castle's side. Now, I hovered just inside the doorway but couldn't move forward. I twisted my head, the only part of me currently able to move. Out of the corner of my eye, I saw the doorway I'd entered through fade out of existence.

I thrashed, trying to break free of whatever held me, but I still couldn't move. A sickly green vapor crept around me from all sides as I fought to loosen myself. The strands coalesced over my arms and legs, forming into a solid rope as thick as my wrist. Suckers, like an octopus would have, grew out of the appendages as they tightened around me.

My Gift wouldn't come to me as I tried to fight off the grasp of whatever had me. I screamed as the vines constricted. Pain and panic in equal parts shot through my system. My heart hammered as sweat poured off me. I could see Powell's face in front of me: the scarred ear, the foul stench of his breath. Brunner stood off to one side, Clint and Ryder on the other, both charred but recognizable. "You killed us," they chanted as I bucked in vain to break free.

I heard someone call my name, but all I could see was the clearing where they'd planned to kill me. Wendi came into view, covered in blood from where Powell had shot her. She joined in the chant.

I heard my name again, louder, stronger. Powell began to fade along with the rest, the echoes of "you killed us" still rolled in my head. Wendi faded last, the final dagger to my heart.

A blue bubble shimmered, forming around me, severing the vines where they crossed the blue light. The pressure holding me vanished, and my energy roared back to life after being suppressed. I pulled the vines from my arms and legs. They turned back to vapor and dissipated as soon as I let go of them.

My stomach lurched as the glowing sphere moved deeper into the vortex of red lightning and swirling clouds. Flares of anxiety spiked as I continued through the storm. Even though I was free of the vines, the blue sphere trapped me as well as the Air-Lock in Redemption ever had. The panicked animal brain wanted to lash out to free myself. I suppressed the impulse since I didn't know where the sphere would take me. Unlike the vines, the softly glowing orb gave off a peaceful vibe.

A door, formed of beige blocks of stone, appeared before me as the ball slowed. The uneven surface of the rock gave it the appearance of being ancient and weathered. As I watched, the stones, a row at a time, flowed apart, leaving the doorway exposed in the center.

Once the doorway stood fully open, the sphere pressed against the entry and forced me through and into the room beyond. I stumbled at the sudden acceleration, catching my balance before I face-planted. Behind me, the all remnants of the door had vanished.

Cold sweat poured off me like Niagara Falls as fear flooded my brain. My heart felt like it might burst, and I worked to control my breathing like Blaze had taught me. I'd like to say I had mastered my anxiety; I hadn't, but at least I had a leash on it.

With nowhere else to go, I stepped out into a vast cavern and gasped at the damp and musty odor which permeated the place. A small lantern hung on a black metal hook, providing a small amount of light. The stone walls faded into the darkness above. I turned, hoping a doorbell would be waiting, but the stone stared back impassively.

"Hello?" My voice echoed into the depths of the cave. The echo sounded small and scared. I tried again. "Hello. I don't know why I've been brought here, but I want to be returned. Alyx the Summoner will come for me."

Nothing. No answer came from the darkness, just the echo of my voice. I took a few tentative steps then stopped to retrieve the lantern. Most of the floor consisted of black sand, but where I stood, dark cobblestones created a path. Off to my right, something hissed. I held the light toward where I'd heard the sound but couldn't see anything. More noises came from behind me, and I decided following the path would be my best option.

The cobblestones led me deeper into the cavern. I hesitated, trying to decide what the best course of action was as I held the lantern out in front of me like a shield. I could feel the energy from the black box swirling through me as I walked, glad Dad had thought of these things that I had not gotten used to doing yet. If all else failed, I could fight, but against who or what I didn't know. I felt like a character in one of Marcel's D&D games. The solo knight stalking the dragon in its lair. I gulped and decided thinking about dragons probably wouldn't lower my apprehension. What I wanted was for Alyx the Summoner to show the hell up and get me out of here.

As I followed the path, an arch appeared out of the gloom ahead, faint traces of light coming from beyond it. Power surged as I gathered it, in case I'd need it. A bolt this powerful would fry a T-Rex.

"Thomas, please enter and be at ease," a female voice came down the hall to me. "I mean you no harm. We have little time and much to speak of."

The darkness receded as she spoke; light flowed up the walls, shimmering as it went. It looked like a firefly convention on overload. I lowered the lantern and headed toward the sound of her voice; the hair on my arms stood on end from the sheer magnitude of energy I held at the ready. I followed the curving hall and entered a throne room. The woman sat on a stone chair which must have been carved from the wall behind it. She wore a robe of white silk, trimmed with ruby and gold beads and embroidery; a matching veil ghosted over her waist-length, black hair.

"Greetings, Thomas." Her gentle voice floated across the space between us. Her accent sounded a bit like Gladiator's but held a musical quality about it. "I am sorry to meet like this, but I have need of seeing you in person."

I glanced around, wary of a trap, but the room was empty of anyone else. I set the lantern down in case I needed my hands free to fight. "Who are you, and how do you know me?" My tone could have been less callous, but it's not every day you get pulled through a magical portal to meet a beautiful woman who lived in a cave.

She smiled. I took a few steps closer and gasped. Her eyes were gone, leaving the sockets empty. The same symbol I'd seen on the door marked her olive skin. "My name is Eiraf. Do not let my lack of eyes disturb you; they are the price I paid for my magic."

My face flushed red with embarrassment. "Why did you bring me here? Alyx will come looking for me. I should have been back by now."

"This place sits outside of time, so you will return without delay." She stood as if to walk to me. I ran up to help her, afraid she would fall. She chuckled softly. "Your kindness is appreciated Thomas, but I see far better than it appears."

I stopped before her, noticing how the symbol in her forehead glowed. She reached out, placing her hands on either side of my face, her skin warm and softer than velvet. "Thomas, I am a seer of all that has happened and may yet come to be. The timestreams flow all around us, breaking and reforming on the decisions we make, taking from us. They grant boons; pain and suffering recede on the loom of time to happiness and contentment before being torn asunder once again. This is how it has always been, and if the fates allow, will always be."

I stood frozen in place, unsure what to do. "Um, what does this have to do with me?" The symbol's glow intensified, its golden light bright but not painful to look at.

"You are a keystone in the path the world is on. You've experienced great loss for one so young and will face more if you continue the path you are on."

I thought of Wendi, her dying with a bullet to the head. I could see the blood spray, the way she collapsed on the ground. If I could avoid losing anyone else, I would in a heartbeat. "What do I do to get off the path?"

Her head slammed back, her back arching as if she were being tortured. Her head lolled to the side as she gasped for breath. Her olive skin had darkened and turned blotchy. I tried to pry her arms away from me, but her grip held like a steel vise.

"Stop!" I screamed, feeling panic grip me. Her mouth still moved, but no sound came. The golden light had taken on a reddish cast. Lights flickered on the edge of my vision, resolving into disembodied heads pelting around the room. Their screams echoed through the cavern, reverberating back until it became a long droning sound.

"You must choose wisely, young one." Her head hung before her, sweat dripping on the floor between us. "You will be tested. You must choose the path you will take. One path leads to losing yourself; the other, the loss of all. Beware the one who offers freedom at the price of your soul. In the end, only you can choose your path. But choose well. The way of fire and blood is not easily put off."

I stopped struggling. It would have been easier to break steel with my teeth than her grip. Spirits spun around us with frantic energy. Occasionally, one would crash into Eiraf, making her back arch and the glow from her forehead pulse.

"How will I know what to choose?"

Her head snapped up, staring directly at me. "Listen to the cursed one, the Phoenix, and the doppelganger. They will help you choose. If you fall to the dreamer or the trickster, all is lost. The way is fraught with danger, fire, and death; choose wisely, or all is for naught."

Her hands slackened, the glow receded, and she wobbled on her feet. I stepped forward, catching her as she fainted. She slumped, forcing me to swing her up in my arms to keep her from falling to the floor. I looked around for somewhere to put her and decided the throne would have to do. Walking up the couple stairs to the dais, I gently placed her on the throne. The realization I was stranded kept me from leaving. I checked her pulse, and it felt strong and steady. Her skin had returned to its original color, and I was struck at just how beautiful she was, even without eyes.

I sat next to the throne, my head reeling with all she had said. The cursed one would help me? That didn't sound good. Cursed how? Seriously, did the Phoenix talk like Big Bird? The only doppelganger I'd ever heard lived in a book I'd read. None of it made any sense.

A faint sound from Eiraf broke my thoughts. I stood up, checking on her. "Are you alright?"

Her eyeless face moved as if she were taking in the surroundings. Her head stopped as she centered on my voice. "Thomas?"

"Yep, I'm here." She started to push up, so I helped her sit. Luckily the throne could hold three large people, so sliding her around was easy. Once I had her propped up, she seemed better. Her head covering had fallen off when she sat up, though the fact it stayed on during the pyrotechnics impressed me.

She shook her head slowly as if trying to clear it. "I'm sorry Thomas. I am a slave to the fates and must read the future as bidden by my masters."

"Masters?"

She raised her face toward me. "The word means something different for me than what you believe."

My head still spun with everything she had said. "Who is the cursed one?"

She held up her hand, stalling the rush of questions. "I know nothing of what I said, and in my mind's eye, I can only see faint images of your possibilities, so please don't ask."

Considering this, I wondered how she could tell me so much and not know anything. "What images do you see?"

Her sightless gaze peered past me, focused on something in the distance, her face absent of all expression. I turned to see, but there wasn't anything there. I turned back to her, puzzled as to what she was doing.

She spoke as if in a trance. "I see a man with a mustache; he is in great pain. Your enemies are holding him near a metal man with a rope, but you should not go alone." The slackness of her features withdrew. "I'm sorry I can't tell you more as I can tell this is of great importance to you."

Any information could be useful though a metal man could be anywhere. "Thank you, Eiraf. I appreciate you trying." She had to be talking about Waxenby. It weighed on me that the Syndicate had taken him.

She nodded once. "Thomas, you should return to your people. I wish you the best, though I have a feeling life will be difficult and painful for you." The symbol flared a deep green, and the vortex opened before me.

I bowed to Eiraf, not knowing why, but it felt right. "Thank you."

She smiled a sad smile. "May the Goddess watch over and protect you."

With the way things were going, I'd need all the protection I could get.

5

I stepped out of the vortex and into the storeroom in Castle. Blaze leaned against the wall, a bit greener than usual, holding his duffel bag. If his hair had stood on end, he couldn't have looked more freaked out. His eyes darted around the room as if trying to reestablish himself in the real world.

I chuckled to myself. The first trip through the vortex did it to just about everyone. "You okay?"

He nodded rapidly. "Dude, it's a bad trip for sure. I think I'll stick with the portals from now on."

I laughed. "Yeah, they are much less intense." I paused and decided to ask my question. "How long have you waited for me?"

Blaze frowned. "If I hadn't moved, you would have stepped on me coming out, so not long, why?"

I shook my head. "Time gets funny in there." I gestured to where the vortex's door had been moments ago. "It seemed to take a lot longer to cross than usual. I thought I heard voices on my trip back."

Blaze's already wide eyes grew larger. "Dude, totally freaky. I think I would have lost it. The trip had been bad enough without any weird shit going down."

The stomping of boots rang out as Abby turned the corner. She wore her normal combat boots, black pants, and shirt. Mom must have helped her dye her hair half neon blue and the other half purple. It looked cool, but I would miss the red/black combination.

"Blaze!" she shouted as she ran over and hugged him. Blaze and my mom were the only ones who ever got that kind of reaction. Everyone else got stern indifference. On the bright side, the last time I'd seen Abby, she was beating the snot out of me; I'll take indifference.

Blaze lit up. "Hey Abby! How are you girl?"

"I'm good. I hear you are going to teach Sparky how to fight so he can actually give me a workout." She laughed, but I caught her as she watched me from the corner of her eye.

I laughed along. Her ragging on me signaled the truce had taken. "Really, I just didn't want to mess up her makeup."

"Sparky, the day you mess up my makeup is the day I retire." She smirked at me and pushed my shoulder. I saw it coming, so I didn't fall on my ass. With age comes great wisdom. I steadied myself, wondering if I should tell anyone about what had happened but decided to wait until I caught up with Alyx. The magical realm was his turf, and he'd have an answer.

"On that note, we should take Blaze to see everyone," I said. No sense standing in the storeroom when we could go sit down. My unexpected side trip had left me drained. Sleep sounded like the most wonderful thing in the universe, but it would have to wait.

We exited the storeroom and took the stairs up to the hallway that connected to the top floor of the living areas. We stepped through the emergency doors, crossed the intervening space, and entered into the living room.

Marcel's head came up as we entered, a smile blossoming on his face. "Blaze!" He stepped over to shake Blaze's hand enthusiastically. Blaze grinned as he tried to retrieve his hand.

"Marcel, you look great. Ready to start training again?" Blaze asked innocently.

That stopped Marcel cold. The shaking stopped as his mouth dropped into a frown. "Well, my Gift is computers, so I really don't need to learn to fight."

Blaze shook his head. "It's a dangerous world for all of us. If someone gets in here, fighting may be your only choice. Susan is going to learn as well."

Mom laughed and grabbed Blaze into a huge hug. "Eugene, we are lucky to have you here." She stopped and held him at arm's length, studying his features. "You look tired. Long trip?"

"I'm fine, nothing a good night's sleep won't fix." He turned and faced Dad. "Cyclone, good to see you."

Dad shook his hand. "Thanks, Blaze. I'm glad you agreed to come. You can call me Mike now since my secret identity isn't so secret anymore."

"No, sir. You'll always be Ranger to me. You fought well in the Gauntlet." Blaze tossed his bag on the floor next to a leather recliner and sat.

Mom and Dad returned to the couch. "I had a lot of extra help." He'd been pissed when we had surrendered, but the plan had worked, except for Wendi's death. I pushed the grief down, concentrating on Blaze.

Abby and Marcel grabbed the other couch as I dropped into the chair next to Blaze. His gaze traveled to each of us. "You did."

When he got to me, his eyes filled with sympathy. I knew what was coming and steeled myself for it. "I'm sorry about Wendi. I know you all loved her."

I choked up but refused to let it out here. Mom sprang into action. "Thank you, Eugene. She was a wonderful young lady, and if not for her, I'd be dead."

Dad held Mom's hand. "She fought like a tiger," Dad said. He chuckled a bit. "When I suggested she hang back, she blessed me out. I'd have ten of her on my team if I could."

Abby glanced at me, a mixture of worry and anger flashing across her features. "She refused to back down. I'm proud she was my friend. Though her choice in men left a lot to be desired."

I rolled my eyes at her, and she responded by sticking out her tongue at me. I'd lost Wendi; I couldn't take losing Abby. Marcel had his eyes affixed to me, waiting to see if I was okay.

Blaze's face twisted up like he had eaten a bad Skittle. "Where's Jon?"

Dad sighed. "Jon took Wendi's death hard, which we all understood. He decided it would be better if he left than stay with us. Dresden was compromised, so we came to Castle."

"Too bad. He seemed like a cool dude." Blaze rubbed his chin before he spoke again. "So, Cyclone, what's the play?"

Dad glanced sideways at Mom, who adjusted herself on the couch. "Play? No more plays. We are going to stay underground until the Protectorate loses interest. Afterward, we can get fake papers and settle somewhere and try to live in peace."

Blaze barked out a wet, harsh cough. He pulled a handkerchief from his back pocket and wiped his mouth. He folded it and pushed it back in his pocket. "Sorry, allergies this time of year are tough. So why train to fight if there's no plan? What about Oliver? Are you going to leave him to the Grim Reaper to turn over for execution?"

Abby tensed, leaning forward as if ready to pounce. Marcel slid away from her, just in case she jumped off the couch.

Dad stood. I'd noticed he preferred to be on his feet during confrontations, and this conversation was heading toward a fight, fast. "Oliver shouldn't have done anything but get the kids and Susan to safety. Grim Reaper is using him as bait, and we can't expose ourselves to any more losses. If anyone goes to find him, it will be me and me alone."

"Who are you to say we aren't going?" Abby shot back. "We owe it to Waxenby to get him out. He gave himself up to protect the rest of the team. Armageddon would have killed us all if not for him."

Dad stiffened. I don't think he expected to have this fight again so soon. He had underestimated Abby's commitment to getting Waxenby back. "I am the only one of us to have ever been on a combat team. Your powers are new and aren't fully trained yet."

Abby leaped to her feet. "I fought shoulder-to-shoulder with you in the Gauntlet. I can hold my own."

"That was different." Dad said, hands on hips as if he'd been declared the victor.

Ding! Welcome to round one, folks.

Abby's eyes widened. "Different how? Because you had no choice but to save the poor, little girl that had been stupid enough to get caught?"

To Dad's credit, he knew he'd blundered in his tactics. "Let me explain."

Her head shook vigorously, hair swaying with the movement. "Or was it that you were faking out the Protectorate when you..."

"Enough!" Dad held his hands up in surrender. "I wouldn't have lived without you all. This will be different. We will be engaging with other Gifted, not robots or Norm troops. They've fought for years together."

I pointed to Blaze. "Isn't that why Blaze is here? He can train us in combat and you in strategy."

Dad looked to Mom, his life preserver.

"Don't look at me," she said softly. "I agree with them. Oliver doesn't deserve to die any more than you."

"Well, it doesn't matter in this case," Dad responded. "We don't know where they are holding Oliver, if he's even—"

"He's alive," Abby said, her voice deep and gravelly. I noticed her face reddening. "I saw him as the Reclaimers were restraining me. Reaper's goons hit him with a suppressor and dragged him away."

Dad paced back and forth. "When we find Oliver, we will devise a plan to extract him. There will be no solo missions to find Oliver or even the score with Reaper or any other harebrained plan the three of you feel the need to launch. Understood?"

He looked directly at me. I could see why people feared Dad. "Understood, sir."

Abby and Marcel chimed in. Abby returned to her seat, her skin returning to its normal tone. I felt bad for the person who fought her at full bore. I still wore the bruises, and she likes me most of the time.

Once Dad had said his piece, he bid us goodnight, signaling our dismissal.

On the way out, I motioned to Marcel as we headed down the hall. After a couple of corners, I said, "I need you to look into something for me, but you need to keep it quiet."

Marcel struck a hurt expression. "Bruh, when did I ever roll over on you?"

"Ummm, never?"

"Exactly. What can Mr. Wizard provide you?"

I laughed. "You really need to lay off the old TV shows."

"Nada. Bruh, this place has every episode of almost every show ever made in storage. It would be like spitting on a masterpiece to ignore it."

I sped up the pace; no sense chancing being overheard. "So, something happened with the doorbell." I proceeded to tell him about Eiraf and the weird things she said. "My guess is they are holding Waxenby near the metal man. Can you see if you can figure out where it is?"

He stroked his still stubbly chin. "Hmmm, Oz?"

I groaned, loudly. His sense of humor left a lot to be desired some days.

"But I'll add it to the algorithmic search I'm running. Can't have too many data points."

I groaned again. Having a geek for a best friend was trying at times.

The next morning at o-dark-thirty, we assembled in the training room. Abby sat on the bench running along the wall, nursing a cup of coffee, as Blaze warmed up. I flopped next to Abby and cracked open a Mountain Dew while I watched Blaze. A commotion arose in the hallway, loud enough for Blaze to stop and see what was going on.

Dad strode in, pushing a protesting Marcel in front of him. Mom followed up, carrying his backpack. "I don't see why I need to train; I already saved my bruh with a chair."

Dad shot me a questioning glance.

"I'll tell you later."

"Marcel, don't be a baby," Abby said in a mocking tone. "On the battlefield, there won't be chairs lying around."

"Well, I'm sure I can find something to hit a goon with. I think outside the box."

Blaze laughed. "Wouldn't it be easier to know how to protect yourself than rely on luck?"

Marcel shook his head, the afro swaying with the motion. "Me? Fighting is totally FUBAR. Bruh has the power-ups, not me."

Dad made a face. "Was any of that English?"

"Marcel has a unique relationship with language," Mom said, tossing Marcel's backpack on the floor next to him. "Well, you all have fun, I'll have breakfast ready when you return."

Blaze held up a hand. "Not so fast, Miss America. Everyone trains in case the worst happens." Blaze grabbed a bag from under the bench. He pulled out a box and handed it to Mom.

She shook her head. "Eugene, the only fighting I do is in court. I'm not Gifted."

Blaze shrugged. "Neither am I, but it never stopped me."

"Mom, you just got done telling me how righteous this is," Marcel chimed in. "Are you joshin' me?"

She shot Blaze a look which would have incinerated a lesser man. "No,

Marcel, it is important. I guess breakfast will wait." She opened the box, revealing a jet-black pistol. "Eugene, I don't do firearms, nor am I licensed to carry one."

"Dude, I doubt the Reclaimers will ask for your carry permit." The surfer personality left as the drill instructor appeared. "Lesson number one: this is a war. The Protectorate already used you as bait once. You," he stopped to eyeball everyone, "all of you, will fight with whatever is at hand until you are dead or incapacitated."

Dad nodded in agreement. "Blaze is right. We can't have a weak link. If we fight, everyone has to be able to protect themselves."

"Okay, down to training." Blaze handed each of us a pistol in a holster. "These are Mark 23s. They hold twelve rounds and have the laser sight attached for easier aiming. I expect everyone to have their weapon on them at all times."

"Why would I need a gun?" I asked. "I can throw lightning at anyone who comes at me."

Blaze rubbed his face. "Tommy, do you remember any of your training?"

"Yeah, but…"

"Why do we learn many styles of fighting?"

I thought back to the sessions at the Secret Lair. "Because every style has its place."

"What happens if a disruptor band catches you?" He turned to Abby.

She growled. "It takes all my strength. I can't fight anymore."

"Wrong!" Blaze snapped. "You weren't trained to fight without it. There will be times immense strength is useless. If I'm on the other end of the room, you can't hurt me, but a well-placed shot could."

Abby grunted. "This is a waste. Powell's thugs got lucky. Next time I won't be so nice." She stood and headed for the door.

Mom spoke up. "Abby, you…"

Blaze interrupted her. "I tell you what. You hit me, and you are free to go."

With a harsh laugh, she turned around. "Blaze I don't want to hurt you. It's not a fair fight."

He smiled back at her. "I agree. It's not fair to you, but sometimes lessons are hard to learn."

Dad stepped between them. "Okay, this isn't necessary. We are all training together."

"No, Ranger. This is absolutely needed." He moved over to the center of the room away from the rest of us. "Abby, shall we?"

Mom and Dad exchanged a glance then took seats on the bench next to me. Marcel hesitantly joined us. Abby hadn't seen Blaze fight before, but we had. What Blaze gave up in size, he made up for in speed.

Abby stopped before Blaze.

"One hit is all it takes. Begin when you are ready."

"Blaze, seriously, I don't want to hurt you."

He smiled at her. "You won't. In fact, you won't touch me. I'd be more worried about Marcel with his chair."

With a low growl, Abby flew at him, arms outstretched. Blaze slid to the side, tripping her. She arced forward, rolling into the fall and was back on her feet in an instant. She pivoted, breaking into a run. At the last second, she leapt, both feet pointed at Blaze's chest.

Blaze's knees bent as he arced backward, limbo style. Abby sped over him and landed behind him. He stood facing her again.

"Just because you're fast, doesn't mean I need your training." She circled her opponent, crouched low and looking for an opening.

Blaze turned with her but made no move to attack.

Instead of speed, she went for a brute force attack. She threw a punch at Blaze's head, which he flowed around. She reversed it, attempting to backhand him. He stepped back, caught her wrist in an extremely painful hold, and twisted her arm. She howled in pain, and he increased the pressure. She pulled back her left foot to kick him, but he swept the right leg, using her unbalanced pose against her. She toppled to the floor. Blaze glided around, pulling her arm with him, eliciting more howls.

"Are we done?" Blaze asked calmly.

Abby thrashed, trying to break free, but it only made the pain worse. Finally, she screamed uncle, and he let go. She clutched her arm to her chest, shrinking away from Blaze. Mom crossed the distance to check on Abby, speaking in low tones to her.

"Okay, do we need any more lessons, or can we begin training?"

Training sounded great given the alternative.

6

We'd been in Blaze's boot camp for over a month. Marcel still hadn't found the metal man, but given we trained six hours a day, he didn't spend a lot of time on it, but he constantly tweaked his neural networking algorithms, whatever that meant. I sat on a stool in the kitchen, talking while Marcel and Abby cleaned the dishes, when Dad strolled in.

"Hello, all. Good dinner tonight. Tommy, you and Susan are a great team in the kitchen." He stopped next to me, placing his hand on my shoulder. "Let's go spar for a bit."

I hopped off the stool, waving to the dish crew. "Sure thing. Catch ya' later."

Abby mock glared at me. "Sure, run off and play with Dad. We'll be here cleaning up your mess."

"Bruh, did you really need to use every pan in the place? I swear there are more dishes here than we own."

I laughed. "You have to suffer for my art." They both groaned, but I noticed the leftovers were still out and being snacked on. Gifted burned through a lot of fuel to keep our metabolisms going at peak levels.

I followed Dad out and down the hall to the stairwells. Having to take the stairs everywhere did wonders for my leg strength and endurance, not that I had any choice since there weren't any elevators in Castle.

The self-sealing hatch opened onto the stairway complex. It led to the old command center that held the training room. "We sparred earlier today, so why a second time?"

Dad glanced over at me; at six-two, I stood about an inch shorter than him. "We need some specialized training, and I don't want an audience. I'll explain when we get there."

Hmm. I couldn't think of a reason why we needed privacy, but obviously, Dad felt the need for it. I guess old habits die hard. Before the Dark Brigade attack, he'd had to keep his personal information away from even his team. Good thing, since the Protectorate had captured a lot of the Gifted from the government teams.

We took the stairs in silence. After growing up with just Mom, having Dad around was nice but weird. At times, he still seemed like a stranger to me.

Entering the gardens at the bottom of the stairway blew my mind. If I hadn't known I was over one hundred feet underground, I'd have thought I was outside. Crickets chirped in the background, butterflies floated around, and birds darted everywhere. Marcel said the gardens totaled over three football fields in area. Everything from wheat to apples grew here, hydroponically. These shelters had to be designed to withstand just about anything. If the world ended while we were here, we might not notice.

Exiting the gardens through another hatchway, we strode along the hall to the training center. We used these every day. The main room took up the majority of the floor. It held a large open area for practice along with adjoining areas for weight training, cardio or whatever else we could want. Blaze had set up a shooting range at the far end of the room. I walked into the room, but Dad had stopped.

"What? I thought we were sparring?"

Dad nodded. "We are but not here." He turned and headed for a section of the left-hand wall. He slid a panel to the side, revealing a keypad. After he punched in a code, the panel slid open with a hiss. Another set of stairs led deeper underground.

"Where does this go?"

Dad smiled. "You'll see."

The door closed behind me as we descended the stairs. On the next landing, Dad entered the code to open the door. Another flight of stairs continued to more levels below us. "What's down there?"

He stopped and looked at me. "Okay, I'll tell you, but this needs to stay with you. If I don't tell you, you'll get Marcel to hack into here and explore, right?"

My face turned bright red with embarrassment, but I didn't deny it.

"I thought as much." He sighed. "There are cells down there to hold Gifted prisoners. Most of the larger teams had them in case they were needed. The worst of the worst ended up transferred to the orbital prison."

"Oh."

"Capturing powerful Gifted who went rogue was exceedingly difficult. Law enforcement couldn't tackle them, so the government formed the teams to protect people. When we did capture one, they had to be hidden until transferred. It was a messy business."

I thought for a minute. "So, they are like the Block?"

Dad frowned but agreed. "Only we held people who abused their Gifts, whereas the Protectorate threw anyone they wanted out of the way in the Block. I'm convinced I met some non-Gifted people the Protectorate wanted removed while I was in there."

I didn't say anything. Honestly, I hadn't ever thought about these types of things before. From my room in Redemption, it was all black and white, Gifted vs. Norms. The more I learned, the hazier things got.

"History lesson over?" He examined me, waiting for an answer.

"Yes, but can I ask questions later?"

He chuckled. "Of course. I'd rather have you ask than unleash Marcel."

I grinned, looking over his shoulder. A hallway stretched out before us, doors in the left and right walls. "So, what is this place?"

"Follow me, and you'll see." He went down the hall and opened the right-side door. A huge gun-metal gray room stood on the other side. The room itself had no features, just metal walls and ceiling, rivet heads studding the walls.

I entered, totally confused. Dad closed the door and walked past me. "Isn't this great?"

So, throwing lightning damages your brain. Good to know for the future. "Umm." The witty replies kept on rolling.

He laughed. "How about now? Sal, load tactical situation alpha."

Lights flickered around the room as I found myself standing in the middle of a shopping mall. People strolled around, carrying bags and snacking on various treats. "Wow!"

"This was a mall in Chicago, before the attacks. The computer can use old footage to recreate environments. We will use them for training."

I stopped. "Wouldn't this help Abby as well?"

"I doubt it. Her Gift is different from ours. In certain situations, your tactics have to change. I could launch a whirlwind in here, but people would be sucked off the upper floors and plummet to their deaths when the winds stopped. These are the things you have to think about."

It made sense. Abby basically pummeled whatever got in her way during a fight. Not a lot of strategic thinking involved.

The clatter of gunfire sounded off to my right. Three men armed with machine guns ran out of a jewelry store. People screamed in terror as they ran.

"Tommy, stop them," Dad said, his voice intense.

I ran toward them, pulling the energy as it swirled within me, preparing to strike. The lead guy leveled his gun at me. Without thinking, I threw a bolt of lightning at him, hitting him in the chest. It launched him across the marble floor, and he crashed through the window of some fancy clothing store. Mannequin parts flew in all directions, like bowling pins hit by a giant ball.

The other two ducked and reversed direction, darting between people as they ran. I tore after them, dodging around the fleeing shoppers as I went. I'd never catch them at this rate. Wait, this was a simulation. I could just run straight through stuff; it wasn't real. A trash receptacle with the mall logo and "Keep the Atrium Clean" on the side blocked my way, so I ran through it, or at least tried to. I landed flat on my back, the air whooshing out of me.

I heard Dad laugh behind me. "Simulation pause." He stepped over, offering his hand. I grabbed it so he could help me up.

"It's a simulation; I should have been able to run through it."

He grinned. "Sal, show the room."

The light changed as the mall disappeared. The floor rose around me, including the solid trash can in front of me. The balconies above jutted out from the walls going thirty feet into the air. Pillars stood indicating where the people in the mall would be, down to a stroller shape I'd seen a mother pushing. My mind shuttered at the possibilities.

"Holy crap! This is amaze-balls!"

"I thought you might like it," Dad said, leaning on the trash-can-like pillar. "We need to discuss your Gift."

I didn't like the sounds of that. "What about it?" I sounded way more defensive than I'd meant. Dad had mastered his long ago; I must look like a chump.

"Tommy, you are extremely powerful. The bolt you used on the criminal would have killed him. Sal, resume simulation in paused mode."

The light changed, and the mall sprang to life around us. Dad walked over to where the criminal lay on the ground. "Sal, run tactical analysis."

The room was silent for a moment. "Tactical analysis complete," Sal's voice said into the room. "Three enemy combatants involved. Two escaped. One combatant dispatched. Ninety-nine percent chance of death. Collateral damage estimate: eighty-two point three-eighths percent chance of bystander fatalities. Structural damage estimate: thirty-two thousand dollars with a ninety-four point two four percent chance of fire causing an additional forty-two thousand dollars in damages."

Dad appeared grim. "Sal, show most likely bystander collateral damage."

The lights flickered, and bodies appeared on the floor. The bolt had penetrated the criminal and hit three additional women who had been shopping in the store. A sales girl slumped against the back wall of the store which had a massive hole in it.

I felt cold as the realization that had this been real, I'd have killed four innocent people. Tears welled up in my eyes, even though my brain screamed it was a simulation.

"Sal, end simulation." Dad put his arm around my shoulders and walked me back toward the center of the room. "Sal, two chairs."

The floor shifted, and two blocky metal chairs rose up. Dad settled me into one and sat in the other. "Tommy, simulations give us a chance to make mistakes and learn. Gifts like ours require all the attention Blaze has been teaching us about shooting on a range, and then some. When lightning flies, it doesn't hit just one person."

"I know," I mumbled, chin down on my chest. The only times I'd fought had been us against the bad guys. I could have hurt one of my own team and not even realized it. Dad preached safety and responsibility every day.

"Do you understand now?"

"Yes, sir."

"Good. Now let's talk about how you use your Gift."

I looked up at him confused. "How I use my Gift? I throw lightning just like you."

He shook his head. "No, you don't."

Could today get any more surreal? First, I found out about the hidden levels of Castle, then, the amazing simulation room, now I don't throw lightning? I came up with a total burn response. "Huh?"

Dad chuckled. "Tommy, I generate electricity." He held up his hand and a small arc shot between his finger and thumb. "You absorb energy. If you are shot, the bullet's force translates into energy within you."

"And it hurts like a bastard."

"I'm sure it does." The arc flared a bit as he spoke. "Any energy you absorb magnifies, and you can release it."

"As lightning."

The arc snapped out of existence. Dad rubbed his face. He sighed mightily. "Yes, but you don't have to. Remember when you were fighting Powell? You hit him and knocked him across the room. I went and re-watched the fight, and your hand glowed. Somehow you had funneled the energy into your punch."

The ton of bricks crashed down on me. I hadn't even realized I'd done it. I thought back and realized I'd done the same when I fought Jon in the boxing ring. "I really did. I don't know how though."

"That is why we are here. You need to think outside of the box when it comes to your Gift. In the Gauntlet, I thought up a way to use my Gift to build a shield of electricity."

I leaned forward. "In the maze."

He nodded. "Yes. I'd never done it before but needed to find new ways to use my Gift the designers hadn't seen before. It was my only chance."

It struck me as odd. After being one of the strongest Gifted around, there were uses for his powers he hadn't uncovered before. "Couldn't you have done that while you fought the Reclaimers?"

"I could have, probably should have." A wistful look crossed his face. "Maybe had the Gifted been more creative, we could have found a way to

41

stop the Dark Brigade. Maybe we could have avoided all those needless deaths. So many innocents killed due to our arrogance."

It didn't sound right. "Arrogance? Mom always said the Gifted fought to protect the people who couldn't fight back."

"Tommy, you've heard the saying 'Absolute power corrupts absolutely'?"

I nodded.

"The Gifted throughout history started with good intentions." He paused as if considering his words. "When the governments of the world built Gifted teams, the goal of protecting the population from rogue Gifted was the most important thing. Over time, teams fractured over personality conflicts and jealousy. Gifted fought more for endorsement deals and fame than they did for the people of Earth."

He leaned back in his chair. "The big news toward the end revolved around who was dating whom and which team could beat the others, who was strongest, fastest, toughest. Huge amounts of money went to teams who won with spectacular footage, not results. When Titan used a city bus, no one cared who had been on the bus, but the footage ran constantly. He appeared on talk shows to pick up construction vehicles. It turned into a circus with the clowns running the show. I know some teams would let perpetrators escape so they could fight again. The Dark Brigade attacks ended it all, and everyone on their team had been stopped many times before."

I couldn't believe what he was saying. My world flipped upside down and stood on its head. "Were you like that too?"

He considered for a minute. "No, I don't think so. All I wanted to do was retire and sneak off with Susan. If the Dark Brigade hadn't struck when it did, we would have been together on the farm where you were born. Well, until the Protectorate came for us."

I studied the man who was my dad. I saw that it cost him to tell me this, risking our new relationship. He watched as I came to my conclusion. "It's in the past, and I wish it had been different, but I'm glad you're here now. How about another simulation, then upstairs for a movie?"

He smiled, and I could see his eyes had become a bit damp; we'd passed a hurdle for sure. "Sounds good." Dad stood up, and as I did the same, he grabbed me in a hug. A good-natured laugh escaped him as he did. Stepping back, he asked, "You ready for another one? Try not to wreck the room this time."

I rolled my eyes. "Well, if the room can't take a bit of lightning."

He snorted. "Sal, launch random combat simulation."

The lights dimmed, and my personal hell arose around us.

7

M y brain screamed in panic as I realized we were on the set from the final round of the Gauntlet. The scattered cars, the red brick buildings. My eyes shot to where Wendi's bloody body would be waiting for me. It wasn't there.

Instead, I noticed dead soldiers littering the battlefield. Their bodies twisted and charred from the primal fury the lightning Cyclone Ranger had unleashed on them.

Dad fell to his knees, tears flowing down his face. "Not again. No, I can't fight anymore," he whispered, rocking back and forth. Anguish flooded his eyes as he stared down at the limp body of a woman dressed in a skin-tight black combat suit. Long blonde hair poking out the back of her combat helmet lay in a pool of vomit. The symbol on her chest—a golden dagger through a downward facing red crescent moon—gave her away: Dominion.

This wasn't Saturday Night Showdown; this was the scene from the day Dominion used Dad to destroy Powell's men. The day Dad surrendered rather than continue to fight. I surveyed the wreckage to see if Powell was in the scene, but he wasn't. He'd fled the battle before then.

I knelt beside Dad and put my hands on his shoulders. "Dad, it's not real. It's a simulation." He didn't notice me. The memories had taken over. The agony reflected in his eyes mirrored my own as I thought of what

Powell had cost me; a moment of mercy had been repaid with the death of Wendi.

"Sal, end simulation," I said causing the room to reappear as it really was. I sat in front of Dad as he fought to regain control. After all these years, the memories of killing those men still haunted him. I thought I understood since I had nightmares of the men in the arena dying under streams of lightning as I fought to save my family. I could hear their screams when I closed my eyes. I'd never realized that the damage I'd done had been to myself as much as the men I fought.

Even worse was the kids I'd vaporized. Something in me broke the day I killed Clint, Ryder, and Brunner. They had deserved it, but their blood would forever be on my hands.

"I can still hear them," Dad murmured as he came back from that horrific day. "I can smell the charred flesh, feel my skin burn as the lightning killed them all. I think Powell was the worst; he had to live with the aftermath of the day."

"Powell's gone, Dad."

Dad's eyes locked on mine. "Yes, he is, but he'll always live on in my memories."

"Mine too, Dad. Mine too."

For the next few days, I felt drained. I couldn't shake the image of the women in the simulation lying dead from the blast I had unleashed. Without fail, those thoughts led to Wendi's blood-spattered body in the arena. It had been over a month, but the pain magnified as the days flowed past. I needed to take it out on someone, but Powell was dead.

Training went on as always. Mom turned out to be an ace with her pistol. Dad called her Annie Oakley. Mom just rolled her eyes at him. My parents are weird. Marcel still dreaded the sessions, but Blaze said his progress was encouraging.

The fourth morning, I hit rock bottom. I could hardly sleep. When I did, horrible nightmares destroyed any rest I could get. Wendi begging me to stop Powell before he killed her, Clint apologizing as the lightning tore him to shreds, people dying under the constant surge of white-hot energy.

The alarm sounding for training ended abruptly as a thin lance of lightning fried it, shattering the plastic housing. The smell of ozone hung heavily in its wake. I pulled the pillow over my head, wishing the world would go away.

Sometime later, I didn't know how long since I'd destroyed my clock, I heard a knock on the door. I ignored it, knowing how futile a gesture it was. A second, louder knock and then the door opened. Mom flipped on the lights as she entered. I looked from under the pillow as she checked out my handy work with the clock.

"You know I usually go for the surrealism in Dali's work, but you've done a fine job bringing 'The Persistence of Memory' to the modern era. The melted plastic face isn't as elegant, but it certainly smells worse."

I pushed the pillow over my face harder. Mom came over and sat on the bed next to me. "Okay, kiddo. What's going on? Marcel skipping practice is usual, but you never miss."

"I don't want to talk about it."

She sighed. "Thomas, remove the pillow and sit up." I knew the tone and did as she told me. Mom reached over and lifted my chin, her gaze holding me. I noticed her eyes were red-rimmed and puffy. She'd been crying.

Something inside of me broke, and the tears rolled down my cheeks. "I'm sorry. This is all my fault. Wendi's gone, and I miss her so much. I can't take it."

She gathered me in her arms and held me like so many nights since we were sent to Redemption. She rubbed my back as I cried. I don't know how long it took since I'd destroyed the damn clock, but I felt better having let it all out.

"Tommy, I miss Wendi too, but she wouldn't want you to live like this."

I nodded. I knew she was right, but I couldn't pull myself out of the hole I was in.

"She loved you, and it hurts, but it will get better."

I didn't say anything. I couldn't put into words all the issues I'd been dealing with.

Mom watched me, assessing her client with practiced ease. "It's more than Wendi, isn't it?"

"Yeah," I croaked out of my over-dry mouth. "I killed so many people, how do I deal with it? I know they deserved it, and I had to protect my family, but..."

She gripped my hand hard. "I don't understand completely, but your Dad went through this after fights when people died. I don't think it ever goes away, but that's what keeps you from becoming like the Grim Reaper and the Syndicate. Once you stop caring, you are one of the bad guys, no matter which side you're on."

"Gladiator said something similar about Jon."

She smirked. "I'd listen to him; he's had a lot of time to figure things out."

"Is he really thousands of years old?" I blurted out, sounding more fanboy than grieving warrior.

"As far as I know, he is. Regardless, he's exceedingly wise when it comes to the world and exceptionally adept at killing." She stood up and ruffled my hair. "Time for a haircut, you're getting shaggy."

"Nada, it's my new style."

It was her turn to roll her eyes. "Honey, I'm always here if you need me."

"I know, Mom."

She turned and left, nearly getting run over by a frantic Marcel as he burst into the room.

He grabbed her arms to steady her. "Sup, Mom."

She shot a mock glare at him. "What's up is you need to slow down. I don't need you huge guys squashing me."

He, at least, had the decency to look embarrassed. "Sorry, Mom. Big news on the street." He held up his tablet as if to prove his claim.

I stood up. "What's going on?" If this were a new tablet release or some new game, I would have to kill him.

He rubbed his chin, which, sadly, still didn't have a goatee, just the lingering patch of stubble. "I poked around a bit and found a signal feed coming out of DC. I thought it might be a Syndicate transmission I could..." Mom gave him her "this better be legal" look. "er...monitor." His eyebrows shot up, waiting for the impending scolding. Mom didn't seem convinced, but she didn't say anything, so he went on. "Turns out it belongs to the Underground. I left a message in their virtual drop box, and they have requested a meeting in Atlanta."

"Atlanta?" I asked. "Why not in DC?"

Mom answered. "The Protectorate has upped the troop levels in the area. Your father is guessing they are trying to bring the Syndicate in since they botched capturing you."

"We got away, but we ended up on Saturday Night Showdown anyhow. What's the dif?" I asked, perplexed. How we got there shouldn't have mattered.

Mom shook her head. "The Protector isn't stable. He's erratic, changing views and policies all over the place. His people are in constant damage control mode. More than likely he views Grim Reaper's failure as a lack of loyalty to him."

Marcel agreed. "Ranger wants to see everyone in the conference room to discuss."

Mom snatched Marcel's tablet, reading over the information.

"Well, can't keep the man waiting." I motioned for them to exit the room. I closed the door behind us as we headed up the three floors to the conference room.

"Bruh, I think this could lead us to Waxenby."

"I hope so." Rescuing him would certainly help to even the score. Besides, we all owed him a huge debt. He'd helped to stop Powell and aided our escape from Redemption and the Syndicate. It had already been over two months with no word of him. "If we do find him, I wonder if Dad will let us help get him back."

Mom, who was walking ahead, still reading Marcel's intel, stopped dead in her tracks, pivoting to face us. "Tommy, when we find Oliver, we will get him back. You don't leave men behind."

Marcel stammered. "I thought Ranger said he would..."

Her face flushed red. "I know what he said, but we are not leaving Oliver with those psychopaths any longer than absolutely necessary, and it will take more than one person to do it." She left, stomping down the hall. If storm clouds gathered around her, I wouldn't be surprised.

Marcel let out a big breath. "That was intense, Bruh."

"Yeah, should be an interesting conversation with Dad." But I knew who'd be winning the fight even if Mom had to go by herself to get Waxenby.

We slowly followed in the wake of Mom's anger, stopping to get drinks before heading into the conference room. Dad stood at the head of the long walnut table, talking in a low voice with Blaze. Abby and Mom sat together on the far side of the table. A knife blurred between Abby's fingers as she flipped it around. She looked over Mom's shoulder, reading what Mom pointed to on the tablet she held. The ceiling-mounted projector hummed in the background.

Marcel grabbed a chair close to the door. I dropped into the next chair. Dad glanced over, finished talking to Blaze, and began. "Marcel has found a way to communicate with the Underground. They are requesting a meeting with us in Atlanta at the Millennium Gate. I'm worried it's a Protectorate trap."

The projector whirred to life as the room darkened. Mom tapped the tablet a couple of times, and an image appeared on the wall behind Dad. He moved to the side so we could see the display. Mom rose and stepped to the wall, pointing. "So, this is the proposed meeting place." A tall stone building stood in the center of overgrown weeds and wrecked cars, one of which had driven up the low stairs before it died. Apartments surrounded the structure; skyscrapers loomed in the distance. "Millennium Gate is north of the center of Atlanta. It's not too far from the Protectorate area of control surrounding the city so it will be easier to get to."

Blaze chuckled. "Crossing a guarded border with armed patrols to enter a dead city infested with giant rats and whatever else has mutated in there. Count me in."

Mom shot him a dirty look before continuing. "There are ways into the city. The drug cartels use Atlanta as a distribution center. They pay the Protectorate a cut, and they leave them alone."

Dad nodded. "I agree with Susan; it's a good spot for a meeting or an ambush. I don't know if the benefits outweigh the risk." He paused and glanced around the room. "Marcel, do you think they have any information on Oliver?"

"I don't know," he said slowly. "They wouldn't discuss specifics since they don't know who we are any more than we know who they are."

"I'm sure they think we are Protectorate." I hoped Dad would see the value of this meeting.

"Cyclone, we need to alli..." Blaze broke off, a wet cough racking his thin frame. Once it subsided, he wiped his mouth on a cloth and sipped from the glass of water. "Sorry, allergies. As I was saying, we need allies on the outside if we are going to be able to move against the Protectorate."

Dad leaned on the back of a chair, his face dark. "Blaze, we barely escaped the arena. Most of the Underground are bit players or non-Gifted anti-establishment types. I understand wanting to get Oliver, but I think our best bet is to wait for the storm to pass, then integrate into society and try to live normal lives."

Abby growled low in the back of her throat. "So, we just take what they are doing to us?"

"Yes, you are all old enough to not be checked. We could have real lives, spend our time on what's important."

Abby stood up, her face red with anger. "What about making the Protectorate and the Reclaimers pay for what they've done to us? How about all the people locked away? Do they get to lead normal lives?"

Dad's brow furrowed. "A lot of those people are criminals, and dying in vain serves no purpose."

"Who says it's in vain? We release all the Gifted and take down the traitor."

"Enough!" Mom was on her feet. "First things first, we need to rescue Oliver, which means meeting with the Underground. Any questions?" She glared at each of us in turn. No one uttered a peep.

Being overly attached to my head, I kept my mouth shut. Who said I wasn't learning?

8

After Mom's proclamation, Marcel contacted the Underground. The meeting would happen in three days at nine p.m. under the Millennium Gate. I headed down to Marcel's lair to see what he found out concerning the metal man.

I knocked on the door and heard a muffled voice say enter, so I went in. The seventh level contained all of the infrastructure for Castle. Banks of servers and cascading Ethernet and fiber optic cables covered the right wall. Marcel slumped in front of the main set of monitors hung on the back wall of the room. Equipment, tools, duct tape and an assortment of various parts lay scattered on the tables in the center of the room. Marcel's talent didn't rival Mr. Fix-it for being able to create new devices, but he could modify anything made of electronic components.

I glanced out the window to the mechanical rooms that ran Castle's physical needs. The room boggled my mind. It amazed me that engineers could build these machines that took care of every facet of Castle's inner workings.

Marcel swiveled to face me. "Bruh, welcome to *Casa de Geek*. What can I do for you?"

I smiled. "Just wondering if you'd had any luck with the metal man with the rope?"

His face twisted into a scowl. "No. I scanned the ruins of Atlanta to see if there were any leads, but no signs of it or Mr. W." I could tell it bothered him we'd hit a dead end. "Do you have anything else I could search for?"

"I wish I did, but that's all I got." I hadn't told anyone else about the strange experience I'd had on my way back through the doorbell. Honestly, I'm not sure I believed it was real and not some strange hallucination. The fact Marcel couldn't find a metal man with a rope made me wonder about the accuracy of the information Eiraf had provided.

He stroked his chin. "Hmmm. I built the algorithm to prioritize metal structures in and around D.C. and the South Western Region. I applied the parameterized constraints to the search matrix. I can expand the range and see if I get any hits."

It couldn't hurt to keep searching though I had no idea what Marcel meant. "Have you scouted out the meeting site?"

He snorted. "You think I'm some noob? I've pulled every Protectorate feed they have around Atlanta." He spun around, fingers clacking on the keys. Images popped up on the monitors showing the Millennium Gate from every angle. A stone statue stood near the base of the monument. At one time, it had been beautiful, but after everything, nature worked to reduce the once beautiful area to a wasteland. "I don't like it; there are too many places people could hide." He pointed at the surrounding buildings, covered with dead vines. I noticed he wore his suppressor watch. "All these buildings overlook the gate. It would be easy to put a sniper up there."

I agreed. I wished Jon had been here; he easily grasped the tactics of an environment. I pushed the thought away, remembering he still blamed me for Wendi's death. I forced my focus back to what Marcel said, having missed a few words.

"Fences could be breached, but the guards have towers surrounding the city." He pulled up a map, red dots showing the guard towers. "They are set up so every stretch of the fence is under surveillance. The good news is the Protectorate has gotten lazy, relying on cameras and motion detectors instead of live guards in most of the towers."

Well, that was good news. Anything Marcel could reach could be compromised. After hacking the Megadrome, this would be child's play. "I'm sure you can handle it." The fact Marcel had his suppressor on worried me. "So, why the bling?" I indicated the watch he wore.

He rolled his eyes. "Mom. She's worried I could epic-fail like Mr. Fix-It." He shrugged. "I keep it on so I don't blue screen. I can remove it if I need to go all Neuromancer on anything."

"Was any of that English?" Dad asked from behind me. I hadn't heard him come in; he could give ninjas sneaking lessons.

"Hey, Ranger." Marcel spun around, pulling up more maps of the area around Atlanta. "I got the intel you wanted. You'll have to take the Gryphon from the flight point to get there."

Dad looked confused. I chimed in. "He's being funny. He means it's a straight shot to Atlanta."

"Couldn't you just say that?"

Marcel grinned at him. "I could, but what fun would it be?" He went back to tapping on the keyboard. More information sprang to life on the screens. "Where do you want the 3D scans sent?"

"Send them to the combat simulator. I'll gather the rest so we can strategize," Dad said as he turned and headed for the door. "See you in fifteen."

I guess Dad had changed his mind on keeping the room a secret or, more likely, Marcel had found it on his own. Marcel stood, resembling a shaggy Cheshire cat. "I really do love messin' with Ranger."

I shook my head. "When he zaps you, don't say I didn't warn you." I crossed the room, Marcel in tow.

"You don't think he'd actually do that, do you?"

I laughed. "You never know, now do you?"

He laughed half-heartedly as we walked to the simulator. Marcel launched into the benefits of the newest Zevion processor and how he needed to figure out a way to get his hands on one. It's not like we had postal delivery out here.

I nodded on occasion as we traversed Castle's corridors and stairs to our destination. My head buzzed with so much to consider. Where had they stashed Waxenby? Was he even alive? Would the Underground be able, or willing, to help? Could the meet be a Protectorate setup? I had no answers, but every question spawned more and darker thoughts.

We arrived at the simulator, walking over to join the Mom, Dad, Abby and Blaze as Marcel pressed the button and closed the door. I couldn't wait to see their faces when the simulator started. Nothing I'd ever seen before had prepared me for its realism.

Dad glanced over at us. "Okay, let's get started. Load Millennium Gate simulation." The room's lights dimmed as the simulation came to life. The illusion of the gate stood over us as the rest of the room became weeds, concrete, and long abandoned buildings. I leaned against the wall and got shocked looks from everyone but Dad and Marcel. So, Marcel did know how the room worked. I should have guessed as much.

"How are you doing that?" Abby asked in confusion. "It's just an image."

Marcel stepped up, knocking against the gate's wall. "The floor is a series of hydro-pneumatic plates. The pistons under the floor lift the sections so it mimics the simulation. It only goes up twenty feet or so. The top of the structure is just an image." He kicked a raised piece of concrete, his foot stopping where it should. "This makes it possible to train in an immersive environment where the landscape is an accurate representation. The mechanism is a remarkable superstructure being made of a poly—"

Dad cleared his throat, cutting off the lecture. "Thanks, Marcel. He's right, of course, the simulation makes training more realistic. What I'd like to do is lay out a plan for how I'm going to get in and out again."

Mom's eyebrows shot up. "How YOU are getting in and out? We are a team. We all go, or no one goes."

"No, Susan." He held up a hand to stop her. I wondered if he'd miss it when she tore it off. "This could be a setup. There is no way I'm risking all of you again. I'll make contact and report in. Marcel can keep tabs on me in case something goes wrong."

Mom folded her arms across her chest. "And what are we supposed to do from five hours away?"

Blaze stepped between them, placing a hand on each of their shoulders. Both looked from him to the hand and back. "Dudes, let's start with laying out the trap and work from there."

Abby frowned. "Trap? We don't know there will be a trap."

Blaze nodded. "If you prepare for everything you can think of, it makes what you weren't expecting easier to adapt to."

"If I were the Protectorate, I would use snipers in the upper windows," Marcel said, bringing up his previous concern while examining the layout of the buildings. "With just a few, you could cut off all exits from this area."

"Computer, load optimal sniper locations for holding a team at the center." Dad watched as snipers with rifles appeared on the roof lines around us and counted them. "So, five snipers. Computer, lay down fields of fire."

Light blue cones emitted from the walls, centering on where we stood. Abby walked to the side, checking how far it went back. "Absolutely no cover. You can't even hide under the arch. Best case is kick in one of the doors and wait them out." Eight metal doors resided under the arch, four per side.

Blaze indicated his agreement. "These dudes are covering you, what else? They have to have a plan for any Gifted you might bring."

Mom paced back and forth. "You'd want to be able to neutralize their abilities, like they did with Dominion."

Dad stiffened at the mention of her. "The launchers have to be used from close range. Computer, add locations an inhibitor band could be fired from."

Two images appeared by abandoned cars that sat on the sidewalk of the arch. "We need to eliminate those two cars?" I asked. "We could hit them with lightning when we get there as a precaution."

"No, I don't think so," Abby said, studying the cars. "They could insulate them, plus we don't want to tip our hand if we don't have to." She stepped the distance from the cars to us. "Computer, place accurate range markers."

I could see the wheels turning as Abby surveyed the area. She'd spent a lot of time with Jon and had learned well. A green line formed in a circle around each car. It didn't quite come to us. "If we stay under the arch, it would be a fluke if they hit anyone."

Blaze stepped over to the door next to Abby. "What's to stop them from loading a team into the gate itself ahead of time? These doors are a blind spot."

Marcel cocked his head. "What if we jammed the doors so they couldn't be opened?"

"It would be almost impossible to stop a determined foe from coming through those doors, though it might slow them down," Dad said, surveying the scene.

An idea blazed in my mind like a comet through the darkened sky. "Why not let them come out?"

Mom gave me an odd look, probably wondering if she had dropped me one time too many as a baby. "Honey, I think the idea is to avoid capture. If those doors open, we'd be surrounded."

"Not if we attach explosives to go off if the doors are opened." I checked Dad and Marcel. They both nodded, appreciating the idea.

Abby snorted. "We kill ourselves in the blast? I don't see how that helps."

At this point, everyone knew I could take a lot of damage, but Blaze and Abby weren't aware that I converted the energy into lightning. "It wouldn't hurt me."

Mom stopped pacing and locked my eyes. "You are not going in by yourself Thomas George Ward."

Blaze put his hand on her shoulder. "He wouldn't be alone, he'd..." Blaze broke off as a coughing fit overtook him. He stumbled over to lean against the gate. Mom moved next to him; concern etched on her face. After a minute, the fit subsided. He wiped his mouth with a cloth from his back pocket. He pushed the cloth back into the pocket.

"Eugene, you need to see a doctor. The coughing has gotten worse." Mom examined him, waiting for a response.

He shook his head. "Susan, I saw a doctor before I came here. It's allergies and bronchitis. I'm doing what I can, but I'll be like this for a while."

He'd mentioned it before, but Mom obviously didn't believe him; still, she let it slide.

"Where was I? Oh, Tommy wouldn't be alone. Michael and Abby would enter with him but not go into the meeting place. If things go bad, they move in to neutralize the threats." He paused and studied the simulation. "It also rules out the snipers since Powell shot him up and didn't leave more than a few bruises."

"Over my dead body! I will not allow my son to be the bait for this meeting." Mom held herself in full lawyer mode, but I could see the fear peeking out of her eyes.

"Mom, I'll be fine." I stepped over and looked her in the face. "We have to find Mr. Waxenby, and I'll have Dad and Abby to back me up." I could see by the set of her jaw she was digging in for a fight.

Marcel moved next to me, pushing the hair back up off his face. "Mom, I know you're worried, but Tommy can take care of himself. Plus,

I'll rig enough explosives to make anyone think twice about messin' with him."

I glanced at Marcel, noticing the lack of slang when talking to Mom. I put my hand on her arm. "Seriously, we go in, meet with the Underground and get out. If it's a trap, between Marcel's tech and our firepower, we can get out."

Dad came over, putting his arm around Mom's shoulders. "Let's sleep on it. It's a good plan, but we may come up with an alternative."

Mom stared at each of us in turn. "Fine, but we will discuss it again tomorrow." With that, she stalked across the room, though the sliding door robbed her of any dramatic exit. We all let out a collective sigh of relief.

Dad smirked. "Well, it could have gone better, but I think she'll come around to see the benefits of the plan." He turned to me. "Tommy, are you sure you are good with this? Things could get hairy if this goes sideways."

My whole life had gone sideways on me. I should be finishing my senior year of high school, probably moving to Granite Falls to work at the Lair with Blaze. Wendi, Mr. Taylor, Brunner, Clint, Ryder, and Powell would still be alive, and Jon wouldn't be on the run. On the other hand, if I hadn't, I wouldn't know my Dad, which would suck. Once the Gauntlet had been announced, my world had spun out of control, destroying anything in its path. "Dad, we have to find Mr. Waxenby. We owe it to him to try. If we have to fight, we have to fight."

I could tell he understood. Dad hated hurting people, especially those who couldn't fight back. Responsibility came with the Gift. "I'll go talk to Susan. I think this is a solid plan." He strode out of the room. Cyclone Ranger, one of the most powerful Gifted who'd ever lived, and my dad. Things had definitely changed, and I had a feeling this was just getting started.

I wished I understood Eiraf's advice better; maybe it would have helped. In reality, if I had comprehended what she said, I would have run away screaming.

9

It had been two days since the strategy meeting in the simulator. As Dad predicted, Mom chilled and agreed to our plan, which kept everyone as safe as could be expected. We drove overnight using back roads the Reclaimers hadn't patrolled for years. We pulled off the road a couple of miles outside of the Atlanta DMZ near the Chattahoochee River. An old apartment complex that had been swallowed by the surrounding forest gave a safe place for the car to wait for us.

Abby handed me a black case out of the trunk before retrieving a waterproof gun bag she slung over her shoulder. We all wore the new combat suits Mr. Fix-It made for us, replacing the ones we'd lost at The Gauntlet. They were solid black, and, after Viper's poison attack during the last fight with the Syndicate, they were now airtight. The visor provided night vision, which would come in handy on this run.

I secured the case to my back, adjusting the straps and fastening it across my chest. Dad stood off to the side, surveying the surroundings.

Abby's voice came through my earpiece. "All ready. We moving out, Maverick?"

"Player One, you ready?" Dad asked, swiveling his head to check on us.

"Maverick, ready to roll," I said, smiling at the names Marcel had assigned us. I thought Abby would pull his arms off when he labeled her

Goose. Even though our channel was encrypted, he thought better than to advertise who made up the team. Dad agreed. Blaze had laughed.

"Good. Goose left, Player right." He moved out through the forest, following an old broken sidewalk. We maintained radio silence as we wound our way down to the river. "Double check your seals then enter the water."

I ran my hands around the face and neck seals even though the helmet read-out showed the seal functioned correctly. Better safe than sorry. According to Marcel, drug runners used an opening in the fence running across the river to access the city like the Syndicate used the Squid. I hoped we wouldn't run into anyone underwater.

"Wizard, how are we looking?" Dad asked over the comm-link. Marcel monitored everything possible, and probably a few things which were impossible, while we were on the ground.

Marcel's voice reverberated in my helmet. "Maverick, you're clear as far as the eyes in the sky can tell." After a short pause, he continued. "Of course, if any of those rat monsters or worse are lurking around, I wouldn't know. Man, what an awesome shooter concept."

Dad cut in. "Wizard, let's keep focused. Anything looks unusual, we need a head's up." I could see him shake his head as he kept us moving forward. We had a long way to go before sun up.

Abby slithered through the forest, avoiding making a sound, ghosting around trees and deadfalls without breaking stride. I, on the other hand, sounded like a stampeding herd of elephants carrying boom boxes blasting out Metallica. Stealth wasn't one of my Gifts to be sure.

After twenty minutes, we reached the back of the Chattahoochee River. Downriver stood the security fence built to keep people out of the dead city. If the intel we had was any good, there would be a large hole in the fence underwater to allow us entry. Even though we'd been over the plan a dozen times, I still worried we had missed something.

Abby's voice crept into my ear. "Man, it's going to be a cold swim." She stepped into the water, wading into its dark depths. She stopped, waist deep, glancing back to Dad and me. "You two coming?"

I heard Dad chuckle. "No time like the present." We both stepped into the river, the current pulling at the box on my back. I checked the straps to make sure it was secure. I pushed forward, and the water closed around me. I let the current move me. Any guards on the shore would have a hard time picking us out, three dark, bobbing helmets under a cloud-filled night sky.

Marcel's voice broke the silence. "You should reach the wall in under a minute. Maverick looks to be dead on with the breach."

Dad floated off to my left, more centered on the river. Abby had over-shot the line. As I maneuvered to get behind Dad, she swam over to join us. I could feel the cold through my suit, but it felt more like an early spring day than the frigid blast it actually was.

The wall loomed over us as we approached, transitioning to a metal lattice over the river. We stopped long enough for Dad to signal to dive. My HUD changed to heat imaging as the cold water covered my head. I pulled myself deeper along the wall. The air in the suit, which had let us float down the river, worked against us as we progressed deeper.

"And there she is," Dad said as the display changed, showing us the hole in the wall. He grabbed the edge and flipped himself around the fence, his momentum shooting him upward. "Careful, the edge is jagged. Don't puncture your suits."

"Good safety tip, thanks, Egon," Marcel quipped over the line. I groaned. Marcel needed to get a life. Abby spun through the hole like a gymnast. I pushed myself through the opening but didn't float up. The box caught on a piece of the wall. I twisted, trying to loosen myself, but couldn't break free.

"Player, you okay?" Dad asked over the comm-link.

Great. Leave it to Captain Klutz to get stuck underwater. I tried to push myself lower, but the suit wanted to go up, and I had no leverage. "The box is stuck on the fence." I could feel my face flush with embarrass-ment. I struggled like a fish on a line but to no use. My stomach clenched, forcing the taste of bile into my mouth. I gasped for air, afraid I was drowning. "I'm stuck; I can't move." My voice betrayed my panic.

Abby's voice broke through the fear. "I've got you." Rough hands pushed on my shoulders, then I began to rise, free of the damn wall.

"There you go, Player," Abby said, giving me the thumbs-up. "Every-body knows water and electricity don't mix, Sparky."

First Marcel, now Abby. Everyone's a comedian. "I'll try to remember that." I crested like a breaching submarine. Abby bobbed up next to me, she signaled, and we swam faster to catch Dad. I gave him the thumbs-up as we pulled alongside. The next hour consisted of floating as we watched for the train crossing, marking our departure point from the river.

I spent the time reviewing how strange my life had become. Last year, I lived in Redemption with Mom, being hassled by Brunner and Powell on a daily basis. Now they were dead, I'd lost Wendi, and we were fugitives from the Protectorate. I wondered if it was worth all the pain and loss. Nightmares tormented me most nights. Images of the people I'd killed: Wendi's lifeless body, Clint and Ryder melting in the blast of energy I'd unleashed, Reclaimer bodies scattered like broken toys around a transformer near Jinx's house. What's done is done, but it wouldn't stay in the past where it belonged.

My mind wandered, a lucid dream-state in the perfect quiet of floating down the river, landing on Eriaf's words. I hadn't seen Alyx to ask about it, and frankly, I wasn't sure if maybe I hadn't hallucinated the whole event. She'd said three people would guide me: the Phoenix, the cursed one, and the doppelganger. I had no clue who any of them could be. Falling to the dreamer or the trickster meant nothing to me; neither description fit the Protectorate or the Syndicate. What use were warnings if you couldn't understand them? When I got back, I had to talk to Alyx. I understood losing Waxenby would be catastrophic, though I had no idea why. He's a great guy, but how could one person be so important? I shook my head, returning to the present.

In the distance I could make out a bridge. An old rotted train lay on the right bank. It must have hit the bridge during the Dark Brigade attack. Dad signaled to head to the left bank. We swam across the river, dragging ourselves out of the water. The cloud cover kept the city in darkness, but we couldn't chance flashes of lightning. In a dead city, lights would be a beacon to the Reclaimers.

I dropped to my knees, glad to be on solid ground again and away from my memories. Dad scouted the woods, looking for a path up to the train tracks. Abby reclined against a rock formation jutting from the ground. I vented my faceplate and breathed in the cold air. It smelled of impending rain and the river. I stood up, stretching as we waited for Dad to return.

Abby raised her HUD, setting her gun case on the ground next to her feet. "Sparky, you had me worried down there." I couldn't see her face, but she sounded concerned. "I'm not losing any more friends, got it?"

I nodded. "I'm right there with you. Thanks for the assist—"

Abby stood abruptly, head on a swivel. "Did you hear that?" She asked, peering around, on full alert and growing rapidly.

Just as I slapped my visor into place, the ground opened below her feet, dropping her from my sight. "Abby!" I screamed as I dove for her arm, missing it by inches. I crawled over to the hole, getting knocked backward as a huge boulder shot into the air, a dirt geyser spraying in all directions.

I leapt to my feet and couldn't believe my eyes. What I had thought was rock turned out to be an alligator of immense proportion. It thrashed on the ground, stubby legs scrambling for purchase on the soft riverbed. It must have been forty feet long and taller than a horse. Beady red eyes glowed in the darkness as it sought to crush Abby in its giant jaws.

The monster whipped its enormous head back and forth trying to dislodge Abby who had her legs wedged against the roof of the creature's mouth, her back laying on its tongue, keeping it from eating his dinner. She screamed in primal rage, her size expanding as she held the giant maw apart.

A flash of light announced Dad joining the fight. He streaked across the distance, barreling into the side of the thing's head. The alligator stumbled, then swiped its head, knocking Dad back into the woods. I pulled the energy together, readying a strike.

"No lightning!" Dad shouted over the comm-link. "We can't alert anyone that we're here."

Marcel crashed the party. "What the hell is happening?" The sound of him banging on the keyboard in the background increased as he spoke.

I ignored him, running toward the monster trying to eat my friend. Far faster than I'd have thought possible, its tail whipped around. I now know how a baseball feels. The solid mass of armored tail crashed into me, propelling me into a tree. The breath whooshed from my lungs as I hit. Slowly I slid down the tree, stunned.

Dad flew back in, avoiding the tail on the back swipe. He drove a fist into the unprotected eye, causing the creature to rear, roaring in pain. The mouth loosened, allowing Abby to roll free of the jaws and land on her feet. She accelerated, delivering a massive blow to the exposed throat. Another bellow of pain erupted from the wounded animal. I thought it would flee, but it attacked.

Abby rolled away as the giant head slammed the ground where she had been. I got to my feet, feeling the surge of power from hitting the tree gave me. I couldn't throw lightning, but I had an idea. I ran at the creature's side, encasing my fist in energy. I hit it full force behind the front, left leg. The force of the blow flipped it on its side, but instead of disabling it, the thing rolled, coming back to its feet. It rushed at me, intent on ridding itself of what had caused it pain.

There is no reason something that huge should be able to move so fast. I backpedaled, but it was on me before I'd gone five steps. Dad swooped in, none too gently putting his shoulder into my stomach, and got me away before the behemoth made me his dinner. Dad dropped me on the ground, out of the way, and shot back into the fight.

The whole scene reminded me of one of the fights on Saturday Night Showdown. Abby, the newest recipient of the Smashing Tail Award, crashed near me. While on the show, Dad had jumped on the back of one of the robots so he could disable it. This thing's armor stood up to just about any blow, but there had to be a weak spot. I ran to help Abby up; the blow had staggered her, which is saying something since she had to be near eight feet of solid muscle. Good thing her combat suit adapted to her changing proportions.

I stopped in front of her. "I need to get on its back. Can you get me up there?"

She looked at me. Normal Abby couldn't pick me up, but Gifted Abby could do a lot more. I heard a growl of assent as she found purchase on my torso and left leg. She sped into the fight, throwing me in an arc as we neared. I flew, stifling a scream that would earn me constant harassment from Abby and Marcel for months, and landed on the monster's back. The ridges made excellent handholds as it ferociously shook to dislodge me. I crawled along the back, searching for an opening. Dad and Abby darted in and out, distracting the beast, keeping him from concentrating on me.

At last, I found what I'd hoped to find. At the base of his skull where the armor plates came together was a gap large enough for a knife. I'd practiced with Blaze in Castle and hoped this would work here. I focused the swirling energy around my fist, willing it into the shape of a fist dagger. The power flowed between my middle fingers, forming the thick base and tapering down to a pointed end. I plunged the dagger between the plates into the behemoth's brain. It roared as I forced the blade deeper, pumping more energy into it as it tore through flesh. Blood and ichor sprayed out of the wound as I put my weight behind the blade. The alligator twitched as the point hit home.

I let go of the stream of energy that fueled the knife, slumping against the still form of the beast. "Will somebody tell me what's going on?" Marcel's shrill voice sounded in my ear.

I grinned. "Just getting Captain Hook's hand back."

10

After the fight on the riverbank, the walk into Atlanta was quiet. Luckily, we all still had the ordnance cases we'd need for the meeting. It had been touch-and-go with mine; it now bore deep grooves where the underwater fence had scored it. Abby's looked in better shape. We saw signs of passage as we followed the abandoned train tracks through the outskirts of the city. Old tanker trucks labeled Georgia Gas sat unused behind a derelict chain linked fence as we left the tracks to move to the gate. The waterworks greeted us as we ghosted through the cold night, and we passed unseen. I heard howling off in the distance and shuddered. I would be thrilled to conclude our business and return to Castle. I'd had enough of destroyed cities.

More abandoned buildings and the remains of wrecked vehicles stood silently as we made our way toward tomorrow's meeting place. We turned the corner onto what had been 7th Street and saw the Millennium Gate. A brown and tan apartment building with rusted metal rails around the balconies was off to our left; that would be our home for the rest of the night. A dilapidated minivan provided an entrance, having crashed into the building, sending the patio door into the living room.

"Radio silence until we're settled," Dad said then shut off his link. Abby and I followed suit.

Climbing over the hood, all the while avoiding the damaged portions, challenged our agility. Well, mine at least. Balancing the box attached to my back didn't make this any easier. Abby finally leapt over, grabbing the top of the opening and swinging in. The rifle case slipping messed up her landing, forcing the Asian Zone judge to score her a six for the stumble. "Terrarium" might have been a better name than apartment with all the weeds grown in and around the rotted furnishings. Something had torn apart the kitchen cabinets at some point, probably in search of food. The large bite marks on the discarded cabinet doors didn't soothe my nerves any. We found the front door of the ground floor apartment still locked, the owner having been disintegrated instantly in the attack.

Dad unlocked the door, peering up and down the hallway. He showed the thumbs-up, and we moved out, closing the door behind us. Spider webs clogged the hallway, and a thick layer of dust on the floor assured us there hadn't been activity in a long time. I silently thanked Mr. Fix-it for the sealed combat suit; the thought of spiders—mutated spiders—creeped me out. We reached the stairway, and Abby and I started up. Dad sent a light breeze along the hall to obscure our tracks. The concrete stairs were in good shape, and we made the climb to the fourth floor through the homes of every insect ever created.

We entered the abandoned hallway, checking for signs of anything passing before us, none of us wanting to tangle with the wildlife. Dad gave the signal. Slowly we made our way to the last door on the right that looked out over the Millennium Gate. Abby twisted the door handle, breaking the lock and opening the door. She silently slid into the room, checking for other signs of entry. Dad and I followed her in, flanking her. I stepped into the master bedroom, the bed unmade, women's clothing scattered on the floor. Mold covered the bathroom, make-up, lotions, and clothing laying around. The former occupant either left in a hurry that morning or was a colossal slob. I hoped for hurry, since many of the cities started evacuating before the second wave of attacks hit.

I stepped back into the main area; Dad flashed the all clear. He went to the apartment's front door, retrieved a piece of metal from a pocket and welded it into place, effectively locking the door. I clicked on the comm-link; I hadn't realized how stressful knowing I couldn't talk to anyone would be.

"Find a spot and get some rest. I'll take first watch. Abby, I'll wake you in three hours. You wake Tommy after."

Abby's helmet nodded. "You want the rifle? The scope has night and heat vision."

Dad shook his head. I wondered what we must look like to an outsider. Three aliens in black exoskeletons wandering around an abandoned building in the middle of the night. "My visor is fine to keep watch on the meeting location. We just need to know if they are up to anything."

I scanned the room, seeing the moldy furniture, and decided sleeping on the comparatively clean tile in the kitchen would be my best choice. I unhooked the banged-up case I'd carried into Atlanta and set it next to me as I tried to get comfortable. Under no circumstances would I remove my helmet in here. Abby peered into the bedrooms, thought better of it, and joined me sitting on the floor and resting against cabinets.

I drifted off to sleep, wondering when my life would ever be normal or if that would even be possible. Way too quickly, Abby shook my shoulder to take my shift. The chrono display in my HUD displayed one in the afternoon local time. Abby held out her hand and pulled me to my feet. She took my spot on the floor as I stepped over Dad and headed to the window where I could best see the Gate.

The Millennium Gate must have been beautiful at one time. Now vines grew up the walls and cars had smashed into the lower level, destroying the ring of pillars in places. Just like the simulation, two cars stood sentry on the median leading to the meeting area below the arch. The cloud cover held, but rain hadn't fallen, and I wanted it to stay that way. Slick surfaces didn't make for much fun. I spent the next three hours watching nothing happen. The HUD flashed at four o'clock, and I went to wake up Dad and Abby so we could finalize the plan.

Dad unsealed his helmet and removed it, a grimace crossing his face as the smells assaulted him. Abby and I did the same, and I regretted it. The air was thick with mold and decay. I fought not to throw up. Dad pulled out a packet of jerky and carefully opened it so his gloves did not touch the meat directly. "Better eat quick, it will be a long time until we reach the car."

I grabbed my packet and chewed the dry jerky. As soon as it was all in my mouth, I reseated my helmet and resealed it. Unfortunately, the stench clung to my skin, but it was a vast improvement over smelling the room.

Dad pushed his helmet back on. "Player, once it gets dark, you can jump over from the balcony and slide down the lamppost to the ground floor. Make your way to the gate and get set up. Everything looks on the up-and-up, but let's not take any chances. Mr. Wizard, can you access everything remotely?"

Marcel's voice boomed in my ear. "Affirmative, Maverick. I've got a link to a satellite in geosynchronous orbit over your location. I've bounced the signal off three—"

Abby cut him off. "Have your nerdgasm some other time; we just need to know if you can back us up if things go south fast."

Marcel's voice had a sulking tone to it. "Yes. Goose. I can access everything."

"Good job. Once everything is set, Goose will cover Player with the sniper rifle, and I'll set up on the balcony in case I need to move in quickly. We need to set the deal and then head out. Unless its life or death, no Gifts. We don't want to announce who we are. If for any reason we get separated, return to the old apartment buildings next to the wall. We don't cross the wall until we are all together. Understood?"

We both nodded our agreement. Abby retrieved her case from the kitchen, opened it and assembled the rifle. She snapped the scope on and loaded the weapon. According to Blaze, the rifle had an effective range of half a mile. The bullets had been designed for use against Gifted and would punch through just about any material this side of Carbinium. She set the rifle on the floor and retrieved a suction cup and glass cutter from the bag. She secured the cup to each window in turn, cut out the window, then placed the glass on the old couch.

Dad exited the room through the balcony door. He carried a device that looked like an electronic grasshopper. In reality, the field generator would provide camouflage by mimicking the surrounding area. Once established, the scene wouldn't change, regardless of what happened behind it.

Abby laid on the living room floor, the tip of the rifle just inside the window frame. She adjusted the scope, moving the dials until she grunted her satisfaction. I headed for the kitchen, grabbing the case I'd carried in. I popped the lock and checked to make sure no water had gotten in, and all the contents were secure. The case held eight shaped charges and a remote detonator. I verified each one sat correctly in the foam insulation and that the detonator turned on. I switched off the detonator, carefully pulled one of the charges from its protective cradle, and activated the device. "Mr. Wizard can you see package one?"

"Affirmative, Player. Package one is ready for delivery."

I switched off the detonator and reseated it. We repeated the process for the other seven charges; Marcel saw each of them, and he could remotely detonate them if needed once they were in place and active on the doors below. I finished my tests and secured the case. I stepped out on the balcony, which I swear groaned slightly. Dad sat in an old rusted patio chair, surveying the area with his helmet off.

I pulled my helmet off; the cold, fresh air tingled on my face. What a relief after the offensive odors of the apartment. The generator ensured no one could see us, but I felt exposed out in the open. We still had a couple of hours before it would be fully dark. The ominous storm clouds left the city a stark black and white.

"You know this used to be a beautiful city at one time." Dad scanned the view, but I doubted he saw what stood before him. "People lived here; the city had a rhythm, a music all its own. In the summer, families would take their kids to the parks, stop for ice cream. We've lost so much."

I didn't know what to say. Until Grim Reaper had driven us to DC, intent on selling us to the Protectorate, the largest place I'd ever been was Granite Falls. The world had been this way my whole life. I pulled over another chair and dropped into it. Part of the rusted seat crumbled under my weight, but it held. I tried to imagine what the city would look like with people in it, cars streaming past as we watched. I thought it probably had been a sight to behold. At some point, Abby joined us, and we quietly watched the thickening storm clouds dance as night rolled in. A portrait of vivid reds and greens painted the horizon.

Dad stood after a long while, putting his helmet on. I did the same and headed to grab the case. Dad helped me secure it to my back as Abby returned to man the sniper rifle.

"It's go time. Mr. Wizard, you ready?" Dad asked, adjusting the chest strap to his liking. He put his hand on my shoulder and squeezed. I grinned nervously inside my helmet, though he couldn't see it.

"Maverick, we are go. Call the ball."

I cleared my throat, trying to calm my nerves and keep my voice calm. "Player calls the ball." I walked out to the patio, gave Dad the thumbs-up, and jumped across to the streetlight. The pole swayed but didn't break as

I slid to the ground. I ducked behind a van with a donut logo and the slogan "Hot Now" in large letters on the side panel. I weaved between the cars, staying low. Panic screamed through my nerves as I kept a lookout for giant rats, alligators, or anything else that might want to eat me. Luckily, the run didn't hold any surprises.

I passed the last of the abandoned cars on the median, peeking with heat vision to make sure they were empty, and sprinted to the gate. I felt an itch as I crossed, fully exposed for anyone to see. I knew Abby followed me with the scope, but anyone else could be doing the same. I skidded to a halt under the dark shadows of the structure. I needed to work fast in case anyone showed up early. I pulled each charge, primed it, and activated it. I pushed one into the center of each door where it affixed. If anyone opened those doors, they were in for a loud and painful greeting.

I pushed the dented case between the wall and marble statue at the front. If things went bad, I didn't need to be tripping over it. "All set, Mr. Wizard."

Marcel's whispered words reached me. "I call the ball, Player." I wasn't sure why he whispered since he was in the control room in Castle, but that's Marcel for you. Now we waited for the Underground to arrive. I laid prone in the middle of the arch, surrounded by the dark like we were playing hide-and-seek. I might have dozed off, but my head jerked up as Abby said, "Player, you've got three headed up the median toward you."

"Player, let's keep this short and sweet. Who they are, what do they want, and do they know where the Commander is? Then we head for base."

I nodded in the dark even though I knew they couldn't see me. I got to my feet and moved to the opening of the middle of the arch. I could make out three silhouettes in the entrance. One kept moving, but the other two stopped, stepping to the sides. A soft, yellow light clicked on, revealing the Underground's representative, or at least I hope so.

My visor adjusted to the light source so I could see. A woman holding a shuttered lantern stood before me. Long, wavy red hair dipped past her shoulders, framing a pretty face and a guarded expression. I'd guess her to be around my mom's age; her posture and stare reminded me of Mom in full lawyer mode. I'd learned long ago to never judge a person by their size.

"Thank you for meeting with us. I'm Warden, leader of the Underground here in Atlanta. What should I call you?" Her voice held a note of authority, not mean, but business-like.

I thought frantically. I couldn't use Enforcer since they would probably know it from Saturday Night Showdown. Player didn't sound right either. I blurted out the next thing I thought of. "Sparky."

"Sparky?" Three voices said in my ear at the same time.

"Seriously, Sparky is the best you could come up with?" Abby asked in exasperation. I groaned inwardly, cheeks flushing in embarrassment.

Warden cocked her head as if she wasn't sure she'd heard me correctly. "Um, Sparky it is."

The figures escorting her stepped toward the circle of light. "You might as well call him murderer." A flat voice I knew all too well reached me as he walked into the light, bow drawn and aimed at my head.

Jon Stevens had joined the party.

ilently, I wondered who I'd pissed off to have such horrible luck. How the hell did Jon Stevens end up with the leader of the Underground? I broke my eyes away, noticing the second person who stood to the left of Warden: Turk. I hadn't seen him since I'd left the Secret Lair. Jon must have freed him of his collar. Asking if today could get any worse would have to wait since I had an arrow pointed at my head.

I heard a growl over the comm-link. Abby sounded as happy as I did. "Can I shoot him?"

Dad's calm voice answered. "No, let's see how this plays out. I don't want to bury anymore Stevens children unless it's unavoidable."

The words hit me like a bucket of cold water. I slowly raised my hands. "I came to talk, not to fight." The last thing I wanted to do was hurt either of them. Both had lost a person close to them, but they didn't realize those losses hurt me as well.

Warden turned on Jon, her face flushing red. "Put it down. We don't have time for this."

The bow tensed as Jon pulled hard on the nocked arrow. "He killed my sister."

"I said put it down, NOW!" Her voice cracked like a whip. The string relaxed as the bow lowered, all the while murderous revenge raged in his eyes. "We can discuss this later, but I'll not have you ruining an opportunity we sorely need."

Turk barked a harsh laugh. "We'll deal with Sparky here another time. We've both got scores to settle with him."

Warden's eyes shot skyward. "I'm sorry." She stepped closer as she spoke. "The boys told me about the Syndicate taking your friend. I know how it feels; they captured my daughter. We've heard rumors they established a new base of operations in the South Western Region. We haven't found out where yet, but odds are good it's one of the no-go sites."

I nodded. "Thank you. You mentioned you needed help?" I tried to focus on Warden, but my eyes kept checking on Jon and Turk.

"Player, you're playing in lunatic mode down there. You could use some power-ups." Leave it to Marcel to turn this into a video game. If it were, I'd have rage quit after seeing the two of them. It made sense they paired up, seeing that they both blamed me for deaths I had little control over, however much they haunted me.

Warden sighed. "Yes. We are in desperate need of weapons and tech. Between fighting the drug cartels, the mutants, and the Protectorate, our numbers have dwindled. We can trade information or assistance in other matters."

"Tell her to leave a list of requests in the drop, and we'll see what we can do," Dad said hesitantly. "Ask her what their plans are and why they need weapons."

I repeated what Dad asked and was rewarded with a laugh. "Plans? We plan to survive. When we fled to the no-go sites after the attacks, we had planned to overthrow the Protectorate. Now I have children to feed and enemies on every side. Even if I pulled all my fighters together, we couldn't overthrow a city, much less the global Protectorate."

"Interesting. Tell her we'll be in touch."

I did. A small smile crossed her face. "Thank you. I'll leave the boys home next time."

"We've got company," Abby's voice came over the comm-link. "Three copters inbound from the north. Player, move now."

I spun to look for the helicopters, but they weren't visible yet. "There are three helicopters on their way. You need to go."

Warden stiffened. "Someone betrayed us." She glanced to where Jon and Turk stood. "There is no way the Reclaimers could have found out."

I followed her gaze. "None of us would survive meeting up with the Reclaimers or Protectorate. Something tipped them off."

Abby shouted into my ear. "PLAYER MOVE NOW!"

"Everyone meet up at the rendezvous. Get going, Player! No Gifts unless you have to." I heard the tension in Dad's voice. Mom had fought him on letting me go, and now we were in trouble.

Lights flooded the outside of the arch. "This is the Protectorate DEA. Come out with your hands up."

"There are boots on the ground converging. Head out the back; there's more cover. I'll buy you some time." The sounds of rifle fire and shouts from the troops outside rang in my ears.

"This is local drug enforcement, not Reclaimer forces." Dad was breathing a lot harder. He'd be running to the ground floor to help me fight. "We'll follow once you get past our position."

I turned to Warden. "Head out the back; it's local DEA. We should be able to get away."

She nodded, signaling for Jon and Turk to follow. Jon paused to point at me. "We are not done, we'll never be done while both of us are alive." He ran to catch up with Warden and Turk.

Even in the middle of a fight, Jon couldn't let it go. The sad part is, if Marcel's theory was right, his Gift fueled a constant need to hunt. He could no more let go of hunting me than I could stop absorbing energy. I fled the arch, leaping to the lower level that consisted of broken Roman pillars surrounding a cobbled patio with a pond at the end of it. Warden stood in the center of the ring, Jon and Turk flanking her. None of them moved as they faced me.

"We need to get out of here," I yelled as I jumped, not wasting time taking the stairs. Landing, I realized why they were doing an impression of statues. Six Protectorate agents decked out in dark blue uniforms with armored vests, utility belts, and leg armor held rifles at the ready. I'm not sure who was more surprised by my entry.

I started at the bark of Abby firing the sniper rifle. "What are you doing? Get out of there!"

Everything moved at once. The lead officer spun, leveling his rifle at me, or at least tried to as I kicked his knee out from under him. He crashed to the ground, gaining the attention of the others. I kicked the side of his head, knocking him out and sending his helmet sailing across the courtyard. "I'm trying to, but we didn't check the downstairs doors. I've got company."

Arrows dropped the two soldiers to my right as my foot lashed out to the left. The blow landed, but his armor absorbed the worst of it. I saw Turk launch himself at the officer on my left, leaving me with two. Out of the corner of my eye, I saw Jon lower his bow. Asshole.

The second soldier stood paralyzed, not sure who to focus on. I pivoted, driving my fist into his faceplate and shattering it. I felt his nose break from the force of the impact. He grunted and dropped to the ground. Momentum moved me past my other opponent, which afforded him the opportunity to slam his shock baton into my head. I heard the helmet crack; cool air rushed along the back of my head. The HUD reported the breach, the electronic voice sounding slightly pissy that I'd let it happen. Like I needed to deal with a passive-aggressive AI. Things kept getting better and better.

I stumbled but kept my footing. Another sharp strike hit my back; power flooded through me like a tidal wave of molten lava. The third strike never landed. I spun to the left, using a two-armed scissor block to stop the baton under a shower of sparks. The shocked look on the soldier's face said everything that needed to be said. I snatched the baton out of his hands and jammed it into his chest. Arcs of electricity leapt across his torso, collapsing him on the spot. From the spreading stains on his jumpsuit I was glad my helmet still mostly functioned. "Didn't your mom tell you not to mess with electricity?"

Turk had knocked out his man and stood over him. Somebody had leaked the meeting. Nothing had come in or out of here for the past eighteen hours. I'm not sure what happened, but it would have to wait for later.

I strode over to Warden. "You need to get out of here; it's not safe." She nodded her agreement, her brown eyes flashing with anger. "We'll be in touch."

"Thank you," she said. The loud noise of helicopter rotors descended, making further conversation impossible. Two Protectorate 'copters hovered just over the pond at the opening of the courtyard. "Throw down your weapons and put your hands up. You're under arrest. Failure to obey will result in the use of lethal force." They had machine guns pointed at us from the bay doors. I could survive the onslaught, but the others couldn't, including the six Protector agents laying behind us.

"Goose, can you hit one of the helicopters?" No response. "Raise comm-link."

The 'ever so reassuring' voice of my robotic overlord chirped in my ear. "Comm-link antenna is malfunctioning." I sighed, thinking frantically what to do next, deciding it was time for a distraction. Reaching into my pocket, I retrieved the remote detonator. "Get ready to run," I said to Warden, who raised her hands in surrender. I flipped the detonator cap up to expose the firing button. With a soft click, everything changed.

A terrible explosion sounded behind me, concrete striking me from behind. I could see body parts and gear bouncing across the open ground. The power surged through me even as I felt the pain flare across my back and legs. The night sky turned white as the eight charges fired in unison. The gate groaned as masonry flew in every direction. Something hit the side of my helmet, and my HUD went dark. OMG, what else could go wrong with this mission? I realized I really didn't want to know the answer.

Warden didn't waste any time. She swept her arms up before her. The clouds roiled and lightning flashed above, the sound of thunder on its heels. She pushed her hands together, and the wind responded. The helicopters rocked like boats on choppy water. The gunner from the first helicopter fell screaming into the pond below. Without my HUD, I couldn't be sure, but I swear something plucked him out of the air. The pilots fought for control, gunfire spraying wildly as they flailed around. When the full force of the wind hit the first copter, it spun out, slamming into the other with a screech of tearing metal. The wreckage fell into the water below as the storm hit us.

The wind drove the rain down in sheets, threatening our footing. I tried the comm-link, but it was dead. Between the darkness and the rain, I could barely see through my visor. At least my suit kept me dry, unlike the uniforms of the Protectorate officers who were trying to catch us. Warden grabbed my arm and gave me the thumbs-up. I nodded, returning the signal. She turned and vanished into the storm like a wraith in the night.

As hard as I tried, I couldn't get my bearings. I moved into the wind, thinking the apartment complex Dad and Abby had holed up in should be that way. Debris flew everywhere before the onslaught of the wind and rain. Lightning strikes pounded the city, leaving gaping holes in the concrete and buildings alike. On multiple occasions, pieces of broken masonry hit me as I pushed toward the relative safety of the surrounding buildings. I jumped as a loud crash sounded from behind me. I wondered if the weakened arch had collapsed in the storm.

After a few minutes of struggling, using the abandoned cars as handholds, I reached a building. I couldn't be sure I had gone to the correct one, but it would have to do. I found a breach in the wall and climbed over the fallen masonry into pitch darkness. The wind still howled as if seeking revenge for having been summoned unexpectedly. A single bolt of my lighting paled in comparison to Warden's storm like a bullet versus a nuclear bomb.

I dropped to the grimy floor, exhausted from the trek through the storm. As I lay there catching my breath, I planned for my next move. With the storm raging, I'd have to stay inside as much as possible. If I was in the correct building, it wrapped around the corner, which would put me closer to the rendezvous site. As per Dad's plan, I needed to get to the train tracks and follow them back. I couldn't afford to wait long. Without the storm, it had taken hours to get here from the river, and I had farther to go now. I forced myself to sit up and get moving.

I pulled off my near useless helmet, feeling for the crack to see if I could fix it. The helmet emitted a bit of light from the faceplate but not enough to let me do repairs. Marcel could fix it later. I looked out into the darkness, listening to the storm rage on unchecked. The storm would keep the Protectorate from launching any attacks against the Underground. After more than fifteen years of hiding here, they knew how to stay hidden; they had information I didn't possess.

I moved to the door, pulling it open and stepping into the hallway. I stopped dead in my tracks. In front of me stood a hooded figure, arms raised toward me. A hissing sound and something wet hitting my face were the last things I remembered as I passed out.

I knew I didn't want to know what else could go wrong today.

I woke with a steady pounding in my head and a sharp pain in my right arm. Without opening my eyes, I listened to see what I could figure out. Someone hummed a melody that sounded a lot like Sweet Caroline as they walked around, accompanied by clinking glass and soft bumps of closing cabinets. A musky smell I couldn't place tickled my nose. Lying down, held in place by ropes, didn't bode well for the situation. I cracked my eyes, expecting to be in a cell of some sort. Instead, wood paneling, caged animals, and a huge reptile awaited me.

A voice came from across the room. "Oh, good! You're awake." The owner was a man in his late forties, bald with a long gray goatee. Large glasses perched on his nose, looking like they would fall off at any moment. His tone held a bubbly excitement that worried me. "I'm so sorry for the inconvenience, but the work must go on, and I can't get volunteers, so I have to snatch people when I can. I do hope you understand."

I gawked at him, unable to think of what to say. He stood next to the table he'd tied me to, but I couldn't feel any power in me to break free. I glanced around, trying to make sense of it all. I saw my suit thrown over the back of a chair and realized my clothes were gone. I wore a green hospital gown under the ropes.

The man tapped his fingertips together rapidly, almost bouncing with contained energy. He reminded me of a kid on Christmas morning. "Ahh, cat's got your tongue? No worries, a minor side effect of the knockout spray. It also keeps you from using your Gift. Man, I wish I could get my hands on a dampening field. Oh boy, would that make my life easier. As it is, the spray works well, but I must keep an IV with the stuff running. Rest assured I won't need you for long." He stopped, tilting his head to the side. "Do I know you? You look so familiar."

I shook my head, part in answer, part to try to clear the fog away. "Who are you?" I whispered. My throat ached from the dryness, making me wonder how long I'd been out.

His hand shot to his mouth. "How rude of me. I have many names, but for the length of your stay here, you may refer to me as Dr. Goat, or just Goat, like everyone else here." He pulled his hand through his goatee in a vain attempt to straighten the unruly hair. "I am in charge of research and development for the cartel. Once I've completed a tissue sample, you'll be released."

I tried to respond but couldn't get the words out. Dr. Goat noticed, crossed the room, and retrieved a bottle of water. Unless my eyes played tricks on me, he wore a green plaid kilt and a faded black Harley Davidson t-shirt. He also had a pistol strapped to his hip. He held my head up and let the pure bliss of cold water slide down the rawness of my throat.

"If they'd just relent and let me sample you people, this wouldn't be necessary." He knelt next to me, letting me drink until I pulled my head back.

"Thank you," I croaked out, but I felt much better after the water. "Why am I here?"

He strolled across the room, dropping the bottle on a cluttered table as he passed. He returned, pushing a surgical tray covered with a blue cloth. "It's a matter of supply and demand. The Reclaimers refuse to use Gifted in any matter, but they certainly want their powers. I've found by culturing cells of select Gifted, I can produce a drug that mimics, though to a much lesser degree, those powers."

I didn't take my eyes off the tray. "So, you test the drugs on these animals?"

"What?" He reared back as if I offended his mother. "These are my pets. The Reclaimers test the drugs on people they don't like; I'd never hurt my animals." An angry glare had replaced the happy demeanor. "Well, good a time as any to turn you into a pin cushion." He chuckled at his joke.

He reached above my head and flipped a switch. A low hum of a motor started, and then the table rotated to the right until I hung suspended above another table. The table I was strapped to descended, gently sandwiching me between the two, making me the cream center of the Oreo.

I heard the instruments being readied on the tray as he went back to humming. "I'm going to take a bone marrow sample. It might hurt a bit but Gifted heal quickly enough." A scraping noise and a flood of cold air announced part of the table exposed my ass to the world.

Cold metal pierced my skin, but the pain barely registered. A tapping noise followed, then the whole process repeated two more times. I drifted off only to jerk awake as the table reoriented itself to the original position. Dr. Goat wheeled the tray back and busied himself with whatever he was doing. A weight landed on my legs; a startled yelp escaped my mouth. The weight resolved itself into a small dog with a black, white, and brown patterned face.

Dr. Goat looked over and laughed. "Booger, leave the poor boy alone." The dog didn't respond to his commands. Instead, he climbed up, put his paws firmly on my chest, and licked my face before he settled across my stomach, his head resting on my right arm.

"His name is Booger?"

Dr. Goat waved a hand. "His real name is Emerson, his nickname is Booger, because pain-in-the-ass is too long to say. Caviler King Charles always think highly of themselves." He trailed off as he banged around the kitchen/laboratory. "Damn, where is the sample kit?" He walked out of my field of view. Emerson's head lifted, and he nipped the IV line. He winked at me and put his head back down. The dog winked at me? These must be some great drugs.

Dr. Goat stomped in, throwing cabinets open and slamming them closed. "There ye are, my pretty," He exclaimed, holding the red plastic box before him. "Thought ye could get away, but not from this old goat." He must be a few bullets short of a magazine to be talking to inanimate objects like that.

I cleared my throat. "Excuse me, sir. How long do you think before you'll release me?"

He stopped, looking off in the distance, all the while tapping his chin. "Hmm, by morning I should have what I need, I'd think. Please don't call me sir; it makes me feel so old."

"Sorry, Goat." I organized my thoughts, which grew clearer as time passed. "Why are you out here? I would think you could do this anywhere."

He chuckled, stopping to grab two glass flasks, one half-full, the other empty with some device hooked to the top. "Believe me, I wish I could." He sat down at the table, pushed an assortment of dirty dishes, paper, and various scientific equipment to one side. Bending behind the table, he retrieved a rubber hose that he attached to the flask. He pulled a long straw-like piece of equipment out and dipped it into the liquid, and then he put it into small tubes from the kit. "You have no idea how much work goes into just surviving out here. Food and water have to be brought in, medicine needs to be made and given out."

"Medicine?"

He nodded as he worked. He filled the upper chamber of the empty flask, which emitted a sucking sound as the liquid flowed through. "The death ray, or whatever you want to call it, left behind a mutagen of some type. Living here messes with you on a cellular level."

I'm sure my eyes were bulging out of the sockets like a cartoon character. "What does the mutagen do?"

Vials clinked as he worked quickly, moving them back into the red box. "The Gifted don't seem to be affected, though every child born to them are Gifted, which isn't the case on the outside." He removed the rubber hose and the attached device. He covered the open top with a waxy sheet that stretched as he pulled it to securely seal it. "The plants and animals that have come in since the attack have changed over the years. Some die off faster, some have abnormal abilities."

"Like becoming giant?"

"Most certainly. I saw a deer with eight legs and razor-sharp antlers that skewered three Reclaimers before they took it down. It's a marvel of evolution." He stood, carrying the flask and red box into the kitchen area. Both went into a silver box. He set an old egg timer in the shape of the Death Star. He strolled over and pet Emerson, who still slept across my chest. "Aww, my good puppy." Emerson's loud snort was the only response he got.

"So, I don't want to be rude."

He cut me off with a wave. "Boy, don't worry about it, ask away. I was a teacher before all this madness happened."

I decided to push ahead, who knew when this information could come in handy. "So why doesn't the Underground wipe you out?"

He spread his hands out before him. "As I've told you lad, supply and demand. I produce an antidote of a sort to the mutagenic effect of the Death Ray residue."

I frowned. "But you said it doesn't affect Gifted?"

"I did, but not all of the Underground is Gifted. Over the years, malcontents of all stripes have entered the abandoned cities. I give them the antidote, they leave me alone and forgive the occasional kidnapping."

"But if they know you kidnap people, why don't they stay away from you?"

He chuckled to himself. "They try, but like tonight, they weren't expecting the trap I set."

"Trap? The Protectorate tried to arrest everyone. They claimed we were part of the drug cartel."

He smiled with the glee normally reserved for the very young. "I know, it was beautiful! I tipped off the Protectorate that a drug deal was going down at the Gate. The Protectorate is not appreciative of us selling to anyone but them. They crashed the party, and my goons snatched you in the process. I'd hoped for Warden or one of those newbies she has, but any catch is a win for me."

I groaned inwardly. Too bad he hadn't caught Jon or Turk. My dumb luck still held true. Leave it to me to stumble into the one building where they had been waiting for us. "Lucky me."

"Oh now, cheer up, Bucko!" He clapped me on a shoulder amicably. "It won't be long, and the boys will drop you back where they found you." He scratched Emerson on the head again as he walked back into the kitchen. He checked the timer, twisting a couple of dials as he hummed to himself.

Emerson lifted his head and gave me an exasperated look. I couldn't help but grin, the dog was a nice diversion from thinking about the mess I was in. Dad and Abby would be frantic when I didn't show up. I mentally kicked myself as I thought about how terrified Mom would be when I didn't return. She'd been against me being the contact person from the beginning. At least I knew the Underground hadn't betrayed us. Once I got back to the rendezvous, I could fill everyone in. Hopefully, the Underground could help us track down Waxenby.

I heard a door open but couldn't see it from where I was strapped to the table. "Seriously, I have company and am culturing cells for examination," Dr. Goat exclaimed. I imagined the wild gesturing which would go along with his statement. He sighed loudly. "Fine, if the Jackal can't wait, he can't wait." Goat stepped back into the room. "I've got to go speak with someone. I'll return shortly, Laddie."

I nodded. The door closed with a bang. I put my head back and thought through the steps I would take to get to the rendezvous. By morning, the storm should be over. I'd need to be careful and stay out of sight as much as I could until I got to the train tracks. I'd have to chance being seen once I got there. Walking through the tall grass didn't seem like a good idea with mutant wildlife roaming free. At least I could use my powers in the daylight as the light wouldn't draw attention.

The biggest question was, would Goat have me followed? I didn't know the city at all, and after everything, I didn't want to lead them to Dad and Abby. Maybe I could get through enough of the abandoned building to make it more difficult to tail me. The fact they had caught me in the middle of the gale that Warden had summoned didn't make me feel overly confident in my abilities. They didn't know what my Gift was or that I'd been trained in hand-to-hand combat by Blaze. I'd take any advantage I could get. I'd also learned a few new tricks, like the energy dagger, which could come in handy.

Emerson growled so low I wasn't sure if I'd heard it or felt it. Goat entered, beaming a megawatt smile. This couldn't be good news for me. "Mr. Ward, it is so nice to see your demise on Saturday Night Showdown was exaggerated. The Protector is extremely interested in speaking with you, and we are making quite the tidy sum to turn you over."

A memory came to mind as I stared at Dr. Goat. While I worked at the Secret Lair, I'd flip hamburgers and catch them on the back of the spatula, showing off for Marcel and Mimi. One day I missed, the hamburger flew across the grill, bounced once, and landed in the deep fryer.

I realized I had become the deep-fried hamburger.

13

I couldn't speak. Nothing would come out. My brain screamed to deny it, but my mouth just hung open like a dolt. Finally, I uttered. "I'm not who you think I am."

Goat guffawed. "Come now, Bucko. I've seen the show, and the young man called 'The Enforcer' is you, though you had far more hair gel. I applaud your courage in volunteering for The Gauntlet, but this is where your crazy train pulls into the station." He bent and double checked the ropes and made sure my IV was securely in my arm. "It seems a poor payback for knocking the Protector on his ass to turn you over, but this is what the Jackal wants, and we all live by his word."

"You could let me go. Say I escaped." I knew it was pointless to argue, but I had to try. "The Protectorate and Reclaimers are murderers, and you know it."

He nodded as he walked away. "Thomas, I salute you, but this is business. The Reclaimers are inbound to take you in." He turned to go. "For what it's worth, I'm sorry."

He strode out of view. Hearing the door slam behind him, I got the distinct feeling Goat wasn't a fan of Jackal's plan. I doubt it mattered since Goat wouldn't be helping me out. He'd been a teacher in the past, he'd said. I could have been one of his students under different circumstances. What should have been an easy meet-and-greet had turned into a major catastrophe. Why did these things always happen to me? At least I knew Jon hadn't set us up. Not that it mattered to anyone at this point. Not only had I let down Mom and Dad, but Abby and Marcel. The Underground wouldn't help find Waxenby either after this mess. I'd finally gotten myself in a situation with no way out.

"Every time I see you, you're locked up." A voice said to me. I lifted my head, Emerson's big brown eyes regarded me calmly. I peered around the room but couldn't see anyone else.

"Hello?" I said, hoping they would reveal themselves or realize the drugs coursing through my veins did a lot more than suppress my Gift.

"Hey, Tommy," Emerson said. Now I knew I was tripping. Dogs don't talk unless they are on TV. Emerson barked, and I swear it sounded like a laugh. "You let me out of the Zoo, so I figured I could return the favor."

"Mol—" I was interrupted by a paw over the mouth.

"No names. I've been spying on the Cartel for a while. I don't want my cover blown."

"Gotcha. Can you cut the ropes? I need to get out of here fast." I hadn't seen Mollie, or Molecular Mollie as she was known, since the Zoo in DC. She could shift into animal form in an instant. No wonder the Cartel didn't know she was here.

"You should be able to free yourself. I shut off the IV a while ago."

I realized when she bit the line, she must have been turning off the drip. Luckily, Goat hadn't noticed; he'd just checked the needle end. I could feel the stirrings of energy, but it was like they were behind a glass wall where I couldn't reach them. "I can't access my Gift. The drug must be working still."

She rumbled a low growl. "Damn, I figured we had more time." She moved so she laid across me, her head next to the rope. I felt the tug as she used her teeth to try to free me.

"Wouldn't a knife be easier?" I tried to summon the energy that would free me. The wall bent, but I couldn't break through. I heard voices and running feet outside the room. The Reclaimers were here, or close by, to have the Cartel so worked up.

"If anyone is watching, I don't want them to see me doing anything. I have a mission to finish. I'm already risking it by helping you this much."

"Yes, sir," A voice said outside the door. "They are on their way down with Jackal."

I redoubled my efforts. Instead of breaking the wall, I focused all my energy in the mental equivalent of a spear and drove it into the wall. I felt it splinter, and the slightest amount of energy trickled through. I summoned a razor-thin, buzz saw of electricity and slashed at the ropes. The first pass scored them; the second severed the outer layer. "I've got it. Start barking like you're warning them."

Emerson rolled on to his feet and leapt to the floor. His barks rang out around the room. I slashed the ropes and heaved, snapping the last of the binding. I wrenched the IV from my arm, splattering a little blood across the floor. The door flew open as I was snatching my suit from the back of the chair. No time to put it on, but I'd need it outside.

Goat stepped into the doorway, his face pale. "How?" was all he had time to say. I pulled all the energy I could and shot a bolt across the room at him, missing intentionally but hitting the box where he'd put my samples. Electricity shot sparks across the metal box. Surprisingly, Goat stood his ground as Emerson danced around his feet barking.

I advanced on him, but he held up his hand. "You're helmet and boots are on the floor behind the table."

I shot a glance to where he'd indicated, and there was my damaged helmet. I grabbed it, the boots, and headed for the door.

"Head down this hall, the stairs on the right go to the surface. The Reclaimers are surrounding the building, but at least you'll have a chance."

I looked hard at him, trying to figure out if he'd lie to me. "Why help me?"

He shook his head. "I told you it seemed unfair. Do me a favor and punch me, hard as you can. If they think I let you go, it'll be bad on the old Goat."

"Thank you." I said, then hit him square in the jaw. His head knocked back to hit the wall behind him, and he slid down it. Emerson barked, standing in front of Goat as if to protect him.

"Good luck, Tommy," Mollie whispered. I'd never get used to a talking dog. I winked at her, jammed my helmet on my head, and ran for the stairs. They were right where Goat had said they'd be. I took the flight as fast as possible. I still felt a bit woozy from the drugs, but I could feel more power flowing into me as I went. At the top of the stairs, I eased the door open. Before me stretched an old warehouse; small trucks, motorcycles, and a single red and orange golf cart sat parked around the cement floor. The large bay doors were all closed. A helicopter's rotors sounded from the roof as I took a minute to pull on my suit and boots. Fighting in a green hospital gown didn't seem like a great idea, especially with my ass hanging out the back.

Glad to be fully dressed, I stuffed the gown in a barrel next to the door and headed for the side exit. I snapped down the cracked faceplate. Air flowed into the helmet, but it was better than nothing. I could barely see out the window for all the dirt, but a three-story building sat across the street. If I could reach it, I'd have a much easier time. Voices from the stairwell announced they had found Dr. Goat. I had to go now or fight here where they could surround me.

Slowly, I pushed open the door; luckily the rotor noise outside would cover any noise I made. Inside it sounded far away, but here, it was deafening. The way looked all clear. I gathered myself for the run as the stairwell door slammed open with an echoing boom.

It might as well have been a starter's pistol. I put my head down and ran as hard as I could for the adjacent building. As I reached the road, shots rang out from the warehouse. A bullet clipped me in the shoulder, staggering me. I fought for balance and barely held on to it. Finally, glorious power surged through me. More shots and a lot of shouting pursued me across the street.

As I reached the building, I jumped straight through the plate glass window, landing in the reception area of whatever business had been here long ago. I saw a door heading further into the building. I threw it open and made my way deeper into the darkness. I really could have used my night vision, but my helmet hadn't magically repaired itself during my medical procedure. The hallway turned, going past empty offices and a mold-ridden breakroom. The hall ended with a fire door, the exit sign hanging by the wires. I pushed on the door, but it wouldn't move. For a second, I thought I would blast my way through, but I didn't want to give away my location to my pursuers.

I backtracked, checking for another way out. Light flooded in as the first soldier swung his rifle, its flashlight attachment illuminating the hall. Without thinking, I sent a blast of energy up the corridor. The far wall shattered from the impact. It would buy me a few seconds.

I ducked into the remains of the breakroom. The pipes must have burst at some point, as a thick green carpet of mold grew undisturbed across the floor. Skeletons from a couple of mice and what I guessed was a cat lay in the sickly green growth. The stench alone could kill a horse. On the far side, another hall slunk off into the darkness. Flickering light from the very cautious soldiers alerted me they were on the move. I held my breath and ran. Green spores plumed as my feet crashed on the mold rug. I gained the far hall and ran to the next turn. I paused, catching the flashlights strobing through the darkness. I heard retching coming from the breakroom's direction. I risked a peek and saw two soldiers losing their lunch. I was glad I held my breath.

I wished I'd run, but I didn't. Spores erupted where the vomit hit the floor, swirling around the soldiers. Their breathing became labored until they started screaming. The soldier on the left fell face first into the mold. More spores flew out, bits of dust floating in the light he'd dropped. The other soldier's head jerked up as he screamed. The skin on his face melted like hot wax, dripping off his bones to cover the front of him. I'll never forget it for as long as I live.

The shock of it got me moving again, sliding along the right-hand wall. I searched for a hallway that would lead to the back of the building. I watched for more of the lethal mold as I went past office doors, but I didn't think they would lead me to safety, and the last thing I wanted was to get trapped in a room. Beams of light appeared before me. They must have entered multiple locations, trying to trap me in between them. I thought frantically. I couldn't go back with all the spores; I doubted I'd fare much better than the soldiers. I couldn't go ahead with more troops headed toward me.

The sound of voices grew closer; time to decide had run out. I found the handle to a door, opened it, and stepped into the office. My hands became my eyes in the pitch black, locating the desk and almost knocking everything over. Following the edge of the desk, I reached out to find the wall. I dropped to my knees and crawled until my helmet bumped the wall.

My heart dropped like a lead balloon as I heard, "We've got him!" from outside the door. I wanted to beat my head against the wall. I hadn't thought about the tracks I left in the dust. They led the Reclaimers straight to my hiding spot. I gathered the energy and formed the energy dagger. Spots flared in my dark-adjusted eyes as it sprang to life. I drove the blade into the wall, slicing through the drywall and aluminum framing with ease. I shoved on the piece and created a hole big enough to crawl through. I dove into the adjoining office. Shots sounded from behind me, the bullets shearing through the interior walls well above where I crawled.

The time for stealth was over. I fired a stream of energy across the room, opening a larger hole in the wall. I kept the energy knife going, using it for light. Bullets cascaded around me as the soldiers opened fire, not caring what they hit.

I pulled myself into the next office, and my hope of getting away flooded back. The top portion of the back wall contained a bank of windows, all with blinds. Once I got through those, I'd have a chance to escape. I grabbed the old office chair and slammed it into the windows. The glass cracked but didn't shatter. A few more blows and the window collapsed out, frame and all. I did a quick check of the parking lot. Lots of cars, but no Reclaimers in sight. I dropped the chair and leapt through the opening into the fresh air and sunlight.

As I landed, a hard blow hit my leg. The knife blinked out of existence as my Gift evaporated.

A blue band wrapped around my calf. A disrupter band.

I looked around as eight Reclaimers approached, walking around the cars they had used for cover, rifles pointed at me. Directly in front of me stood the leader, holding the launcher across his chest. "Mr. Ward, you are under arrest as an enemy of the Protectorate."

The troops inside weren't trying to capture me, they were herding me into the trap they'd laid. I'd fallen for it. I reached for the band; if I could pull it free, I could fight.

The leader laughed. "By all means, go ahead and remove the band." The soldiers stayed out of reach. I bent and pulled, but it didn't budge. I knew it wouldn't, but it gave me a moment to think.

"Not so tough without your accursed powers, are you?" The leader glared at me, just like Powell had done before I broke free in the clearing. "Bind him and get him on the 'copter. The Protector wants him delivered post haste."

The leader turned to leave. His head whipped around as a silver ball flew past his face to land by my feet. "Grenade!" The Reclaimers dove out of the way, I had nowhere to go, so I covered my head and waited. A loud whine erupted from the orb then burst with a loud bang. The grenade hadn't detonated, but the blue band slid down my leg. Power surged back as the disrupter died.

The leader came to his feet, screaming. "Hold your fire!" but it was too late. A slow learner fired his weapon, striking my back. The force of the impact supercharged me. "Form up." The leader stopped mid-sentence, two arrows sprouting from his chest.

More arrows dropped the three men to my left. I turned to face the four on my right but couldn't believe what I saw. Turk stood behind them, green tendrils of smoke slithering across the intervening space. Each tendril attached to one of the soldier's legs. Their skin shriveled as their veins pulsed beneath. They tore at their faces, screaming as the toxins killed them. Turk smiled as they fell to the ground, dead.

Jon walked over to me, bow still at the ready. "Let's go. Ranger and Abby are waiting with Warden for you."

I tore my eyes away from the gruesome scene. "Why save me? I thought you were going to see me dead."

Jon smiled at me. "When you die, it will be me killing you and no one else. Until then, you need to live."

Wonderful—my own personal, psycho bodyguard.

14

I followed Jon and Turk away from the building, leaving the corpses behind. More dead Reclaimers wouldn't be welcome news to anyone, especially the Underground. We entered a dilapidated strip mall and took a set of well-used stairs between stores down past an old bar-and-grill, slipping by it to a covered flight leading further underground into a basement storage area.

Warden waited at the bottom, flanked by two guys. One stood at least six-five and over three hundred pounds, mostly muscle. He wore a tank top showing off his full sleeves of tattoos. The other came up to my shoulder and was whipcord thin. A scruffy dark beard covered the lower half of his face. His expression made me want to stay on his good side.

Warden checked me over as I stepped off the last stair. "Well, you certainly led us on a chase, Sparky." She emphasized Sparky with sarcasm, which spoke volumes.

I flushed with embarrassment. "Thank you for getting me out."

She waved her hand. "You had already escaped, we just helped you find your way out. Were you followed?" The last was directed at Jon.

He shook his head. "No, we took care of the Reclaimers who had Sparky."

A concerned expression crossed her face. "Took care of? How?"

Turk spoke up. "We iced those asses. We'll teach them not to mess with us." His eyes glittered with excitement as he spoke. His hands were out in front of him as if reliving the kills.

Warden's face hardened with anger. "I explicitly told you there would be no killing of any Reclaimers or Cartel members. Do you have any idea what you've done?"

Turk barked a harsh laugh. "Saved Sparky's lame ass is what we did."

Jon shot Turk a withering scowl. "Warden, they had an inhibitor band on Sparky and weapons leveled. We couldn't chance an itchy trigger finger. I assumed you didn't want him returned dead."

The big man stepped toward Jon. "I don't like your tone." His voice rumbled like thunder.

Warden put a restraining hand up. "Not now, Boulder. We have bigger things to worry about than an impertinent tone. We need to get back to base." She gave Jon and Turk a very hard glare. "We aren't done talking about this or your place with us. Come."

She turned and passed through an opening in the back wall. I followed Jon and Turk; Boulder and his silent friend brought up the rear. We moved through a long hallway, lit with a string of Christmas lights. Another set of stairs led even deeper into the bowels of the city. Warden stopped at the end of the hall, motioning us to keep going. "Salvo, blow the access. We can't chance the Reclaimers finding this route."

The thin man shot us a dirty look. "Warden, it will limit our access to the Cartel and Mol–"

Warden's response cracked like a whip. "I know what it will cost us, but we can't chance it. There are other ways that are usable. Now close this off and return to base."

Salvo bowed his head to her. "But of course, Warden. You are correct as usual." He spoke with a strong North Eastern Region of the European Zone accent. Mom referred to it as British. I wondered if the Underground operated out of London as well as Atlanta.

Our band of Gifted wound our way through an elaborate series of halls, stairs, and sewers. Noises echoed while we crept through, not wanting to draw the attention of anything living down here. Salvo rejoined the group on the far side of the sewers. The thought of walking through here alone sent shivers down my spine.

Thirty minutes later, we arrived at an underground city. Children ran and played in the streets as adults worked on repairing structures, laying out food for the afternoon meal, and otherwise keeping busy. There must have been over a hundred people living in the hollowed out remains of several buildings. Arches held the roof up in between the old structures, giving it an open feeling. Light filtered from above, adding to the impression of daylight. No wonder they had been able to avoid the Protectorate for so long.

Warden noticed my swiveling head and laughed. "You look like a tourist in the big city for the first time, Sparky."

I didn't bother trying to keep the awe out of my voice. "This is amazing. I'd have never guessed at how much you have here."

Turk barged into the conversation. "We should be taking the fight to the Protectorate. The Reclaimers couldn't match our firepower."

Jon glared at him but stayed silent. Warden sighed. "Boulder, can you escort these two gentlemen to the reserve? I'll be along shortly."

Turk opened his mouth, his temper flaring, but Jon's hand slashed out, striking him in the stomach. "Warden, we'll wait on you with no problems." Daggers flew at me with his glance. "Sparky, we'll meet again."

"I'll be counting the days," I said wearily, surer of Marcel's theory every moment I was around Jon.

Jon grabbed Turk's arm and led him away, Boulder and Salvo trailing them.

Warden studied me for a second. "He really doesn't like you, though his reasons only make sense to him."

I watched them go. "It was my fault, and I deserve it."

"Actually, you don't, but from personal experience, teens have a harder time grasping the realities of the situation. If you'll follow me, I have a couple of people anxious to see you."

It got my attention. "After you, ma'am."

A quick walk later, we entered through the door into what had once been a bank vault. Dad and Abby sat at a card table, waiting. They leapt to their feet when they saw me. Abby virtually tackled me in a hug, knocking the breath out of me in the process. Dad hugged me far more gently. "Welcome back. You don't look worse for wear."

I pulled off my broken helmet. "A functioning helmet would be nice. Sorry if I worried you."

Warden cleared her throat. "I hate to break up the family reunion, but it's time for some straight talk. Why the hell is the cast of Saturday Night Showdown standing in my operations station?"

We all glanced at each other.

"Oh, come on! Even if Jon and Turk hadn't betrayed your identities, everyone in the world saw you on the show. I'm not stupid."

Dad explained about Waxenby and the run-in with the Syndicate. Abby and I chimed in details, though she stopped us when we mentioned the Zoo. "That was you?"

Abby indicated it was.

"Well, I guess we are even then. You freed my daughter from that bastard, and we got you away from the Cartel."

Stunned, I blurted. "You're Molly's mom? She helped get me away from Dr. Goat. Without her, I'd have been handed over to the Reclaimers."

Warden wilted. "I asked her not to go there, but she's so stubborn, just like me. She's trying to find the formula for the mutagen drug. Then we could shut down the designer drugs Jackal is selling. Some of them do horrible things to the kids who take them."

"Dr. Goat calls her Emerson, and he dotes on her. She'll be spoiled by the time she comes back." I tried to sound upbeat, but I still worried I'd exposed Molly on accident.

She chuckled, sounding very tired. I recognized it from watching Mom all the years in Redemption. "I'm sure she will be. Well, if we are going to be allies, I should show you something. Please come this way."

Warden walked through the bank vault door. I entered into a massive room with a silver metal structure sitting in the middle of the chamber. Twice the size of a normal door frame and covered with circuitry, it dominated the room with its presence. A thick rope of cables trailed across to a desk by the far wall, holding a bank of monitors. A slight dark-haired woman looked up, waved, and went back to what she was doing.

Warden gestured to the doorway. "After the Dark Brigade attacks, a group of Gifted correctly concluded we were fighting a losing cause. With the Protectorate gaining strength, their reach made staying outside of the ruins impossible. The Underground formed around the original group. They put out the word that any who entered would be safe."

Abby's scowl deepened. "Safe? We've seen giant rats, and some alligator monstrosity almost ate me. Not what I'd call safe."

Warden sighed. "In the years after the attacks, nothing lived here.

Later, we realized the death beam had residual effects. Non-Gifted who entered sickened and usually died. The Cartel developed the mutagen drugs, which allow people to live here without adverse effects."

I didn't want to interrupt, but something she said gnawed at me. "You said usually died? What happened to those who didn't die?"

She grimaced. "Some developed Gifts of their own. Others became twisted, grotesque, and in constant pain, and we ended up killing them to put them out of their misery. A few fled to live on their own; we try to avoid them. Things don't go well when we meet up."

I heard a low growl from Abby, but thankfully she dropped it. I'm sure it hit close to home seeing how she'd been hunted like an animal before her parents turned her into the Reclaimers. I watched out of the corner of my eye, but she didn't appear to be growing.

If Warden heard Abby, she didn't show it. "We had a Gifted, Technokid, who could build just about anything. He created these transporters. They transfer matter between places, allowing us to move from city to city. We built them in places we could close off easily and destroy if necessary. The idea of one of the transporters falling into Cartel or Syndicate hands keeps me awake at night. If it ever happened, they would eradicate the Underground." She fell silent as if pondering the future of her people.

Dad stepped closer to the transporter to examine it. "Will your people flee to escape the Protectorate response to rescuing Tommy?"

After a moment, she responded slowly. "No, I don't think it will be necessary." She straightened her jacket and went on. "The Protectorate will scour the area, but they know they can't find us in the ruins. We have rigged traps around the city as have the Cartel. Nosing around will lead to more loss with little to gain. I'll pull all my people back here so we can escape if needed."

Dad continued to study the structure. "This is impressive. I met TechnoKid early on. Nice kid, but extremely odd sense of humor. He set up a continual loop on Golden Avenger's sword recall device. Took him a week to figure out how to stop it. Avenger wasn't pleased when he summoned his sword, and it returned to base."

It got a laugh out of Warden. "He was a sweet kid. Luckily, he finished the transporter project before..." She trailed off.

Abby prodded. "Before?"

Warden took a deep breath and continued. "TechnoKid couldn't stand authority, but he couldn't fight. He brought his wife with him to live in Boston with the Underground. After a couple of years or so, his wife fell ill from the mutagen. She transformed into a monster, killing most of the medical staff who'd been trying to reverse the effects." She paused, collecting herself. "TechnoKid entered the building and killed her, which was truly a mercy. In his grief, he turned the gun on himself." She turned away from us, wiping tears from her eyes.

"I'm sorry," Abby said, her eyes unfocused for a moment. "I know how hard that kind of decision is. There are no winners."

I put my hand on Abby's shoulder. I knew she'd be thinking about her murdered parents and blaming herself. For the millionth time, I wished Wendi were alive. She could reach Abby when no one else could. I sometimes forgot how important Wendi had been to everyone else besides me. Her death had a domino effect reaching farther than I would ever know.

Warden turned to us, her mask back in place. "Thank you. We've all been through terrible ordeals because of the Protectorate."

"If you could, would you free all the Gifted?" I blurted out, getting a sharp look from Abby and a concerned one from Dad and Warden.

She studied me carefully as if she had taken me at face value only to find something different. "That's an interesting question. On one hand, all people deserve to be free." She glanced at Dad before continuing. "On the other, some Gifted use their powers irresponsibly, on both sides of the law. Freeing the Gifted could lead to the same issues that put us here. I'm just glad I don't have to make those decisions."

Dad moved to stand next to me. "None of us will be making any decisions. The Protectorate has eliminated our choices quite thoroughly. Our immediate need is tracking down Oliver Waxenby. The Syndicate captured him in a failed rescue attempt."

Warden cocked her head. "Would that be the attack on the school buses in the South Western Region we've been unable to confirm?"

Dad nodded. "It was. The Protectorate destroyed two school buses and eliminated most of the students from Eldorado High School to explain how they caught Abby."

She whistled. "Every time I think the Protectorate can't sink any lower, they do. Slaughtering children to frame Gifted." She paused, taking a deep breath. "I've got my people in all of our cities looking for clues as to where they are holding him."

"Thank you," I said quietly. "He was captured stopping Armageddon from killing us all."

She flashed me a quick smile. "Even more reason to find him then. And when we know where he is, you are free to use the transporter to gain access to the city. Let's not float down any more rivers?"

Abby laughed. "The floating wasn't the issue; it was the greeting party that bit."

Abby had been spending way too much time with Marcel. "That was awful." I groaned. Marcel's horrible humor had infected her, which reminded me, "Before we go, something Dr. Goat said is troubling me."

Warden's keen stare affixed me like a lizard on a skewer. "Is it about Molly?"

I waved my hands frantically. "No, nothing like that." The intent glare softened, allowing me to breathe. "He told me he'd called in about a drug deal to get the DEA to crash the meeting. How would he have known?"

"Damn it!" Warden punched one fist into her open hand. "I knew a DEA bust was far too convenient on a meeting only a few of us knew about."

Dad's brow furrowed. "How sure are you about your people? The two who accompanied you to the meeting could have been planted."

"No, they weren't told until we were leaving, I was the only one who knew about the meeting. Our secure channel must not be as secure as I thought."

"Mr. Wizard can fix it," Abby said.

"Mr. Wizard?" Warden's face twisted in a grimace. "You guys really need help with code names."

Dad winked at Abby. "He's our tech-op. If he can't find the source, no one can. I'll have him reconnoiter the comms and determine the root cause. Maintain radio silence until he's had time to work."

I waited for a barbed comeback over the obvious radio silence statement, but she let it slide. "Let's get you back to where you belong."

We followed Warden out of the transporter room and down another basement beneath the rock ceilings of the cavern. Three large men stepped out to meet us, Boulder at the lead. "Boulder will show you a tunnel that comes out near enough to where you hid your car. They'll sweep the car for trackers, just in case. Have a safe trip back. We'll be in touch."

"Thank you, Warden," Dad said earnestly. "Tommy falling into the enemy's hands would have had dire consequences for us all."

She smiled. "We need to stick together if we are to survive."

She motioned to Boulder, who set off toward our exit. We stepped in behind him and the other two guides. Warden's voice followed after us. "Oh, and Sparky..." I turned to look back at her. "Please come up with a better code name before we meet again."

Abby barked out a laugh. My cheeks flushed as I resumed walking.

Wonderful, the world is full of comedians.

15

B oulder led us through the twisting, turning labyrinth of passages of the undercity. He set a good pace as we traversed the abandoned buildings of Atlanta. Abby walked next to me, taking any obstacle as a chance for parkour practice.

"It is amazing how the Underground has set this up," she said as we went through an old warehouse. Crates and pallets were stacked around haphazardly, but small, unobtrusive markings showed the inhabitants where to find supplies or contact points. "No wonder the Reclaimers haven't found them."

I agreed, amazing would be a good term for it. "I don't know how anyone could find their way around down here."

Boulder answered my question, causing me to flinch with surprise. "Most of us have lived here our whole lives. My parents brought me here as a teenager to avoid being sent to the Block. By fifteen, I could lift a small car, so everyone knew I was Gifted." He paused as he ducked under a metal pipe to jump down to the next section of pathway at the end of the warehouse. We hopped down behind him. "As soon as they announced the testing, we fled here and were welcomed by Warden. I've been here ever since."

I started to ask about his parents when Abby elbowed me hard in the side. She glared at me, daring me to open my mouth. The question ended then and there. Most likely, his parents had died from the mutagen, so asking would be stupid. I grimaced at Abby and got a satisfied nod in return.

We continued through unseen passageways, through wrecked buildings, and once back into the sewers for a short, scary trip. I swear I could feel eyes watching me as we passed. Several areas had mold, trapping skeletons of unwary animals that we avoided. Unnerving would be an understatement.

At last, we came to a large room stacked with crates and boxes. People moved around busily opening the containers and repackaging the contents into smaller bundles. The far wall was entirely made of metal, with a small door set off to one side. "This is one of the landing docks. We bring supplies in, and then they are carried to the main community."

Dad looked impressed. "How do you get the supplies in past the Protectorate?"

"We are outside the wall here, so they don't watch as closely. We have Gifted who make this easier, but darkness hides a lot of sins."

"Makes sense," Dad said. "Do we exit from here?"

"I will show you how you can signal your arrival, so you don't have to use the river passage next time." Boulder chuckled. "I bet it was an amazing fight with the armordile. I've always wanted to try myself against one."

Abby grunted. "Armordile? Is that what you call that nightmare?"

Boulder shrugged. "The name fits, we have no idea what it actually is. It has armor plating, gator jaws, and burrows underground, waiting for prey. You live here long enough, you see all sorts of strange things."

I'd be adding it to my list of things to never do. The giant rats and armordile were bad enough. I'd hate to see what else the freak show had to offer.

We followed Boulder to the exit door and stepped through into an old storm runoff tunnel. He showed us the location of the hidden panel then gave us a friend code, and a hostage code in case of emergencies. "Don't mix them up, the hostage code will collapse the tunnel on you."

Abby snorted. "Important safety tip, Egon. Isn't that a bit extreme?" I really needed to get Abby away from Marcel more often.

Boulder turned to face Abby. "No. Everything we have and everyone we love is beyond this door. If you are forced to open the door, we expect you to die rather than betray us. Understood?"

She swallowed hard and nodded.

"Good." Boulder snapped the plate back over the keypad and stomped down the tunnel, dim light outlining the end. We followed him as he went. Night would be here soon, and with it, the darkness to cover our return to Castle. Boulder stepped over to me, reached into his pocket, and handed me a small wrapped package. I opened it to find a pair of goggles. "I thought you might need those since your helmet is a bit worse for wear."

"Thanks." I pulled off my helmet, attaching it to my belt hook, and seated the optics in place, noticing the hazy green of the night vision. "My helmet broke during the explosion."

Boulder shrugged. "Least I could do for the guys who beat the Gauntlet." He watched the darkening sky for a moment. "Let's go. It will be full dark before we near the wall."

It took over an hour to get to the car. Boulder pointed out where we could enter and hide our vehicle on any future trips. He ran a hand scanner over the car and grunted his approval. "It's clean. Safe trip." He shook each of our hands and then slipped away into the night.

"Shotgun," Abby said quietly. I shot her a dirty look and climbed into the backseat. Settling in, I stored my useless helmet on the floor next to me and watched behind us to make sure nobody followed us. Dad used the night vision to get us closer to a main road then handed his helmet back to me. We slipped into the stream of cars, just another group of Norms headed to wherever they wanted. Even though we didn't live in the confines of Redemption any more, we were still caged. Castle made a much nicer cage than say, Atlanta's Underground community, but we weren't free. Even Tracy Stevens, Wendi's mom, who couldn't be detected by the Protectorate, lived in an invisible cage of fear.

I laid down on the backseat, remembering all the trips to Granite Falls with Mom. She'd have a CD playing, singing along, off-key, and I'd drift off. The memories could have been someone else's given how distant they seemed. I wondered if Molly had found the formula or just returned home. I know I couldn't wait to see Mom, and I'd only been gone a couple of days.

A small laugh escaped me as I thought of Warden giving me crap about using Sparky as a code name. It's not like I'd thought of it before then, and I certainly wasn't using "Executioner" as Saturday Night Showdown had dubbed me. I didn't think Abby or Marcel had names picked out, though Marcel would be Mr. Wizard since we used it when we were away from base. My Gift didn't lend itself to an easy name like Firework Farley or Super Samurai—even Dad's Cyclone Ranger referenced part of his Gift.

I could absorb energy, but names based on that would suck. I inwardly laughed at the pun; I'd have to remember to tell Marcel later. I'd sound more like a paper towel than a Gifted. No, Absorption was out. I could amplify energy, but Magnify or Intensify didn't lend itself to a cool name. Plus, I didn't want to advertise my Gift. It helped to have everyone thinking I threw lightning like Dad. If my enemies didn't know I needed to absorb energy before I could unleash it, so much the better. Dead end on that train of thought.

Running through names of other heroes didn't help either. Golden Avenger or Titan reflected their physical appearance. Energy might be better, something non-descriptive. MegaWatt came to mind. It sounded cool, like a metal band, or...a light bulb. Something else. Bolt could work. Or Taser, since they referenced throwing energy. Maybe. Then it hit me: Surge. Short and to the point, and it sounded cool, kind of like Salvo. You didn't know what to expect, but it would be intense. Surge. The more I thought it through, the more I liked it.

We got back past midnight, Dad being extra careful we weren't followed. Since the mission went sideways, we were all a bit tense. Finally, assured no one had seen us, we drove into Castle's parking area. A tunnel connected it to the main complex and, like Atlanta's, could be collapsed in case of an emergency. I'm not sure why a group of Gifted fighters needed a backup plan, but it made me feel better knowing it was there.

As we entered the living area, Mom flew across the room to envelop me into a bear hug. I hugged her back, careful not to hurt her. Having put on so much muscle over the past few months made me a lot stronger than I had been when collared. She held me at arm's length, examining me for injuries. After years of bullying in Redemption, I knew the drill.

She tsked as she looked me over like a chef eying her ingredients. "I swear you've grown again, but you don't appear to be injured."

I smiled at her in what I hoped was a reassuring manner. "Mom, I'm fine." Dad and Abby ran down what they'd told her since the Cartel had captured me. "The doctor drew some blood. He uses it to make drugs, but after, I left and joined back up with Dad and Abby." I answered Marcel before he even asked, since his afro had bobbed significantly when his head snapped up from the laptop. "I destroyed the samples before I left."

Mom scowled, trying to figure out if I held back any information. "You're sure you're telling me everything?"

Inwardly, I kicked myself for wanting to tell my mommy everything: the fight with the Protectorate, Warden's storm, the Reclaimers, Jon and Turk killing those soldiers, but I knew I'd never be let out again. I plastered a bigger smile on my face and plunged in. "I'm sure. The Underground is huge and really cool. They agreed to help find Mr. Waxenby."

I don't think she believed me, but she let it go. Did every kid have to go through lying to their parents to preserve their freedom? I didn't know about anyone else, but I did, and it sucked. "I'm glad you're back, sweetheart. Go take a shower, you smell like dog and stale sweat, then get some sleep. You all look tired."

I kissed her on the cheek and headed toward my room. Abby caught up quickly, bumping me with her elbow. "Race you?"

"No way," I said, stifling a yawn. "I'm out of juice."

She laughed. We took the stairs down and into our rooms. I showered and fell into bed. My first mission had been a disaster, but it had worked out.

We started back on the regular training schedule while we waited for Marcel or the Underground to find Waxenby. It had been a week since we'd been to Atlanta, and we were no closer to locating him. The longer it dragged out, the more concerned I got. Waxenby could be dead, and we'd not know it. He could have been turned over to the Reclaimers. Marcel pointed out the Protectorate would have had the news as every headline on Earth, but I still worried.

The only avenue I hadn't explored further was Eiraf's message. I had run it through my head a million times, but nothing made any sense. I decided I needed to use the doorbell again and speak with Eiraf, if I went there, or at least Alyx. I found Mom and Dad sitting at the dining room table, eating breakfast.

Mom looked up as I entered. "Good morning, Sweetheart. How did you sleep?"

"Fine. I wanted to ask you both a question."

They shared a glance before Dad said, "Sure, what's up?"

The best way to do this was to rip the band-aid off. "I want to use the doorbell to talk to Alyx about Mr. Waxenby. Maybe he has a way to help us locate him, since Marcel and the Underground haven't heard anything about his location."

Dad leaned forward, putting his crossed arms on the table. "Why now? It's only been a week, and Warden said it wouldn't be easy to find him."

I sat back in my chair, pulling my thoughts together. "I don't know. I woke up this morning, and it just felt like I should at least try."

Mom's eyebrows went up, but she didn't say anything. Dad shrugged in response. My parents are weird or telepathic, possibly both. Mom broke the silent conversation. "Okay, there and back, no side trips to the California malls and definitely no surfing; water and electricity don't mix." She smirked at her joke. I face-palmed. Even my mom's a comedian. "I'll tell Blaze you're skipping practice this morning."

"Thanks, I won't be long." I pecked Mom on the cheek and ran for the door. I didn't want them to have time to change their minds. I took the stairs two at a time down to the doorbell's storage room.

Taking a deep breath, I pushed the button. The swirling vortex greeted me, and my stomach clenched. Once we got Waxenby back, I vowed never to use this thing again. I stepped out into nothing and fell through the nothingness, lights twisting and dancing around me as I moved toward Alyx's end of the maelstrom. "Eiraf!" I yelled into the emptiness, hoping to feel the pull that proceeded my last visit, but nothing happened. I continued to try until I landed at the doorstep. I opened the door, stepping out into the basement of the hideout.

Nausea hit me like a runaway freight train coming down a mountain. I clenched my teeth to keep from vomiting all over the terracotta tile, which might have helped it look better. Lurching to the couch, I fell onto it, feeling my stomach roiling and vertigo spinning the room around me as if I sat on a merry-go-round. I put my head in my hands and waited for the sickness to pass.

Before, I'd been dizzy after the doorbell, but nothing like this. I wondered if all the yelling had upset my system more since I'd been in the vortex longer than usual. I heard the creaking floorboards above my head; Alyx or Gladiator was here, so one good bit of news.

My stomach slowly stopped its impression of a bucking bronco and let me off the ride. A few deep breaths later, I felt better but not great. Well enough to take the stairs and speak with Alyx, hopefully. I like Gladiator, but I doubted arcane, eyeless woman babbling in strange riddles were his speed.

Over the last month, Mom had replaced all the 80s vintage furniture with a large sectional and a flat panel monitor. Marcel had automated everything in the house, so the lights kicked on as I entered through the wall, or door, depending on how you looked at it. I stood, noticing tasteful tapestries had replaced the surfer decor. The tapestries were probably Gladiator's, procured over his long lifetime.

I gently eased my way up the stairs, taking care not to upset my stomach any more than necessary. A ginger ale would be greatly appreciated at this point, though I doubted they had any in the house, even though they kindly kept the fridge stocked with Mountain Dew for us. I reached the door and opened it into the spacious living room. "Alyx, Nico?" I called out. I turned the corner to head for the kitchen, stopping dead in my tracks.

A large man dressed all in red robes stood peering into the open refrigerator. He reared back, spotting me, eyes widening. In his left hand, he held an ornate wooden staff with something affixed to the top. I'm not sure what it was, since he pointed it at me, screaming "Foul demon, I hereby abjure you in the name of the mighty Rexgarr!" A bolt of red energy sprang to life, speeding across the distance between us. I rolled to the side, just missing the coffee table as the blast nicked my shoulder. The living room fireplace behind me imploded from the concussion.

I flipped over onto my back, the robed figure looming over me, staff gripped in both hands ready to strike. "Any last words, demon?"

Only one. "Help!"

16

I knew full well getting thwacked with a wooden staff couldn't hurt me, but my lizard brain panicked at the sight of a tall man, bald, but with a bushy gray beard, preparing to turn me into shish kabob. I held my hands before me, ready to block the blow, but the guy seemed like he knew what he was doing.

"Charles, stop!" Alyx's voice came from inside the kitchen. I snuck a peek, without taking my focus off the butt of the staff. "Tommy is a friend."

A frown creased Charles' face. "Do you not smell the stench coming off him? He is in league with the darkness."

Alyx sped across the floor in his wheelchair to the living room, the small motor humming as it propelled him toward us. A concerned expression etched his features as he came closer. "I do, but there has to be an explanation. Please sit down, Charles."

I got to my feet. Charles glared at me but said nothing as he adjusted his dark red robes and took a spot on the gray couch that sat against the wall. I noticed he gripped the staff as he tried to appear relaxed. Runes ran the length of the light-colored wood staff, a carved dragon's head adorned the top, and unlike its owner, its eyes shone with wisdom and knowing. I studied Charles, thinking that if he pulled out a lightsaber, he couldn't have looked more like a Jedi knight. "Alyx, I came here to talk to you. Could we discuss it in private?"

Unlike the older wizard, Alyx wore jeans, the openings neatly seamed shut where his legs ended, and a faded blue Storytellers Brewery t-shirt. His hair had the same messy style that took others hours to accomplish. He shook his head slowly. "Charles is right. Tommy, you have the remnants of a terrible power surrounding you. I need you to stay still while I investigate." Blue light sprang to life around his right hand. He mumbled under his breath as he wove a circle around my feet, the design so intricate that I couldn't follow it.

Time slipped away, consumed by the glowing lights and swirling colors dancing around me. Sparks shot in all directions as the magic leapt up, surrounding me in a sphere. Shapes twirled around me. I concentrated on them, trying to figure out what they were. They shifted, twisting from one form to another in rapid succession. My brain ached from the strain of attempting to identify them before they evolved. Dark red and black flowed off my skin, imploding on the inside of the sphere wherever the two streams met. Time had become meaningless before the colors pouring off me ebbed.

The circle flared as Alyx lowered his hand, watching intently as the blue swirled, bits of red and orange mixing into the kaleidoscope colors. A few seconds later, the light died and winked out.

"Interesting," Charles murmured from his place on the couch. He stroked his long beard as he spoke. "It would seem I owe the lad an apology."

I glanced back to the shattered fireplace on the far side of the room. "I think you owe Alyx a new fireplace as well."

Charles glowered at me, which I returned. I didn't appreciate being ambushed in our safe house. Alyx broke the silence before it could escalate. "Tommy, come over and sit down. Charles overreacted, but you have to understand the miasma that clings to you is the same as the enemy we are sworn to protect the Earth from."

The room held two light gray couches with a metal coffee table in the center with enough room for Alyx to get his wheelchair through. A large TV hung over a long, oaken sideboard that was probably older than dirt. Dust from the marble fireplace drifted around.

I sat on the unoccupied sofa and ignored Grumpy, who rearranged his robes again. He reminded me of Mom as she did and re-did her hair before a big trial. The dark brown fabric didn't look any different now than it had before his fussing with it. "I came here to discuss what happened after I got Blaze."

Alyx rolled over to face me. "So please tell me what happened?"

I cleared my throat as I organized my thoughts. "I've used the doorbell on multiple occasions and never had a problem."

Charles interrupted. "Doorbell? What in the world is the boy talking about?"

"I created an intra-dimensional gateway so Cyclone Ranger's team could come here as needed. It's coded to allow only the six of them to use it," Alyx said, irritation creeping into his tone.

"The covenant strictly forbids us from meddling in human events. I must protest this use of your magic in aiding a group outside our sphere of influence." Charles' voice sounded overly pompous. I'm not sure what size pole needed to be shoved up your ass before you sounded like him.

Alyx waved him off. "We can discuss the proper application of magic as prescribed by the covenant later. Frankly, the Gifted have always been thought outside the realms of the covenant, but it can wait until Tommy has told his story. I have the feeling it will be important."

Charles stopped himself before he launched into another sermon. "Very well, continue."

I waited until Alyx nodded to me. "I sent Blaze then stepped through. The colors changed immediately. The blue of the vortex turned red. I heard a voice call my name before being wrenched away from the door. I landed in a huge cave."

Charles mumbled. "Hmm, interesting," as I spoke.

"I followed a path to the back of the cave, where a woman named Eiraf…"

Alyx blanched, all the color sliding out of his face. "What name did you say?"

"I'm sorry, I might be saying it wrong. I thought it was the name she gave."

"Holy mercies above," Charles said, crossing himself. "Why has she returned?"

"I don't know, but it doesn't bode well for us. Tommy, continue."

I went on telling of the ghostly heads crashing into Eiraf as she spoke.

I repeated what she'd said as close to word-for-word as I could. Alyx and Charles would stop me to review at particular points, but finally, Alyx seemed satisfied with my recall of the event.

Alyx pushed his head back, peering at the ceiling as he thought. "Is it prophecy?"

Charles stroked his beard. "If the apparitions were truly there, what else could it be?"

"Tommy wouldn't be able to ken a true apparition from an illusion as one of the Council could. The enemy could be laying a false trail for us, especially after what we faced in old-world Argentina."

Charles grunted. "Regardless, we need to protect ourselves." Without warning, he muttered something I couldn't hear, and red rings materialized around me. They collapsed on me, holding me so I couldn't move. "What the..."

Alyx responded far faster. He flicked his hand at me, blue dart streaking across to destroy the rings. "Tommy is not an enemy, and I won't have him treated as such." Alyx had risen from his wheelchair, hovering as if he stood on legs. His face flushed with anger, blue energy crackling along his clenched fists.

I pulled from my reserves, preparing a bolt to return fire if Charles tried anything again. "I don't know who you think you are, Obi-Wan, but if you try that again, I'll burn you to a crisp."

Charles rose to his feet at a leisurely pace, straightening his robes as he turned to face me. "I am the Grandmaster of Protection, and I've fought your kind before, whelp. Stand down before you force me to put you over my knee like the impudent brat you are."

My anger flared, and so did the electricity arcing up and down my arms. "You might think you're some bad-ass Yoda, but I'll go supernova and fry you where you stand."

Charles laughed. "Boy, you are testing my patience."

"Enough!" Alyx roared, a blue shield forming between us. "We are on the same side. This is only doing the enemies' work for them. NOW SIT DOWN!"

I let go of the power roiling in me and sat back on the couch. Charles glared at me, then did the same. Alyx shot us both dirty looks. "Like dealing with children," he muttered.

"Well, he is a child."

"I meant you, you pompous ass. Sit there and shut up while I think."

Charles straightened his back, a haughty glower on his features. "I've been the Grandmaster Protector for over 500 years. I'll not be spoken to like that, especially by you, who has only been on the Council for a score of decades."

Alyx bowed toward the older man. "I beg your forgiveness, Lord Protector. Now can we get down to what we need to do about Eiraf?"

Invoking her name snapped Lord Douche Nozzle back to the present. "Yes, it is the issue now, isn't it?"

Alyx sighed. "Did you have any encounters on this trip through the gateway?" He rolled his eyes at me, as the musty old wizard took his seat. I stifled a laugh.

"No, I thought I might get pulled back to speak to her more, but nothing happened. Can I ask what is going on?"

Charles harrumphed but held his tongue when Alyx glared at him. He paused before addressing me again. "It's extremely complicated, and I'm not at liberty to discuss most of it, but I can tell you this." He rubbed his eyes then launched into it. "The Council was created by the strongest wizards to ever walk the earth, in direct response to the enemy."

I broke in, my curiosity getting the better of me. "Who's the enemy? Evil wizards?"

He shook his head. "I can't explain it to you, but let's stick with they are evil. There is a third group who attempts to maintain balance. Think of them as the fulcrum of a cosmic balance beam."

My eyes widened in shock, the implications that Eiraf could be using me to hurt my friends shook my confidence a bit, though I should have seen it as a possibility. "Are you saying they will help the enemy?"

"They be honorless curs that swing as the wind blows," Charles exclaimed. "We should be hunting them down. Better to know you don't have a dagger at your back wielded by a supposed ally."

I swear I thought I could see steam rising off Alyx like an overheated radiator. "They believe the balance keeps the universe from being destroyed. They don't help or hinder either side but will act to address threats. Whether they are allies or not makes no difference." Alyx shifted in his wheelchair, adjusting his position. "Eiraf is a seer, older than any other being we've ever encountered. She'd not harm you, but she could point you in a direction that would serve their purposes. The real question is, what are you doing that would warrant her interest?"

I shrugged. "We've been searching for Mr. Waxenby. I don't see why it would matter."

"I agree. It would seem a small matter in the scope of things. We should destroy the gateway as a safety precaution."

"But how will I get back? Or come here to get supplies or travel?" I mostly kept the panic from my voice. I think.

Alyx held up his hands. "There are other ways we can travel between two places. The doorbell represents the easiest way, but not the only way. We can discuss this later."

I couldn't see why searching for Waxenby would have an impact on a magical war that had been around since the beginning of time. I went over Eiraf's words again and again in my head, looking for a clue, but honestly, if Alyx and Oldy-wan couldn't spot it, I doubted I would.

Charles rose, banging the butt of his staff on the floor. "The time has come to see this doorbell. We should remove it until we can ascertain if there is danger present." This guy must be a blast at parties. Gladiator never sounded like he fell out of a middle school production of Shakespeare.

Alyx glanced at me, his eyes twinkling with mirth. "Aye, me matey, let us go in search of booty!" His pirate accent hit the mark as Charles reddened slightly. "Sorry, Charles." He didn't sound sorry though.

I rose and followed as Alyx rolled to the basement door. A few feet away, he floated out of his chair and descended the stairway. Charles stomped along behind him, grumbling under his breath the whole time. I distinctly caught the words "whelps" and "banishment" as we went.

I entered the basement and my jaw dropped. The door to the gateway stood wide open. The green lights from the vortex tinted the room. "How did it open without one of us pushing the doorbell?" I asked worriedly.

The question answered itself as a tall, pale figure stalked through the opening, three huge hounds following close behind. The face swiveled toward us. I couldn't tell if it smiled because four tentacles had replaced the lower portion of its face where a mouth should have been. Its skin reminded me of a drowned corpse; it had four talons instead of fingers that I got a good look at as it pointed at me. It said in a sibilant, raspy tone. "I have come for you." The hounds spread out, lowering themselves to leap. They stood three feet at the shoulder, red skinned with flames flaring along their spines. The lead dog barred teeth the size of daggers.

Charles bellowed. "Begone, foul beasts, or feel my wrath!"

The lead dog advanced as the squid dude laughed, a ball of light growing in his hand. "Ha, your magic cannot compare with the might of X'nthar. Prepare to die, mortal."

I knew I should have brought Abby with me. "Nice puppies. We don't want any trouble." The dog growled as the three advanced slowly, red eyes tracking me as I stepped back.

"We do," Squid-head hissed.

I unleashed a stream of electricity at the nearest dog. "Bring it on, ugly."

17

The bolt slammed into the lead dog, eliciting a howl of pain as it slid across the floor. The second dog leapt over the downed hound. A flash of blue light formed around me as I launched a shot at the second hound just as the third crashed against the shield Alyx had thrown around me. The impact jarred me to the point I only scored a glancing blow.

"The hellhounds can teleport, so watch yourself," Alyx yelled, moving out of the way as Charles pushed past him.

Charles swung the staff at the rebounding dog, striking it with a solid thwack, red sparks erupting where the staff struck. The dog flew across the room, headed in Squid-head's direction. A quick flick of the thing's taloned hand diverted the airborne hound. He responded with a glowing ball thrown toward Charles.

Charles bellowed a laugh. "You'll need better than that." He held the staff before him, releasing a stream of fire from the dragon head's mouth. The ball vanished into the flames.

Alyx coughed behind me. "Try not to burn the place down, Charles." Alyx threw four blue spheres across the floor. They rolled like marbles, growing in size as they went. The surfaces shimmered, shapes revealing themselves under the pulsating surface. Arms formed as the head pushed upward like a swimmer breaking the surface of the water. One turned, expelling a stream of water over the sectional smoldering from the pyrotechnics. The remaining three closed on the tentacled horror at the other end of the room. Shards of ice flew in rapid succession like an ice machine Gatling gun.

"Water against a kraken-born? You jest," It batted the ice aside with ease. The shapes flowed and became water that once more splashed to the floor. A slash of energy ripped across the room and hit another hastily readied shield. Alyx swore under his breath as he fought to keep the shield intact.

Three more hellhounds joined the fight from the open doorbell portal. Charles chanted as he launched return fire against Octo-man.

"We need to close the portal," I yelled at Alyx.

Alyx stood near me, sweat pouring down his face as he held the shield around us. Charles fought on, but Squidy seemed to have no worries holding the two of them off.

I'd have to close the portal myself. I pulled on my source, letting a fist-sized ball of energy fly to hit the lead dog in the face, pulping its head in the process. They could die, that's for sure. I leapt over the dog I'd fried earlier, putting a bolt into its injured pack mate on my way. No sense leaving an enemy alive at my back.

I closed in on the two remaining hounds, readying my attack, when they vanished. I dove forward, tucking and rolling like Blaze had taught us. It saved my life.

The two dogs struck each other as they collided where my head had been seconds earlier. I unleashed twin blasts, hitting one in the neck but missing the second entirely. The bolt sent an avalanche of drywall and dust scattering. The dog turned, flames flaring to life as it crouched for its next leap.

"Tommy, grab the doorbell before more come through," Alyx yelled, sending a burst of blue flame at the squid thing.

I glanced to my right, where the bell sat affixed to the wall. The hound pounced as soon as my attention shifted. I took a page from Abby's playbook and rolled back as the weight landed on me. I'd just gotten my foot under its belly in time and used my momentum, and a liberal amount of juice, to propel it through the portal. Unless it grew fingers, there wouldn't be any way for it to get into Castle.

I rolled to my side and lunged for the doorbell. Unfortunately, it wasn't there. I turned to see the device resting in the taloned hand of our enemy. "Squidbert, I'm going to need that back," I snarled as I readied a bolt to blow his ugly head off.

"I think not, mortal." A slash of light appeared behind him as he stepped back into an alien looking landscape. The portal started to close, but its progress stopped as a blue barrier flashed into being.

Alyx flew past me, headed toward the new exit. "We have to get it back!"

He disappeared through the portal. Charles went through a second later. I ran but saw the web of blue energy fading. I dove for the opening. As I passed through, I wondered if I'd be sliced in half if it closed on me. Luckily, I belly flopped on the red sand, all my extremities in the correct places.

Charles wielded his staff like a battle axe, attacking the sorcerer with wood and flames, being countered with the glowing, golden magic the other used. Alyx spun in the air, bolts of blue energy streaking away from him, dropping the bats as they dove at the two.

Something struck me in the back, talons digging into my shoulders. Energy from the impact filled my depleted reservoir, sharpening my focus. What I had thought were bats, weren't. They looked like a cross between a pterodactyl and a Rottweiler, blood-red eyes glowing above a mass of long, razor-sharp teeth. I reached up, grabbed the thing's leg, and delivered a shock strong enough to light up a house. A howl of pain rattled my brain. I'd expected a bird's screech, not a lion's roar. Thankfully, it let go, flapping its giant wings to escape. I sent a shaft of energy slicing through its torso; green ichor fountained out of its back as it spiraled into the ground.

I noticed blood running down from the puncture wounds in my shoulder, but I didn't have time for injuries right now. I went street fighter on the next monster who closed in on me. I struck it just under the gaping maw, shattering its teeth with the impact. It flipped backward through the air, striking its brothers in the process. I put my back to Alyx, and we fought on. Nothing got close as we delivered a rain of death to the things.

The numbers dwindled once one of the brighter bird things decided there were easier ways to get lunch. "I've got this, help Charles!" Alyx shouted to me.

I didn't like what I saw. Charles had talon marks across his face and torso as Squidy and he fought. He seemed to be slowing, the squid mage striking more often. I ran, leaping at the last possible second for more momentum. On the down stroke, I punched, my fist glowing with built-up power. I caught the sorcerer across the tentacles, splashing slime on his white robes and the sand next to him. His head snapped back, eyes wide in surprise.

His hands flashed toward me, but I blocked them, stopping both with my wrists. Blaze would have been proud of that maneuver. I lashed out with a front thrust kick, striking him in the sternum. He folded like a fancy napkin at Thanksgiving. The doorbell landed in the sand near my feet. I grabbed it, keeping an eye on tentacle head as I backed up to where Alyx stood as he supported Charles, the larger man's arm over Alyx's shoulders. "What should we do with the terror from the deep over there?"

Alyx grunted. "He won't be bothering anyone for a while. We need to get out of here before the dangerous stuff comes."

I did a double take. "Those things weren't dangerous?"

"Not in comparison." Alyx spoke a couple of words, and a portal appeared in front of us. "We need to get Sir Charles to the Council for healing. The Kra-kelal tore him up pretty good. Nasty fighters."

I pulled the fire lord's right arm up and settled it over my shoulders. He still clung to his staff. "Tommy, watch out for his staff, it's warded..."

Alyx didn't get to finish before the butt of the staff swung, hitting me in the shin. A shock like I'd never experienced before went through me, and I crumpled to the sand. A strange energy swirled inside me as I lay there with two hundred pounds of Sir Charles collapsing on me.

"Are you alright?" Alyx asked, concern etched on his face as he lifted the Lord Master Fire Protector Dragon Staff.

I nodded slowly, rising to my feet. My ears felt like a gong struck by King Kong, and my whole body tingled with a strange sensation. "I think so." I stumbled after them through the portal into a marble-lined hallway. As I stepped through, I heard the familiar ding of an elevator arriving. Funny, I didn't see an elevator.

Down the hall raced at least twenty men, armored and carrying swords and shields. All had red tabards over their chainmail, a lion

UNBREAKABLE STORM

symbol in gold adorning them. "Halt trespasser!" yelled the guard in the lead.

Alyx swung around, facing the men, his eyes burning with anger. "Bertron, stand down. Sir Charles has been injured in battle. We need to get him to Lady Makeda for healing."

The man held up a hand, and the weapons behind him were lowered but not put away. "Sir Alyx, you have a trespasser with you that we dare not allow."

"Allow!" Alyx's voice cracked like a lightning bolt across a clear sky. "That 'trespasser,'" the word was layered with scorn and dismissal, "just fought a Kra-kelal and saved your master's life. Now, put up your swords and carry Sir Charles to Lady Makeda for healing."

"Yes, sir," Bertron said, crisply saluting Alyx by placing has a right hand over his heart. He signaled, and two uniformed men scooped up Charles, a third gently pulling the staff from his grip. Alyx noticed my raised eyebrows as I watched the guard walk away carrying the staff that had shocked the crap out of me.

"The guards are bound to Sir Charles, so the wards don't activate." He gestured for us to follow along. "Mages invest a lot of time in building items of power, but if you fall in battle, someone has to be able to bring them back."

"Makes sense." I glanced at Alyx as he floated along next to me. "Why don't you have a staff?"

He shrugged noncommittally. "They take a lot of time and energy to build properly. It's also difficult to wield them without legs. I have other trinkets that serve me better."

I took in the surroundings. We walked down a corridor large enough to land a plane in. The stone walls glowed faintly, and giant columns soared to the ceiling thirty or more feet above. I gasped as the celestial bodies above moved in unison along the hallway. Everywhere I looked, marvels stood barely noticed by the inhabitants as we strode along. "What is this place?"

"Speculo Regis. The first Council built it here to act as a gathering place for all the mages." Alyx paused as a group of robed and hooded people crept pass, chanting as they went. "Magic has diminished on Earth over the millennium, but we still protect our realm from things like the Kra-kelal and much worse."

117

"I'd hate to see worse than that." We approached a massive, ornate door. Bertron halted the company; Alyx floated up, placing his hand on the door. It shimmered and disappeared. Alyx waved the men holding Charles in; the rest took up positions along the hallway, hands on swords. I took a step to go with Alyx, but Bertron stood before me, hand against my chest.

"I'm sorry, lad, but strangers aren't allowed into the Physicka." He gestured toward an ornate bench. "Please take a seat until we work the situation out."

My mouth wanted to shoot a snappy comeback that included a reference to his mother, but I realized we were in a hospital, so instead, I let the exhaustion take over. "Thank you." I flopped onto the bench that was larger than most of the couches I'd seen. I leaned my head back and closed my eyes, amazed at how tired I felt. My stomach ached. I tried to figure out when I last ate but couldn't focus enough to remember. A vague recollection of breakfast with my parents was the best I could do.

Voices rose, pulling me from my fog.

A tall, dark-skinned woman dressed in a vivid blue robe exited the Physicka, yelling for Bertron. He stepped over to intercept her. "What exactly ya thinking keepin' the boy out here? He's a guest of Lord Alyx, not some poacher."

Bertron, who'd been dressed down by Alyx without flinching, blanched. "Ummm," was all that came out as he stood still as a statue. She waited for more, but his witty banter had fled him.

The woman threw her hands to the sky. "Ummm. Best you can do is ummm. If you'd spend as much time readin' as you do trainin' to stick people, you might be worth talkin' to." She pushed him aside, walking to where I sat. She appeared to be in her early thirties, but like Gladiator, had to be a whole lot older. A simple head wrap, which matched her dress, covered her hair. Her face broke into a soft smile as she spoke. "Thomas, I'm sorry for these brutes, they don't think much. Same as when I was a girl, the more muscle, the fewer brains they've got. Makeda at your service." She stopped, a penetrating look in her eyes. "I see the ichor from your run in, but did you lose blood in the fight?"

Did I? My thoughts seemed full of static. I tried to clear my head, but it didn't help. Maybe if I stood up, it would make things better. I pushed away from the wall, lurching to my feet. The hallway spun, but revolutions slowed. Makeda said something, but I couldn't tell what it was. She placed her hands on either side of my face, then pulled my ruined shirt off my shoulder. Pain flared through my sodden brain, but I couldn't find the energy to react.

Makeda held me up as my knees began to buckle. A couple of guards caught me as I fell, and then the lights went out.

18

Consciousness slithered its way back into my brain, pushing out the foggy recollection of what had happened. A pulsing pain flared behind my eyes. I forced them open and regretted the decision immediately. My shoulders were straight out of a mummy movie, but the bandages weren't soaked with red, which was a step in the right direction. I checked around me. I laid in bed in a small, white room. Dad sat in a chair at the foot of the bed, reading a battered book. He looked up as I pushed myself to a seated position.

He closed the book, a smile on his face. "You know your mother doesn't appreciate your adventures. You're giving her gray hairs."

I rolled my eyes, the pain reminding me why it was an epically bad idea. "Good thing she's blond. Where are we?"

The answer presented itself as Lady Makeda entered the room. "Welcome back, Thomas." Her tone was warm, but serious. "Lucky for you, the creature that pierced your skin uses a sedative, putting its victims to sleep so they can eat warm meat. I'm sure you've got a hell of a headache for your troubles, though."

I thought about nodding and decided against it. "I do. Thank you for helping me." My dry throat caused my voice to sound like a croaking frog.

"Think nothing of it. Sir Charles would probably be dead if not for your intervention. He'll take longer to mend than you, I'm afraid." She stepped over and checked my forehead with the back of her hand.

"What happened to him?" Dad asked. For being brought to a magical fortress to see an unconscious son, he had a firm grip on things.

She tsk'ed as she let go of my face after closely examining my eyes. "Kra-kelal's talons are extremely poisonous. We have an antidote, but the toxin is nasty and hangs on for a bit." She adjusted the front of her dress before continuing. "In the morning, once you've had a meal and some much-needed rest, the Council would like to speak to you."

"I can go now."

Makeda stopped me with a gentle hand on my injured shoulder. "Take your time," she scolded softly. "When you've been alive as long as we, you develop patience. The guards outside will escort you in the morning."

Dad stood up and put his fist over his heart. "My thanks, Lady Makeda."

Makeda chuckled. "Ranger, you never change." She swept out of the room as if she floated on air.

"You know her?" I blurted out before I could think better of it. Every time I thought I had a handle on Dad, some new fact or story came out that set me back to square one. Did other kids feel like that? Did one day they find out something that changed their image of their parents? I didn't know if it was because he'd been gone for most of my life or if he had lived such a large life, I could never know it all.

Dad returned to his seat. "Yes, there are times when the Council's goals line up with ours. Alyx worked with the teams as a liaison. We helped out on several occasions, though I've never seen anything like you saw today." He retrieved a bottle of water from beside him and tossed it to me. I opened it and drank most of it, water splashing across my face and chest in my rush.

"Thanks," I finished off the bottle, setting it on the bed next to me. "I didn't have time to think about it. One minute we were going to the basement to remove the doorbell, then next we were standing on red sand fighting giant bat things."

Dad chuckled. "It's the way of combat."

A light tap on the door announced a man pushing a silver cart. I could smell the food from my bed; my stomach rumbled in response. "A good appetite is a sure sign of recuperation," the man said, shooting me a smile.

"Mistress Makeda left instructions for you both to eat everything, but I don't see it being an issue."

"You never turn down a meal when you don't know when the next one will be."

"Words to live by, Master Ranger." The man busied himself setting out plates of food for each of us before excusing himself. We devoured the food in silence. Once we cleared the plates, Dad left to check in with Mom. I dropped off into a deep sleep.

D ad shook my shoulder, waking me from the dead. "You up for getting dressed? The Council may have infinite patience, but where you're concerned, your mother doesn't."

"Oh, yeah." I grimaced thinking of the lecture I'd be getting when we reached Castle. "I think I can manage."

"I'll be outside if you need me." Dad handed me a bag with clean clothes, a silver Pop-Tart pouch, and a bottle of Mountain Dew before stepping out of the room to allow me some privacy. I pulled on the faded Nike t-shirt and jeans and kicked on my sneakers. It took longer than normal given how stiff my shoulders were, but the pain was manageable. I devoured the pastry and chased it with a couple of gulps of Dew. I headed out the door, wiping at my mouth in case of crumbs as Dad signaled the three guards. We made our way down the long hall, taking a series of turns before we saw our destination.

A bridge arced away from the marble hallway, sun cascading through the glass arches that enclosed it. You could have driven six tanks across it with room to spare. Whoever designed this place wanted to be able to accommodate a whole lot of people. As we approached it, I realized the entire walkway had been constructed of glass, allowing an unobstructed view of the clouds scudding below. Stepping onto the smooth panels was unnerving; my senses screamed that my foot wouldn't meet anything but air. The surface could have been rock for there was no give or sway to the bridge. We continued our journey to see the Council, the wonderful Council of wherever we were.

Embedded stained glass symbols decorated the walls and ceiling as we went, the colors dancing across the floor like facets of a giant diamond.

We crossed over the apex of the bridge, seeing a floating castle turret before us. My stomach flip-flopped as we approached.

Where the bridge ended, it opened out, revealing the Council hall. The floors were cream colored along the edges with onyx through the middle of the room. The room ended in a raised dais with six ornate thrones, each painted to match the mage who sat on them. I noticed the red throne was empty. Behind the thrones was a wall of floor-to-ceiling windows looking out over the cloudscape below. Giant pillars rose majestically to the ceiling. Each had been carved to represent a man or woman who grasped a staff with an ornate animal head, like Charles' dragon staff.

We strode silently across the center of the chambers. Arched windows dotted the outer wall with murals between. All sorts of mythical creatures were represented, as well as huge and vivid fights between mages. I'd seen smaller football stadiums than this place. My head swiveled as I tried to see everything at once. Dad, unlike me, peered straight ahead as we went.

The lead guard stopped in front of us. In a booming voice, he declared, "The outsiders have been delivered as you commanded."

A middle-aged woman with long, black, braided hair and dressed in a long green robe stood. "You have our thanks, Tarlon. You are excused."

"Thank you, my lady," the guard said, bowing his head with his fist over his heart. His unit did the same before pivoting and marching out of the room single file. The Reclaimers had nothing on these guys.

The green mage extended her hands before her, palms up in a welcoming gesture. "Please, you are honored guests. There is no need for formality. Join us, will you?"

I glanced at Dad. He inclined his head slightly. "We would be honored, Lady Maya." He went up the half-dozen steps, and I followed behind him, hoping I wouldn't embarrass myself or him in the process.

Two chairs that hadn't been there earlier awaited us. Maya leaned back in her throne as we took seats. I settled into the straight-backed, gilded chair, surprised by the soft, comfortable seat. I wish we had these in Castle. I sat so I could watch Dad for guidance out of the corner of my eye.

Alyx spoke up next. "Cyclone Ranger, you've met everyone before, but I'd like to introduce the remainder of the Council." Alyx, wearing blue robes I'd never seen before, shot me a quick wink. I relaxed slightly at that. I'd known Alyx wielded magic, but this setting intimidated me.

"You've met Makeda the Arcanist." She nodded to me, a small smile on her face. "Lady Maya the Wanderer greeted you." Maya pulled her long braid over her shoulder as Alyx spoke. "Next to her is Pimiko the Seer." In the golden throne was a small Asian woman who could have been a teen or forty, I couldn't tell. Her eyes appeared to be two different colors and slightly unfocused. If she knew we were here, it was hard to tell. "And on the end is Yatu the Elemental." The white mage smiled broadly; his teeth gleamed against his tanned skin. Large, bushy eyebrows and salt and pepper hair made him look like a kindly old man. Having seen what Charles could do, I didn't think I'd want to make him, or any of them, mad.

Dad glanced at me before speaking. "I'd like to thank you for the hospitality and a special thanks to Lady Makeda for saving my son."

Makeda waved a hand in dismissal. "Thomas is young and strong; he'd have slept it off. If you'd like to repay the small debt of a clean bed and bandages, maybe you could talk Lord Alyx into letting me restore his legs."

Shock sped through my system. She could fix Alyx's legs? Why wouldn't he allow her to? Knowing Alyx, I wouldn't be getting any answers about that. Alyx's scowl confirmed this subject was off limits.

"And if Lady Makeda could leave long ago arguments in the past where they belong, it would be appreciated."

Yatu belly laughed. "You two squabble like two walruses over a seal carcass. May we know why you convened us?"

Alyx composed himself before continuing. "I've called us together. Dark times have come again. Eiraf has returned."

A chorus of gasps and exclamations mingled in the wake of the news. Alyx restored the quiet and told them what happened to me.

The gold mage spoke first. "Who is the man she speaks of? Why would he be so important as to upset the balance that Eiraf claims to protect?" Her eyes never landed in one place, constantly moving as if in REM sleep. It was deeply disconcerting. Chills ran up my spine watching her. I averted my eyes.

"He is a good man, a Gifted, who fought to save my family. He fell to the Syndicate, and we've been attempting to rescue him." Dad paused for a moment. "I hadn't heard about this before now, or I would have brought it to your attention."

His tone left no doubt in my mind I would be hearing about it later. I'd screwed this up, bad. I wondered if Marcel could get me into a witness protection program.

"Do not be hard on him, Cyclone Ranger," Maya said softly. Her coppery skin almost glowed in the shadows that her seat drew around her. "When we first encounter the mystical realm, it feels unreal, a dream perhaps, and makes us question reality. Many of the greatest of us were convinced they'd gone mad before they were found and trained."

I jumped in quickly, sensing an opening. "I thought I had hallucinated it. I told Alyx as soon as I could."

Alyx indicated his agreement. "Ranger, he did come to tell me, and we were lucky he was there, or we'd be searching for a new red mage." He returned to the main question. "I've met this man, and he is not strong in his Gift. The prophecy Eiraf gave makes little sense, though they never do until after it's too late."

Yatu grunted. "No sense worrying if the ice will break. It will in its own good time. The question is how we stop a plunge into a watery death?"

Smoothing the fabric of her emerald robes, Maya smirked. "You can take the boy out of the Arctic..." A friendly look passed between them before she continued. "Well, it would seem you should find this man."

"We have enlisted the Underground in finding him. I owe him a great debt, and I mean to see it paid." Dad's voice had a note of pain to it. I wondered if Waxenby would feel the same. By his accounts, Dad had saved his life in Washington. Would he consider them square?

"We dare not lend aid to the task at hand," Pimiko said dreamily. Her head lolled to the side like a junkie sliding into the haze of their latest fix. "The balance is in jeopardy. The enemy is preparing a massive event intended to destroy all life as is their wont. We need to be here to defend, to respond to the looming threat. Death, death is coming!" Twitching, she slumped against the arm of her throne. The room sat silent, no one making a sound.

"Well, that was enlightening," Makeda said, standing and moving to check on the unconscious gold mage. "Pimiko's power is great but glimpsing the many paths of what may come fractures a mind over time. She needs to rest."

A guard, gold tabard over his uniform, approached as if summoned.

Makeda spoke to him softly. He picked up the slight mage and carried her as if she were a child, not one of the six most powerful wizards in the world. The purple mage returned to her seat, carefully arranging her robes as she sat. "Based on her visions, I think the Council will have to leave you to your own methods until we know more of the situation."

Dad stood. "Would the Council be willing to scry where Oliver Waxenby is? It would be of great help."

"Ranger, we would, but Pimiko would need to do magic, and she's not available. When she awakes, we will..." Alyx stopped dead as his eyes widened. The others on the dais had adopted the same expression. I turned in my seat to see Eiraf standing to my left.

Just when you thought your life couldn't get any stranger, you drop into the twilight zone.

19

The silence shattered as words returned to the collective council members, ranging from 'how dare you' to 'get out of here right now,' all delivered as befitting the era each mage came from. Eiraf stood as still as a boulder, the symbols on her forehead glowed softly under the white cloth that covered her hair. If the commotion from the assembled mages bothered her, it didn't show on her face.

Yatu restored order with a loud, "Stop your blubbering, and let the woman speak."

Eiraf nodded to him before directing her eyeless gaze to the assembled group. "You'll have to pardon my unorthodox method of procuring your attention, but the balance has shifted, and it is in peril of collapse."

"The balance, by its very nature, cannot collapse," Maya said, her tone prickly with anger. "Are you accusing us of imperiling the universe?"

"Not at all, wise Maya. The Order of Midnight facilitated the Dark Brigade attacks in the attempt to destroy all life on the planet." Eiraf's open hand gestured toward Dad. "Cyclone Ranger and his peers thwarted their plans."

Dad cleared his throat. "We lost the fight, the Dark Brigade escaped. They wanted to subjugate the people of Earth, not destroy them."

"To what purpose would destroying the people of Earth bring the

Order?" Alyx asked, his face a mass of warring emotions. "And why divulge this now? You didn't warn us before the attacks."

"The sole responsibility of my sisterhood is to protect the balance at all costs. We knew the attacks would not succeed."

I knew not to interrupt, but my mouth ran before my brain could stop the avalanche of words. "Billions of people died. The Gifted were shackled. You didn't think we deserved a warning?"

The eyeless face turned toward me. "Thomas, there are bigger concerns in the universe than people dying. Wars have killed more than those attacks. My sisters aren't concerned with the trivial."

I gasped. "Trivial? Trivial!" My voice rose in pitch as my anger flared hot and raw. "Billions of people died, never to be seen again. Those people had done nothing to provoke their mass extinction." Dad put a restraining hand on my shoulder; I had not realized I'd been getting ready to attack. I settled down, seething as I stood there.

Eiraf's demeanor hadn't changed. "The human race survived. Innocents are always the price for power. The Order is actively blocking our sight. The echoes have become waves across reality. It will be years before the waves drown us, but the loss of Oliver Waxenby would set off a chain of events culminating in the elimination of the human race. It can't be allowed to happen."

Dad squeezed my shoulder hard. I got the point.

"The loss of the human race would not collapse the balance, most certainly," Makeda said softly. Her shrewd eyes hunted for any hint of a lie.

Eiraf spread her hands wide. "Most certainly not, but the end we see is the ending of everything, which is what the Order is sworn to. We cannot ascertain how this would happen, but it begins with the loss of Oliver Waxenby and ends with the destruction of reality. The rest is being blocked by a power we've never experienced before. This is why I am here to warn you."

Yatu grunted like an angry walrus. "This could be a trap."

"The worst harm comes from where you least expect it. Forget about your enemies and think what your friends will do." Eiraf faded as she spoke. "May the balance preserve us all."

"I hate all these cryptic clues and warnings. First Pimiko, now the snow-blind Sisterhood." Yatu spat on the floor where Eiraf had stood.

Maya sighed, looking exhausted as she sat back in her seat. "And they are at odds with each other, though neither is known for being overly explicit in a path forward."

"What is our next move?" Dad asked patiently. His hands were behind his back and clenched together. "We have been unable to locate Oliver through our means. It sounds like we share an interest in his continued safety. How accurate are Eiraf's prophecies?"

Alyx shrugged. "After events have occurred, it is easy to find ways to make them appear true. Beforehand, there are so many words you might find meaning in. It does trouble me she can't see the possible futures. The Sisterhood of Delphi is renowned for its power."

"We will need time to regard her words," Makeda said cautiously. She rose and straightened her robes. "We should return you to your home so we may deliberate on a plan. I would have a few words with Thomas before Alyx returns you."

"Of course, Lady Makeda." Dad bowed to her. Alyx floated down the stairs to talk with Dad as the purple mage led me to the side by a gigantic window set into the outer wall.

"Thomas, first I'd like to thank you for your assistance yesterday. Losing Charles would have been catastrophic. Magic has faded as technology has grown. It took us over forty years to find Alyx."

I didn't know what to say, so I settled on a quick, "You're welcome, Lady Makeda." Her smile was warm and motherly. After the day I'd had yesterday, being cared for made me realize how much I'd missed my mom and needed to see her.

"Know I would be your friend, and with the times to come, we will need all the friends we can find." She glanced over to where Dad spoke with the other mages. "You need to be careful; things are not always as they seem. I know not what it is, but things feel wrong to the marrow of these old bones."

"I understand and will try my best to be careful." Once again, my mouth took off while my brain screamed on the roller coaster. "You mentioned you could re-grow Alyx's legs. Were you serious?"

She gave me a sly look. "Good to see you pay attention. Yes, I was. The magical arts are powerful, but the subject has to have the desire. Magic doesn't cure anything, just enhances the body's abilities. Alyx is healthy and, if he wanted it, the magic would return his missing legs. It would be painful, but he's strong enough to endure it. Why do you ask?"

My brain screamed for me to shut up, but my mouth had momentum. "Can you heal anything?"

She shook her head, the beads she wore tinkling musically as if accompanying her. "No. Sometimes the person is too far gone or doesn't desire to be healed. Some feel they deserve what happened to them and fight the process. Magic isn't a cure-all; there are many facets to what we do."

And here it was, the gold medal-winning question. "Could you heal someone who's died?" My voice barely broke a whisper. I felt the heat rise to my face. I knew I shouldn't have asked. Alyx had said no, but he wasn't a healer. I waited for a harsh rebuke or a stinging response. I couldn't let any stone go unturned; if there were a chance to bring Wendi back, I had to take it. I glanced up at Makeda's face, expecting anger, and received a surprise instead. Tears flowed down her face. She pulled me into a hug as the tears sprang from my eyes. I had thought I couldn't cry anymore. Obviously, I was wrong.

"My poor boy," she whispered while she held me as I cried. "Loss comes to all of us, but your loss was unusually cruel. I am sorry, but those arts are beyond all."

I nodded dumbly, unable to speak. After a few minutes, my tears subsided, and she let me go. "I'm sorry, Lady Makeda. I shouldn't have asked. I loved her so much, and I miss her until I feel like I'd rather die than go on."

"I've lost loved ones; I know how raw those feelings are. Would you allow me to show you something? It won't make your pain easier to bear, but it will help you understand why I say no."

"I'd be honored." My brain had resumed control, late to the party as always. She muttered under her breath and flicked her wrist, and a door-sized portal opened. We stepped through. The portal winked out behind us.

"I've no talent for those damn things. Alyx can summon them in his sleep and hold them open for hours." She oriented herself then set off down a set of stairs. "I never put them in the right place."

The stairs ended at an ornate metal door covered in runes and a design made out of metal studs. Marcel would have loved the steampunk of the piece. I doubted Abby, or Titan for that matter, could penetrate the door. At a touch, the runes glowed, and the door disappeared. We entered a long hallway. I looked back and saw the door as solid as ever, back in place.

The hallway had a hint of decay in the air. Warmth flowed at us from all directions, inducing sweat across my brow that dripped as we walked the hundred or so feet. We walked to another door, identical to the first. It swung open as we reached it, booming shut after we passed through. A gray-skinned man lay on the floor, enclosed in a shimmering field of energy. A small bed and a toilet were the only things in the room. The smell of decay assaulted my nose, almost making me gag. "What is this place?"

Makeda glanced at me before beginning. "Thomas, magic is a funny thing. Many more people have a latent talent for it than ever will use it. Sometimes a person will use it in an extreme circumstance, find an explanation that fits, and never use it again. It is the same as the Gifted after a fashion."

I watched the man in the cube. He writhed on the floor, screamed incoherently, and then fell silent again. White bandages wrapped his hands, which ineffectively ran up and down his face. He arched his back, howling like a wolf. I decided he must be ill. "I'm not sure how people get their Gifts since we are all collared before we develop them."

She held herself straight as an arrow, face unreadable. "I've spoken to your father, and the two processes are similar. We find most of our apprentices after a traumatic event when they need their powers. Many don't survive their initiation into the magical arts." She paused. I didn't want to interrupt her with more stupid questions. "I survived mine, but for centuries I wished I hadn't. For some things, the price is so great you wouldn't want your worst enemy to experience it."

I knew exactly what she spoke of; the words crashed in on me, threatening to sweep me away under waves of depression. Memories of Wendi filled my mind: the way her hair shone in the sunlight, the smell of lavender, the warmth of her kiss, the echoing of laughter. Gone. Gone except for my memories of her. The pain burned hotter than any fire ever could. I'd cried for her and avenged her death, but they were the barest of payments for what she had given to me.

Makeda's hand settled on my shoulder, a life preserver in the sea of misery I drowned in. "I do not tell you these things to cause you pain, but I know they do. Pain brings knowledge, knowledge brings understanding, understanding brings peace."

I had learned a lot, but none of it had made things any better. In my opinion, pain brought more pain and nothing else. I focused myself so I could listen, knowing what she told me was important.

"You are young, so my words seem like platitudes, for how could an old woman know how it feels?"

I started to deny it, but she laughed warmly. "I see I have you back." The smile faded, the mask slid back into place. "I was no older than you when I bore my husband a strong son. He grew and surpassed the older boys as a warrior. The gods had blessed him, and he returned with captives to be sacrificed, to honor the gods. I know now how untrue that was."

Human sacrifice? She looked in her late forties, but there hadn't been human sacrifices in forever. I saw an image of Makeda, young and strong, watching her son grow. A fierce and protective mother. I wondered if she showed me the image or if it was my imagination.

"Asad, a tribal elder, grew jealous as my son bested his son over and over again. One moonless night while we were away from the tribe, Asad struck, killing my husband and son. He cut me open and left me for dead, laughing as he went."

The image in my head shifted to the dead bodies around a small fire on a windswept night. Grunts of the predators sounded nearby in the night. Blood covered Makeda, but she pulled herself over to where her son lay, his eyes open to the stars above.

"I prayed to my ancestors to allow me to strike Asad, to hurt him as he'd hurt me. I mourned my husband, but I called to the gods to bring my son back to avenge our deaths. I felt a sensation I believed were my ancestor's hands pulling me to the afterlife. I fought, I screamed to the skies, invoking Ogbunabali's name, offering my life for his."

I could see the scene as she spoke, entranced in the rhythm of her words and the images as they floated through my mind. The body in front of Makeda twitched. Unnoticed, she continued screaming, even as the blood dripped from the cuts Asad's knife had left. The blood stopped flowing, the skin knitting back together. As she continued her pleas to her god, her son flopped over, then struggled to his feet. Her screams of pleading turned to shouts of joy until her son rose to his full height in front of her. Shrieks of agony followed as she saw his face in the flickering light of the fire. His lifeless eyes had no irises, just a flat white of his eyeball. Drool ran from his gaping mouth.

"I'd been given my miracle." The last word heaped with scorn. "My beautiful son had become a monster. I tried to restrain him, but he knocked me down and walked off into the night. He killed the entire tribe that night. In the morning, the Council came and stopped him before he could harm anyone else. They explained I had power and could use it for good. I went with them and became an apprentice."

"The council killed your son then?" I blurted out, mentally slapping myself for having a big mouth. "I'm sorry, that was rude of me."

"No, Thomas. This is why I brought you here." She raised her hand, pointing at the man who thrashed on the floor, screaming in agony. "That is my son. He is an example as to why we never break the law of crossing the barrier."

My head swam in disbelief. The words slammed into me like a runaway tractor-trailer carrying tons of cargo.

I did the only thing a reasonable person could do in this situation. I threw up.

20

Makeda offered me a cloth to clean up after the unexpected expulsion of my stomach's contents. I mumbled an apology, my cheeks flaming red with embarrassment. I flicked my eyes over where I'd left a mess, but the floor, wall, even my clothes were clean. A faint whiff of ozone reached my nose, but not the acidic smell of vomit. I wiped my face thoroughly before turning back to the purple mage.

"Nothing to be sorry for. I took care of the mess and, frankly, even had I not, the smell couldn't get worse in here."

I glanced back at her son, who rolled into a ball, whimpering like an injured dog. His skin lacked any hint of color, as did his hair. It wasn't white like an albino, but gray like he'd been pulled out of a monochrome picture. The only color on him was his shredded clothes. "What is his name?" I asked softly. He'd been a person before this, and it seemed disrespectful to refer to him as an It.

"I called him Femi, short for Olufemi. It means God loves me, and I realize how ironic it is, because my magic caused this, not the touch of God."

I stood watching him as the silence stretched on. "Hello, Femi," I whispered, realizing just how much Makeda understood how I felt. She'd trade anything for him to be alive. He had come back, but not in the way intended. "Why is he here?"

"We tried everything we could to heal him, but there's nothing to heal. He's not in there; Pimiko delved his mind, and Femi is gone." She stared off into the distance as she spoke, seeing things beyond my knowing. "I've kept him here as a reminder of what uncontrolled power can do. The field is tied to my heartbeat. When I die, he will disintegrate."

I watched as he flailed on the floor, banging his head repeatedly. It seemed cruel to endure watching your child like this. How could you ever move on? "Wouldn't it be easier to let him go?"

"It would. Do you understand why I must refuse your request?" I could feel her eyes boring into the side of my head as she waited for the answer she knew could be the only answer.

"I do."

She put her hand on my arm, gently squeezing it. I looked, seeing her in a much different light. "You must listen to me well and good, Thomas. Your loss is a weakness that can be exploited. The Order will promise anything to sway you to their side. Your love brought back whole. Your friends reunited. They are lies. They use black magic to deceive before they destroy everything you love. It is their way. You must be strong if they whisper in your ear."

I understood to my core. She had said understanding would lead to peace, and I realized what she meant. I had tried everything possible to bring Wendi back and came up with nothing. "Thank you, Makeda. I'll never get over losing her, but I know she can't come back. Can I ask one more question?"

"Of course," she said with a chuckle. "At your age, the questions are a flood over fertile soil, germinating into the ideas that will grow into the man you become."

I smiled at her. "Do you believe in the afterlife? That you'll be reunited with your family one day?"

"Technically, two questions." The smile returned to her face like a sunrise after a terrible storm. "I've seen things nothing could explain. I have bent reality with the power of the cosmos, and yet, I have the knowledge of a babe fresh from her mother in comparison to what is out there. I do believe I will see them again, or I will pay for what I did. Either way, I believe there is more than what we can see. Do you?"

PATRICK DUGAN

I thought of Wendi and then of all the people who had died at my hand or because of me. I shuddered inwardly. "I do, but it might be better for me if there wasn't." If there was a God, how could I not be called to answer for all the lives I had destroyed.

"I understand your meaning. I have something for you, and then we should return before your father worries I've stolen you to be my new apprentice." She reached into a pocket I hadn't seen, and pulled out a small, deep purple, glass bottle. The glass felt like ice, cold and smooth, but not unpleasant. I peered into it, seeing a swirling mist within. "If you ever have extreme need for me, a life or death situation, break the bottle, and I will come."

I wrapped the bottle in the cloth Makeda had given me and placed it in my pocket. "I will be careful with it. Thank you."

She muttered a soft word and flicked her wrist, forming a portal. "Let us return."

Dad and I said our goodbyes, and Alyx returned us to Castle. It took a long time to get Mom to let go of me and assure her I was fine. I sat and ate while she peppered me with questions. She walked me to my room, holding on to my arm like I might vanish if she let go. After a few more hugs and goodnight kisses I had to bend down for her to plant on my forehead, she went to check on Dad.

I carefully got the bottle out of my pocket and found a small box to store it in. I wrapped it in a couple of shirts and hid it away in my backpack. I stripped off my dirty clothes and showered like I'd never seen soap and hot water before. Any longer and I'd have sprouted roots. I got ready for bed and climbed in.

Thoughts ran around in my head as I tried to process everything I had seen and learned today. Images of Wendi mingled with those of Femi, which didn't help me drift off to sleep. I'm not sure how long I laid there before I heard a knock at my door. I reached over and switched on the lamp next to my bed. "Come in."

The door opened to reveal a distraught Abby. She shoved the door closed as she ran over and tackled me. I couldn't get my arms up to return the hug. She held me at arm's length, examining me. "Are you okay?"

I laughed. "Other than being crushed, I'm fine." I would have made a joke, but her fist rapped me across the jaw. "Ow! What was that for?"

She stood and glared at me. Her index finger shot up. "One, you left without me. Two, I find out not only did you leave without me, but you almost got killed by some magical monster or dogs or something." Fingers kept flipping up as she counted off the ways I'd let her down. "Three, you get to go to some magical palace in the sky, and I'm here waiting and worrying you won't come back like..." She stopped, suddenly aware of what she almost said.

"Like Wendi. I get it." I rubbed my jaw; it hurt, but she had pulled it. I'd been under the twin sledgehammers enough to know what kind of damage she could do when angry. "I should have come to get you."

She flopped on the bed in front of me. "I promised her if anything happened, I'd watch your back. I can't keep my promise if you take off without me. Got it?"

I held up my hand. "I swear on Marcel's tablet I will never leave without taking you with me." I could see the tension drain out of her. I keep forgetting everyone had lost Wendi, not just me. The new reality took its toll on all of us. I promised myself I'd do better in the future.

"Thank you. Now, I want a rundown of everything that happened while you were gone. Leave something out, and I'll hit you for real." She flashed a grin that made me laugh. If Marcel could be my brother, then Abby was my sister. One day I'd stop hurting the people around me.

She settled back as I ran through the whole story. I started with the first meeting with Eiraf and went straight through until Alyx dropped us off at Castle. She asked to see the bottle, which I retrieved and showed her. "It's only for life or death emergencies, but Makeda said it would bring her." I put the bottle away, careful to not break it. It appeared solid but I wasn't taking any chances.

I hopped back into bed. "What happened here today?" It felt good to let someone else do the talking.

"Nothing much." She thought for a second. "Blaze almost passed out after a quick sparring session. I still think he needs a doctor. Mom made chicken piccata for dinner. There were leftovers."

"I know, Mom heated a couple up when I got back." Even though I'd eaten while I spoke with Mom, I was starved. Healing required a lot of energy. My stomach grumbled loudly. Time to remedy that. "Snack time."

Abby didn't need to be told twice. She ate more than any of us, but you couldn't tell. Olympic athletes would kill to be built like her. We climbed the stairs up to the kitchen. I grabbed the leftover chicken after giving her crap about lying to me. She fetched the plates, and we set to preparing our late-night dinner. The kitchen table could hold twelve people, so we sat at the corner closest to the island where the steaming hot food sat. Mom's cooking was legendary, and we enjoyed another round of dinner. "Man, this is the best."

Abby burped. "You know if you have to hide out, having a master chef and fresh vegetables makes it a lot easier." She got up and put the plates and glasses in the dishwasher. "Don't get used to it; I figured you had a very long day."

In response, I yawned and stretched out my arms. I really did need some sleep. The food coma setting in would help. "I guess I'm going to crash."

She leaned back across from me. "Um, have you talked to Marcel?" I shook my head, stifling another yawn. "I think he's upset about something, but he won't tell any of us. Mom tried to talk to him while Ranger was gone to get you, but he kept saying things were fine."

That didn't sound right. Marcel always had some issue to worry about. Either it was his newest phone not having the correct OS version, or he couldn't train because it might hurt his hands. "Things are fine?"

"I know, right? He's worse than an old man yelling at kids on his lawn. Maybe you should talk to him. He's been holed up in the control room since yesterday. He says he's fine." She gritted her teeth on the last word and then gave me the 'you should really go talk to him' look.

I sighed. It wouldn't take long, then I could get some sleep. I stood, pushing in my chair. "You coming?"

She slid her chair in, and we descended the stairs, through the connector and down to computer central. I knocked on the door. "All hail the computer king!" He didn't answer. I keyed the door and walked in. Marcel sat with his back to the door, his head cradled in his hands as he cried. His giant 'fro flopped over like an avalanche of hair. "Mr. Wizard, what's going on?"

Marcel's head rose slowly. He turned the chair so he faced us. Huge bags hung under his red-rimmed eyes, making him appear a lot older. I'd seen him after all night coding sessions, but he'd never been this ragged before. Tears still rolled down his cheeks. "Hey Tommy, glad you're back."

My jaw dropped open. Marcel hadn't called me Tommy since third grade. I exchanged a shocked look with Abby, whose eyes had grown three sizes bigger. "Um, Marcel, what's going on, man?"

He sunk into the chair further. "Things are fine."

I walked over and grabbed two office chairs, rolling one over to Abby. She swung it around, taking a seat. I did the same. "What's really going on? I've known you my whole life, and there is something wrong."

"I'm fi..." He mashed the tears away before casting his eyes around as if to escape. "Never mind. It's...it's happened, going to come out, all of it. Just watch." He spun back to the control panel, his fingers tapping out a rhythm on the keyboard. The monitor above flickered to life. Grainy camera footage loaded as we watched. It must be a surveillance camera. From the time stamp, it had happened about ten minutes ago.

"Granite Falls?" Abby asked as she squinted at the screen. Making out the details was tough with how grainy it was.

"Yes, it is." Marcel pushed away from the keyboard. His eyes had a haunted look to them I'd never seen before. This must be really bad.

From the right side of the screen, a large man stumbled along. He swayed dangerously as he went, tripping over his own feet. "He's drunk. Why is that a problem?" I asked, totally confused.

"Just watch."

I resumed staring at the screen as the man bumbled along. From the far side of the screen three Reclaimers came into view; one had his shock stick out. They pushed each other as they stood in plain sight of the drunk. He didn't notice.

Abby sat up straight. "Is he Gifted? He has a collar on."

Marcel nodded mutely.

Now that she mentioned it, I could see the edge of his collar just above his leather jacket. Oh, man. Being caught drunk by bored Reclaimers would be bad. They wouldn't kill him, but he'd be in the hospital for sure. The other two soldiers produced their batons and circled him. The guy's head jerked up as he heard the Reclaimer in front of him. They were all laughing at him, shocking him in turn. He spun like a trapped grizzly bear, arms flailing at the air, trying in vain to stop the pain. One of the soldiers stepped aside and delivered a blow across the back of his knees.

He went down hard. They converged on him, striking over and over as the man curled into a ball. I'd been worked over enough times by Brunner to know how it felt, how helpless you were.

The screen flashed white, startling Abby and me. "What the hell was that?" I asked, jumping up from my chair. Abby's exclamation was a lot more colorful. The image slowly returned. All three soldiers were charred beyond belief as was the drunk they'd been beating.

"How could that have happened?" Abby paced back and forth, nervous energy pouring off her in waves. When Marcel didn't answer, she grabbed him. He flinched away, but she held fast. "How did it happen, and why is it our problem, Marcel?" She came close to snarling in his face, she was so upset.

Marcel chocked back a sob. "I turned off their collars to prove it would be better. I didn't know this would happen."

The Reclaimers would kill or lock away all the Gifted.

Welcome to the Reclamation War 2.0.

21

I rubbed my eyes to clear my head before I spoke. "Abby, can you get everyone down here?"

"Tommy, it's 2 a.m. Can't it wait until morning?"

I thought about it for a second. I wasn't sure if we could do anything, but we had the chance now, and it might disappear by morning. "No, I don't think so."

She didn't look happy, but she ran out of the room to do it. I turned back to Marcel. "This is only ten minutes ago. Did anyone else see this footage?"

Tears welled up in his eyes as he bowed his head. "I'm sorry. I thought turning off a couple of collars would prove we could free a few at a time and that the Reclaimers wouldn't notice. Then they disappeared, and I couldn't find them. Now this."

"I don't care about that crap now. Did anyone else see the footage?" Marcel jerked back as if I'd slapped him across the face. He'd screwed up, but we might have time to minimize the damages.

"I intercepted the feed and sent a virus to destroy the hard drive. They only use the camera feeds as evidence if they need it." His tone dripped with misery. "I should have listened, but I couldn't leave all the rest behind when they could be free."

I sighed, wishing Mom and Dad would get here. I should have known he would do something like this. Marcel hadn't stopped talking about freeing the kids in Redemption. At least he hadn't done that or shut down the Block. The headache I thought was gone returned full force. I just wanted to go to bed and sleep.

The door opened and a disheveled set of parents entered, Abby in tow. "What is going on, you two?" Mom asked, her face etched with concern and lack of sleep.

I swallowed hard, not wanting to talk about it, but wishing hadn't brought Wendi back or accomplished anything else for that matter. "We have a situation we need to discuss." I checked with Abby. "Is Blaze coming?"

Before she could answer, Blaze entered. "Dude, chill." He walked in carrying a pot of coffee and three mugs. His hair had been pulled into a ponytail, but loose pieces stuck out in all directions like a haystack after the kids had finished jumping in it. "Nobody's gonna function without some coffee to get us going." His voice carried a rasp to it that hadn't been there before. For the first time, he looked old to me. Blaze handed out coffee to Mom and Dad before drinking his. "What's so all-fired important you've got to drag us out of bed? If it's a new gizmo Marcel wants, you'll regret it at training."

"I wish." I gestured to the screen. "Go ahead and run the video. Marcel got this off the Granite Falls camera feed." Nobody said anything, but their worried expressions changed to ones of horror as they realized the implication of a collared Gifted exploding and killing three Reclaimers in the process.

"Good call, Tommy," Dad said, setting his coffee cup down on the junk table he stood by. "Do we know how this could happen?"

I caught Mom's eye and glanced at Marcel, who sat staring at his shoes. She got my meaning right away. She lightly touched Dad's arm, letting him know. He nodded slowly.

"Doesn't matter, what is important is what do we do now?" Mom's voice held a note of sympathy that penetrated Marcel's fog.

He got up and faced everyone. "It was me. I found a way to turn off the collar without releasing it."

Dad put his hand on his shoulder. "Thank you for telling us. How many people did you release?"

"I used the network at the Secret Lair to broadcast the signal through the sound system." Marcel sniffled, wiping his nose on his sweatshirt sleeve. "I did it right before closing, so there wouldn't be many who were affected."

Blaze whistled. "Dude, you are amazing. I'd never thought anyone could bypass the built-in security at the Lair." He poured himself a second cup and walked over to fill Dad's cup as well.

Dad thanked him, retrieving his steaming mug. "Blaze, how many people would be there at close?"

"Maybe three or four at the most. Max isn't Gifted, so he wouldn't be affected."

Marcel blurted out. "I thought I could prove it wouldn't cause any harm but let them get away from the Protectorate. I'm sorry."

Mom gathered him up in a hug as he started to cry. She moved him across the room, her voice quiet and reassuring. I knew he meant well, but this had gone sideways fast. I worried about Mimi. Was she working? Did her Gift manifest like the guy in the feed? I'm sure I wouldn't know, but I realized I was scared for her.

"The guy had his collar on, so is that our main concern?" Abby asked from her perch on the windowsill overlooking the maintenance area. "If the Reclaimers find out about it, they'll freak."

"I agree with Abby." Dad took another swallow of coffee. "We have to get the collar. Any ideas?"

Blaze grinned. "Max is right there. The time stamp is only twenty minutes ago, and they were in a parking lot near the Lair. He can get over there and at least pull the collar. I'll go call him." He tottered out of the room. I'd seen him jump over a person to break a board on the far side. Maybe he pulled a muscle during training.

Dad lowered his voice. "This is bad; we're lucky he didn't burst into flames in the middle of a school or someplace with an audience. Can we trust Marcel?"

I gaped in shock, how could we not trust him. He got us out of the Megadrome. He found Castle when we had to burn Dresden and Oberon.

"I can see from the look on your face that's a yes."

"We can trust him, but we should talk it over with him." Dad agreed, so I called him and Mom over. Abby hadn't moved, though if she grabbed a bucket of popcorn to watch the show, it wouldn't have surprised me much. Mom pulled up a chair next to Marcel, still holding his hand.

Mom pushed a chair to Dad. "Take a seat, Ranger. You are a bit intimidating standing over everyone."

He gave her a wry smile and sat. "Marcel, we talked about this. Can I ask why you decided to release the Gifted at the Lair?" He started to say something else, but stopped, waiting for Marcel to answer.

Marcel's size made it easy to forget he hadn't reached his eighteenth birthday yet. People expected him to be mature and make the right decisions, but just like me, he screwed up unintentionally. We didn't know much about our Gifts, having grown up in Redemption.

He sniffled. "I know, but I thought with how gradual Gifts developed, they would realize it and be able to get away from Granite Falls since they aren't watched like the school kids." He pushed his glasses back up his nose. "I'm sorry. I didn't know something like this could happen."

"None of us did, Marcel," Abby commented from the ledge. The three of us were closer than anything. We had to stick together through the bad stuff. "Tommy screws up a million times more than you do."

"But his screw-ups didn't get people killed." Marcel returned to staring at his feet.

I don't know if no sleep, the stress of the day, seeing Femi in the energy cell or what, but something broke in my head. "Seriously? Wendi. Freaking. Died." I bit off each word as I spewed them at my best friend. "I screwed up, and she died. I screwed up, and Ryder and Clint died. The botched rescue attempt cost all those kids. I've killed more people than the Reaper. We need to fix what we can, not sit here and wallow in pity."

Mom stood before me, shaking with anger, face beet red. "Thomas George Ward, I am ashamed of you. If anyone is wallowing, it's you. We all lost Wendi; we all made poor decisions that hurt others. You will apologize to Marcel right this instant, and I will never hear that kind of garbage come out of your mouth again."

Mom had never spoken to me like that before. My face flushed as I realize how badly I'd screwed up. She stared daggers at me as she waited.

"Mom, Tommy is right." Marcel leapt to his feet. "He said what I needed to hear. We must fix this before anyone else gets hurt. Sometimes it takes your bruh to set you straight."

My eyes flicked back and forth between Mom and Marcel. "I'm sorry, I shouldn't have lost my temper. Will you forgive me?"

"Bruh, we're all good." He punched me in the arm. "I need to fix this if

I can." He pulled his chair back to the control panel, fingers flying across the keyboard. The screen lit up as new information flashed across it. "I used the Lair's security system to deactivate the collars. For some reason, they aren't responding to any of the commands like they should."

Mom stepped up to stand next to me.

"I'm sorry; I don't know what happened." I kept my voice low so she could hear me, but no one else. Dad and Abby had flanked Marcel, going over the information he accessed from the Granite Falls systems.

She rubbed my arm. "You're growing up is what's happening. You needed to see the same thing Marcel did." I put my arm around her and squeezed.

Blaze's coughing fit echoed down the hall before I saw him. He entered the room, wiping his mouth with a handkerchief, and I thought I saw blood on it. He pushed the cloth into his back pocket, returning the phone to his ear. "Yeah, I'll ask." He joined the group at the console. "Max wants to know if you have the camera shutdown?"

"I loaded a loop from last night, so they won't notice it was replaced. It took a bit to fake out the timestamp on the recording. Max is good to go. The camera feed is here." He swung his arm up and dramatically hit the enter key. The footage filled the screen, showing the three lumps of burnt men around a middle lump that had been the Gifted.

Blaze gave the go ahead. "We got lucky; the parking lot is off the beaten track; I'm surprised there were Reclaimers in the area."

A shiver cascaded down my spine. Why had Reclaimers been there that late at night? Headlights illuminated the parking lot. I tensed until I saw Max climb out of his beater and head to where the bodies were. He reared back a bit, held his nose, and plunged into the ash pile. After a minute or so, he pulled something from the center pile and shoved it into his pocket as he kicked down the ash piles. He ran back to his car, started the engine, and left the scene.

I hadn't realized I'd been holding my breath until I let it out. The stress flowed out of me. There would be a lot of questions, but without the tell-tale collar, they wouldn't know the pile of ash had been Gifted. From the look on Marcel's face, he felt the same. We had dodged a bullet, but who else had been affected? Given the range of powers Gifted developed, they could have them and never know it.

"Well, this was exciting. Dudes, could we do this during the nine to five?" Blaze resumed sipping at his coffee cup as if nothing had happened. The man could give statues lessons in patience.

"I think I know what went wrong," Dad said, grabbing his cup off the table. He pushed his finger into the mug, and wisps of steam curled away from the top.

Everyone stared at him.

"What? I like my coffee hot." He blew on it before he took a sip. "Most people's Gifts come on slowly over years unless faced with a traumatic situation."

My conversation with Makeda came to mind. She had said mages had a similar experience. I wondered how many Gifted in Redemption would have never fully developed their powers? A lot of those people would have never been a threat to anyone.

"The Gifted we saw had his powers come on too rapidly. It was like thirty years of growth happened in a compressed time frame and over-loaded him. I'd seen spontaneous genesis before, but they were kids, so they weren't at full power. The poor guy imploded."

Marcel gulped. "I didn't realize it could happen. We had the watches to slow down our Gifts; he didn't."

"Bottom line, genius, is not to mess around with people's Gifts." Abby scratched at her cheek. "I do like that you tried to free our people. It took balls of Carbinium to pull it off."

Mom flushed. "Abby, could you try not to sound like a sailor?"

Abby had the decency to look ashamed. Mom had been working on Abby's manners, though I don't know why she bothered when we couldn't go to nice restaurants or fancy parties. "Sorry, Mom."

Blaze chuckled. "Dude, she's a warrior, not a Disney Princess, and I agree. It took a lot of brains and courage to free them. It didn't work out, but we have to keep fighting." Blaze choked out the last as another coughing fit took him. He got himself under control, gasping for breath as he sat down.

"We need to get you to a doctor, Eugene." Oh no, the-mom-knows-best tone. I hated that one almost as much as mom-as-lawyer voice. "You've had 'allergies' since you got here. I know it's more than you are telling us."

"Susan, when you get to be my age, you'll understand. Things take a long time to heal. I'm fine; it's probably bronchitis. I'll get some antibiotics from the medical kit."

She glared at him but didn't argue anymore. She leaned back on the console; I could tell she was worn out.

"Marcel, as admirable as your motives were, we can't take those kinds of risks unless we are all on board. Promise me you'll discuss any other plans you concoct before you..."

Marcel nodded like a bobblehead in a hurricane as his hair exaggerated his gesture. "Yes, sir. I promise."

"You guys can talk until dawn," I said, stifling a yawn. "I'm going to..." I never got the chance to finish as the alarms went off, blaring loud enough to wake the dead.

So much for getting any sleep.

22

Marcel launched into action, hands blurring across multiple keyboards to locate the source of the alarm. Feeds from hidden cameras popped up on the screen, hazy green images from the night vision lens. One centered on the monitor, enlarging to fill the whole screen. A parked car stood a hundred feet from the underground bunker where the vehicles were stored. Marcel zoomed the camera to get a better look.

A dark colored car grew, making the details painfully obvious. Fog coated the windows; the car rocked gently as it sat there. Mom cleared her throat. "I think we've seen enough. I guess that's a false alarm."

"The car belongs to a Caroline Brenton, a cashier at Quiky Stop." Marcel glanced up at the screen, his jaw dropping open. "Oh yeah, false alarm." He quickly closed the feed window.

Everyone laughed. Tension ebbed a bit after the false alarm, but not by much.

"I think it's time to get some sleep," I said, waving over my shoulder as I returned to my room. "Good night."

A chorus of good nights followed me out. I retraced my earlier path, ending under the warmth of the comforter on my bed.

A few minutes later, I dozed off and found myself standing in the center of a formal dance. Women stood dressed in wide-bottomed gowns of every imaginable color. Some wore elaborate headdresses, others veils covering their hair. The men wore tunics with belts around their waists, glittering hilts of knives hung at their side. Couples bobbed in time to the classical music playing around me.

I stood on a low pedestal, above the dancers, seeing the intricate patterns they made, the colors swirling like a kaleidoscope. The enormous room holding the festivities could have been plucked out of one of those period movies mom liked. Deep red walls with gold symbols rose in delicate arches to meet at the top of the dome. The images on the dome were intricate, elaborate depictions of people. As I focused, the details became sharper, and I gasped. The paintings depicted people being tortured and killed by demons of all sorts.

"It is a striking piece of art," a woman said from behind me. The platform had grown to accommodate a second person. She wore a velvet gown of a red so deep it could have been mistaken for black from a distance. A gold corset enhanced her breasts, so they were prominently on display. Her waist-long, silver hair held a gold circlet, like a crown. The scent of roses tickled my nose as she stepped closer to me.

"My, you are much taller than I thought." She circled me, studying me like one of those mannequins in the clothing stores whose eyes always followed you. Her hand slid across my back as she passed behind me. Finishing her loop, she put her hands on her hips, pouting slightly. "Well, you can't be dressed improperly for a gala."

I glanced down, realizing I stood in the middle of the room in the t-shirt and sweats I'd gone to bed in. Luckily, this being a dream, there wasn't a dress code.

"This won't do at all." She waved her hand and my clothes changed into a red and gold vest that hung to my knees, leggings, and knee-high black boots with a blue velvet cape. I looked like a reject from the Three Musketeers: Sir Doofus. "No, not for this type of event." Another wave and the outfit turned into a black and gray patterned doublet with puffy shoulders and red and gold cording running to the elbows. Tight leather pants and tall boots completed the ensemble. I'd seen couches with less cording than I wore. She cocked her head, lips pursed. "No, too fanciful." This time I wore a blue and red tunic with silver buttons running up the front over a soft white shirt. In addition to leather pants and boots, I now wore a large silver belt wrapped around my waist.

"Now you look stunning." She clapped like a little girl who'd gotten a special present.

I had to admit I liked the getup. Too bad I didn't have a Halloween party to go to. My fashion designer stood before me, one hand on her slender hip as if waiting for something. I just stared at her, trying, unsuccessfully, to not notice how impressive her breasts were.

She huffed. "Aren't you going to ask me to dance?"

My face flushed hot with dread. "I don't know how." I wished it had come out more smoothly, but it sounded more like a rap record. My next number one single. "I..I..d.d.d.don't.kn.kn.know.how.how.how." And people say I can't sing.

She giggled a giggle straight out of a princess movie. "Of course you do, darling."

I bowed and then extended my hand to her. She took it gracefully, and I spun her slowly around into my arms. Keenly aware of all the curves pressing against me, I began to wonder what kind of dream this was.

My feet began a stately dance as we moved around the pedestal in time with the music. I relaxed and tried to enjoy my brain's strange fantasy. I guess hanging out with the magi had put me in a medieval sort of space. My mouth decided to cooperate by producing actual words. "Just for the record, who are you?" Yes, charming as ever. You can dress me up, but you can't take my foot out of my mouth.

"You may call me Yelena." She nodded regally to me as we moved in time to the music. "You are an interesting young man, what should I call you?"

I started to say Tommy, but something nagged at me. "You can call me Surge." Using my new code name. It felt right and much better than the Sparky fiasco in Atlanta.

Something like anger flashed in her eyes, but it fled quickly. "Surge it is. Might I ask why you were with the Council?"

Warning bells rang in my head, but I snoozed them like the morning alarm. "Just talking about weird stuff that happened. Some lady name Eiraf showed up. A bizarre sort of day."

"Anything else?" A small grin lit her mouth as she pressed against me harder.

I barely heard her, distracted as I was by the feel of her soft, warm breasts against my chest, and the view didn't hurt either. "Yeah, I think so."

We twirled through a series of intricate steps, the music swelling around us like a wave. I twisted her back, pulling her close as we returned to the original rhythm.

"Eiraf plays a dangerous game, Surge." She tightened her grasp on my hand. "She claims to protect the balance, but she does so at your expense. I do not believe this is right. I need to warn you things aren't as they seem."

I knew something was wrong but couldn't focus enough to think. The whirling dancers beyond us blurred until they were just colors revolving in a strange pattern. The music sounded wrong to my ears. I tried to wake myself up but couldn't. I wondered if this had slid into a nightmare.

"I would gladly protect you," she said as we executed the elaborate steps of the dance.

It would be nice to have someone to protect me, and Yelena certainly would be a pleasant distraction. I thought about how her mouth would taste if I kissed her.

She continued. "The Council will expend you to advance their plans. You must be watchful." She smiled at me, her white teeth gleaming in the darkening room. I peered around. The dancers were gone, and the room completely dark, though I could see shapes moving at the edge of my vision.

I pulled away, or at least attempted to, but she held me, her grip becoming painful. A thought sparked across my sodden brain. "Was the Kre-kelal there to protect me?"

She laughed. Gone was the tinkling giggle of earlier, replaced by a cold, harsh one. "What an unfortunate accident. He overstepped his authority, and you were good enough to punish him for me. Thank you. See, we already make a great team. Come to me, and I will give you anything your heart desires. I will do things to you that you would enjoy immensely."

This time, I pulled out of her arms successfully. My senses cleared, allowing me to see the true nature of the room. Still beautiful, but a hard, cruel look etched her face. The soft smile had been replaced by a sneer and an air of superiority. "Do I not please you? I can be anything you desire." Her face melted, reforming in an instance. Wendi peered back at me. My heart leapt up my throat to lodge in my mouth. "Would this be your preference or..." She changed, and Mom smiled at me. "Maybe this." She laughed at my obvious discomfort. "Maybe, you'd prefer something completely different." Another change and Jon stood before me. I backed up, heedless of the edge of the pedestal. She resumed her original form, but she wore a tight leather jumpsuit, unzipped to her belly button. "I can be whatever you desire, but you must pledge yourself to me."

I screamed no, beating at the wall of sleep that held me in this nightmare. I wanted, no needed, to wake up. I ran for the edge of the platform. If I could leap into the darkness, I could force myself awake.

"You'll not get away so easily." Hands of all types reached out of the darkness for me. Some had fingers with rotting skin and crumbling nails; some were talons or paws. I reared back in full panic mode. I searched for an exit, any exit, but Yelena pulled me back to face her. She produced a silver hairpin with an exaggerated gesture. "We will speak again, Surge. You can count on it." She stabbed down, driving the pin through my left shoulder. I screamed in pain.

And I kept screaming as I sat bolt upright in my bed. Still in my pajamas, I pulled my t-shirt over my head, checking for the wound I would surely find there. Nothing. I looked around, and nothing had been disturbed other than my bedding, which tangled around my legs. I moved the pillows and saw nothing out of the ordinary. The clock said ten after eleven in the morning. I grabbed clothes, deciding wakefulness was preferable to the nightmare I'd just experienced.

If I had known what kind of day it would be, I'd have gone back to sleep.

23

Mountain Dew and Pop-Tarts are the best breakfast ever created. I opened my second pack of Wildberry, rejoicing in the indulgence of breakfast. Given the late night, training had been canceled for the morning. Eating, then being kicked in the gut by Abby, tended to make you lose said breakfast.

Abby stomped into the kitchen, took a muscle-building drink, which tasted like chalk and death, and snatched a protein bar with the density of concrete. I don't know how she could stomach it. She dropped in across from me, grunting what I took for a good morning. She shoved half of the bar into her mouth, and I swear I heard a tooth break.

"Did you get any sleep?" I asked, popping another glorious piece of toaster pastry into my mouth. I took a long draw on my soda to chase it down. A satisfied "ahh" followed.

She gave me an exasperated look. "That shit will kill you. I couldn't go back to sleep after all the excitement. You?" She destroyed the rest of her bar, pushing her hair out her face, now half fire engine red and half Barney purple.

"Dyed your hair last night?"

She nodded as she chewed the brick she called breakfast.

"I slept, but only out of exhaustion." Something tickled the back of my head as if I forgot an important fact. "I think I had a nightmare."

"You don't know? I guess I need to stop hitting you in the head; you're going soft." She chuckled at her joke. "I couldn't sleep so I decided to change up my hair. What do you think?"

To the outside world, Abby is all warrior. Tough, fierce, and virtually unstoppable in a fight. The obvious answer here would be something snarky that would probably give my Gift a lot of energy to absorb. In reality, she wanted to be appreciated, and she wanted her appearance to be cutting edge. There are a lot of things I'd play with her about, but not this. "I love it! If I'd been more awake, I'd have mentioned it when you walked in."

Her eyes lit up, sitting straighter in her seat. "Really? You aren't just saying that, are you?"

"Nope, it's awesome. Wait until Mom sees it." It's always nice when the truth is on your side. She had the style and swagger to pull off any hair color; the wilder it was, the more it fit her. It was easy to forget she wasn't just a battering ram.

A frown crossed her face. She lowered her voice. "How do you think Marcel is after last night?" She glanced around to make sure nobody walked in.

I shrugged. "After everything we talked about, it was a cringe-worthy mistake. We've all made mistakes though, so we'll see."

"The timing sucked, but we will need to do something to free all those people. The Protectorate has to go." She finished off her protein drink and crushed the bottle flat. At least it was empty this time.

"If we don't find Waxenby, none of it will matter from the sounds of it." Another half memory floated through my head. I started humming a melody that sounded like something off the classical channel.

Abby cocked her head at me. "Am I boring you?"

I shook my head. "I have this damn song stuck in my head, and I don't know where I heard it. Maybe I didn't sleep as well as I thought."

"Good morning," Mom said as she came in. She went for the coffee, and the pot was full. "Thank you for making coffee."

"*No problemo.* I figured you'd want it when you got up." I finished off my drink, tossed the empty can in the recycling, and grabbed a new one from the fridge. I cracked it open and returned to my seat. I saw the look on her face, so I held up a hand to stop her before she started. "Abby already lectured me on the soda."

Mom grinned, sitting next to Abby. "As she should." Mom took Abby by the shoulders, turning her to examine the new hair color. "Oh, I love that combination. I didn't think I would, but it is fantastic, honey."

Abby beamed. I might have an opinion, but Mom had the only opinion that truly mattered. "I'm so glad. It's not too much?"

Mom sipped her coffee. "Absolutely not, the color suits you. You have a great style."

"I wish we could go shopping. I found this leather jacket that would be so incredible…" Abby stopped talking, her eyes going to the door. Marcel stood there, obviously worse for wear.

Mom might not be Gifted as we were, but her gift was for taking care of her kids. She flew to his side in an instant, sitting him in a chair at the end of the table. "What's wrong?"

Tears welled in his eyes. "I went back through the logs at the Lair. There were four people in the building the night I deactivated the collars. Max doesn't have a collar, but the other three did." I jumped up and grabbed a cherry Pepsi from the fridge, opened it, and handed it to him. He took a long swallow before continuing. "We know what happened to the one guy, but I can't find the other two. It's like somebody has taken them and is masking their signal. I've been looking at every feed in Granite Falls for any sign of them."

Mom glanced at Abby and me, but we didn't know any more than she did. "Marcel, with their collars off, you wouldn't be able to find them, so it makes sense that they've vanished."

He shook his head, sending his hair waving like a wheat field in a storm. "Each collar has a dampening unit in it, and I terminated the processing, but the collar remains in place. It allowed their Gift to return, a lot faster than I would have thought." He stopped for another drink, wiped his mouth on his sleeve. Mom handed him a napkin from the pile on the table. He gave her a guilty look, wiped his dry mouth with the napkin, and continued. "There is a multitude of systems incorporated into the collar. The nanotech involved is incredible. The Protectorate engineers knew their stuff, that's for sure. With the level of miniaturiza-tion, they achieved—"

Abby slapped her palm on the table. "Professor, stick to answering the question. Why do you think they're gone?"

I stifled a laugh, earning a kick in the shins from Mom.

"Oh, sorry." Embarrassment flared across his face. "One of the components is a tracker. Each has an encrypted code assigned to it. I left it on because the Reclaimers' readers get the ID from the collar when they do identification sweeps. If they saw a collar but didn't get a reading…well, you see what I mean."

I did. I'd been on the receiving end of the sweeps the Reclaimers did almost daily at the Secret Lair. The soldiers would come in and push us around, hoping someone would start trouble. The Granite Falls Reclaimers were bullies for the most part. I couldn't imagine what they'd do if they found a collar not working. They might kill the person "subduing" them.

"I backtracked through the hack and found the codes and pushed an update through to re-activate the collar, so nobody else got hurt. All three failed."

"What failed?" Dad said as he came into the kitchen. Mom caught him up as he grabbed a cup of coffee, taking a minute to top hers off. "Interesting. Do you think when you deactivated the collars, it could have shut off the identity protocol as a byproduct?"

"No, I ran a test to make sure they were responding and returning the correct information. After the update failed, I hit the Protectorate server housing the personal information and their collar codes for all the Gifted. Two of the people I didn't know, but Mimi was the third, and I can't find her. I don't know why. Her tracking chip should still be active." Tears raced over his cheeks. Mom hugged him tight, murmuring in his ear. Like I said, she's got powers all her own.

Dad pondered his coffee cup. "There has to be an explanation for it. If they ran, would you be able to get the signal?"

Mom let go of Marcel after checking to make sure he was okay.

He thought for a moment. "I don't know. I would think so, but the transponder would switch. The Protectorate would know if they went outside the zone of control. They don't monitor inside since they don't want alarms every time a Gifted goes from Redemption to Granite Falls." He stroked his chin, thinking over things. "They could be on the move but not outside the zone yet. Let me go ping the collars from all of the transponders. I'll know once the test is complete." He picked up his soda and almost ran out of the kitchen.

Dad took a long pull from his cup. "Testing should keep him busy for a bit, but I think he's right that it's a problem."

"I know we could have a problem if another person explodes or something along those lines, but if their powers aren't strong or obvious, why would it be an issue?" I asked. If Mimi could turn her hair orange now, who would notice? Well other than Abby, who would love to be able to switch hair color at will.

Mom sat down next to Dad with her coffee cup in hand. "We would have heard if some Gifted had started throwing their power around, wouldn't we?"

"Dad, what if they have a Gift like Tracy Stevens? She didn't get larger or have anything that would out her as a Gifted. If they could remove the collar and leave, we'd never find them."

The furrows on Dad's forehead deepened as he contemplated my question. "Tommy, I think Marcel's right, and someone has them. The question is who. We know Jon recruited Turk from Granite Falls; has he taken more kids to build a team? Has Reaper returned to collect new bodies for his army? All the unknowns are the problem."

"We could go and find them before anyone else does," Abby said, cracking her knuckles for emphasis. "The three of us can wipe the floor with anything they can throw against us."

"I'd rather avoid another fight like Atlanta. The less noise we make, the better." As he spoke, I noticed how exhausted Dad was. After all this time, he had to be tired of being Cyclone Ranger. I bet he would like to be a nothing more than a husband and father. No more missions, no more fights, just peace and quiet. He'd more than earned it, but I doubted he could stop any more than he could give up his Gift.

The wet, ragged cough preceded Blaze's arrival. He stumbled into the kitchen, hair undone and his skin slicked with sweat. He lurched over and dropped into the chair two down from me.

"Eugene, you don't look so well," Mom said, moving over to check on him. "You're burning up. We need to get you to a doctor."

He waved her off. "I'm fine. I need some antibiotics and some extra sleep. I've been pushing too hard, but you can train without me now."

Marcel stood at the head of the table. I hadn't noticed him come in with all of Blaze's coughing. "Is Blaze okay?"

Blaze answered with a hacking cough. He wiped his mouth, and this time I saw blood, and from the concern etched on her face, so did Mom.

"Eugene, enough. What is going on?" Her voice carried the same iron tone I'd heard her use to dress down an uncooperative witness.

He sighed. "I knew you'd figure it out, but I thought it'd be Marcel hacking my doctor's office before I had to tell you." He took a deep breath, suppressing another cough. "I have lung cancer. It's metastasized to my other organs."

"What?" I couldn't believe it. I knew he was sick, but nothing like this. The looks of horror around the table reflected mine.

"Why didn't you tell us?" Mom asked, her hand over her mouth, tears running down her face.

"Susan, I promised Ranger I'd take care of you and Tommy. I'm already dead, but you needed training, and I only had a small amount of time. I needed to make sure you could protect each other. I've completed my task."

"There has to be something we can do," Abby said. "We need to take you to the hospital."

Blaze shook his head. "The doctors told me it's too late. I did what I set out to do."

My brain seized on an idea. "We can contact the council. They could cure him."

"No. We don't have a way to contact them," Dad replied.

"I do." All heads turned toward me. Abby smiled. I pushed back the chair and ran for my room. I jumped down the stairs two at a time, running as if my life depended on it. I threw the door to my room open, tore open my backpack, and grabbed the box containing the bottle Makeda had given me. She said life or death, and this certainly counted. I retraced my steps to the kitchen, hope blossoming as I thought about Makeda healing Blaze. The cancer would shrink and disappear, leaving my friend and mentor healthy.

Abby must have explained while I was gone. The barrage of questions didn't hit me as I entered the kitchen. "Makeda told me she would come to me in a life and death emergency." I opened the box and extracted the purple bottle. The wisps of smoke swirled inside, just as they had when she gave it to me.

"How does it work?" Mom asked in a whisper.

158

"I smash the bottle, and Makeda should come to help. She promised she would." I took the bottle and set it on the floor. I glanced around the room; everyone seemed to be holding their breath, leaning in to see what would happen. I lifted my foot and brought it down on the bottle. I heard a loud crack from under my shoe.

I stepped back from the shattered bottle. Mist swirled up from the remnants of the vessel. The tendrils twisted and spiraled, rising from the floor as if dancing to unheard rave music. They jerked and spun, growing thicker as if the motion enhanced the effect. Purple suffused the mist as a shape began to form. A moment later, Makeda the Arcanist stood before us.

"Thomas, I'd hoped to see you again, but this is much sooner than I would have thought." She surveyed the room, nodding to Dad who saluted her in return. "What can I assist you with?"

I indicated to where Blaze sat. "My friend, Bl—, err, Eugene, is dying from cancer. The doctors say it can't be cured. Can you help him, please?"

"I make no promises. As I told you, magic is limited in what it can do, but I will do all I can." Makeda turned to Blaze. "Hello, Eugene. You looked much better the last time we met."

"What? You know each other?" I'd had too many shocks over the past couple of days. I hadn't meant for it to come out so harsh.

Makeda gave me a stern glare and turned me into a frog.

24

So she didn't actually turn me into a frog, but the look she gave me made me wish she had. "Um, sorry, Lady Makeda. You just startled me."

A smile creased her ageless face. "I will need to lay Eugene down so I can examine him. Is there someplace close by?"

Mom took over. "Lady Makeda, I'm Susan Ward, Tommy's mother. If you'll follow me, please. Michael, bring Eugene to the living room."

Dad swept a protesting Blaze into his arms like a groom does his bride in one of those cringe-worthy movies. He strode with purpose into the living room. He placed him on the couch, gentle as if he were one of Marcel's tablets. Mom adjusted the pillow under his head. The rest of us stood at the entry watching, wondering what would happen.

"Eugene, be at peace. This will not hurt, but it may feel strange."

Blaze indicated for her to start. His face had little color and none of his usual good-natured humor. Coughs racked his frame. He appeared to have dwindled to nothing. Blaze had never been a large man, but he could have been a child, he seemed so small on the couch.

Mom stepped next to me. "Lady Makeda is the person you told me about? She healed your wounds?"

"Yeah, she did. I like and trust her." I hadn't taken my eyes off where Makeda stood, hands outstretched over Blaze. Her hands glowed with golden energy as they moved above Blaze's body. As they passed over his chest and abdomen, the gold flared an angry red that spiked in all directions, mimicking an angry porcupine. With an effort, she pushed her hands down to his feet. The glow subsided, leaving spots dancing in front of my eyes. She reached out and touched a finger to Blaze's forehead. "Sleep, my friend. Be at peace."

Blaze's body went limp. The coughing stopped, but his breathing was still labored. Makeda joined the group of us where we stood anxiously waiting for news. From the look on her face, I didn't think it would be good news.

"Eugene is very sick. The disease has ravaged his organs, and he will not last more than a few weeks at best." Lines that hadn't been there before now etched her face. "I can try to heal him, but he is weakened, and the strain could kill him."

Mom almost vibrated with the need to pace, something she did when she needed to think. "We can't make this decision for him."

"Blaze is a fighter. He'd want to fight not just give up," Abby said, her tone hard with conviction. "He'd skin one of us for quitting in a fight."

Makeda spread her hands apart in front of her. "Eugene is a warrior spirit, but he's fighting me in this. I know not why, but he resists."

"Lady Makeda, why would he resist? I'm sure he wants to live." Marcel rubbed at his chin, thinking his way through things. "He did say he had completed his purpose in training us. Could that be it?"

"I can't tell what lives in his heart of hearts." Makeda sounded as tired as she looked. "I need a decision before progressing."

"Can you ask Blaze?" I asked, not knowing what else to do. "It really should be his decision."

"Tommy is right. I don't think any of us should answer for him if he can answer for himself," Dad said, catching each person in the group in the eye. "We will abide by his decision though."

"I can make it so one person can enter his dreams and gain the answer. It should be the person closest to him, or he may reject them. I can only do this once. I will await who you choose." She returned to the couch, knelt beside Blaze, and gently held his hand.

Dad pulled us together. "We need to decide quickly. I know from the mages that magic takes a toll."

"I'll go," Mom said into the quiet. "I've known Eugene for years, and I'll not risk any of you."

A cold chill ran up my spine. Makeda hadn't mentioned any risk. Did Mom know something we didn't? "She said the person closest to him should go. I spent a lot of time with Blaze working at the Lair and so did Marcel."

"I'd go, but I'm not sure how close he feels to me since I can't master any of the stuff he teaches," Marcel said hesitantly. "Abby is his best student, but Tommy spent a lot of time with him."

Mom opened her mouth to say something, but Dad touched her shoulder. "I'm not close with Blaze. Abby, any feelings on the subject?"

"I think Tommy is closer to him," she said reluctantly. I could see she wanted to go warring with Blaze's health. "They've been together the most."

"Mom, I'll be fine. Makeda didn't say anything about risks." I held up my hand to stop her protests. "We have to know."

She pulled me into a fierce hug and whispered "I love you" in my ear. I told her I loved her too and went to Makeda. I knelt next to her, noticing how shallow Blaze's breathing had gotten. "Is he going to make it through this?"

She nodded slowly. "Part of what I did reduced his metabolism, sort of a semi-coma to give his body a rest." Reaching over, she took my hand in hers. "Place your hand on his forehead. You will feel a force behind your eyes; don't fight it. Speak to Eugene, ask him if he wishes to be healed. When you are done, close your eyes and think of returning to us."

"Okay," I said, wishing my voice sounded more certain like Dad's always did in a crisis. I set my hand on Blaze's smooth brow. Ever since he'd come to Castle, he'd been tense; now we knew why. I closed my eyes and listened to the soft words roll around me and through me. The force behind my eyes felt more like a kick in the ass by a three-hundred-pound horse.

Unlike the trips through the doorbell vortex, I slid through an empty space, landing in a deserted warehouse, the smell of dust and oil mixing in the air. If I'd had a nose, I would have sneezed, but I found myself translucent. I'd never been a ghost before.

I ran toward the voices I heard ahead of me. A long salt-n-pepper ponytail stood out against a black and gray combat suit. I moved to stand next to Blaze, though he didn't see me. He must be dreaming. "Blaze, I need to talk to you." No response.

Blaze pulled a pistol from its holster, crouching into the stance he'd spent hours teaching us. I noticed his finger wasn't on the trigger; nice to see he practiced the trigger discipline he pounded into our heads. He slid around a stack of boxes, coming into view of three semis parked in the loading dock.

Someone closed on Blaze, setting us moving in unison as a tall man floated down next to us. "Dammit, Jack. What are you doing?" Blaze asked, annoyance thick in his voice. He spoke into his comm-link "The Guardians are on site. Be advised."

Jack? My jaw dropped as I realized it was Jack Taylor, my high school teacher who Powell and Brunner murdered. He looked every inch the hero I knew he was, or would be to me, in a custom combat suit of silver and black. His hands stood out against the black legs of the suit, his fingers being stone. Taylor had told me that losing his Gift had saved him, and now I understood why.

"Blaze, we are guarding the trucks. UN supplies to be shipped out tomorrow." He glanced over his shoulder as another man slithered up alongside us. He carried a sniper rifle slung over his shoulder. The person behind him caught and held my attention. Bright orange hair announced Pepper Spray as she joined the group. Her suit didn't fit well and had a hole in one knee. The irises of her eyes were jet black and not natural. The picture Blaze had shown me didn't do her justice. She must be around thirty, though Blaze must be a lot older than she was.

I tried again to get Blaze's attention, but his reality was this dream, and nothing I did changed that. I'd have to wait out the sequence and try again. I moved back to watch as the rest of this play out. Something gnawed at the back of my brain, but I couldn't figure out what.

A small woman, with short, dark hair ran from the trucks to where the assembled group stood. "Jackhammer, we've got problems. Ruby Lash and the Death Angels are moving in fast. We're outnumbered and outgunned." As if to emphasize her point, the front wall exploded, throwing chunks of concrete and glass through the warehouse like shrapnel.

"Thanks, Siren," Jackhammer said into the comm-link "Guardians, move out." The man with the sniper rifle called his team to action at the same time. I saw Alyx and Gladiator charge into battle as the Death

Angels stormed the loading dock through the dust and debris. They brandished all sorts of tech weaponry, though they could have passed for extras in a biker slasher film. The smallest was over seven feet tall and a solid three hundred pounds of muscle. I'd never seen anything like them before.

The room was in chaos. Blaze fired shots at an Angel armed with a shotgun that sported a whirling blade for up-close fighting. The boom of the shotgun added to the commotion but missed Blaze by a mile. Like a surgeon, Blaze shot out pieces of his foe's gear, until the giant tumbled to its back, unable to get up again.

Gladiator held off two Angels with his sword as Alyx sent blue fire against another who tried to flank them. Jackhammer screamed by, slamming his hands into the behemoths, blood spraying from wounds as he smashed them. The woman who had warned them screamed a high-pitched wail, causing the Angels in her wake to collapse, holding their ears as they bellowed in pain.

The back of the closest truck erupted, throwing the doors out into the loading dock, one of which downed Siren as it clipped her leg. Her scream shattered the ceiling above her, launching metal in all directions. Out of the smoke stepped a tall, dark-skinned woman dressed all in red, swinging a glowing whip. Unless I missed my guess, she would be the Ruby Lash that Siren had warned Jackhammer about. She joined the fray, whip snapping out, pushing Gladiator back.

As I saw who stood inside the trailer, I started to run, summoning my power as I went. Grim Reaper strutted to the opening in the ruined trailer, jumping down to stand over the fallen Siren. "I claim Siren in the name of the Underworld!" The scythe pulled back; the sickly green glow intensified as if it knew it was about to taste blood. As the blade fell, an orange blur stepped between Reaper and his victim. She slashed four furrows into his chest as her hand struck out.

I stopped running, realizing the Grim Reaper wasn't here, but my anger had made me stupid. A possibly fatal flaw in a fight. Ahead of me, Blaze finished off the Angel in front of him with a well-placed head shot. He quickly double tapped, then noticed Pepper Spray facing off against a Gifted foe. "Pepper Spray is in trouble. Collapse on her position."

I heard Alyx scream from across the room, blue energy racing to encircle Pepper Spray as he had done for me against the hounds in the basement. I glanced over in time to see Ruby Lash's whip wrapped around the lower portion of Alyx's legs while he was distracted. She pulled hard, and the whip cut through his legs, toppling the mage.

Blaze fired shots as he ran, but I knew he'd be too late. I now knew what had been troubling me. I watched as Grim Reaper's scythe descended on Pepper Spray, parting the shield to embed in her chest. The green light pulsed as she died, impaled by the blade.

Blaze screamed as he ran. Jackhammer swooped in to impact Reaper in the chest, sending him flying out of the loading dock. Ruby Lash laughed as she avoided Gladiator's sword and made her escape. The whole thing had been a setup, and neither team realized it. Blaze fell next to Pepper and pulled her limp body into his arms. Jackhammer landed next to him but couldn't console Blaze; his grief poured out of him like a broken dam.

I stood mutely watching as the love of Blaze's life died in his arms. There weren't any last words exchanged as the movies would like us to believe always happened. Gladiator knelt next to a legless Alyx, who had passed out, probably from shock. I'd meet them later, prisoners of the Syndicate in the Zoo. I don't know how long I stood there, watching a grieving Blaze, unable to do anything about it.

The edges of the dream frayed like an old blanket as Blaze's world telescoped down to Pepper in his arms. I was unsure what to do next. As I watched, a ghost rose out of Blaze; the one I knew, not the one I'd watched live through the worst day of his life. He came to me, his face haggard and streaked with tears. "Do you understand?"

Understand what? I just watched as the woman he loved more than life died. Saw one of his friends have his legs amputated by a psychopath. I understood pain, I understood loss, but I didn't know what he was asking me for. "I don't."

He looked me straight in the eye, still as a gravestone for a long moment. "Do you understand why I want to die."

25

I stared wide-eyed, mouth hung open as if to catch flies. My brain whirled, Blaze wanted to die? I know the loss of Pepper Spray had been painful, but it had been years ago. "No, I don't. How can you die knowing there are people who love and depend on you?"

"Dude, I've lived with this for over twenty years, dreamt of it most nights, crying over my loss. Time doesn't heal all wounds. If there is an afterlife, I'll get to be with her again. Don't you see? I'm tired, Tommy."

How could a seventeen-year-old understand how tired someone over sixty feels? I'd lost Wendi. I knew the ragged hole in my heart had closed and, in some ways, it had deepened, but I couldn't just give up. "You always told us you never give up the fight, but it's okay for you to quit?"

"That's different. You've got things to live for."

"SO DO YOU!" I hadn't meant to scream, but there we are, my big mouth running the show while my brain is off taking a nap. "Everyone at Castle loves you, and regardless of what you think, we still need you. The people at the Lair need you, especially with Mimi missing."

"Dude, you will all be fine without me. I've trained you; you're ready to face anything."

"You're right. I guess we'll take care of your mess." Time for the low blow.

His eyes narrowed. "What mess?"

I steeled myself and begged Blaze would forgive me later. "Grim Reaper. You haven't settled the score with him. He has Pepper Spray trapped in his scythe. I guess we'll handle it while you drift off to the great beyond to see Pepper." I snapped my fingers. "Oh, that's right, until we destroy his weapon, her soul is stuck in the scythe." I turned on my heel to leave. I shot back over my shoulder. "I'll tell Makeda not to bother with you."

Blaze caught up to me in a flash. Fortunately, being a ghost, he couldn't turn me around or beat me like a drum. I faced him. Anger coursed over his face, and his eyes burned with fury. "Dude, that's not fair. I couldn't beat Reaper if I wanted to."

"No, but you could help us do it." I wanted to say more, but I'd already hurt him. He had to realize we needed him and he needed us. I watched as emotions raged in his eyes. Part of him wanted the pain to end, but the warrior craved revenge, and it could push him toward living. Honestly, I'd played my cards; I'd have to see if it had been a winning hand.

He sighed at last. "Tell Makeda to heal me if she can. When I'm better, I owe you a thrashing, Dude."

"Well, in that case," I trailed off, catching him smiling at me. "Makeda did warn me the healing could kill you, but I figure you're too stubborn to die so easily."

He laughed. "We'll see." His smile faded. "Tommy, thank you for making an old man see the ocean instead of the wave."

"I'll see you when you're feeling better." I closed my eyes and thought of being home. I opened my eyes to find Blaze laid out before me. "He said to heal him." I decided I'd never share what I'd experienced in Blaze's memories, except maybe with Alyx, if the need arose.

Makeda nodded once. "I need to start; he's fading." She squeezed my hand then stood. Words in a language I didn't understand flowed out of her like lava from a volcano. I returned to stand with the rest of my family. Funny, they really were my family, and the only ones I'd ever have.

Mom put her arm around my back, pulling me close. "Good job, kiddo." I don't know what I'll do when Mom passes. I'd just hope it was a long time before I'd find out.

Golden light gathered around Blaze, lifting him off the couch, buoyed on the currents surging around him. Thicker bands swirled, looping around his torso and legs, tightening to hold him in place. Motes danced, small stars spun above his chest, all in time to some unheard rhythm. They darted into Blaze over and over. He shuddered each time one vanished into his body. Chest, head, and abdomen were shot through with the particles of energy. The room flashed with the light show.

Makeda hissed. Her words took on a rushed quality I hadn't heard earlier. Black tendrils oozed out of Blaze, coating his skin like an exoskeleton. The motes died as they touched the darkness that consumed him. The golden light flared, and the blackness retreated slightly. Blaze screamed in agony. Mom's grip tightened as the terrible sound erupted out of him. The light dimmed before going out completely, dropping Blaze on the couch. Abby ran and caught Makeda before she fell.

Mom ran to check Blaze. "He's still breathing, but his skin is warm."

Abby set Makeda in a chair. Marcel returned with a glass of water, which he handed to the weary mage. She took a deep drink, closing her eyes as she did. Her breath slowed as she sipped at the water. I could see a definite trembling in her hands. When she had emptied the glass, Marcel took it from her.

"I'm sorry," she said, her tone laced with exhaustion. "The sickness is deep within him. He doesn't have the strength to help me rid his body of it. I did manage to reduce it, which will keep him alive longer, but without intervention, he will die."

"Thank you, Lady Makeda." Dad sketched a quick bow to her. "We know you did everything you could."

"It wasn't enough, I'm afraid." She rubbed her eyes, trying to remove the tiredness from them. "Where magic has failed, science may prevail."

"I'm not going to any hospital." Blaze laid on the couch, eyes open. "If it's my time, it's my time."

Mom shushed him. "You aren't Gifted, so you'd be safe to go."

His face twisted into a scowl. "I went to three doctors before I came here. All three said the same thing. The cancer had spread too far to treat. Medical science hasn't progressed enough to remove it."

Marcel's head whipped around, causing his hair to rebound, hitting him in the face. "I'll be back." He almost ran out of the room. I knew from the look on his face, he had An Idea. The last time he had An Idea, he'd had us surrender so he could break into the Megadrome's security systems.

Makeda's eyes had returned to normal. Tired lines etched her face but

168

had reduced in intensity as she sat. "Before I return to the council, I have something for you."

She rolled her hand over, holding it out to me. In her palm sat a black rectangular device with a gold piece attached to its face. I took it from her outstretched hand. The gold part hinged so it could be opened. I flipped the top up, and a familiar sound made me laugh. "Is this a Star Trek communicator?"

Her eyes traveled to the ceiling. "Alyx asked me to give it to you after Pimiko told him I would see you soon. He said Marcel would know how to use it to contact him until he can make a more secure mode of travel for you. Now I will take my leave of you." She rose and went to kneel by Blaze. "I'm sorry, I tried my best for you."

"I know you did, Lady Makeda, and I am honored you would expend so much to save me. I am grateful for your assistance." Blaze's eyes held a haunted distance to them.

She touched her fingers to his forehead before rising, facing the rest of us. "I have much to do, so fare thee well."

"Thank you," we all said. She inclined her head, spoke a soft word and vanished from the room. It felt like we had lost our one chance to help Blaze.

Blaze pushed himself up to a sitting position. The color had returned to his cheeks, the mischievous spark to his eyes. "Well, I can cross that one off my bucket list. I don't know about the rest of you, but I could eat an elephant."

"I'll make you some soup," Mom said as she headed toward the kitchen.

"Screw the soup; I need real food." Blaze started to stand but fell back on the couch. "Whatever Makeda did has at least helped for a bit."

Abby stepped over, assisting Blaze as he climbed to his feet. With an arm around his back, she guided him across the room, toward the kitchen. I noticed as they passed, Blaze's feet were about two inches off the floor.

I stopped next to Dad as he watched Abby carry Blaze to the kitchen. The open area in the center of Castle had beds of plants and flowers basking under the artificial sun. Living underground took a lot of extras to make it habitable. The living quarters all had simulated windows which tracked the weather outside Castle. Without such things, you'd go insane after an extended stay.

"You okay?" Dad asked as we stood there. "Traveling into another person's mind can mess you up quick."

I shrugged. "I'm fine. I'm glad Blaze is doing better. I thought we might lose him today." I started across the atrium for food, my Pop-Tarts a long, distant memory. I kept seeing Pepper Spray dying when my mind wandered. I couldn't imagine how hard those memories were for Blaze.

"You did well." Dad stopped just short of the kitchen. "Don't let how he is today fool you. Without treatment, Makeda's actions have only given him a couple of months if I had to guess. At this point, any additional time was better than the alternative."

I heard the heavy foot treads coming from behind us. Marcel ran, yes, actually ran, toward us down the hallway leading to the stairwell.

"I think I have a way to help Blaze!" He yelled though the huffing and puffing from his run, distracted from his enthusiasm. He bent over, catching his breath while Dad and I watched. He really needed to work on his cardio. Too many hours at the computer.

"I have to talk to Blaze, but I think there is a chance we can help him." Marcel resumed his trek to the kitchen. Dad glanced at me, to which I shrugged and followed.

Abby sat at one end of the table, feet propped up on a chair. Mom had enough food set out to feed a small nation, but when I saw Blaze, I understood. The man ate like he'd never tasted food before. Three empty plates sat stacked in front of him as he ate a chicken pot pie. I'm not sure "ate" covered it. More like he inhaled it. Within thirty seconds, he had finished it off and looked about for more.

Mom slid over a salad bowl of pasta salad she made so that we had late night snacks. His fork blurred as he attacked it without mercy. At this rate, he'd eat more than his weight in food by dinner. I slid into a chair at Abby's end of the table. I didn't want to lose a limb to the shredder going at the other end. Dad flanked Abby on the other side from me. Marcel stood near Blaze, waiting for an opening. It came a minute later when he pushed away the empty bowl.

"Blaze, I need to ask you something. I went through the systems here, hoping to find a registry of all the safe houses and underground complexes the Gifted teams had. There isn't one. Do you know where we could get one?"

Blaze sat back, his usually flat stomach bulging from all the food he'd packed away. "Dude, there wasn't one."

Marcel's head dipped in defeat. "Oh, thanks." He turned to go, but Blaze put up a hand.

"I said there *wasn't* one. I created one when it became likely the Gifted would lose." Blaze burped, quickly excusing himself. Abby laughed heartily. "You wouldn't find it here. Gifted teams never shared intel between them."

"So where can I get it? If I'm right, that list might hold the key to helping you." I swear Marcel held his breath while waiting for the answer.

"It's on the system back at the Lair."

"You put the master safe house list on the cash register system? It's totally unsecure. I could hack it with a toothpick and a piece of gum." Marcel spluttered at the thought.

"Whoa, dude." Blaze held up both hands as if trying to stop a speeding car. "There's a lot more to the Lair than you know. The system is disconnected from everything. You can only access it through the control panel in the underground portion."

"What underground portion?" Abby had her head cocked with a confused look plastered on her face. "We've never heard about anything along those lines. Have you, Tommy?"

I didn't have to say anything; my silence did the talking. She threw up her hands. "Of course you knew."

"I had to hide out after Mandy's boyfriend tried to kill me in the parking lot. I was sworn to secrecy." She rolled her eyes at me. "My lawyer told me to keep it under wraps." She nodded once but wasn't happy about it.

If Marcel cared about being kept in the dark, he didn't show it. "We need the file. I found a report detailing out a prototype medical device that could re-write a person's DNA. The team who had it was called Crisis Patrol. If we could get you there, we might be able to reverse the cancer by fixing the genetic codes."

Silence hovered over us, no one knowing what to say. Could we possibly find a way to eliminate the cancer killing Blaze? Mom spoke first. "If it's true, it would cure you. We have to get the file."

171

Blaze shook his head. "Way too dangerous. We can't return to Granite Falls; every Reclaimer in the world is searching for you. The public might think you're dead, but finding you is the Protectorate's first priority."

"We could go at night, slip in, get the file, and be gone before anyone knew we were there," Abby said quietly.

"We'd want to download the systems, so we don't have to make a second trip." Marcel rubbed his chin. "I've got just the tool. Ten minutes and we'd have everything and be gone." A dismayed look crossed his face. "We'd have to drive to Granite Falls in order to do it. That's going to add to the risk."

I smiled. "I've got just the thing to help out." I held out the device Makeda had left with me.

"Is that a Star Trek communicator?" Marcel's eyes widened. "Does it work? Where did you get it?" His words stumbled over each other as his mouth tried to keep pace with his brain, a problem I've never experienced.

"It works. I'll tell Scotty to beam us up."

26

Nothing, ever, goes as planned. Cooler, less geeky heads prevailed, pointing out we would need an actual strategy more than Alyx dropping us in Granite Falls. I guess waltzing through the front door, going to the hidden safehouse under it, and retrieving files the Protectorate would kill everyone in the city for wasn't the best idea. Marcel and Dad went down to the control center to prepare the gear we'd need to replicate the system. After, we'd nuke it, so if it did fall into the wrong hands, there wouldn't be anything left.

We had gathered in the living room once Blaze had finished eating everything in sight. Mom announced his color was better, but he needed to rest. Since the mission involved infiltrating his store in the middle of the night, we needed his input. He sprawled on one couch, with Abby and me on the other. Mom sat in her favorite chair as we waited for Dad to return from the control room. It wouldn't take long since Marcel was in full geek mode.

Dad strode into the living room. "Marcel has what we need to be able to extract the data and wipe it from the systems there. We've also got a couple surprises to leave in case anyone enters. At least we'll know if the place is compromised. The three of us..."

Mom, however, wasn't having it. "Michael, can you handle this? After

Atlanta, I don't want Abby or Tommy in the line of fire again. They are children, not soldiers."

I felt Abby tense next to me. She didn't like being called a child, maybe more than the thought of being left out of a mission. I nudged her, shooting a silent plea not to explode.

"Mom, we aren't kids. We've fought for our lives, and we are stronger as a team than apart."

Mom's icy glance told me I wasn't included in this conversation. "Tommy, you were captured in Atlanta, and if not for the Underground, the Protectorate would have killed you. I'm done taking chances with my children, and I mean all three of them."

"Susan, it is a dangerous world for all of us. Tommy is right, we are stronger together. But I will go with Alyx and handle it." Dad's tone held no signs of emotion. I doubted the lawyer voice would work on him.

"What about Mr. Waxenby," Abby asked softly. "Is Ranger supposed to go it alone? What if this seer is right and losing him ends everything while we sit until our eighteenth birthdays?"

Shock crossed Mom's features; Abby had hit home. "Abby brings up an excellent point." She paused, collecting her thoughts. "In that light, I can't refuse you going, though it worries me sick when any of you leave."

Dad moved to her and set his hand on her shoulder, squeezing it. "I know it's hard, but we don't have another choice."

She lowered her head. "I know. We have to try to save Eugene and Oliver. I just wish someone else could be fighting this and leave us alone. We've lost enough already."

My heart dropped through the floor and burst into flames at the Earth's core. We had lost enough. I'd lost everything in one terrible moment I'd relive forever. Three months of forever down and an infinity to go. I kept my mouth shut. Everyone had lost Wendi, not just me, as Mom rightly reminded me last night. The Darkest Storm had consumed millions of people in a failed attempt to conquer the world and more during the war. Would it ever be enough? I returned my attention to the conversation at hand.

"I think the point is that we try not to lose anyone else." Abby glanced at Blaze, who appeared to have drifted off on the other couch. "If there's a chance medical help could cure him, I say we take it."

Mom nodded. "Agreed." She turned to Abby and me. "I'm sorry. I don't doubt either of you. You go off, and I sit here and wait. It's terrifying."

A rumble from the couch made me flinch. Blaze rubbed his eyes before looking around at us. "There is a simple fix. Susan, you are going with the team. It's about time you get some field experience."

Her eyes grew wide. "No, I'm not a soldier."

Blaze cut her off. "Nonsense. Dude, you're the best shot here by far, and with every weapon we've trained in. What you don't have is experience. You won't know if you'll freeze until you've experienced a mission."

Dad chimed in. "I agree, Susan." He held up a hand to stop her protests. "This is an easy in-and-out mission. You stay with Alyx and me; the kids go into the Lair and duplicate the system and set the traps. Anything happens, you're there to help out."

She wasn't any calmer. "What if I make a mistake?"

"Same thing we do when I screw up, Mom. We improvise and run like hell." I'm sure the smile on my face didn't reassure her at all, but it was worth a try.

Abby smirked. "He does it a lot, so we're kind of used to it."

"Hey!" I tried looking offended, but ended up with pathetic loser instead.

Marcel walked into the room carrying a duffel bag and his epic laptop. "Hey, Blaze. Feelin' any better?"

"A bit. Makeda is quite the woman."

Marcel flopped on the floor, next to my feet. He opened the duffel and started pulling out items. "I modified an old backup drive case, so we can dump the whole system and bring it back up wherever we are. I'll explain the connections to Abby and Tommy so that they can complete the transfer." He set down the case, pulling out a gadget best described as if a Nintendo and a piece of weird alien tech had a baby. "This will allow me to verify the system is up and running on the backup before we wipe the system at the Lair. No room for accidents on this one."

Blaze coughed hard, but no blood showed up, so that was a relief to everyone. "The security systems won't allow an outside system to connect. You won't be able to verify the system. We should just booby trap it and leave it in place."

Marcel rolled his eyes. "Do I tell you how to do martial arts?" He didn't wait for an answer. "No, I don't. The device is linked to a geo-synchronized satellite the old USA claimed was a weather nav-sat. The thing could record conversations through fifty feet of concrete. I'll remote into the backup, and we'll know if it's working. It can double as a secure line if anything happens to your helmet." The pointed look I got could have frozen a woolly mammoth. He laid it next to the backup case and retrieved a USB drive. "This has the logic bomb to destroy the system, rewriting it so it thinks it's monitoring the internal cameras. It won't fool them, but they won't be able to see what was there."

Now that show-n-tell was over, Blaze ran down the security and how to bypass it if his codes didn't work. After the fiasco in Atlanta, nobody was taking chances with walking into a situation we weren't prepared for. We adjourned to the tactical simulation room to lay out where everyone would be located and the extraction points. The last stop was the armory for combat suits and weapons. Mom balked but eventually selected an HK G28 sniper rifle. We all carried P320s as a sidearm since no one left Castle unarmed. For me, I could always shoot myself in the foot for a power boost. It also hid the fact there were Gifted in a fight.

The rest of the day raced by as we finalized plans, ate, and got some sleep before Alyx arrived at 4 a.m. to transport us. I tried to sleep, but I mostly tossed and turned. I finally gave up and went to the training room to loosen up. Abby had the same idea, and from the amount of sweat on her, she'd been there for a while. With a shared nod, we fell into our routines. I'd been practicing some of her less suicidal parkour moves to improve my agility. I only face planted occasionally now. She flew through the course over and over, stopping at places to mimic pulling her pistol to fire. At three, I showered and suited up, ready to be going as the nervous energy cranked throughout my body.

I headed for the control room to go over the gear with Marcel one last time. After Atlanta, I didn't want anything to go wrong. Alyx stood by the window that overlooked the mechanical room talking with Mom and Dad. I gave a quick wave and sat next to Marcel. Abby joined us a few minutes later. Dad ran us through the procedure three more times, making sure we had the sequence and timing down. The plan was simple, but so had been the meeting with the Underground.

The last step consisted of suit checks by Dad. Normally, Blaze would have done this, but his strength was limited, and nobody wanted to push him. Dad finished with Mom and turned to the group. "Stick with the plan. If things go sideways, we bolt and come up with a new plan. No heroes." I swear he was looking at me when he said it.

"No heroes," we all echoed.

"Helmets on, and we are hot." He gave Alyx the thumbs-up, and the portal opened on the roof across from the Secret Lair. Mom, for all her protesting, moved like a seasoned vet, dropping to the ground, shimming over and dialing in the rifle's scope. "We're clear."

Dad raised the signal. Abby and I took the fire escape to the ground. I tried to be quiet while she swung like a gymnast. I hopped over the last rail and landed next to her without falling flat on my face. I doublechecked the bag with all the gear we needed. Without it, we were screwed. We scanned the street level, making sure no roving Reclaimers were about. Shift change would be at six local time, so most of the Reclaimers would be asleep at this point. Granite Falls never had issues with the Gifted population. Two thumbs-up and we moved.

Crossing the snow-covered street left us exposed, but we made it to the door unseen, though the tracks were still in the snow. I pulled the key from my pocket, slid it home, and the heavy door opened with a shove. It had seemed a lot heavier when I had worked here. A lot had changed and not all of it for the best. I dismissed any more thoughts and focused on the mission at hand.

Abby locked the door behind us as I moved to the front desk. I turned off the cameras; no sense leaving any evidence of our mission. Max would probably wonder in the morning why they were off, but he'd assume it happened at closing. I turned the corner and had to stop myself from blurting out "What a mess." Before we left every night, Blaze insisted everything be cleaned spotless. Not anymore. The tables were dirty, the floors hadn't been swept, and I could see a bin of unwashed plates sitting in the window to the kitchen. I ignored it and moved to the office.

The office door slid open to reveal an even bigger mess. Half-eaten food and empty beer bottles lay strewn around the room. Blaze would skin Max alive if he saw this. I found the elevator controls, and the door hissed open behind us. Abby stepped in, and I followed after, putting the trash back where I found it. I shouldn't have bothered.

The door opened on to the safehouse, or the city dump, depending on your viewpoint. I froze. Nobody besides Blaze knew about this place. "Mr. Wizard, we may have a problem. Somebody has been in here."

Dad's voice came through next. "Abort, and we'll come back."

"I think we're fine," Abby said softly. "It looks like someone has been partying, but nobody is here. We might not get another chance."

"I agree. We need ten minutes to get what we need." I held my breath while I waited for the response.

"Eyes open and fast." The way Mom clipped her words told me how hard she was fighting not to pull us back. "Move, you two."

We moved. Pistols out, we flowed through the space, checking for hostiles. Nothing there. We stepped into the main living area where the bank of TVs and monitors cover the walls. It smelled like a brewery from all the leftover bottles. Alyx would be happy they were all from Story Tellers. I cleared the console of bottles since an avalanche of breaking glass would wake the dead. Abby crouched next to me, gun trained on the doorway leading into the part of the Lair I hadn't seen. I got the control panel up and connected the backup. It lit up and started working.

I couldn't shake the feeling of wrongness about this place. Maybe the mess that Blaze never allowed disturbed me. Something played at the edges of my perception that fled when I tried to examine it. I focused on the data dump, knowing it was all that mattered. I caught Abby looking over her shoulder.

"Do you hear a clicking noise?" she asked, confused.

I shook my head, trying to ignore whatever was setting me on edge. The need to scratch the back of my brain to get rid of the sensation drove me crazy.

The light on the transfer flashed green. "The dump is complete," I reported to Marcel. I removed the cord and plugged it into the cyborg Nintendo Marcel had given me. The device lit up as the contents passed through a validation check. We didn't want to drop the logic bomb before we knew the copy had completed. I didn't take time to disconnect it, just shoved it all back in the padded bag I carried it in.

"It's good to go, Surge," came over my comm unit. "Go ahead and deliver the payload."

Abby had the drive with the logic bomb on it. She had turned from the console, facing the other direction. I nudged her with my elbow. "What?" she stammered. "Oh, sorry, payload." She inserted the drive and typed in the command Marcel had her memorize. The screens flicked then faded to black. She slid the drive out and back into her pocket. "Completed."

"Excellent. Move to extract position," Marcel said.

I was missing something but couldn't figure out what. I pulled my helmet off and looked around, trying to figure out what was wrong. Click. I heard it. Well, not really. I put my helmet back on and listened. Click. "Mr. Wizard, are you hearing a clicking noise?"

"Negative. All audio channels are clear."

Click. I didn't hear it as much as feel it in my head. A quick examination of the entry and kitchen didn't reveal anything but the mess we saw when we got here. Abby had crossed the main room, heading toward the door in the right-hand wall. I jogged over to check on her. I put my hand on her shoulder but got no response. Usually, it would have earned me an elbow to my ribs. I tapped on her faceplate, and she flinched. "What's going on?" I asked, fighting back the uneasy sensation I had been experiencing.

She pulled off her helmet; I followed suit. We both used the belt hooks to hold the helmets out of the way. "Tommy, there's something in there. Can't you hear it?"

"All I hear is a clicking noise."

"It's more than that. Something is trying to break into my mind. I think my head may split wide open."

"Well, there's only one way to find out." I closed the remaining distance and opened the door. The smell of a gas station bathroom in the middle of summer hit me like a sledgehammer. Trash covered the floor of the thirty or so feet of hallway. A moaning noise came from one of the rooms down the hall. Each wall had three doors set into them; another sat open at the very end. I moved slowly, focusing my energy so I could respond to any attack. The clicking noise stopped, replaced by a voice in my head. "Help me," it repeated over and over. The edges of my sight went foggy as the voice demanded my attention. I followed the sound, unwilling or unable to resist its pull. I stepped into the open doorway and froze.

The sight of a bloody body laid against the far wall snapped me out of my fog. Our easy mission had just gotten hard.

I wish I'd been startled, and the person laid out across from me was just sleeping or unconscious. I stepped closer to get a better look. Something cracked under my boot. Blood oozed out from where my foot had landed. I lifted my foot, and something red and wet dropped to the floor. I focused on the man's corpse ahead of me. He'd been mutilated; deep scorch marks crossed his arms and chest. His right arm ended in a burnt, severed stump. One of his eyes hung from the socket; the other socket sat empty. I fought not to vomit.

Bloody handprints decorated the wall in a grisly piece of art. I followed the wall, seeing other body parts, discarded by whoever ran this house of horrors. One of the beds held two arms still chained to the bedpost. A low snarl from behind notified me Abby had snapped out of her fog as well.

I followed the gruesome path, checking each bed as I went. The furthest bed held a person.

I signaled Abby to watch behind us as I moved closer to the prone figure where they laid chained to the bed. "There's a dead body and another captive. I'm investigating now," I whispered into my mic, eyes scanning to make sure nothing else lurked here.

I came to the foot of the bed and gasped. The captive turned out to be a woman dressed in a hospital gown that barely covered any of her. Her right arm had an IV drip attached to it, the needle piercing a tattoo of the deathly hallows symbol. I'd know her blue and purple hair anywhere.

I holstered my pistol and took her hand. "Mimi, it's Tommy. Can you hear me?"

Her head lolled toward me, mouth dropping open, allowing saliva to drool down her cheek. "Hey, Sport." Her eyes closed, and her breathing stilled. I reached out and checked her pulse, which was still there. I grasped the bedside cuff, thinking to shock it open, but stopped, wondering if the shock would hurt Mimi in the process. "Abby, I need you."

She moved quickly, never lowering her pistol in the process. I pulled my helmet off the clip on the back of my belt, settled it in place, flipped open the visor, and pulled my revolver to cover the door.

Abby stopped dead in her tracks as she saw Mimi's bruised face and emaciated body. "I'll kill whoever did this." Her voice was thick with anger. She broke the bars holding the handcuffs, snapping the free cuff around each extremity. She tore strips from the bedsheets and padded each set of cuffs to reduce the noise. Since stealth was the main objective, it made a lot of sense.

A soft beep sounded, but I didn't see anyone approaching from where I stood. "We need to go," I said, moving closer to the door.

Abby pushed her helmet on before sweeping Mimi up to carry her like a sleeping child off to safety.

I cued the comm-link. "We've found a survivor. Bringing her out with us."

Marcel's shocked voice came over the earpiece. "Survivor?"

"Stow it." Dad snapped. "Surge, meet us at the extraction point."

"Affirmative."

I signaled to Abby, and we moved slowly up the hall. I took in all the details I'd missed on the way in. Specks of blood on the floor, smears of something dark on the floors and walls, and dents in some of the doors along the way. My heart warred with my head, wanting me to stop and check for other survivors, but we'd been there too long, and every moment could be the one that got us caught.

I stepped into the living room, noticing I'd left the console up in my fog. I ran over and closed it but decided against putting the mess back because of the clock ticking in the back of my head. It would have to be enough. Abby had her back against the wall, out of sight of the entryway and kitchen area. I turned to signal her when I noticed we weren't alone. A figure dressed in black stood in front of the elevator door. I knew him instantly since he'd been the assistant manager at the Lair for as long as I'd been coming here. It was Max, who'd been left in charge when Blaze left.

"We've got company," I said softly into my comm-link. I snapped my faceplate down. "Get out of the way; I don't want to hurt you."

He laughed. "You can't hurt me, even if you wanted to. I thought I smelled food and there you were."

I'd been called a lot of things in my life, but never food. "Whatever." I needed to get us out of here as fast as possible; who knew if he'd contacted the authorities. "Step aside, and I'll be out of here."

Max scoffed at me. "Why would I want to do that?" He pulled a pistol from the back of his pants and pointed it at me. Blaze would have had a fit; you never carry a gun anywhere but in an approved holster. It's an accident waiting to happen. Though in this case, I wish he'd shot himself in the ass.

"I'm walking out of here regardless." I glanced to where Abby stood. She gently lowered Mimi to the floor, so she had her arms free. "You can get out of my way or I can move you, your choice."

He laughed again, a joyless sound like fingernails on a chalkboard. "Tommy, I knew your Gift would be strong. I could smell it on you when you came in the store."

I froze. My faceplate had been up, but I doubted he'd seen my face. I didn't have to wait long for an answer.

"You see, every Gifted has a unique smell about them, and the stronger the Gift, the more obvious the odor." He stepped closer. "The silent alarm triggered when you turned off the cameras. I thought maybe some kids had broken in, but when I smelled your scent, I knew you were here."

"Scent? Are you a dog of some kind?" I asked, trying to lure him closer to where Abby could grab him.

An irritated look crossed his face. "Hardly. I feed off Gifted and become more powerful when I do so. I'd always been forced to procure my own sources, but then Blaze left me the Lair, where I could pick who I wanted."

"Procured?" Shock registered in my already blown mind. "We saw the murder victims on the news before we left Redemption. You were the one killing those women?"

He smiled at me like I was an idiot. "Just figuring it out, are we? I needed their Gift to sate my needs. Problem is, I had to cut the collars off them, and they didn't live long afterward."

"You murderer!" I fired a bolt of lightning across the room, striking him in the chest. The bolt flashed out and hit the table in front of the kitchen.

"Tsk, tsk," he said with that damn smirk on his face. "Your power can't touch me, so now you can head down the hallway, and we'll see how long you can sustain me for. The others' Gifts took time to mature, no matter what incentives I gave them."

"The guy who exploded in the street. It was because of you?" Could this get any stranger? Max was a serial killer and a vampire to boot.

He shrugged. "I got sloppy, and he escaped, but his Gift engaged too rapidly without me taking off the excess, and he blew up. I won't make the same mistake again." He came at me, waving the gun toward the hallway. "Move."

As he passed the wall, Abby leapt out, catching his wrist. The gun discharged; the bullet pulled at my side but not enough to add to my power level. Abby swung at Max, striking him in the face. Her arm recoiled like she'd hit a Carbinium wall. She fell to the floor clutching her hand, swearing her head off.

"Oh, you brought dessert. How nice." He pointed the gun at Abby's head. "Now you help her up, and we go together down the hall." He cocked the gun to emphasize his point.

"You win, Max," I said, putting my hands up in surrender. "We don't need anyone else getting hurt."

I glanced at Abby; she still swore, but hid a smile behind her fist. Max turned the gun on me, not realizing it couldn't hurt me. Abby scissored her legs, knocking him to the ground. The gun fired, bullet flying past me. I wrenched the weapon from his hand. Abby leapt to her feet, snatching Max by the front of his shirt, and threw him into the wall next to the hallway door where he'd been planning on imprisoning us.

I started to help Mimi up, but Abby threw her over her shoulder, and we ran for the elevator. The door hissed open as we jumped in. I banged the up button, trying to get the doors to close faster. Max ran around the corner, but he was too late. The doors closed and we sped up to the main floor. I pulled Blaze's office chair over and wedged it in the elevator door to keep it from closing. There were other ways out of the safehouse, but they would take longer.

We pelted across the store. As we hit the front door, I slowed to retrieve the key. Abby had other ideas, slamming her booted foot against it, shattering the door frame as the lock ceased to be. Out and across the street we ran, heedless of prying eyes. Suddenly, the comm-link sprang to life. "This is Mr. Wizard. Respond please." Marcel's voice sounded frantic with worry.

I hadn't realized we'd been cut off from the team. "Mr. Wizard, we are headed to extract location Alpha. We need immediate pick-up."

"We've got your back trail covered, and you aren't being followed. Two minutes to pick-up." Dad's solid voice reassured me things were okay. I didn't know I'd been holding my breath until I let it out explosively.

Mimi muttered incoherently when Abby lowered her to the snow-covered ground. Man, I didn't miss the snow and gloom of Montana winters.

Even after carrying Mimi for two blocks, Abby didn't have the decency to look tired at all.

"How's the hand?" I asked as we waited.

She shook her head. "Hurts and it's broken." She grasped her right hand in her left and pulled while rotating it. A few sickening cracks and pops later, she stopped. "I think that will do it. Don't want it to heal wrong. Couple days and it will be good as new."

The sudden appearance of blue lights interrupted the conversation, not that either of us minded. The portal opened onto the control room back in Castle. Abby hoisted the unconscious Mimi and stepped through. As I started to follow, I heard a voice from behind me.

"Tommy, I'll be seeing you!" Max yelled down the street from where he stood. I flipped my middle finger at him and stepped into the safety of Castle and my family. I arrived to see Marcel grabbing a sweatshirt off the table and bunching it into a makeshift pillow for Mimi's head. I got out of the way of the second portal, which popped up a minute later. Mom, Dad, and Alyx entered from the rooftop they'd been staking out.

Helmets came off, hugs were exchanged, and there was a bit of Mom checking us over for wounds. You would think having the ability to absorb most damage-causing events would make Mom worry less. Not so.

Alyx rolled over to me. "You guys know how to keep things lively. I'd love to stay and help out, but I've got another convergence in the great white north to go investigate."

"Alyx, can I speak to you before you leave?" Dad asked. Alyx nodded.

"Meet up in the living room in thirty to go over what just happened," Dad said, then spoke softly with Alyx as they moved away from the rest of us.

After the quick checkup, Mom had Abby carry Mimi to a room to get her settled. Marcel ran off to tell Blaze, and I decided a shower sounded like the thing to do with my time.

In clean clothes and freshly washed, I even had time to grab a box of Pop-Tarts and a Mountain Dew before we discussed the mission. I brought the mission bag with me, setting it by my feet as I dropped on the couch.

The others filtered in, taking seats around the room. Mom arrived last. "Blaze is watching over Mimi. She's in bad shape, but nothing sleep and food won't cure." She turned to where Abby and I sat on the couch. "What the hell happened down there?"

Abby told the story, explaining about the trashed conditions and the weird clicking noise. I filled in about finding the body and Mimi since Abby had been out of it for that part. Abby finished up with fighting Max and making our getaway.

Dad interrupted Abby, looking to me. "Wait, so did your shot miss?"

"I don't think so," I said slowly, pulling up details from the fight in my mind's eye. "It was like it bounced off him. The energy hit the table instead of him."

"Abby, what happened when you punched him?" Dad's tone didn't betray the concern, his face did.

"I might as well have punched the wall. I felt it connect, but then the force seemed to come all the way up my arm. I felt the bones snap." She shook her head. "Actually, punching walls has hurt less."

Marcel whistled. "Do you think Max has some sort of feedback Gift?"

"I don't know, but the fact he's feeding off Gifted makes him extremely dangerous. We need to keep well away from him." Dad wasn't pleased. Obviously, he knew more than he told us.

"We can't let him keep torturing and killing Gifted," I said, a little more unsure than I'd have liked. The scene in the room had unsettled me quite a bit.

"Tommy, we have larger objectives than chasing this down. Blaze and Oliver need to come first. We'll deal with him later." Not stopping a serial killer pissed Dad off, but he'd stay on the mission regardless.

Marcel started to laugh. All eyes went to him. "Sorry." He adjusted his glasses before speaking. "We don't need to handle him. I can hack the Reclaimers database and put an arrest warrant out for a Syndicate Gifted. If I list the Secret Lair as the hideout, they'll handle Max for us."

Mom smiled. "Now I like this plan. Let the Reclaimers handle the dirty work. I'm sure Max not having a collar will raise some questions, but it's worth the risk."

"Not really," Marcel explained. "By marking him Syndicate, they'll assume he's with Reaper, and none of them are collared."

"Marcel, you're a genius." Mom gave him a quick grin.

"Agreed. Marcel, take care of it." Dad sighed. "You two did well keeping your heads about you. Good job retrieving the data we need. Marcel, can you find the machine you were telling us about?"

Marcel nodded enthusiastically. "I just need the backups, and we're all set."

I reached down, grabbing the bag to retrieve the device.

Mom frowned. "Tommy, what happened to the side of the satchel?"

I looked, and my heart sank. Unseen by me in all the excitement was a ragged bullet hole. The shot had missed me but had struck the bag. I barely felt the tug on the bag. I'd forgotten about it until now. I reached in and found jagged pieces of metal as my hand fastened around the destroyed backup device. My head lowered in defeat as I held it out.

Our last chance to save Blaze sat dead in my hand.

2 8

The room fell silent as everyone took in the view of the destroyed backup. Worse yet, we had eradicated the systems to make them irretrievable. I couldn't believe my bad luck.

Marcel grinned at me.

"You think this is funny?" I asked, my anger rising.

"Not really, but I have a backup."

"Huh? This is the backup." None surpass my grasp of the English language.

Marcel shrugged. "Once I verified the system, you didn't turn it off, and since you said there was somebody down there, I backed up the system to the control room. I figured if you started throwing lightning around delicate electronic circuits, it might fry the drive."

I could have kissed Marcel. "Seriously?" If he had a backup, we could save Blaze, and that was the only thing that mattered.

"Yeah, my gear doesn't have a great track record around you." He smiled his shit-eating grin at me. First taking out Turk with a chair, now this. I'd never have any peace. "Since I still had a full connection, I figured it didn't hurt anything to be safe."

"Good call, Marcel." I could tell Dad was pleased. "How long will it take you to get the location of the medical site?"

"Geez, rush the miracle man, and you get rotten miracles." Marcel grabbed his tablet and swiped across it rapidly. "Boo-yah! I've got the location already. The safehouse name is Harker, and it's in the Adirondack Mountains in the North Eastern Region. The odd part is there isn't a team's name associated with it." His hand started racing once more across the screen.

"Why is that odd?" Abby twisted her watch as she asked, obviously nervous about something, or maybe just shaken over the chamber of horrors we'd encountered.

Mom glanced at the distracted Marcel before answering for him. "These safehouses were huge investments. A team must have owned it."

"True." Dad scowled a bit as he thought. "Could be it wasn't completed before the Dark Brigade attacks. I hadn't heard of any bases so far north."

"Nada. It will take some time to figure out where the entry is and any security there, but the intel says there is a Cellular Regeneration Immersion center in Harker. It's what we need. I'll hit the Bat Cave and geek up the particulars together." Marcel hopped up, gave Mom a quick hug, and headed for the control room.

Mom studied us for a minute. "Abby, are you okay?" Worry flooded her words and for good reason. Abby spun her watch manically as we sat. "You look upset, honey."

Before Abby could deny it, she broke down and started sobbing. Mom shot across the room to console her, holding her as she cried. I moved to the couch where Marcel had been seated. Dad dropped into the seat next to me.

"How about you, Tommy? You've been through a lot, but the room sounded like a scene from a horror movie." Dad put his hand on my shoulder awkwardly. Our father-son bonding hadn't progressed as far as I'd have liked, but when you're running for your life, such things drifted to the background.

I thought about it before giving my answer. I wasn't upset, not really. I still felt numb after seeing Wendi dead on the floor of the Megadrome. I forced the image out of my head, focusing on her the night of our first kiss. She meant the world to me, and I refused to forget the amazing times we had together.

"I'm fine. I've seen worse." Wendi disappeared, replaced by the remnants of Cliff and Ryder rising in my brain instead, charred husks of guys who hadn't done anything wrong other than be friends with a psychotic bully. Brunner had always been that way, but not them. I'm sure each time he bullied a collared kid for laughs, Clint and Ryder had become deadened to his casual cruelty. Kind of like putting a frog in a pot and raising the heat. It never saw the situation as dangerous until it was too late.

Dad squeezed my shoulder. "You have. I don't think I tell you enough, but I'm proud to have you as my son. I've seen veteran soldiers panic in situations far less intense than what you've faced over the last few months. I know how hard it can be to discuss the terrible things we see or are forced to do. If you ever need to talk, I'm here for you."

I didn't know what to say considering how many times I had panicked, so I settled for "Thanks, Dad. It means a lot to me."

The ten-year-old in me screamed that I'd waited for years to meet him, and I was blowing it. It would have to be enough for now. Maybe one day we could do the stuff the Norm kids did with their dads: fishing, hunting or whatever else. I'd fight the bad guys of the world to find a place where we could be safe, if such a place existed.

A loud wail shook me from my reverie as Abby launched into another crying jag over what Mom had said to her. Dad gave me a shocked look. "I'm going to get some coffee."

"They were torn to shreds when I woke up," Abby said among the tears. "When I walked into the room, it was like stepping into a scene from my past."

The words stopped me cold in my mental tracks. Abby had told me she had hunted to survive but never about dead bodies. I felt for my sister, knowing the burden of killing a person. The guilt and remorse of being responsible are horrible. I struggled with it and could see she did as well, and she'd been younger than I was when it happened.

Dad cleared his throat from the entry into the living room. "Look who I found wandering around."

Mimi stood next to him, one hand holding on to his arm for support. "Blaze is sound asleep, and I didn't know where I was." She smiled when she saw me. "Hey, Sport. I'd hoped to see you at the Lair but not like that."

I laughed. "Hey, Mimi." I crossed over to her, and she threw her arms around my neck. I returned the hug, but thought she might break my back before she released me.

"It was Max killing those women."

I swallowed hard. "I know. We put an end to it."

She pushed me back to arm's length. "You did? How? He's crazy. He kept hurting us, rambling about powers and how hungry he was. That dude is seriously messed up."

I led her over, sitting next to her on the couch across from Abby and Mom. They took turns hugging Mimi, though I'm not sure if Abby intended to let go. Dad took the empty chair, waiting for Abby to finish.

Once Abby had returned to her spot, Dad asked. "What happened to you, Mimi?"

Mom hissed. "Michael, the girl's been through hell. You know what happened enough for now."

Mimi held up a shaky hand. "Mrs. Ward, it's okay. I need to tell you what happened. Tommy said Max is gone?"

Abby barked a bitter laugh. "By the time the Reclaimers get done with him, there won't be a greasy spot left."

"Good." Mimi withdrew into herself as we waited. She looked around at each of us. "Once you'd left, it was the same as always. I ran the diner, and Blaze took care of the rest. When Max finally showed up again, being his old creepy self, sniffing at me, telling me how wonderful I smelled. Then bang, back to disappearing for days at a time. Blaze and I struggled to keep up with everything. Mandy started helping out after school, so Blaze hired her to run the front."

Mom's eyebrows shot up. "Mandy?"

Mimi smirked, some of her normal personality shining through her pain. "Yep, Tommy's kissing partner." She elbowed me. "I think she kept hoping Tommy would come back, but then we saw you all die on Saturday Night Showdown." She paused for a bit, wrapping her arms around herself. "I thought she would stop coming, but she didn't. The Lair was all she had left of you."

I felt guilty as I hadn't thought of Mandy since I'd left Redemption. The idea that she'd worked there because of me made me feel awful. I hadn't considered the people who thought we'd all been killed. The teachers, Mom's co-workers, the other kids. They all thought we were gone, and it had to stay that way.

She continued. "Blaze left shortly after you all died. He left Max in charge, which didn't make me happy. I started to notice a few of the regulars stop coming in."

Dad frowned. "Regulars?"

She shrugged. "Guys like Benji, Gary, and Turk. They all ran together. There were rumors some Gifted had freed them and left Granite Falls."

Well, it explained how Turk had gotten out. I remembered Benji and Gary. They hung with Turk, so I'd steered clear of them.

"At first Max worked at keeping the place just like Blaze liked it. A couple of weeks later, he started disappearing again. Always some new girl he'd met. I couldn't figure out how any girl could like that creep, but I caught on too late. One night I was there about to close; Max had been back three days or so and acting totally freaky. He sniffed at me all the time. Griggs threatened to kill him if he smelled him again. One night he'd sent Mandy home early. It probably saved her life." She reached over, gripping my hand in hers. "Something happened. Thompson and Griggs were hanging out to walk me to my car. Three more Gifted women had been abducted, and I was scared. I'd been feeling strange for about a week. Occasionally, I'd hear mumbling voices. I figured I was over-stressed with the long hours."

Mimi paused, so I ran to the kitchen and poured a glass of water for her. I returned, handing her the drink. She thanked me and took a mouthful of water before continuing.

"Max came into the diner, carrying four beer bottles. I pointed out Blaze didn't allow drinking here. Max shrugged it off, saying we were closed and had made our numbers, which deserved a toast. It's not like one beer would hurt, so we each took a bottle. Surprise, he'd drugged our beers. When I woke, we were chained to the beds where you found me."

Abby's face reddened. "Did he do anything to you while you were unconscious?"

Mimi shook her head and took another sip of water. "That's not what he wanted. He told us our collars had stopped working, so he would help us activate our Gifts." She shuddered, her voice dropping as she spoke. "He said trauma would be the easiest way to get them to surface. Each morning he would try something new and more painful. He shocked, stabbed, and burned each of us. Thompson's power began to manifest first. When he started glowing, Max would stand over Thompson and place his hands on his head until the glow flickered out. Max got off on it, called it 'feeding time.' He spent more and more time with Thompson."

"Was that the body we found in the room with you?" I hadn't wanted to ask but couldn't help myself.

Her voice cracked as she answered. "No, that was Griggs. Thompson escaped one night. He somehow melted the chains. He said he'd go for help and come get us. We begged to go with him, but he ran, promising he'd send help. None came until you and Abby showed up."

I jumped as a thump and a sharp crack sounded from the doorway. Marcel stood there, eyes wide, hands limp, a shattered tablet on the floor in front of him. Oh man, this was so not good.

Marcel stammered. "I'm sorry. This is all my fault. I was trying to help, I swear."

Mimi looked at him, confusion written across his face. "Marcel, you weren't even there. How could this be your fault?"

"I turned off the collars." He stared at the floor as he spoke. Agony laced every word. "I thought your Gifts would activate, and you could be free of Granite Falls. I'm sorry."

Mimi's face flushed red. "Why the hell would you do that? Who asked you to? Do you know what I lived through because of you?" Mimi dove toward Marcel, but Abby caught her and set her back down.

The words hit Marcel like a wrecking ball, destroying his resolve. "I'm sorry." He tried to leave, but Abby had him in a bear hug before he took two steps.

Abby released Marcel, turning on Mimi. "Max had been killing Gifted before the collars were turned off. Do you think he wouldn't have taken you anyhow? You were right there, and you have a Gift."

"You don't know that. He hadn't bothered me before." She shot back. "He only drugged us because the collars were off."

"You told me he smelled you all the time when he was at the Lair." Abby's tone grew angrier. "He could have had it all planned, and it was a coincidence the collars were off. Marcel shouldn't have turned off your collars, but at least you had a fighting chance against him, unlike the murdered women."

That stopped Mimi dead in the water. It was her turn to study the floor. "It doesn't make it any less wrong."

Dad cleared his throat. "I don't think assigning blame does any good. The past is behind us, and now we need to fix what we can."

"You're right." She took another drink. "After Thompson left, Max worked on Griggs, but his power never manifested, and he ended up killing Griggs in the process."

Mom reached over and put her hand on her arm. "Honey, you can stop. You're here now and safe with us."

"No, I need to finish."

I glanced over to where Abby stood with Marcel, one arm still around his shoulders. It was hard to see the consequences of your actions coming home. I hoped he'd be alright, if that was even possible for any of us.

"I must have been developing my power since he'd come down and put his hands on my head a few times a day. I could see him, but he felt like a blank space to me. If that makes any sense."

"The clicking noise." I caught Abby's eye, and she nodded. "We both kept feeling a clicking noise, but not one you could hear. It must have been you."

Mimi cocked her head, considering. "Maybe. It's weird. I see you all, but I also can feel you all in here." She pointed to her head. "It's like you exist twice."

"Most likely you've got some mental ability." Dad rubbed his forehead unconsciously. After Dominion, I doubted he trusted anyone with psychic powers. "We'll have to discuss this part later."

I wondered if discussing it would be putting Mimi as far from him as possible. I looked at the broken tablet at Marcel's feet. Time to change the subject. "Marcel, did you find out where we're going?"

He started at the question. "Sorry. Yeah, I have the information, but it's not why I came up here."

Mom's eyebrows rose. "You came up here why?" I think it drove her crazy that Marcel always left out the important parts until asked.

"Oh, they found Mr. W."

And that would be the most important news we could get.

29

"Who's Mr. W?" Mimi asked as we all stared at Marcel. I'd begun to believe we'd never find him, that he'd been killed, or hidden so well he might as well be.

Mom answered absently. "Um, Oliver Waxenby. He was a teacher in Redemption."

"Oh, Ollie. I know him. Very nice man, though his car had seen better days."

"How did you find him?" Dad asked Marcel, ignoring the commentary on Waxenby, while Mom went over what had happened for Mimi without a lot of details.

"Warden sent a message. They found the building he's being held at in the Dallas site. She wants to strike tonight before they can move him and was hoping we could help."

"Tommy? Abby? Are you two up for a mission? I know earlier was rougher than we expected."

We both nodded, but it was Mom who answered. "If they are going, so am I."

Dad frowned. "Susan, this is going to be a war with Gifted on all sides. You'll be vulnerable, and I'm not sure we can protect you."

Her chin rose as she addressed her husband. "Michael, I am going. You can put me on a rooftop with my sniper rifle. I can at least be your eyes and can eliminate any of those bastards who get in your way."

"Mom, what if they have fliers?" Abby asked, clearly unhappy with the idea. "We almost lost you at the Megadrome and..." She stopped short of mentioning Wendi trying to save her had cost her life.

She didn't have to, based on the pained expression that briefly crossed Mom's face. Pure determination erased it quickly as if it had never been there. "I know what happened in the Megadrome, but I've spent months training alongside you. If you are going to hide me away every time there's danger, why did I bother? I could have just cooked and cleaned while you all ran off to save the world. Well, it's my world too. I've lived through the losses, the collars, the beatings, and the ridicule with all of you. I will not be left behind."

Dad shot me a quick questioning glance. I shrugged. Knowing Mom, she'd hide in the trunk after packing it.

"Well, I know when to take my lawyer's advice." I winked at Mom, getting a warm smile in return. "It's a five-hour drive to the rendezvous site, and I'm going to go get some sleep." I stood up, stretched, then headed for my room.

"Good idea," Dad said, stifling a yawn. "Meet up in the armory at fifteen hundred hours. Get as much sleep as you can; it's going to be another long night."

I grasped Marcel's arm as I passed, dragging him along. "I know it seems like this is your fault, but we've got to move past it." I kept my voice low so it wouldn't be overheard. Mimi's emotions were raw, and I didn't want to upset her unnecessarily.

I heard a sniffle from Marcel. "Bruh, I appreciate it, but it is."

I cut him off. "No, it's not. Max killed those people, but he'd been killing long before he took Mimi. Turning off the collars doesn't equate to a serial killer imprisoning you, no matter what. Understand?"

With a great upheaval of bobbing hair, he nodded his agreement. "Thanks. I am sorry, though."

"You want to even the scales? Put Max where he can't hurt any more people."

What I got in return looked like a cross between a shark smiling and mad scientist plotting his revenge. "I put out an emergency bulletin, and the Reclaimers grabbed it like a power up. Turns out they were on overdrive with three missing soldiers. They caught Max behind the Secret Lair putting Griggs body in the dumpster. Last I checked, Max was being transported to the Block as a known Syndicate member."

I smiled at him. "Excellent work, bro. You done did good."

He cringed. "I know English isn't your native tongue but could you not butcher it so."

"I've always spoken English."

Marcel shook his head. "I don't know what you speak, but it isn't English. More like bastardized pig English."

I feigned shock. "I'm very unique-est is all."

Marcel plugged his ears. "I'm going to bed before you set the language back any farther than you already have." He turned down the corridor and slid into his room. I'd missed hanging with Marcel. It seemed like the whole world depended on everything we did, and there wasn't time to banter over a night of Xbox and junk food. Even though my family, both biological and chosen, were here, things had changed since Wendi died. All I could do was hope time would set things right.

I entered my room, tossed on my sleeping sweats, and was asleep before the lights had gone out.

M om pulled the van off into the building Dad had indicated. According to Warden, the building held shields to block the Protectorate drones and satellites from detecting anything. We geared up and waited.

A few minutes later, three figures emerged from the shadows of the derelict building. I tensed, figuring Jon and Turk would be with the party. Luckily, they weren't. Instead, I recognized Boulder and Salvo from our previous mission in Atlanta. The third person turned out to be a small Asian woman dressed in black, her hair pulled up in a bun on top of her head.

Dad flashed the hand sign at the group, and they visibly relaxed. They returned the correct response gesture, and everyone settled down. "Ranger, we are on a tight deadline. Looks like there are at least six Syndicate members with Grim Reaper. Warden has the plans, but we'll need to move."

"Let's go." Dad pushed his helmet on as Boulder led us deeper into the building. We descended a series of stairs that led to a hidden trapdoor in an out-of-the-way side wall. I still couldn't get over how elaborate the network of tunnels had to be for the Underground to move around unseen by the Protectorate watchers.

We emerged into a tunnel big enough to hold three trains side by side. An old truck sat at the bottom of the stairwell. The woman and Salvo jumped in the front cab as the rest climbed into the bed. Boulder banged on the side of the truck. "Warden doesn't want to miss this opportunity. If we could stop the Syndicate, we could actually work toward freeing the Gifted from the Protectorate."

I just wanted to get Waxenby back before whatever fate Eiraf had seen could come to pass. If I got to kill Grim Reaper in the process, so much the better. His was one death that wouldn't haunt me. I owed him more than I could count.

A quarter of an hour later, we pulled up to the massive doors we had left from last time. Salvo parked the truck, and they led the way to where we'd met Warden and the transport machine. If what she said was true, we'd be in Dallas in under an hour.

We entered the old bank vault that held the device. I preferred using Alyx, but since he was off on another magical mystery tour in Canada, this would have to do.

Warden turned from where she spoke with the control panel operator. The young woman wore overlarge glasses that made her eyes swim behind the thick lenses, more cute librarian than weird, goo-goo eyes. She wore her dark hair held back by a bright pink headband with a matching sweatshirt.

Warden sported dark circles under her eyes and slumped shoulders. "Thank you for coming on such short notice. One of the Dallas surveillance devices spotted the activity, and we got eyes on the building. Your man is in there, but we don't know what shape he's in."

Dad reached out and shook Warden's hand. "We appreciate your assistance. Do you know who is in the building?"

She shook her head slowly. "Grim Reaper has been spotted. It worries me that after all this time, we saw him. It's unlike him to be this careless."

"You expect a trap?" Dad asked though I'm sure he knew the answer.

"I always expect a trap," she said with a harsh laugh. "Yes, I think it's a trap, but I'm not sure for whom."

"He's looking for us. He's got a score to settle with Abby and me. He took Mr. Waxenby to get even with us."

"Makes sense." Warden signaled the woman, and she spoke into a microphone on the desk. Outside, the speaker transmitted her words, but I couldn't make it out.

Mom touched Dad's arm. "Ranger, knowing it's a trap, do you think it's wise to step into it?" The concern in her voice was evident to me but only because I knew her so well.

Warden answered for him. "If we don't take this opportunity, we'll never get another. Even if you decline, my people are going."

"We aren't backing out." Abby's anger could have set concrete on fire from the heat contained in it. "I owe those bastards." She'd grown since we'd been standing there. A fact Warden hadn't missed.

"Excellent. My team is on route. We have five going, plus your four will make nine."

A bright, happy voice came from behind us. "Make it ten." Molecular Molly came bouncing into the vault. Warden immediately started rubbing her temples.

"We've been over this; your talents aren't useful in a combat situation."

"Bullshit, Mom. I can change into a mountain lion and kill faster than your storms can."

"Enough!" Warden's face had turned fire engine red. "You aren't going, period."

Molly folded her arms across her chest, defiant glare aimed at Warden. "You can't stop—"

I cleared my throat. "Warden, may I have a word?" All eyes swung toward me. "In private."

She checked for objections and seeing none, crossed to the far side of the transporter. "I don't mean to intrude, but you know Molly will follow as soon as we leave. So instead, can you have her stay by our sniper? And if things get bad, both of them can get out of harm's way."

Warden's eyes narrowed. "Why? I saw Saturday Night Showdown, and I can guess who's in the combat suit since the other young lady..." She stopped before saying it. It always came back to Wendi's death.

I sighed. "Yes, my mother is a great shot, but she's not Gifted. If the fight gets bad, the two of them can get out of Dallas, at the least. Molly still gets to go, but she'll be overlooking the fight and not in the middle of it."

She thought it over. "Can she really use the rifle she's carrying?"

I laughed. "She's the best shot around. With two sets of eyes, we'll be warned if anything goes wrong before it's too late. It's the best you're going to get."

"You're right." She didn't sound happy, but it would be far better than the alternative. Molly had been captured once already. No sense chancing a second time.

"Thank you." I felt relief flood through me at the thought of Mom having backup.

Warden and I rejoined the others. "Molly, you can go under one condition."

"What condition?" Her eyes narrowed in the same way as her mother's.

"Your job is to go with..."

"Snapshot." I provided Mom's alias, which probably earned me a glare, but she had her helmet on to conceal her identity.

Warden nodded. "Snapshot. She'll be covering the building, and we need your eyes to warn us if there're any issues. If things so sideways, you two get to the Underground facilities. Agreed?"

Molly started to protest, but Warden cut her off. "That, or I cage you while I'm gone. Your choice, peanut."

"Fine." The smile ruined a perfectly good pouting tone.

My comm-link chirped in my ear. "According to Blaze I need a spotter, so we'll go with it." I knew Mom wouldn't be happy, but she'd not been in a real fight before. I'd live with the scolding if it kept her safe.

The rest of the Underground team entered. Boulder and Salvo were joined by the woman from earlier, and an older lady who wouldn't have looked out of place at a quilting bee. At least Jon and Turk weren't there. "Um, I thought Jon and Turk would be going with us?"

Warden's jaw clenched, not a good sign in my experience. "Turk killed two of my people in an argument over a card game. I banished him, and Jon decided to join him."

Dad stiffened. "Don't they know the layout of the Underground facilities here?"

Warden's thin lips creased in a bitter smile. "They did, but we have a young man who can eliminate memories. He wiped their brains of anything having to do with us."

"Isn't that a bit excessive?" Abby said, almost snarling. While she was pissed at Jon for abandoning us, he was still family to her.

"The other choice was death. They gladly accepted the wipe. We did ask if Jon would like his sister's death removed or at least dimmed in his memory, but he declined. He is an angry young man."

Didn't I know it all too well? I wish Jon had taken their offer to lessen his memories; maybe then he could forgive and return to where he belonged. I doubted it would ever happen. Who was I to tell him what to feel? But hanging out with Turk would only lead to more trouble.

"I think we should get to Dallas, so we have time to scout the area and come up with a game plan," Dad said evenly. Standing around wasn't how you rescued people.

Warden agreed. "Angela, prep the cyclontron for translocation."

Tammy gestured she'd heard and began whatever sequence she used to move people from one place to another. Warden walked on to the transport pad, followed by her team. Dad led us up next to them. "How long will this take?" Dad asked Warden.

"Long enough for introductions," Warden said, turning to her team. "You know Molecular Molly, Boulder, and Salvo from your last visit." Molly waved enthusiastically; the two men simply raised a hand in acknowledgment. She indicated the Asian lady from earlier. "This is Izanami." I'd seen statues more animated than Izanami. Warden then gestured toward the older woman. She wore a loose-fitting black top and pants that were pushed into her boot tops. Her graying hair held a myriad of barrettes and clips to keep it in place. "And Specter." She smiled warmly at us.

It was Dad's turn. "I'm Cyclone Ranger. This is Snapshot, our sniper." Mom nodded to the group. "and..." That's when he realized Abby hadn't picked a code name.

"Oh, for God's sake." Abby startled me with her abrupt entry into the conversation. "The Protectorate called me 'The Butcher,' of all the dumb names, or you can call me Abby." She jerked her thumb at me. "He's Tommy. Makes it a whole lot easier, and it's not like we have a secret identity to protect."

And there you have it, the bull in the china shop. I'd been outed. Warden knew who we were, but Abby had just confirmed it for the rest of the Underground. Though she was right, Saturday Night Showdown had used our real names as part of the introduction. I pulled off my helmet since it seemed silly to hide our identities at this point. Mom and Abby did the same.

The speaker above our head instructed us to stand still. I did as I was told. Lights whirled around us as metal circular rings rose from the floor, spinning ever faster until they blurred. With a slight popping of my ears, I knew we had shifted locations. The lights slowly dimmed to reveal the transport surrounded by men with rifles pointed at us. "Don't move!" One of them shouted.

We weren't in Kansas anymore.

30

"What's the code word!" yelled one of the men. With the bright lights, I couldn't pick out who spoke.

"Oh, for God's sake, Squad, you know who it is since we just radioed we were translocating." Warden snapped at whoever had spoken.

The lights dimmed down to normal level as the rings dropped back into the floor. At least thirty identically dressed men pointed rifles in our direction. Warden didn't seem worried as she strode off the disk we'd been standing on, toward one of the men. "Knock it off, you'll spook our guests, and you don't want that." She headed for the console where a guy in a helmet and darkened goggles sat behind the controls.

Like an accordion collapsing, the men blurred as they combined into one man standing across from me. Molly whispered. "That's Squad; he can make copies of himself. He thinks it's funny to startle new people."

Great. We're on a mission to save Waxenby, and we get a practical joker. He's lucky one of us hadn't fired. "Got it." I looked around the room. Gone were the clean lines and metal fixtures from Atlanta's bank vault. Dallas consisted of thick, stocky cement walls, whitewash faded from years of neglect. Power lines snaked across the ceiling and down to the translocator, metal brackets holding them in place.

Dad looked around as well. "Warden, what was this before the war?"

"Munitions bunker that the Reclaimers had built. Walls and ceilings have three layers of Carbinium plates encased in the concrete. There's a certain justice in using it to defy them." She hadn't looked up from the laptop she typed on.

"Good use for it." Dad looked impressed.

I followed Molly across to where Warden stood beside a projector. She had an aerial view on the wall of the greater Dallas region. Everyone gathered around it.

Warden pointed at the image. "Here is where the Syndicate is holed up. According to the records, it used to be a bank. It's constructed with bulletproof glass and reinforced walls. We are going to have to go in through a door." She looked around for questions. Seeing none, she continued. "We can set Molly and Snapshot up on the roof of the old Prosperity bank building. It's fifteen or so stories tall and has a good view of the area. It also has an access hatch to the underground if things go bad." That was directed at Molly with "the mother" stare, which made you know she meant it.

Molly nodded. "I've got it."

"Good. We need to scope the surrounding area and make sure things are what we think they are. We'll send two groups. Ranger, Sparky, Abby, and I will scout the western side. Salvo, Boulder, and Izanami will take the eastern. Once we are secure, Specter will scout the building for us."

I glanced at Specter, wondering how she would penetrate and scout a building full of Syndicate goons. I think she read my mind. "I create a spiritual copy of myself. I'll ghost through the building and get the general layout. I can't see the small details, but it's something."

Warden snorted. "She's selling herself short. She'll be able to tell us what's going on in there. Once we have the intel, we move on the building, get your man out, and take down as many of the bastards as we can. Any questions?"

There weren't any.

"Squad, get the rest of your team back to Atlanta. I don't want our home base unguarded in case things go bad here."

He saluted crisply, as four more copies peeled off behind him. "Yes, Warden!" They all jogged out of the room.

Warden shook her head wearily before leading the group out and through the underground town that held her people in Dallas. People called greetings to her as we walked, which she returned good-naturedly.

Exiting through a steel portal, we entered the labyrinth of tunnels that connected the Underground to a good portion of the remains of the Dallas area. Large sections of the city had burned to the ground about ten years ago, making it even less hospitable. After half an hour, we stopped for a break while Salvo and Boulder went for a vehicle to quicken our journey. Specter slumped against the wall in exhaustion.

Dad pulled Warden aside, talking in soft tones. Mom joined Abby and I where we waited. "I'm glad Blaze pushed us so hard in training," Mom said, her tone light over the comm-links. The helmets provided thermal imaging that cast the world into shades of green. Aboveground, the night vision gave a better view, but not underground. "I hadn't realized how out of shape I was being a lawyer."

I chuckled. "You were in great shape compared to me. I'd have dropped from exhaustion ten minutes after we started."

Abby chimed in helpfully. "He would have. I'd never seen someone so out of shape. Well, except Marcel."

"Thanks," I said dryly. Normally, Marcel would have been monitoring the missions, but the Syndicate knew we were coming; no sense chancing them intercepting the long-range communications to boot. Loneliness crept in, knowing my best friend wouldn't be riding shotgun.

"I miss Mr. Wizard." Abby sounded like how I felt. Abandoned. We were always together since we'd beaten Powell, even if it were on the comm-links.

Dad joined our conversation. "We need to keep our eyes open; I don't have a good feeling about this one." He stood near Warden, but she spoke with Specter, who had regained her feet. "The Underground getting this tip, and the fact Grim Reaper is on site for a prisoner move is a setup. Reaper is spoiling for a fight."

Ever the pragmatist, Mom chimed in. "Of course he is. I'm sure he expected us to die in the Gauntlet."

"It would be great, but they've got something up their sleeves. Grim Reaper wouldn't risk losing Waxenby if he weren't positive he'd win this fight or get something of greater value."

"You think he could be after one of us or the Underground?"

"Hmm. Could be. No one gets left behind. We can't free one just to give him another pawn." A click announced Dad had left the channel as he resumed his conversation with Warden.

Lights came around the bend, and a beat-up old van pulled up next to the ledge we stood on. "Thank goodness," Specter said with a delighted tone in her voice. "My poor old feet wouldn't take the long walk."

We all hopped into the truck, and Salvo drove us to the exit point. It only took about twenty minutes, though the van never got much over fifteen miles an hour in the tunnel. We stopped next to a flight of metal stairs that rose up to what I guessed would be the basement of the Prosperity building. Salvo and Boulder led the way, checking the door before opening it and inspecting the area beyond. Salvo gave the all clear. Specter headed up next, followed by Izanami and Warden. Mom and Molly went ahead of Abby and me. Dad brought up the rear. Nothing seemed out of place, though it didn't soothe my nerves any.

The Underground had stocked the basement in case of a forced evacuation or mission prep. The Underground team pulled weapons out, checking the condition before loading them. Molly grabbed a rifle that could have been the little brother of Mom's HK G28. Once they were ready, Salvo and Boulder opened the hidden door carefully, but nothing waited for us. We climbed up a set of stairs to the lobby of the building. Mom paused on the landing. She hit her external speaker. "Do Molly and I climb to the roof?"

Warden shook her head. "We have battery packs to operate the elevator. We keep some of the taller buildings accessible since the snakes here are enormous and extremely poisonous. I always hated snakes, but these are nightmare-inducing."

Good to know. Killer crocs in Atlanta, giant rats in D.C., and now poisonous snakes in Dallas. These cities were a biologist's dream come true. Who said animals didn't evolve?

We moved across the wastelands of the lobby to the elevator bank that once had taken people to their daily jobs. Salvo eased a panel off the wall, connected two wires, and the door opened with a chime. He replaced the panel.

"Molly, you two head to the roof and stay low. Keep your eyes open and evacuate at the first hint of trouble." Warden turned to Mom. "This shaft has a working elevator. The last shaft is empty, but we rigged a rope system that will drop you into the basement with an exit to the tunnels. If things go bad, ALL of you need to escape and wait in the tunnel. Understood?" She directed the last word firmly at Molly.

They both nodded. Mom gripped Dad's hand, then Abby's, then mine, before the elevator took her to her post. I didn't like that none of us were there to protect her, but Molly had saved me before and would do the same for Mom. Specter followed Mom and Molly to the roof to do her work.

The rest of the group split into teams and moved to scout the area around the Syndicate base. We crossed through the building's parking lot, staying out of the deck, which didn't appear overly safe. Across the street stood an expansive building. Warden had pointed it out as an old megamart. The back of the building held the loading docks; the bays looked like empty sockets in a skeleton's skull. Vines emitted a strange scraping sound that set my teeth on edge.

Three cars sat where they had collided years ago. Warden slid between two mangled bumpers, getting to a small clear area in the center of the triangle. We crouched behind them, hiding from any Syndicate watchers. "I need a few minutes to pull a storm up in case we need it. In the middle of a fight isn't when I want to wait for the clouds to form."

I watched as she focused her Gift, but much to my disappointment, her eyes didn't go all white or glow electric blue; nothing formed around her or anything. I'd thought a power as expansive as controlling the weather would have a show associated with it. I guess Mother Nature didn't worry about being upstaged. I checked overhead as the clouds scudded together, increasing in quantity. They darkened as they formed.

I saw Dad's head tilted upward, watching the spectacle of summoning a storm from nothing. I switched to our private channel on the comm-link. "She's powerful, isn't she?"

Dad's head shifted slightly in my direction. "In certain ways, I guess she is."

I frowned, not that he could see my face since we had helmets on. "What do you mean? She can summon a storm from nothing."

"It is impressive to be sure. Before the attacks, she'd been support personnel." He sat, his back leaning against the remnants of a blue van that now sheltered us from prying eyes. I flopped on the broken asphalt of the road.

"Support?" I had thought all Gifted had been on teams. Waxenby and

Tracy Stephens had shown me that not all Gifted used their powers to fight. As Marcel said, my concept was binary. You were on a team or not. Support was a new concept.

The reflection of the cloud's movement gave Dad's visor a strange streaming effect, kind of like a lava lamp. "When the call came, you couldn't wait fifteen minutes for someone to ready their powers; you had to go. A lot of times we leapt from planes to our target sites. Powers like hers aren't practical in those situations." He paused for a moment. "Having said that, I'd not want to fight her in Atlanta where she keeps the storms close by. Gifted like her usually went to drought areas to bring rain, or were flown over the oceans to break hurricanes before landfall. Things along those lines. Mr. Fix-it was support for a lot of teams."

"Oh, I didn't know that." There was a lot I didn't know since history consisted of the Reclaimers winning the war and imprisoning us for being born with Gifts they didn't like. As far as the Protectorate was concerned, time began with their rise to power. The rest had been thrown out.

Warden signaled she was done. I switched back over to the team comm so I could listen in. "Ready?" she asked before leading us out and around an old shopping center. Vines crawled over the building, engulfing it in vegetation. We gave a wide berth to the plants as they writhed and stretched toward us when we moved past. I had no interest in seeing what would happen if I got too close. The Atlanta mold gave me a new healthy respect for plants.

We reached the front of the building. Nothing moved. The parking lot held a multitude of rusted-out vehicles that had been parked when the Dark Brigade attack hit the area. We leapfrog advanced through the jungle of abandoned junkers until we could see the front of the Syndicate base. Warden spoke softly into her comm, which was linked up with ours. "Anything moving out there?"

Mom's voice came back. "No, everything is quiet."

Salvo agreed. "Nothing here, Warden, except those creepy-ass plants."

Warden nodded to herself. "Specter, give it a look-see."

"On it, Warden. Back in a jiffy."

Warden knelt next to where Dad and I had stopped behind the remains of an old station wagon. "I don't like this. They should have people on the roof or patrolling the perimeter."

"Agreed, they are up to something. I don't know what, though," Dad said thoughtfully. "How good is Specter?"

"The best. You think I'd drag an old lady out here for fun?" Warden smiled, but her eyes never settled in one place as she scanned the area for the trap we all knew would be waiting.

The minutes felt like hours before Specter broke the silence. "Grim Reaper is in there with four others and the target. He's tied to a chair in the middle of the old lobby. Three of the perps are on the far side of the safety glass of the teller line. Probably don't want to taste any of Ranger's lightning."

"Great job, Specter. Get to the bolt hole and wait for us." Warden's clipped tone freaked me out. We weren't seeing something.

"Will do, Warden."

"No sense wasting time," Dad said, peering off into the darkness. Nothing showed on night vision or thermal. If Grim Reaper had only brought five, we'd have the advantage.

"On my mark..."

Mom's voice over the comm-link cut her off. "Heads up, somebody is coming out of the target." I pointed across the asphalt to where a figure, dressed head to toe in black, strode out of the Syndicate's base. There was no doubt in my mind as to who that was: Grim Reaper. Four others followed in his wake.

"Tommy, why you hidin' over there? We are friends. Come, let's talk."

I didn't know what to say, but talking was the last thing on my mind.

31

As I began to rise, hands grabbed my arms from either side. "Don't be crazy," Warden hissed between clenched teeth. "He's baiting you."

I knew he was; I'd seen him do it to Jon in the boxing ring time after time. I relaxed, letting myself be pulled back out of sight. "What do we do then?"

Dad tapped me on the shoulder, pointing back toward where Mom oversaw the terrain. "You guys got eyes on this joker?"

"Oh, yeah." Mom's voice almost purred. She had a score to settle with Grim Reaper. "I've got the shot."

Warden smiled. "Take it."

I heard the report of the rifle over the comm-link. A bright blue flash flared in front of Grim Reaper's face. "Oh, that's low, Ward," He yelled into the night. "Good thing we've got Commander Gravity at our disposal. So how about we talk now before I slash old Ollie?"

I don't think any of us thought we'd capture him so easily, but it had been a nice thought while it lasted.

Warden glowered "Salvo, give him a bit of fire, and see what he thinks."

"Got it, boss."

Streaks of fire arced into view from our left, crashing on Grim

Reaper's position. The shield held, until a stroke of lightning arced into the right side of the shield making it flash and disappear. Dad's voice came over our secure channel. "This is why you never let people know your weakness."

I thought back to the night we fought the Syndicate. "But Waxenby held in Armageddon's blast the night in the desert."

"Oliver can contain just about anything inside a shield, but they collapse if they are struck from multiple directions at the same time from the outside."

It made sense. Grim Reaper dodged the flames as he dashed for the safety of the doorway.

I heard a satisfied chuckle from Warden. "That'll teach him to run his mouth." She signaled for us to move out. "Start the assault. We need to hit while they are disoriented."

We weaved between the vehicles in turn, keeping the hideout in sight. Salvo's team moved in from our left, flanking the side of the building. I knelt behind a husk of an old SUV and waited, Dad to my right, Warden to my left. I saw Abby take up a position beyond Warden.

Fires flickered across the landscape where Grim Reaper had stood. On the ground, I saw a grimy, metal statue of a cowboy, lasso above his head. It had been snapped off at the ankles and obscured by the grass that grew around it. Eiraf's metal man that Marcel couldn't find was right there.

The door opened, and Grim Reaper stepped out, but not from under the overhang. Smoke drifted off his leather jacket from fresh scorch marks. A smear of soot crossed his right cheek where he had rubbed the reddened skin left from the firebombing. "I warned you!" The sickly green light of the scythe illuminated the darkness. The windows on all sides of him blew out, and the rest of the Syndicate fighters rushed to engage us.

It would have been nice of Chip Calloway to announce each of us like he did during Saturday Night Showdown. A flashy graphic overlay with their name, height, weight, and power would have come in handy right then. As it was, we only had four figures moving through the darkness toward us. Floodlamps flared to life from the hideout and two of the neighboring buildings. Our advantage had been effectively negated.

Thunder boomed to answer the explosions as Warden whipped the wind into a frenzy.

"Call your targets. I'm on Reaper," Dad said as he launched into the air. During the Gauntlet, the shield contained his blasts, but here he went full out. Bolts of lightning impacted on the force field in front of Grim Reaper. A stray bolt blew apart the roof, causing a small avalanche of bricks to crash into Reaper as he dove out of the way.

The winds picked up, driving debris and ash before them, as the storm surged toward the fight. I headed for the closest of the Syndicate soldiers. Imagine my total lack of surprise to find before me stood Turk, wearing a leather vest, jeans, and combat boots. His long, dirty blond hair streamed away from his face in the wind.

"Oh, how I've waited to pay you back, Ward!" I could barely make out his words over the maelstrom. For the briefest of moments, I thought about trying to reason with him, but if he'd joined up with the Syndicate, it was already too late. Jon blamed Reaper as much as me for Wendi's death, so I didn't have to worry about him.

I pulled energy together and launched an arc of lightning at him. I'd give him this: Blaze had trained him well. He rolled sideways, came up on his feet, and threw a blob of something green at me. The wind whipped it down the street before it ever got near. Blasts of flame seared the air as Tenji unleashed his attacks, trying to hit Dad as he threw bolt after bolt at the Syndicate members.

"I can't get a clear shot; the wind is too strong." Mom's helpless tone betrayed her anxiety. "Warden, roll it back. You're going to wipe out our team."

Warden stood, swaying in the wind, staring off into nothing. The storm continued to intensify all around us.

If Mom said more, it was swallowed by the roar of wind and the shrieking of metal as the abandoned cars fought to hold their ground. The air filled with projectiles made of rusted metal, broken glass, and every other type of debris known to man. A door tumbled across the parking lot, bouncing over cars until it clipped Warden in the head, driving her to the ground.

"Warden is down!" I shouted into the comm-link, though I couldn't be sure anyone could hear me. A small figure scampered away from her prone body. I tried to follow it, but something grabbed my head.

I could see the fingertips of whoever held my head but nothing else. I threw my head toward my attacker, but a knee in the back stopped my progress. The green ooze spreading across my faceplate informed me it was Turk. I'd seen him kill with his Gift before, and I knew I was in trouble. I tried to break his grip, but Blaze had trained him to avoid all the tricks he'd taught us. The smell of decaying, putrid meat invaded my helmet as the sludge bubbled across my view. The warping of the material grew as I fought in vain. The smell intensified as did the need to puke my guts out. I could feel my strength failing me. I had to do something he'd never expect.

"I never thought killing you could be so easy, Tommy." With a hard push, Turk dropped me against the pavement, laying on my back, effectively immobilizing me. The power I held swirled, but I knew I couldn't get an arc anywhere near him. I heard Dad's voice in my head. "You need to adapt, to use new aspects of your Gift if you're going to survive."

I spit up dinner, fighting to stay conscious as the poison tried to do its work on me. My healing might keep it at bay, but not for much longer. Change, adapt. Tenji threw flames, which I couldn't do, but could I transform energy to heat? I concentrated pushing out power in all directions, but not releasing it. After a moment, steam swirled inside my helmet, making the smell worse, as if it could be worse. A scream came from above me as I saw blisters swelling on the fingers touching the visor. A sharp crack and a flood of fresh air were a welcome change. My head jerked around as Turk flailed, trying to let go of the red-hot helmet. I reached up and pulled the release and got my head out, the edges scorching my skin and burning parts of my hair in the process. Turk tumbled to the ground, screaming in agony as his charred hands fused to the helmet.

I ducked as a piece of bumper flew by. I could absorb the energy of being hit, but a rusty cut could still be trouble. I stopped and emptied my stomach into the gutter. The roaring had intensified as the winds continued to increase, swirling as it progressed at a rapid pace in our direction.

Suddenly I rose into the air. Not by wind, but Abby. She threw me boldly over her shoulder and ran for the shopping mall, stopping behind an old tractor trailer that had seen better days. She'd lost her helmet in the fight too, her purple hair trailing out like a wave of Kool-Aid. Boulder joined us, Warden's arm over his shoulder as she stumbled along. The roar increased as the vortex formed into a full-on tornado. We couldn't fight it, especially with Warden in her current condition.

From somewhere deep in my memory, I realized I knew how to fix this. Marcel always went on about whatever he'd been researching. We had spent a night discussing how Dad could spin up cyclones, and it had to do with the cold downdraft his winds created. No cold air, no cyclone. I had to try.

I got to my feet. Abby tried to pull me back down, but I waved her off. She couldn't hear me even if I screamed. Pushing around the nose of the semi, I felt the full force of the tornado. I concentrated, running into the vortex, driving the heat out of my raised hands toward the maelstrom. Still the storm moved on, unaffected, as my skin blistered from the intense heat I generated. I screamed in agony and elation as I threw more energy into the heat until blisters burst, spewing clear liquid from the palms of my hands. None of it made a difference.

I caught sight of Dad as he streaked in, circling the tornado against its churn. He threw lightning into the vortex. Between the two of us, the winds weakened and slowly it broke apart. I slumped, most of my energy drained from the exertion.

Reaper, seeing his opening, swooped in while I recovered. He swung the scythe at my unprotected back. "Say goodbye, Ward!"

His victory turned to defeat as a tire from a dead semi slammed into him, knocking him to the ground. Abby howled in rage as she pursued him. Fire erupted from the ground in front of the prone man as Tenji rejoined the fight. Grim Reaper would be a goner if Abby reached him. Abby avoided the fire shield, moving to attack Tenji. He fired gouts of flame, trying to drive her back, but she moved like a jungle cat, always a step ahead of him. The distance shrunk between them as she advanced.

I staggered to my feet, trying to help, but the heat had drained my energy surplus. Dad floated down in front of me. Concern etched his face as he flipped up his visor. "You okay?"

I nodded, or at least tried to. "Just drained." With the tornado gone, we could hear each other, though the driving winds still made it tough to move.

Dad checked me over quickly before setting his hands on my shoulders. The intensity of the shock was nothing like I'd ever experienced before. Power bloomed through me as my deprived body absorbed every drop I could get. I felt revitalized. I must have been smiling like an idiot.

Dad laughed. "I thought it might help. Let's get Oliver and get out of here." He launched back into the air and sent lightning streaking toward Tenji.

"He's gone bleedin' crazy!" Salvo crossed the parking lot, throwing bombs at someone I couldn't see. "I don't want to hurt him. He's my best friend."

I ran to where Salvo knelt before the prone form of Warden. A huge silhouette emerged from the smoke: Boulder. Like his name, he had transformed his right arm into rock.

"What the..." was all I got out before taking a massive swing from Boulder, straight in the chest. I flew backward, slamming into the old station wagon, which crumbled like a sheet of paper as I struck it. I focused in time to see Boulder crush Salvo under the weight of his massive fist. Blood splattered everywhere as Salvo's head exploded beneath the force of the blow. Boulder shook his head as if seeing everything for the first time. Pure agony released as he fell to his knees screaming. "NO!" He pulled his friend's lifeless body to him, rocking as he screamed his name over and over again.

I got to my feet, disoriented from the blow, but energy coursed through me like a tidal wave. That's when I noticed a child-sized creature climbing up Boulder's back. It put its hands around Boulder's neck and the screaming stopped. He shoved Salvo's corpse off his lap and stood, turning to where Warden lay against the ruined tractor trailer.

I pulled the energy into a thin beam and targeted the clinging parasite. I didn't think I'd hurt Boulder but didn't want to chance a larger strike. With the precision of a surgeon, I struck. The thing screamed, falling to the ground. It thrashed a couple of times before righting itself and fleeing the scene.

Boulder came to, seeing Salvo again. Agony caused him to scream again and again, but we would have to deal with his grief, this loss...later. Abby and Dad still fought Tenji; the smaller man bounced around attacks like Tracer. I saw Izanami fighting a man who threw spikes at her as she advanced. I'm not sure what warned me, but I dodged left, just missing the glowing green of Grim Reaper's scythe.

He growled, taking another wild swipe at me as I danced back. I'd seen the results of the scythe in Blaze's memory and wasn't excited to experience it firsthand. I threw a blast of energy at him, but in my haste, it went wide.

"I'm going to enjoy gutting you, Ward." I knew Jose had never been a friend, but I thought we were on the same side against the Protectorate. Turns out I was wrong about everything where it concerned Grim Reaper. "You cost me a lot, and I'm gonna take it out of your *gringo* hide."

I grinned at him. "You're not man enough to take me down, Jose." I'd watched him goad Jon enough that I knew I could get under his skin. "You couldn't handle me with all the Syndicate around you."

He swung wildly as his anger took over. I dodged past one swing, which impaled itself in an old car husk. I uppercut him, adding some extra juice for payback. The same punch that had sent Jon flying barely moved him. He smiled, his teeth coated with blood. "I wish I'd taken some time with that *puta* before you got her, *murio*."

The backhanded sweep almost took my head off. I leaned back in time for it to pass in front of my face. I punched a blast of pure energy into his chest, launching him across the pavement. I started toward him, intent on finishing the bastard off once and for all. A noise reached me, causing me to pause and turn. Helicopters were landing around us as we fought. From above, a new floodlight illuminated the struggle. Everyone paused mid-fight as a voice boomed over the loudspeakers.

"Grim Reaper and all members of the Syndicate. You are under arrest by command of the Protectorate. Everyone lay down, hands behind your heads, and you will not be harmed."

Right, because the Protectorate never hurt Gifted. I saw troops forming in a circle around the building and parking lot. They carried plastic combat shields meant to stop electrical or fire attacks. This was bad, and we still had not freed Waxenby. Without my helmet, I couldn't communicate with my team. We had to get out of here and fast, but I had to get Waxenby at all costs. I turned to run into the hideout but didn't take the first step.

The scythe hit me in the back, and everything went dark.

"Tommy?" A feminine voice called to me from a million miles away. "Tommy, you need to focus."

I opened my eyes. Well, I would have if I'd been in my body. I held up my hand, seeing the translucent outline of my body. In front of me stood the ghostly shape of Raychel Downs, or as I knew her better, Pepper Spray.

"What happened?" Half memories flooded my dazed brain. Fighting Grim Reaper, the Reclaimers showing up, piercing pain in my back. "That bastard stabbed me in the back."

Pepper grabbed my intangible arms and shook me, though I'm not sure how, being a ghost and all. "You've got to focus, or you're going to die. Reaper pierced you with his scythe, but he hasn't severed your soul yet. You can still fight him."

I felt a tug from behind me. I glanced over my shoulder to see a ribbon of light twisting off into the gloom. I knew my body was tethered to the other end. The whole scene screamed of the surreal, like the painting with the melting clock in it.

"Where am I?" The landscape around us lacked any details, just an endless white expanse. "I can feel my heart beating, so I'm not dead."

Raychel solidified, the same face as the picture Blaze had shown me.

Her spiky orange hair enhanced her features in a way I couldn't define. Freckles lightly dotted her nose and cheeks, giving her a youthful appearance. Her eyes danced with the energy of a kid that was up to something they knew was wrong but funny. I bet she teased Blaze unmercifully.

"You're in the scythe as far as we can tell."

"We?"

She gestured over her shoulder. "There are a lot of us, but for some reason, I can move around in here better than the rest. I felt you enter when you were stabbed. You've got to get out of here while you still can."

"How do I do that?" My brain worked in slow motion, clouded with a fog I couldn't shake. "Do you know?"

Raychel shook her head. "How the hell would I know? You think I'd still be here if I did?" She paused for a minute. "Did you tell Blaze what I said?"

"I did. He thanked me, but I know it hurt." I didn't want to hurt her any more than she was, stuck in here with no way out. Never being able to see the sky or touch anything or taste your favorite food. "I'm sorry. When I lost Wendi, my world ended, and some days I think things will never be right again. I know he loves you."

Tears welled in her eyes, but not a single drop fell. "I'd give anything to see him again. I miss him so much. Time is weird in here, so sometimes it feels like yesterday and other times forever since I've seen him."

"I'm sorry, Raychel."

Her head jerked up at the mention of her name. The look of shock faded into a chagrined smile. "I guess my secret identity isn't important anymore. Just caught me off guard."

Way to go, Tommy. Freak the dead girl out. "Should I call you Pepper?"

"Yes, I don't care for my given name; too much baggage attached."

"I'm sorry," I stuttered, flustered by the numbness I felt in my head. "I didn't know. It's Pepper from now on."

"You say sorry a lot. How would you know? Blaze is the only one I've told."

"Oh, thanks," I said anxiously. Even dead, I couldn't get out of my own way. The whole place unnerved me, which I suppose was an effect of being trapped in a reality that didn't exist outside Grim Reaper's scythe. I'd never been any good at consoling people. Wendi, Abby, even Mom; I never thought of the right things to say or do to make them feel better. I could now add Pepper to the list.

"My father was a drug addict who made and sold his own supply. It's bad when a junkie can just make more when they need a fix. Unfortunately, he dealt to the daughter of one of the big shots in New York who had been marked off limits. He needed the money, and she was an easy mark." She stopped talking, lost in her memories.

"You don't need to tell me. I know it's painful to discuss your past; I know mine is." Thoughts of Wendi exploded in my brain. The way she looked, how she laughed, her lying on the floor of the Megadrome as the masses cheered while she died before them. I tamped them down; I needed to pay attention to what Pepper told me, not dwell on my pain.

"I have to get it off my chest if it's okay with you." I couldn't blame her. Sometimes the pain became so intense the only thing to do was vent it before it destroyed you. I knew the feeling all too well. To make it worse, she lived, if you could call it that, in the scythe of the man who'd killed her. How much worse could Hell be than this? I nodded for her to continue.

"Preash." She straightened her back as she pressed on with the story. It took guts to reveal a pain that had become part of you. "When the goon found out his daughter was dying from all the drugs, her docs needed a donor."

"Oh, no!" I gasped, hoping I was wrong.

She grimaced. "Yeah, and my piece of crap old man had a spare daughter laying around: me. He'd offed my mother the prior year but set it up like an OD to keep the pigs off his back. His new girlfriend hated me, so I was on my own. At thirteen, nuthin' I could do. Dad traded my organs for not being killed, though I heard they found him dead after the guy's kid OD'ed on prescription drugs."

It never ceased to amaze me how terrible people could be to one another. All the people who'd been hurt over things outside their control. Pepper hadn't wanted a junkie parent, nor to be sold off for spare parts.

"The doctors left me for dead. One of the nurses took me to Doc Campbell, who'd been working on man-machine interfacing. He ran a human chop shop, so he had the opportunity to experiment on me without interference. Whatever the reason, he saved me by bolting on a lot of cybernetic parts."

She stopped, but I waited since I didn't think she had finished her story. For once, I made the right choice. She cleared her throat and continued. "Campbell fostered me with a family to help me recover. He needed to protect his investment. They were good people, and for the first time, somebody gave a shit about me. It didn't last, never does. Just after I turned eighteen, a bunch of toughs took me from my bedroom in the middle of the night. I found out later Campbell sold me to a Cartel to be an enforcer and drug mule. Dr. Campbell put a sealed case in my gut which could transport contraband undetected. Bastard put in an explosive plug that would kill me if I didn't do as I was told. The Cartel's leader, Jerrico, trained me to be an assassin. I had more surgeries to enhance my abilities and make me more useful. I killed a lot of people for them until I ran up against Jackhammer. He beat me, and the Tech Guy removed the plug and freed me. He introduced me to Death Adder and Blaze, who were assembling a team. It's how I ended up working on Stryke Force."

She blinked a few times as if waking up from a nap. "You didn't need to hear all that. We should be finding a way to get you out of here and back to your body."

The fog in my head had dissipated to the point where I could think. "Can I follow my tether back to my body?"

She shrugged. "Try it. He severed mine so fast I didn't have a chance to return."

I pulled on the tether. Nothing happened. I used it as a lead and I walked, but nothing changed. I did everything I could think of, but I was still in the empty void of the scythe. Despair raised its ugly head as my ideas ran out.

Pepper's yelp seized my attention. "You've got to fight. He's coming." She stepped around me as if to hide from the intruder.

A figure floated toward me as I stood there. Its black robes hung straight, unmoving as it came at me, gleaming, steel scythe held in its bony hands. The skeletal face peeked out from under the heavy hood that covered its head. I'd seen this image a million times around Halloween, but the chill of death radiated off it like cold in the frozen food section of the grocery store.

I swallowed hard, trying to find my voice. My mouth lacked even a touch of moisture as the undead eyes focused on me. "You've been called. Your time is up, mortal." Its voice sounded raspy and harsh with no emotion whatsoever. "Come with me." It began to turn, expecting me to obey.

"The only place I'm going is back to my body to kill Grim Reaper once and for all." I wish my voice hadn't quivered at the end but facing down death isn't easy.

Slowly it revolved until it faced me. "I see. I will sever your soul, and you will serve with the rest." It glided across the intervening space, raising the scythe as it went.

I focused, reaching for the energy I felt surging back in my body, but nothing happened. The power couldn't follow me here. The panic rose in me. How could I fight death without my Gift? The scythe descended; I instinctively moved, pulling the tether out of the path of Death's weapon. It snarled at me as it advanced again.

Pepper spoke from behind me. "The rules of the physical world don't apply here. Use your mind to fight him."

My mind? Marcel would say it wasn't a fair fight since I'd be unarmed. Armed? I thought of Gladiator's sword, and it solidified in my hand. Luckily, Blaze had taught us swordplay in training, since you never knew who you'd end up fighting or what would be around to fight with. I parried the next blow, catching it on the blade.

"Mortal, your time has ended. Allow me to complete your passage and be done." The skeletal mouth never moved as the words come out. It creeped me out.

"Why don't you just put that stick back up your ass?" I swung at his head, only to be parried so hard I almost lost my sword. I needed to focus more on the fight and less on the semi-witty banter. We traded blows, but my sword passed through him without even ruffling his robes. We could stay like this for all eternity, at least until my tether severed.

I could feel the power residing in my body, and while I couldn't pull it here, maybe I could bring it into being like I did with the sword. I retreated a few paces, threw the sword at Skeletor, which he easily dodged, and imagined a fireball. I couldn't do this in the real world, but here it worked. I pitched the ball at him, striking him squarely in the chest. Flame burst over him, flaring up to consume his head. The fire grew then disappeared.

"I am not of your world, Mortal." The last word was loaded with dismissal like a worm he'd step on if he so chose. "Only things of my world can harm me."

His world? Did Death have a world? Death. A thought crossed my mind. "Pepper, help me."

Pepper ran to my side. I grasped her hand. "Call to the others Grim Reaper has killed."

"They can't come here. I told you that."

Death closed the distance between us, readying the scythe. This would work or I was toast. And who wanted to be toast? "Just do it."

"Gabriella, Mark, George, Ron, Amanda, Meghan..." She kept on calling names as I concentrated on what I wanted to do.

The scythe rose above my head, readied the final blow. "As I said, you..."

A woman rose out of the ground before him, dressed in a colorful, patterned skirt with an embroidered white blouse. She wore an elaborate headdress of flowers. Death stopped as she confronted him.

"Jose has gone too far, killing an *el niño*. I will not allow this." She turned toward us. Her face had the elaborate design I'd seen around the Day of the Dead celebrations some of the Redemption kids held. Her eyes burned with a ghostly blue flame.

Death raised his weapon. "Gabriella, this is none of your concern. Be gone."

"No." She stretched out her arms, lifting them to the sky. Death gasped as the first hand broke through the ground below. The hand grasped the hem of its robe, pulling it downward. I yanked Pepper back as bodies broke through the floor, between Gabriella and their killer. Boney swiped his weapon through them, but they were already dead, so it had no effect. She laughed as the mob surrounded him, played pile-on, and drove him to the ground.

Gabriella faced us. "Please, go. Only pain lives on here." Her head bowed to her chest as the tears fell.

I still held Pepper Spray's hand. "Thank you, Gabriella. I couldn't have stopped him."

Her eyes locked on mine. "I loved him long ago, but it wasn't enough. God has punished me to this hell. Now leave me to my pain."

The fire in her eyes intensified until they glowed a solid blue. Her form grew darker, more menacing, as black clouds billowed around her legs. "Go!"

The force of the words struck me like a burst of lava. My body blew apart until I could no longer feel anything other than Pepper's hand in mine.

The last thing I saw was the gaping abyss that stretched out before me.

33

Opening my eyes for real this time, I was happy to see a fully formed body holding me up. I pivoted to face Grim Reaper, only to find him out cold on the ground behind me. His scythe had disappeared, not that I expected to take it from him.

Well, it went better than expected. Honestly, I wasn't sure you had it in you.

I froze. The voice I heard in my head wasn't mine.

Hey, pay attention. You're in the middle of a fight, dolt. A bullet whizzed past my head to emphasize the point.

"Pepper?" I asked to the empty air. I wondered if I'd lost it coming back from the dead. Maybe my mind had finally cracked from the strain.

Yeah, but you've got company. At least her voice didn't echo like in an abandoned building.

I concentrated on the situation, which hadn't changed since I'd left. Reclaimers flanked us on two sides. Boulder rested on his knees next to his friend, dead at his hands. Bullets dotted the air as the troops gathered behind the Ceramiplas shields. We couldn't defend the parking lot, and we hadn't gotten to Waxenby yet. Lose him and, if Eiraf spoke the truth, nothing we did mattered. Time to rally the troops.

"Boulder, get Warden and follow me!" He didn't move, just stared at Salvo's corpse. I grabbed his chin and turned his face to me. "Warden is hurt, and we are all going to be dead if you don't get moving. Mourn later; we need to fight now."

Recognition dawned as he nodded. "You're right." He gathered Warden up in his arms and jogged along behind me.

"Abby, get Grim Reaper and let's go."

She stared at me, mouth open in shock. "That rat bastard can rot for all I care."

Keep going; it's not over yet. Pepper said, unheard by anyone else than me. Every day, my life got stranger.

How do you think I feel? I'm stuck in here with no way out.

I swear she was laughing at me.

I am, she replied. *I can hear your thoughts, you know?*

I wanted to beat my head against the pavement. "The Reclaimers think we're Syndicate. We may need him to bargain with."

That got her moving. Selling Jose to the Protectorate for a trip to Saturday Night Showdown would be worth carrying his limp form. In a few seconds, she secured his arms with a zip tie I didn't know she had and hoisted him over her shoulder. Izanami ran to meet us as we reached the steps of the Syndicate hideout. Dad settled down next to us as we entered.

Just as Specter had described, Oliver Waxenby sat in a steel chair, head slumped against his chest. He'd never been a big man, but he appeared skeletal strapped to the chair as he was.

Abby threw Grim Reaper on the floor and started untying Waxenby. She caught me watching and scowled. "If I'm carrying anyone out of here, it's him."

Wow, he looks like shit.

I didn't know if I'd get used to having a second person in my head, but it would have to wait.

Dad came over to where I stood, pulling off his helmet so we could talk. "Your mother told me to tell you she's supergluing a comm-link to your ear next time." He glanced around the room. Boulder had Warden sitting up, her head lolled to the side. Izanami stood guard over the two of them, quietly surveying the room. Abby had found a bottle of water and was helping Waxenby drink. "This is bad. We look more like the walking wounded than an elite Gifted team."

Unfortunately, I agreed. "Where is Mom?" I wasn't sure how we were getting out of this mess, but she could get us to safety.

"I sent her and Molly to the safe room. We need a plan." Dad rubbed his forehead. "There are at least three platoons out there. If they bring in more helicopters, we aren't getting out of here."

Even with the shields, Dad and I should be able to cut a path through the troops to get us out.

Wow, that's the best plan you've got? The sarcasm dripped off like glaze on a donut. *What about the others? Do you think they will make it while you go out with guns blazin'?* An image of a cowboy blasting away with two pistols surfaced in my head, right up until a bullet hole appeared in his forehead.

Well, if you can do better, I thought at her.

I'm just a lowly passenger on the S.S. Minnow. You're the Captain. She paused for a second. *Nah, you're Gilligan.*

What are you talking about? How any of this helped, I didn't know.

Never mind, you're too dense to get it.

"Tommy?" Dad asked. I guessed it wasn't the first time he'd tried to get my attention.

"Just thinking." I looked around the room. Pepper had it right; fighting our way out would be a bad decision. "Did Specter say this used to be a bank?"

Warden pipped up from where she sat on the floor, leaning against Boulder for support. "Yes, it was. Why?"

"I don't see a vault." The bank in Granite Falls had the vault behind the teller line. The one in Redemption had it in the main room.

"It's in the basement." Boulder helped Warden to her feet. She swayed a bit but steadied herself enough to approach us. "What are you thinking?"

A thought popped into my head.

Me likey that plan. Pepper purred in my brain.

"I think I know a way we can get out of here."

Warden grinned.

About a half hour later, I stepped out of the old bank building into the night air. "I want to discuss terms of surrender!"

I waited for a bullet to hit me or the sound of rushing footsteps, but none came. The clouds still roiled, but the rain had mostly stopped. A few minutes later, an older woman approached. She wore the standard issue Reclaimer combat gear, but I noticed the pin that marked her as a major. We had gotten someone's attention.

"I'm Major Black of the hundred and fourth terrorist response unit. I've come to accept your unconditional surrender." I heard a slight Midwestern accent, so she must be from the North Central Region.

I cocked my head at her, hand holding my chin with a perplexed expression on my face. It would have been easier to pull off if Pepper hadn't been cackling wildly in my head at the time. "Unconditional? I don't remember offering that. Hmmm. Maybe you are in the wrong place, Lieutenant?"

She stiffened. Military officers hate to have civilians downgrade their rank. Powell always bristled when it happened to him. "First off, it's MAJOR, not Lieutenant. Second, we have you surrounded with crack troops, trained in removing threats such as yourself. There will be no conditions. Surrender now." She smirked self-satisfyingly at me as if she'd won already.

"I know you are currently a Major." I held her eye, making her sweat out the answer. "But Lieutenant is what you'll be when you report in that Grim Reaper is dead, which he will be by the time your troops can get to him."

Her face blanched as she processed what I told her. Dad had guessed it would be the main objective of this raid. "So, you want a few more shiny medals, then we give you what you want, and we get what we want."

She cleared her throat, but it didn't help. "And you want what?" she asked, much less confidently than she'd started this conversation.

"We want safe passage out of here." I spread my hands out in front of her. "See how easy that is. We walk, you raid the building and grab Grim Reaper. Protectorate himself will probably give you a medal."

The glint in her eye gave her away. "I'll have to discuss this with my superior officer. I'll return within the hour." She turned on her heel and marched across the space to where her team stood by.

Applause sounded in my head. *Bravo, that was magnifique, Thomas,* Pepper said in a thick accent followed by a kissing noise. *You deserve a Tony for that performance.*

I was baffled. *Who's Tony?*

Never mind.

Warden looked far better than when we brought her in. "How did it go?"

I smiled. "She took it faster than I would have thought." I walked behind the teller line to a door leading to the basement. The vault door and all its valuables were untouched, but we had what we needed. Boulder, Dad, and Abby were in front of the concrete wall across from the vault door. It had the distinction of being closest to the street and, by extension, the sewer main that ran under it. Abby had spotted the manhole cover out front.

Boulder turned to face me. "Are you sure this will work?" I could see his red-rimmed eyes and understood. I knew the pain and guilt he'd face in the months ahead, but we needed an exit and soon.

"I hope so. If we can tunnel through and get into the sewer system, we can get back to base and out of here." I checked each person, and they nodded at me. "When I yell, dig like hell."

"Tommy, we've got a problem up here," Warden yelled.

"Coming." I turned to Dad. "Wait until my signal. If they hear the noise, they'll rush us."

Dad smirked. "Unless I missed my guess, they are testing us now. Go."

I ran. Taking the stairs three at a time, I got upstairs and into the lobby. Warden and Izanami crouched in front of the windows. Most of the floodlights the Syndicate used still functioned. A squad of eight soldiers, armed with Ceramiplas shields and stun sticks, approached the front. I knelt next to Izanami to watch.

"Ranger says they are testing us." I watched as the Reclaimers approached the building. A full rush would have worked with half our team downstairs, but they didn't know it.

Izanami stood up. "I'll dissuade them."

I put a hand on her and removed it when she shot me a glare.

"I'll come, too. We can work together."

"I work alone. Just watch for disruptor bands." She pulled her long, straight black hair back and fastened it. She exited the building and stopped about ten feet past the doors. The squad halted, obviously not expecting a petite Asian woman to greet them alone outside their target. "The weak are meat; the strong eat," she said to them.

Watching carefully, I spotted the one with the disruptor launcher. I aimed and sent a thin line of energy at it. The gun flew from its owner's grip. Smoke drifted off it where it lay in the street.

Izanami shimmered slightly before launching herself into the squad of soldiers. I expected a smooth flowing attack like I'd seen Blaze execute a hundred times.

I couldn't have been more wrong.

Izanami became a wrecking ball. Stun sticks bounced off her, as did the men who wielded them. As she waded into the middle of them, she tore a shield from one of the soldiers. He screamed as his arm stayed attached to the shield. The severed arm flew while she used the shield to batter the closest attacker until it cracked. Discarding the broken shield, Izanami drop-kicked a man twice her size, knocking down two of his squad mates as he fell. She landed back on her feet and throat punched an unfortunate soldier who'd tried to stun her. Before he could even attempt a gasp for air, she performed a Reverse Piledriver and slammed the man's head into the pavement. Two Reclaimers moved in to attack in tandem. Her hand whipped out, grabbing a smaller woman by the chest plate. A series of quick revolutions and the soldier sailed across the intervening space to crash into her partner. A couple of well-placed kicks ended their struggling to get off the ground. Screams of pain and fear erupted from the remaining soldiers, the best the Reclaimers had according to Warden's people.

The severed arm splatted outside the window, coming to rest. *OMG, that's gross.*

I had to agree with Pepper.

Warden and I watched for a few more moments before Izanami strode back into the building. I ran over to meet her and make sure she wasn't hurt.

Who the hell could hurt her? Did you see her tear that guy's arm off? I ignored my personal play-by-play commentator.

"It is done," was all she said. She shimmered slightly, and then I noticed bruises and burn marks growing across her skin. She noticed me noticing. "I must pay for my Gift after I've used it. I will heal."

I nodded. We all paid a price for our Gifts. "Can I ask where you learned to fight like that?"

She looked at me oddly. "WWE, of course."

Pepper burst into laughter, and I joined her for a moment. Izanami winked at me before sliding against the wall to rest.

Warden limped over. "She'll be fine."

I nodded. "Can you call up a huge storm? We need a distraction."

"I think so, if the energy hasn't dissipated from earlier." She strode to the windows, and a few minutes later the rain and wind started until you couldn't have heard a freight train going by. I ran to the basement. Boulder smashed the wall repeatedly; Abby and Dad cleared the debris as they went. I hoped we would be gone in under an hour.

Returning to the lobby, I thought I'd better check on Waxenby. Abby had been taking care of him, but with us needing to build a tunnel out of here, I picked up the duty. As I knelt next to him, his eyes opened, and he stared at me.

"Mr. Waxenby, it's Tommy. Do you know who I am?"

His eyes focused in the low light. "Tommy, where are we?"

"In Dallas. We rescued you from the Syndicate." Hope rose in my chest that he'd be okay once we got him away from here. Then the laughing started.

"You'll never get away. No matter what happens, there is no escape!" He screamed, froth coming to the corners of his mouth. His shouts echoed through the room until he collapsed back into the oblivion that held him. It freaked me out.

We finally had Waxenby back. Time would tell if there was any of him left in the shell we'd rescued.

34

The storm raged outside as the work underground progressed. The wailing of the wind reminded me of the old cartoons when they wanted something to be spooky. The four shattered windows didn't help keep us dry or lessen the noise. Warden's color had faded to waxen pale. I didn't think she could hold out much longer.

Dad tapped me on the back, causing me to jump. I hadn't heard him with all the storm noise. He gave me the thumbs-up. A very dirty Boulder came to get Warden. She nodded but slapped his hand away when he tried to pick her up. She pointed at Izanami, who glared and rose to her feet with barely a wobble.

Abby, no less dirty than Boulder, had Waxenby slung over her shoulder. She smiled at me, and I returned it. We had accomplished what we'd set out to do. Boulder and Izanami came over to me. I indicated the wrestler should follow Abby and motioned Boulder to carry Grim Reaper. As much as I hated him for what he'd done to us, I wasn't leaving him for the Reclaimers to capture and hand over to the Protectorate.

I stopped next to the unconscious Grim Reaper. It took all I had not to kick him in the face.

It's not worth it. I could feel Pepper's anger, her voice clear in my head, but it didn't stop her from doing the right thing. *Believe me, I know it's tempting, Tommy.*

I sighed. Sometimes playing by the rules the other side ignored sucked.

A light flared around us as the storm noise dropped to nothing. Everyone in the room froze except for me. On the other side of Reaper stood an amazingly beautiful woman. Silver hair flowed down to her waist, partially covering what was surely a very expensive black dress. The sheer material hugged her curves in all the right places; the neckline plunged to her navel, revealing her large...

Hey, wake up. I know you're a teenage boy, but this isn't normal.

I guiltily jerked my eyes up to see sparkling violet eyes set into her beautiful face. "It is so good to see you again," she said, her accent thick and drawling. "You are very handsome, and you have steel in you. I see why Eiraf chose you for her cause."

Eiraf? What the hell is the Natasha knock-off talking about? Pepper sounded confused. *This whole moose and squirrel schtick is so old. Snap out of it, will you please.*

I shook my head. I'd never get used to magic as long as I lived. "Who are you?"

A low, deep laugh answered me. "Surge, I am distraught you don't remember me. Our lovely dance together. I am Yelena." Her voice almost purred as she pulled me in.

The dream cascaded back. The dancing, the horrible murals on the walls. "You stabbed me."

"Let us not worry about such trifles." She smiled as if we were discussing the weather.

Are we in some sick S&M fantasy? Pepper exploded in my head. *You need to torch this bitch quick.*

Yelena cocked her head like a bird considering which worm to eat first. "Who speaks to you? This is unexpected but matters not."

"You're very pretty. What do you need?" My mouth started to engage itself; unfortunately, my brain hadn't rebooted yet.

Really!!!! That's all you've got? I'm stuck in a testosterone-laden moron. God, I'm glad I'm a woman.

"You are a good boy." Yelena patted my cheek before pointing to the unconscious Grim Reaper. "I come for this one; I still have need of him."

"What?" Reality flooded back in, replacing the confusion I'd felt.

Oh, good! You've finally joined the party, Pepper snapped at me.

"No, you can't take him. He's got to pay for what he's done to us."

Yelena smiled like I was an idiot child until she realized I had broken free of her hold. The icy glare of anger pierced me like a sword. "Ah, there it is." She made a grasping gesture with her hand, and Reaper vanished from view. "A free piece of advice. Stay out of things you don't understand. I'd hate to hurt a pretty boy like you." She blew me a kiss and disappeared.

The storm noise assaulted my poor ears when it returned. Seeing the body still missing in this version of reality, I signaled Boulder to follow me.

Pepper was annoyed. *Boy, you showed her who's boss. A few more minutes and you'd have been licking her boots.*

Enough, I don't know what happened, but she isn't with the Council. I couldn't even summon Makeda or Alyx to discuss this with. She'd mentioned Eiraf, so she had to be part of the Order of Midnight.

Pepper's confusion was palatable. *What are you talkin' about?*

I'll explain it to you later. We need to get out of here.

Boulder made a slashing gesture and pointed at the space Reaper had occupied. I shrugged. Boulder frowned, but he accompanied me as I went through the door to the stairs. Dad fused the door shut, and we all headed to our planned escape route. I had to duck to get through the hole they had made through the wall, which opened out on to the old sewage tunnels. Water poured from the street grates like a million waterfalls. Boulder moved everyone away from the opening, then Dad collapsed the tunnel with a stream of lightning. The storm above would slacken without Warden to keep it going.

"Everyone alright?" Dad asked, checking each of us. A ball of lightning hovered above his hand, providing us with light. We'd gotten Waxenby, but I felt like we lost. From the dirt, bruises, and blood, we looked like we lost. "Where's Grim Reaper?"

Pepper prodded me. *You're on. Try not to screw it up.*

Thanks. "He got away. Our legless friend can explain it to us later."

I could see the unasked questions in Dad's eyes; then a light flicked on. "Oh." He dropped any other questions. "Boulder, can you get us to the safehouse?"

"I can." Boulder turned and walked into the darkness. Dad followed with the light so the rest of us could see. My body ached from fighting;

my head ached from the encounter with Death and having a stowaway locked inside. I needed a giant Mountain Dew, a hundred Pop-Tarts, and a month of sleep.

We came to a place where two branches of the sewer system joined. Boulder held up a fist in front of us. "Drop the light. Nobody move a muscle."

Dad extinguished the light, plunging us into darkness. I heard a faint scraping noise as we stood there like statues in a cemetery. The sound got louder as we waited. Ahead of us, phosphorescent mold grew on the walls, bathing the tunnel in an eerie green that reminded me of Grim Reaper's scythe. I ignored the instinct to run from the mold as my heart sped up in full flight mode. Something big moved.

I held my breath as a head the size of a truck paused in the intersection, forked tongue licking the air, cold dead eyes peering into the gloom. At that moment, Mom not being here turned out to be a blessing. She is phobic about snakes. Her screaming and running away wouldn't have been the best strategy.

Slowly, the behemoth decided nothing good was around and slithered off, away from us. I guess Warden hadn't been kidding about the snakes. We waited for the train of scale and muscle to pass, like at a grade crossing minus the barrier guards and the annoying bell. The tail finally passed. No rattle. Just a giant water snake, if my guess was right.

"You can light the way now," Boulder said as if nothing had happened. We took the passage the snake had emerged from.

Whoa! That was intense-a-rama. What the hell was that thing?

Weird stuff happens in the destroyed cities. I pictured the rats in D.C. and the croc outside of Atlanta.

Ewww, I hate rats. I could feel Pepper's revulsion. *Looked like a close call. You guys have certainly screwed the world up since I've been gone.*

For the Gifted, it's incredibly messed up. I wondered if the Norms would agree with that. With one government, there weren't any wars; the Gifted were collared, eliminating the collateral damage from powered fights. Things for the Norms were better, though they weren't free, but was anyone ever truly free?

You need to boot these Protectorate goons. Bust out the Gifted. You'd be a freaking hero.

I don't know. Right now, we are trying to get Waxenby someplace safe. It shocked me a bit to realize I had no plans beyond getting back to Castle. Had I ever had a plan? In Redemption, I had limited choices. Granite Falls offered a few more, but most jobs Gifted did were either menial or dangerous. Was being a janitor or working in a grocery store better than working in the mines or the smelting factories? The people who hired Gifted wanted cheap, replaceable workers. In a flash of understanding, I realized something that bounced loudly in my head. *My future died the day I was collared.*

That royally sucks. Grim Reaper liked the new world order, but he's scum.

Could you talk to him like you do me? Trapped in his cesspool of a mind would have been a cruel fate for anyone. I focused on walking for a minute while we climbed a set of stairs back to the safehouse where Mom and Molly were hopefully hidden.

Boulder found a latch and opened the door. It swung in smoothly, barely a whisper of sound escaped.

A sharp metallic noise came from beyond the door. "Step in slowly, hands where I can see them." Mom. I released the breath I hadn't realized I'd been holding. She was safe.

Dad stepped through the door first, pulling off his helmet as he went in. She slung the gun over her shoulder and hugged him fiercely. Warden led the rest of us into the cavernous supply room. Mom seized me in her iron bear hug, then checked me for wounds. For a small woman, she could crush you good. Abby had her turn in the hug-o-matic and body scanner, once she'd set an unconscious Waxenby against the wall.

Warden, Izanami, Molly, and Specter had a much different reunion. Salvo's death was reported, and Molly wept while tears ran down Specter's face. Boulder stood apart from the group, head bowed. Warden said something else to the group. Molly ran and threw herself at Boulder. He flinched but caught her.

"It's not your fault," she said around her sobs. "Those bastards killed him."

Boulder's shoulder slumped. "No, I killed my best friend. I couldn't stop myself." Tears streamed as he held Molly as gently as a porcelain doll.

I turned away to give them some privacy.

Pepper wasn't having any of that. *You shot that thing off his back. You need to tell him, so he knows what happened.*

I'll tell them later. I didn't want to intrude on their grief. We had to get back to Atlanta and then to Castle.

I swear she kicked me in the brain as pain shot through my head. *Do it now, Tommy. Sometimes there is no tomorrow!*

Okay, I will. Stop whatever it is you're doing. Geez. My own personal Jiminy Cricket is a pain in the ass.

"Excuse me." All eyes turned to me. Boulder released Molly even though they both still cried. "Um, so during the fight, I saw Boulder." I ran a hand over my face trying to think of how to phrase it. "Well, I saw him…"

Warden came to my rescue. "When Salvo died?"

I flushed. How could I be so bad at speaking to people? "Yes, ma'am. Just after it happened, I saw something clinging to Boulder's back. I shot it, and Boulder returned to normal. I think it controlled Boulder, made him do it."

Warden laid her hand on Boulder's arm. "Pull it together, Boulder. There will be time to mourn once we're safe. The same thing happened to me. I couldn't control the storm while it had me."

I might be able to help. Grim Reaper used a Gifted called Parasite. I don't know the details, but Reaper used him to control others when he wanted them to do something they wouldn't.

That would explain what happened. I repeated what Pepper had told me, though I spun it like I'd heard Reaper ordering Parasite around.

"Well, that explains a lot," Dad said as he watched Waxenby. "I wondered how they got Oliver to use his shields to protect Grim Reaper."

Warden turned to me. "Speaking of Grim Reaper, where is he?"

"Gone," I said, not wanting to explain what had happened.

Warden's eyebrows shot up. "Gone? GONE? You're going to have to do better than that. One of the most dangerous Gifted around and all you've got is gone?"

I froze, not knowing what to say. Dad pulled me aside, telling Warden. "Give us a minute, please."

Warden's face reddened. "I don't think so. You big-time heroes always leave us out but not anymore. If we're working together, then no more secrets. I lost a man tonight."

Mom moved between us, but Dad held up his hands. "Everyone calm down. Susan, can you check Oliver?" Mom glared at him but went to do as he asked. "Unless I'm mistaken, Tommy is protecting one of our friends. If you'll give me a moment with my son, I'll clear things up."

"Make it fast." Warden stalked to her team, a thunderhead of pent-up fury. If death rays had shot from her eyes, destroying me, it wouldn't be a surprise.

Mom and Abby stood close by watching. I didn't miss the fact that Mom had her hand on her pistol.

Dad put his head close to mine. "This is about the Council?"

"Yeah." I kept my voice low, trying not to be overheard. "Some woman, she called herself Yelena, took him. She mentioned Eiraf picking me for her cause. She must be part of the Order of Midnight. She said she wasn't done using Grim Reaper."

I glanced over to see Warden's face as she stared daggers at me. We couldn't afford to lose her trust, but I'd promised Alyx as well.

Dad rubbed his eyes. "Handing out tactical details is usually on a need-to-know basis, but given the circumstances, we'll have to concede this is necessary. I'll try to cover this, but I doubt she'll accept an explanation from me. Tommy, stick to the basic story and leave out the more interesting details. We can fulfill her request without divulging everything we know."

I nodded. We returned to face the group.

"It's as I thought, we were asked not to discuss this particular matter."

Warden cut him off. "Isn't that convenient?"

Dad interrupted before she could go any farther. "But you are right. You've fought and bled with us and deserve to know what happened. I can explain it."

"No, I want to hear it from Tommy. Sorry, Ranger, but I'm done trusting you until I get some real answers."

Heat poured off Mom. "You listen here…"

"Enough. I'll explain as much as I can." This had to stop before it got any worse. I checked my parents. Dad gave me his 'I tried' look and stepped back. It took Mom a few extra seconds before she nodded, but it didn't stop the glare she shot Warden.

Pepper and I had a brief aside. *You've got this. I saw what happened; there was nuthin' you could do.*

You mean there was nothing a male could do.

Pepper laughed, and it helped loosen me up.

I cleared my throat, collecting my thoughts. "After the fight, I went to check on Grim Reaper. While I was there, a woman appeared—"

"Appeared?" Warden sounded a lot like Mom when she badgered a witness on the stand. I fought back a smile as I realized this wasn't any different than dealing with Mom when she was angry.

"Yes, ma'am. The sound of the storm stopped, and a woman appeared next to Grim Reaper. She goes by Yelena."

Molly cocked her head, a very birdlike gesture. I wondered if she took on attributes of the animals she became. "Was she a Gifted? I haven't heard her name before."

"I don't think so." I glanced at Dad, and he nodded for me to continue. "I think she's a warlock like Alyx the Summoner. She told me she needed Reaper for her plans, so she took him and vanished after that."

Warden's eyes narrowed a moment before nodding. "Oh, I've met Alyx before, so I see where you're coming from. I don't like it, but..." She let out a deep breath before continuing. "Did she give any indication of her plans?"

The conversation may have gone on, but a red flashing light and a low alarm went off in the safehouse.

Molly's face had lost all its color. "The base is under attack. We've got to help."

Warden jerked open the far door leading to the truck.

And just like that, conversation over, and we were all running.

35

Everyone dove into the truck. Waxenby, still unconscious, laid out in the bed with the four of us. Boulder drove a lot faster than Salvo had on the way in. We reached the enormous metal doors in minutes. The alarm blared out its warning as we got out of the truck.

Warden jumped out of the passenger seat and made a run for the door, but Dad restrained her. "Have Specter check out the situation; we need to know what we're facing."

She tried to pull her arm away, but Dad's grip didn't budge.

"If we lose the translocator, everyone in the Underground dies. I'm not going to let that happen."

"Neither are we, but if we are all killed walking into an ambush, we can't help anyone else."

"Fine." Warden snapped. In the backseat of the truck, Specter had already dropped into a trance.

After a few seconds, she climbed out of the truck. "The Reclaimers haven't breached the far doorway yet, but they are close. They are evacuating all the non-Gifted."

Warden's grim smile answered her. "Excellent, they are executing the plan."

Specter wasn't finished. "Warden, they have some mechanical monstrosity outside the door. We need to get out of here."

"I'm not abandoning my people to die here." She ripped her arm from Dad's hand. "I'm going to fight."

"You aren't thinking." Specter straightened herself before she got in her face. "We aren't outside. You are powerless down here. You need to get the people out and destroy the translocator before it falls into the Reclaimer's hands. If they get control of a working translocator, they can access every Underground base we have."

Warden nodded curtly, but she stopped arguing.

Dad agreed. "I'll take Tommy, Boulder, Izanami, and Abby. We'll hold the door while you get your people out of here. Get Susan, Molly, and Waxenby back to Atlanta. We'll hold until you signal us everyone is clear. Susan, you've got the rear-guard action, just like Blaze laid out in training. Sound the horns, and we'll get out and blow the translocator."

Warden's face reddened as if she'd explode soon. "I don't like it, but it makes sense. Let's go."

Abby threw Waxenby over her shoulder, and we got through the outer door. A golf cart sat there with a terrified teen at the wheel. "Warden, they told me to wait here in case you returned."

Abby got to the cart and strapped Waxenby into a seat before joining us. She cracked her knuckles, spoiling for a fight.

Mom finished hugging each of us and said, "Be safe." She climbed into the back next to a strapped in Waxenby, unslinging her rifle and readying it for action.

Warden jumped in the passenger seat. "Thank you, Gerome. You did well." Molly perched on the footboard as Warden told Gerome, "Get us to the munitions dump."

Dad motioned us into a circle. "I'll take the lead. Tommy and Abby on my right, Izanami and Boulder on the left. No heroes, we hold the door until the rest are safe. We'll get revenge when it's on our terms."

He directed the last at Boulder, who nodded back.

Izanami led us through the streets making up the base, past people carrying what they could as they ran to the translocator. The boom of the Reclaimers battering the door could be easily heard now. We turned a corner, stopping as we saw the thirty-foot metal door, the only thing standing between the Reclaimers and us. We spread out, giving each other enough room to maneuver.

The area around the door was clear back to the walls, allowing the doors to be swung open without striking a building. At about forty feet back stood low buildings that had the look of homes. A basketball hoop here, roller skates sitting next to the front door over there. Each building had been painted in lively colors to brighten the confines of living underground.

You did good back there. Pepper's cheerful voice seemed out of place considering the situation.

Thanks. I'm not very good at speaking to people.

Get outta here. She laughed, giving me the equivalent of a mental hug. *You think they could make any more noise out there? It's like sitting on a jackhammer.*

I shook my head, but it was giving me a headache. With a rapid boom, boom, boom, boom, the door creaked before it toppled over, crashing to the ground. Dust billowed out, covering us with grime. I wished I'd had my helmet, but as far as I knew, Turk was still fused to it.

Reclaimers fired as they ran in. Boulder went to one knee, arm up and expanding to protect himself from the gunfire. His free hand threw chunks of rock at the oncoming army. I saw a head burst from the impact of his projectiles.

Dad launched into the air, fanning lightning across the front row of soldiers. Nothing happened. They ran through the arcs of electricity unharmed. I could see why. The Reclaimers were encased in a non-metal armor than left no skin exposed.

Abby roared as she charged, growing over seven feet. One of the troops dropped to one knee, firing a disrupter band at her, but the arcing electricity Dad laid down destroyed it mid-flight. Abby and Izanami crashed against the advancing troops. I ran behind them, using my energy to enhance my punches. Armor and bones cracked under the assault. Boulder slammed his colossal arm into anyone that got too close, shattering whatever it hit. Dad swooped around and destroyed the disruptors before they could be launched against us. A few minutes later, we stood in the middle of a junkyard of broken men and armor.

Dad landed next to us. "Specter said they had a mechanical monstrosity, but all they sent in were foot soldiers."

Is the ground supposed to look like that?

Like what? But then I saw it. A faint green haze slithered across the ground. Too late, I knew what it was. "Turk is here." I promptly vomited as the poison seeped into my system. Dad tried to take off, but he fell to the ground, spewing the contents of his stomach as well.

From the shadows of the door came Turk, green miasma spreading out in front of him. "You thought you'd killed me, didn't you, Ward?" I noticed the charred remains of his hands minus a few fingers from each. "I cut a deal with the Protectorate. I help them take out the Underground once and for all, and I go free."

Tommy, you've got to get up. They'll kill us if they capture you. Panic laced Pepper's voice. The sickness continued making me retch even though there was nothing left.

I'm trying, but I can't feel my power.

Forget your powers. Just get up.

I pushed myself up from the ground. "Make sure they give you a ring for your service. It will look great with your new manicure."

"Funny, asshole," Turk said as he kicked me in the ribs, flipping me over. Shadows of Brunner's beating raced through my mind. If I could get out of the green mist, I could fight back.

"I guess you'll need a hand taking a piss from now on, huh?" Another kick in the stomach. *Just a bit farther.*

"The Protectorate wants you alive, but the Reclaimers are okay with a couple of fatalities, so shut it before I shift to poison and off your sorry, murdering ass."

"I've got to hand it to you, never thought you'd lick the Protectorate's balls for him. Always thought you were more of a hand job kind of guy."

Turk pulled back to kick again, but then he noticed he'd stopped pumping out toxins since he lost his temper. A thicker stream poured off his ruined hands, bubbling across the floor. "Nice try, Ward. It almost worked, but I'll have the last laugh."

The sickness returned full force. The sounds of retching came from all around me. *I'd tried and failed.*

Keep trying; you almost had it.

I knew, and so did Pepper, it wouldn't work a second time.

Turk barked a bitter laugh. "I'm going to enjoy watching you pay for what you did to Uncle Jack."

I heard a shrill noise from above Turk. He'd been talking, so he didn't hear it. I needed to distract him, so I flipped him off.

"That's the best you can do, I'm so disapp—" He heard the sound I had noticed far too late.

As a falcon dove from the ceiling straight at Turk, it shifted, becoming an albino panther. Its claws took him fully in the face, muffling his screams as the weight of the big cat drove him to the ground. Turk tried in vain to get away, but the vicious claws raked across him, tearing deep grooves into him, blood spraying in all directions. The screams lessened as the panther finished its work.

With the miasma gone and my healing ability kicking in, I could get to my knees. Molly ran over, still covered in blood and gore from Turk. She helped me stand and steadied me. "What are you doing here?" I mumbled.

She punched me lightly in the arm. "So much for a thank you. Mom sent me to tell you they need twenty more minutes and the evacuation will be done."

Straightening up sounded like a good idea but one it would have to wait. "I'm thrilled you came when you did, but why didn't you just radio Ranger?"

She rolled her eyes at me.

Seriously? Pepper echoed the same in my head.

"They are jamming our communications gear." She looked everywhere but at me. "And maybe she doesn't know I wanted to help."

And there it is. Pepper laughed. *I knew she was up to no good.*

"Oh, I see." I attempted a grin, but I don't think it worked overly well.

Molly grimaced and held her nose. "Um, you should clean up when you get a chance. You don't look any better than you smell." A noise from the entrance caught our attention. A loud whine of engines followed by a dull thud. Over and over. Everyone had climbed to their feet, in various stages of health. Boulder and Izanami had taken the least amount of damage, so they appeared ready to go. Abby started growing as she prepared for another battle. Dad was worse for wear, his helmet gone, but he stood tall as we waited for whatever approached.

"Molly, head back. Specter said this thing is bad news." I strained my eyes, trying to see into the darkness beyond the door. The thuds grew louder, and I felt a tremor through the floor as it came.

She shook her head in defiance. "These are my people, and I will protect them. You'd all be dead if it wasn't for me."

"Molly!" Izanami snapped at her. "Get yourself back to the transloca-tor. We will delay this thing, but you need to let us know when we can leave."

"But..."

"GO!"

"Fine." Molly shimmered, returning to falcon form, and beat her wings to gain altitude and speed. I watched her go for a moment.

Now that is one cool Gift. Did you see her tear up Turk? Oh, of course you did, we share the same eyes.

I had seen it and silently added him to my list. Another death that hadn't been necessary. In another time, Turk and I could have been friends, but someone had turned him against me with lies and deceit. Everyone that encountered me ended up dead.

Pepper didn't respond. How much of what I thought could she "hear?" I thought *tacos* and promptly got a response.

Are you freakin' kidding me? Of course, you're thinking of food at a time like this. Once again, I'm glad I'm a woman.

As we watched the doorway, lights illuminated it, causing us to guard our eyes. The ground bounced at the weight of the mech as it entered the base. At least twenty feet tall, it had the appearance of a giant bug. Six legs propelled it forward as the articulated head swung back and forth. Giant mandibles had been attached to the head; each had a chainsaw blade embedded in it. Along the top, arms with spinning blades swung back and forth. At the far back, a giant missile launcher turned as it aimed.

"Move!" Dad yelled seconds ahead of the first missile launch. Everyone scattered. Well, everyone but me.

WHAT ARE YOU DOING? Pepper's fear hit me like a tsunami.

Watch. The first of the small rockets crashed into my chest, exploding. The impact threw me across the street, flinging me into a bright blue door with yellow daisies painted on it. The rush of energy flowed through me. My combat suit didn't fare as well, but I could get another one if we made it out alive.

I watched as the rockets destroyed most of the homes around the entrance in a vain attempt to kill one of us. Dad soared overhead. Boulder imitated his namesake by hiding under a massive outcrop of rock he'd created. Izanami rolled out from under it as the firing stopped. Abby had leapt up to the rooftop and run out of harm's way but now sped back to the fight.

Power surged through me to levels I'd never reached before. The hairs on my arms danced like they were water on a hot pan. I gathered my power and fired a bolt of lightning across the intervening space, striking the head as it turned my way. The electricity arced across the armor plating, leaving scorch marks but nothing else.

Boulder heaved a massive chunk of what looked like granite to smash against the mechanical beetle but, other than scratching the paint, it did no damage. Abby and Izanami couldn't do anything since they couldn't get to the people driving the mech. Another barrage of missiles launched, but a massive updraft from Dad hurled the rockets over our team. The damage to the buildings further in the base would be terrible, but we were abandoning it anyway.

We moved back. Power thundered through me screaming to be used, but I didn't have a target I could damage. Buildings crashed to the ground as the beetle chased us deeper into the base. Rubble cascaded everywhere as the massive mech crashed through anything in its way. More missiles launched, striking buildings and the walls of the base. Dust and dirt dropped from the ceiling.

I stopped to rest for a second, watching as the beetle had slowed to crush another of the larger buildings. The top floors had fallen on the back of the beast, stopping the rockets for the moment.

Dad flew down. "No word from Molly. We have to make a stand soon, or they'll be at the munition dump in minutes."

I stood next to a two-story building that had a sign saying Supply Depot. The rumble of the beetle freeing itself on the other side was deafening. Pieces of stone fell from the ceiling as I examined the roof. I had an idea. "Get everyone back to the dump. If this works, we can get everyone out of here."

Dad looked at me like I was insane. "No. I'm not leaving you."

"You just said we have to make a stand, and I know how. But you have to get everyone to the translocator now."

"Your mother is going to kill me." He launched into the air. I only had a minute to get in position.

Are you crazy, or do you have a death wish?

Neither. This will work.

It had better, or I'll hate you for rest of eternity.

I knew I probably wouldn't live through this, but I had to save the others. Time to roll the dice.

36

I ran into the supply depot as fast as my feet could carry me. I went through the door and past the front desk that guarded a room full of shelving. On the far side of the room, a stairwell ran to the second floor. I tore up the stairs, orienting myself to where the back of the building was.

At the top of the stairs, hallways branched in either direction. I turned left, heading for the end of the hall. I found a door and threw it open, revealing a huge office with two large windows overlooking the destruction of its next-door neighbor.

Extricating itself of the rubble and various items that had, until recently, resided in the destroyed building, the mechanized armor beetle turned to follow the fleeing members of my team.

Time to see if my crazy plan will work, I thought

You know we could make it to the translocator and get out with everyone else.

No, they still need more time to get everyone out. This is the only way they get out of here alive.

But not us.

I knew this was my last stand, but if it saved everyone else, it would be worth the cost.

No, we don't get out.

Well, it's been nice riding shotgun with you, partner.

There wasn't anything else to say, and time was running out.

I shot an arc of electricity at the beetle, putting nothing into it. I needed to save my power.

The head swung ponderously toward me. I sent a second light show and then ran back into the hall. The outer wall exploded as the barrage of missiles impacted it.

I ran back in, firing a third and fourth electric arc at the mech. The beetle turned slowly, bearing down on the building. I shot a couple more harmless bolts to keep its attention. When the head reached the building, I ran, fighting for balance as the structure rocked. At the end of the hallway, I threw open the window and stepped out onto the fire escape. The building lurched as the beetle tore away at the foundation. I pulled myself up the ladder to the roof. I heard part of the wall collapse and braced for the jolt. The building listed, throwing me into a wall hard enough for my power to increase.

I swung up to the roof. *This had better work*, I thought as I gathered the swirling power I contained, focusing it into one solid flow of pure energy. The base's roof was under twenty feet from where I now stood.

Good luck, Tommy.

I unleashed a blast rivaling the one that tore a hole in the Megadrome. Instead of a single, sustained burst I'd used to get rid of the energy Powell forced into me, I focused the power to cut a square directly over us. The Underground's bases had been carved under the city by a Gifted of enormous power. The ceiling of the base was the foundation of the buildings above. Marcel might have been able to figure out the physics of it, but all I knew is the weight above us would come down if the support under them disappeared.

I finished connecting the square, but nothing happened. The building jerked as the beetle crashed through the main floor, removing the supports from under me. I steadied myself on a piece of machinery. Dirt and dust covered me. I'd tapped my power to the point I couldn't have fired again if I'd wanted to.

The noise from the mech grew as it tore the building apart. All I wanted to do was curl up in a ball and wait for the end, but Mom hadn't raised a quitter. Across a small alley sat another building, its roof slightly lower than I was, at least for the time being. I got a running start and jumped. Unfortunately, at that moment, most of the backside of the building decided to crumble. My graceful jump became a flailing fall. Pepper screamed in my head. I reached out and caught the lip of the roof. The momentum of my fall slammed me into the brick exterior, forcing the breath out of my lungs. I held on with my arms burning, and my fingers complaining loudly that the blisters hadn't quite healed yet. I found a foothold and forced myself to pull up and over the edge.

Wow, that was close!

No kidding.

The building started to sway precariously and then collapsed. If I didn't bring down the city, this had all been for nothing. The impact had restored a bit of energy, but I didn't have another big shot left in me. I need to learn to hold back some power instead of bleeding myself dry.

Don't beat yourself up over this. It's not like you destroy cities every day.

I studied where I'd made my cuts. *Why isn't it falling? The weight alone should have collapsed the section.*

The beetle shifted, freeing itself from the pile of concrete and brick that had been the Supply Depot.

I've failed. I dropped on to the roof; I couldn't stop this thing. The Reclaimers would take the base, and more importantly the translocator, along with everyone that Warden couldn't send to Atlanta before the base fell. It had been a risk, but I thought it would work.

For the record, it shoulda worked. I've got nuthin' to lose, I've been dead for years. She paused a moment. *I'll take goin' down swingin' than living forever stuck in Grim Reaper's scythe.*

Thanks. The sound of missiles launching roused me from my reverie. What are they shooting missiles at? I got to my feet and watched the rocket trails. To my amazement, Dad flew over the beetle, firing bolts into the monster. The projectiles hurtled toward him, but he dodged to the side and let them strike the ceiling above him.

Each impact deposited more rubble to the already clogged streets of the base. The second launch proved to be too much for the already weakened section of roof. Metal shrieked against stone to announce that whatever held Dallas up had stopped working. A large fracture appeared, but not in the nice square I'd cut; the fissure ran lengthwise through the center of the base's ceiling.

I guess I did too good of a job. I ran for the far end of the roof. The next building had only one story. I leapt, landing with a thud as my legs couldn't adjust to the tremors that had started. The crack widened, dropping the husk of a car into the middle of the street.

We've got to get to the translocator. Pepper said as calmly as she could, but the trickle of dirt had turned into an avalanche of concrete, cars, and city. *Well, there you go. Just needed a little push to get started.*

Dad streaked through the falling debris. "Jump on my back."

I did as instructed. In a second, he threw himself off the building. We plunged for a scary moment before he compensated for the extra weight.

He skimmed the ground, swerving as larger chunks of Dallas crashed into the soon-to-be former Underground base. We spun, twisted, curved, and soared in and around the unfolding disaster. A tanker truck crashed in front of us, causing Dad to veer frantically to clear it. I tried to pull my arms away from his neck so he could avoid it easier, but his grip caught my wrists as we just missed the jagged tangle of broken metal.

I looked up, and we had passed the crack, though billowing dust chased us as the buildings of Dallas crashed down into the base below. There was no way the beetle could survive a city block falling on it. Dad pulled up short, and I jumped off his back. We stood outside the translocator, but my heart stopped as I saw where he pointed.

Before us, gray repelling lines hung just outside the munition dump's entrance. I wanted to smack my head. The beetle hadn't been the threat; it had been a distraction. They led the fighters off so they could get to Warden and the translocator.

Turns out the Reclaimers had left someone behind to protect their people. Two sharp cracks of a weapon firing were all the warning we got. I felt the disruptor band hit my leg, wrapping itself around me, knocking me to the ground. The small coil of power I hadn't been able to use vanished. Dad laid out next to me.

What the hell?

Disruptor band. They shut off my Gift.

Three armed Reclaimers pointed rifles at us. The lead one barked. "Don't move or we'll shoot you. You're under arrest in the name of the Protectorate."

We both put our hands behind our heads and waited. They pulled Dad to his feet, then me. The one behind me jammed the muzzle of his rifle into my back hard. "Let's go."

"Sure thing, but we might want to hurry," I said, looking back to where the ceiling continued to crack open, raining more of downtown Dallas.

"What the..."

That moment of distraction was all I needed. Blaze's morning boot camps had prepared me to take advantage of any opening to end a fight quickly. Three of the guards stopped to gawk as a line of faded yellow taxis crashed to the ground thirty feet from us. I spun and kicked my guard straight in the crotch. His scream rose a few octaves as he collapsed, holding his injured manhood.

Dad, having many more years of combat experience than I, swept the second guard's legs from under him before upper cutting the third, knocking him out cold. I kicked the downed guard in the head before he could regain his feet. We left the whimpering man who'd curled into a fetal position. He wouldn't be going anywhere soon.

I tugged at the band, trying to get it off, but it wouldn't budge.

"Don't bother; we'll need help to get them off. Right now, we need to get out of here and fast." Part of a glass skyscraper crashed through the widening fissure. In a matter of minutes, the Underground's Dallas base would be no more.

With no powers, I did the next best thing. I retrieved two rifles from the sleeping beauties and tossed one to Dad. He caught it and started checking it over. I did the same, turned off the safety, and headed for the door.

The room outside the translocator stood empty, but loud voices yelled inside. A couple of kids cried wails of anguish. Inside, you couldn't fail to notice the increasing volume of the base being destroyed from above. I stole a peek around the corner; it wasn't good. Four Reclaimer's held a group of evacuees and our team at gunpoint. Izanami and Boulder were laid out in front of the control panel, disrupter bands wrapped around their legs as well. Abby's head lay in Mom's lap. A once white wrapping around her leg seeped red. Mom stroked her hair as the men interrogated Warden.

I stepped back and told Dad what I'd seen. A putrid smell had invaded the room through the open door. I didn't want to know what had collapsed out there that smelled so horrid.

How much time do we have left? Pepper asked quietly. The good thing about conversing with a person in your brain is that even the loudness of a dying city didn't blot out her voice.

Not long. We've got to get the rest out of here.

"Only thing we can do is shoot them quickly and hope. You take the two on the right." Dad squeezed my arm. I smiled back at him. We'd made it through a lot today. We needed to get everyone to safety. "On the count of three."

I knelt in the doorway; Dad stood above me. He tapped me on the shoulder. I counted one, two, three, and pulled the trigger. The closest guard's head burst as the round took him just behind the ear. The second didn't have time to process his buddy's death before the bullet took him. The other two soldiers didn't fare any better.

I ran over to check on Abby and Mom. Dad went to Warden, who wiped at the gore covering her face. Any closer and the man would have fallen on her. Dad gestured, screaming to be heard over the roar of the destruction outside.

Mom hugged me and pointed to Abby's leg. All I could make out were "shot" and "doctor."

My heart dropped into my stomach. At least she didn't have a disruptor band on; she'd already be dead if she did. Her healing would have to see her through for a little longer. "Go! Now!"

She nodded and ran to the group huddled off to the side. She got them moving. Dad had a wide-eyed Warden at the control panel to get us out of here. Something large impacted on the room's roof.

Thank God for Carbinium, Pepper whispered in my head.

The munition dump's walls and ceiling were embedded with Carbinium plates, an alloy that could withstand any known Gifted. I doubted it could withstand a building landing on it, however.

I pulled Izanami to the launch pad and returned for Boulder and Molly. He'd regained his senses, so we guided him over. Dad carried Abby, and Mom followed. Then he ran and grabbed Warden, who tried to fight him off. Finally, Dad threw her over his shoulder, hit something on the control panel and dashed to us, leaping over the spinning rings of the translocator.

Warden punched him after he'd set her down. "I didn't arm the self-destruct! The Reclaimers will be able to use it to enter all our bases."

Dad pointed as the concrete roof sagged under the weight of the destroyed city. The light flared; the last image I saw was the munition dump's roof collapse as we teleported to Atlanta.

A frightened-looking girl sat at the control panel in Atlanta as we all exited the translocator. Specter stood next to her, relief plain on her face. We had made it.

We had rescued Waxenby and finally completed our mission. Hopefully it was enough to stop the future Eiraf had predicted.

The girl, I think her name was Angela, ran over to Warden. "We received a message a few minutes ago."

She dragged her fingers through her dust ridden hair. "What message?"

"Return to Castle. Blaze collapsed and is still unconscious."

So much for being done.

37

We must go now! Pepper's anxiety raged in my head like an angry metal fan in a mosh pit.

We will. Just calm down. I might as well have been yelling into an empty room for all the good it did.

I checked out our team. Dad and I had disruptor bands still fastened to us, Abby had a hole in her leg, Waxenby swung in and out of consciousness, and Mom bordered on complete exhaustion. It'd had been a long night for us.

Dad broke the silence of the group. "Warden, can you assist with the bands and patch Abby's leg up? We'll be leaving as quickly as possible."

Warden nodded. Her eyes had a dull cast to them, exhaustion and sorrow having taken its toll. "Thank you for the assist back there. Losing the base would have been problematic."

Molly and Specter hovered around Warden like nervous bees around a flower.

"Of course. I know we see things differently at times, but we are on the same side." Dad's complexion had an ashy cast to it. I couldn't tell if it was from the fight or if the loss of his powers was taking a toll on him. I noticed bright red blisters covered his arm where his suit had been torn. My hands were somewhat less blistered, but I'd been healing since using the burst of heat in Dallas.

She studied him for a moment before turning to Angela and sending her off with instructions. "I'm not sure we are, but we can discuss that another time. Angela will bring a tech and a med to look at Abby's leg. Someone will take you back to your vehicle when you're ready."

She gestured to her team. Izanami, Molly, and Specter followed, but Boulder didn't move. Warden glanced over her shoulder at him, a quizzical expression on her face. "We need to figure out what to do next. You coming?"

Boulder shook his head. "No, I'm going with them."

Warden spun on her heel and closed the distance between them. "Boulder, your place is here with us. We need you."

He blanched a bit but held firm. "I can't stay here. Too many memories."

Specter put her hand on the big man's arm. "Please, Boulder. We've already lost so much. Losing you would be too much to bear." A tear ran down her cheek.

Boulder lowered his head but shook it all the same. "I can't stay."

"We'll miss you," Molly said, hugging Boulder around the chest. He gently hugged her. "Will you come back?"

He didn't say anything. His eyes never left Warden's face.

"It isn't your fault," Warden said simply. "That thing used you to kill him."

Nothing. He could have been made of stone for the amount she moved him.

Finally, her shoulders slumped, and she gripped his arm above where he held Molly. "Stay safe and come back to us when you can, if you can."

"Thank you."

Molly and Warden released him and left the room. Izanami and Specter said their goodbyes and were gone.

Mom stepped over to him. His eyes had followed his friends as they left, and he still stared after them. "Why?" was all she asked.

Boulder turned to her. "I want to fight, and Warden will close up and ride the storm out. That wouldn't avenge Salvo."

"You can kill Reclaimers until there are none left, but it won't bring him back." Mom's voice was soft and gentle like the night I'd had a nightmare and couldn't sleep.

"I know, but it's all I've got."

A few minutes later, a technician and a nurse entered the room. He attached alligator clamps to the band on my leg, pressed a couple of buttons, and the thing fell off. I could feel my power swirling again. He did the same for Dad and Boulder before leaving.

The nurse took longer. He examined Abby's leg thoroughly, including prodding the hole with a metal probe. "There is a foreign object in there. We'd have to get her to a surgeon to remove it."

Mom glanced at Dad before addressing the nurse. "Is she in any danger if it's not removed now?"

He scowled as he thought. "I'd recommend you seek immediate treatment, but given how fast Gifted heal, I don't think so. I would get it removed as soon as possible."

"Thank you."

A few minutes later, Abby had a clean bandage on her leg and could get around well enough to walk.

Once the nurse had left the room, Boulder spoke. "Salvo was my best friend." He paused, wiping the tears from his eyes. "I will do whatever you ask of me if you'll allow me to accompany you."

Dad reached out and shook his hand. "We'd be honored to have you join us."

"I'll carry Mr. Waxenby and get you back to the van." Without another word, Boulder slung the unconscious man over his shoulder and led the way out of the vault.

I would hate to be on the wrong side of Boulder. Pepper remarked as I watched his back. As we wound our way through the Atlanta base, a low alarm rang, alerting the citizens that an attack could be imminent. People rushed around, readying weapons and getting barricades erected. The guards at the gate let us through without issue. Warden must have called ahead.

Fighting won't solve anything. Wendi's memory isn't any less painful for all the Reclaimers I've killed.

It's tough, but gets easier, I promise.

It would or it wouldn't. So many things in my life were outside my control to the point I had a disembodied ghost using my head as her crib. I felt like Ashe from League of Legends running through the mazes, fighting a never-ending battle I couldn't walk away from.

At least we had rescued Waxenby, but other than a few bouts of screaming, he'd been dormant. How could he be important to Eiraf's cause?

We walked until we reached the Underground's vehicle. Funny, the walk felt much shorter when we had first arrived, but that was hours and several lifetimes ago. Boulder laid out Waxenby in the bed of the truck, then started up the engine as we all climbed in. Abby rode shotgun with her leg out the window. I sat with Mom and Dad in the back, holding on to Waxenby so he didn't bounce too much.

Dawn was a couple of hours away by the time we reached the van. Exhausted, we stored what little gear we had left and got in. Dad got us out of the Atlanta site fast since we were short of time. I crashed in the backseat, only waking when Dad and Mom traded driving duties as the sun rose. We hit a convenience store and bought out half their food. Stale hot dogs taste great when you haven't eaten for a long time. I washed it all down with a couple of Mountain Dews and was back asleep as soon as my head hit the seat.

After a few double backs to make sure nobody followed us, we arrived back at Castle. Mimi met us at the garage entrance; the dark bags under her eyes indicated she hadn't slept much. Mom swung herself over the side and was next to Mimi in an instant. They conferred for a second before Mom yelled back to us. "Blaze is in the control room. I'm going to go see what's going on."

The rest of us climbed out of the van. Waxenby had gained a somewhat conscious state, like when Jose would drunk-stumble around. Boulder helped him to walk as I helped Abby limp along. Her leg looked better but whatever was lodged in there needed to come out at some point. Dad gathered up the gear and headed for the armory. I admired his attention to detail even though he had to be exhausted.

By the time Abby and I had navigated the stairs and entered the control room, Dad was leaning against the wall by the window to the mechanical room. Marcel had drinks and sandwiches laid out on the table for us, the junk normally on top of it piled underneath. A cot sat next to the control panel. Wires ran from the console to Blaze. The wall reflected all his vital signs. Mom knelt next to Blaze, holding his hand and speaking softly.

Abby pulled away, choosing to slide down the wall to take the weight off her good leg after the long descent. Boulder helped Waxenby into a chair where he stared off into space but was conscious. Mimi brought a bottle of water, trying to get him to drink. Boulder slumped next to him on the floor. Marcel delivered drinks and sandwiches like when we worked at the Lair.

I need to see him, Pepper said, urging me to move faster.

All I wanted to do was sleep but worry and Pepper's prodding won out. I crossed to the opposite side from Mom, grabbing Blaze's free hand.

"Oh, you. It's been so long since I've seen you," came out of my mouth.

Mom gave me an odd look.

Blaze didn't move, his breathing shallow and his complexion gray.

"You've got to hold on Blaze. I can't lose you all over again." Without my permission, I leaned forward and kissed Blaze full on the lips.

Now I had everyone's attention.

WHAT ARE YOU DOING! My body stopped, and I pulled back, staring at the floor.

If you think for one minute I would let him die without kissin' him, you're a bigger fool than I thought.

I felt my cheeks go red.

Mom studied me as I pretended nothing had happened. Here it comes, the lawyer is about to strike. "Out with it. Something happened in Dallas."

Abby perked up. "I could have sworn Grim Reaper hit you with his Scythe but a second later you were fine, and he was out cold." She slurped her Pepsi, watching.

I sighed. I'd hoped to discuss this later but thanks to Pepper it had to be now.

OK, kissin' him might not have been the best play in hindsight.

I sighed again, much to the annoyance of everyone in the room, including my best friend I hadn't even greeted. "This is what happened. Grim Reaper hit me with his scythe, and I somehow absorbed Pepper Spray in the process of breaking free. Not much else to tell."

Questions exploded from the assembled people. I half expected Blaze to sit straight up and ask me for more information.

Mom shushed everyone, and they quieted down. "You skipped a lot of details there, don't you think? Let's start at the beginning, shall we?"

"Yes, counselor." I got an evil grin from her, plus she knew it was me talking. "We were fighting the Syndicate, and Turk jumped me."

"He did?" Dad interrupted. "I didn't see him until later in the fight. He ran off screaming."

Oh yeah. He was screaming like a little bitch. Pepper sounded way too happy about that fact.

"He came up from behind me and used his Gift to poison me. I thought he had me, but I found a way to get him off me. He ran off injured so I thought he wouldn't come back." Remembering the nausea and pain from the second attack left my stomach a bit unsettled. I could smell the miasma in the back of my sinuses. "Obviously, I called that wrong."

Boulder grunted. "Gifted are hard to kill. Is that why his hands were gone?"

I nodded. "He took my helmet with him; it kind of, umm, was fused to him. I thought he'd run for it, not attack us." I paused for more commentary but getting none, I moved on. "When the Reclaimers showed up demanding our surrender, I'd been fighting Grim Reaper. I stupidly turned, and he stabbed me in the back, literally."

"Oh, that sucks. What happened?" Abby asked, her face deeply lined. Her injured leg must hurt worse than I thought.

I went on to describe the meeting with Pepper and fighting Death and finally returning to my body and realizing Pepper had been brought back with me. I popped open a Dew and drank deeply.

Marcel stroked his chin as always. "It must be an aspect of your Gift that nullified his ability to absorb your soul into the scythe." I appreciated how carefully he worded his response as to not give away any information on my powers. "We know from the Zoo that Pepper's soul, for lack of a better term, still resided in his weapon. Interesting. I have some ideas we should discuss later."

"Yes, Professor. I'll make an appointment during your office hours." I shot him my best eat-crap smile, which he returned.

"Why, thank you, Mr. Potter."

Having lived with our banter for many years, Mom simply rolled her eyes. "Can we stay on topic?"

"Sorry, Mom," we both said in unison. Like I said, the three of us had been together for a long time.

"Losers," Abby interjected from where she sat.

Mom gave her "the look" before continuing. "You can talk to Pepper?"

I thought about it, not sure on how to answer. "I can talk to her. She can hear some of my thoughts."

Only the surface ones. When you use your brain, I can't hear you.

I repeated what she told me. "I don't think she can take over except in stressful situations when I do what she asks me…but without her asking me. Do you understand?"

Marcel pursed his lips, still rubbing his non-goateed chin. "It does. She can influence your actions by appealing to the emotional centers of your brain. Well, what little brain you have. I would think it'd be fairly easy, especially with all the extra unused room for her to occupy."

I flipped him off, firing back. "At least I have a girl in me." *Wait, that didn't make any sense.*

Oh, man. You're a tool. Pepper laughed at my embarrassment.

I grimaced. Things were going downhill fast. "Anyhow, I don't think it's an issue, and she helped me get through the fight in the base."

Don't say it. Pepper warned.

"She noticed a lot I missed."

Too late.

Abby snorted. "Maybe we should move you to co-pilot. Sounds like she'd do a better job."

Marcel cracked up. For the most part, the rest tried not to laugh.

Dad intervened on my behalf. "What is Blaze's status?"

To my surprise, Mimi answered. "I got him hooked up to what little medical equipment Castle has. My mom was a nurse, and she wanted me to follow in her footsteps, regardless of the collar. I can tell he's still in there…" Her eyes darted around as if she wanted to run.

Mom stepped over to her. "Everyone here is Gifted, except Blaze and me. It's normal to use them to help others."

She nodded. "I could feel Blaze's thoughts. They were erratic and didn't make much sense. I get the feeling his body is protecting him from the cancer."

Marcel rubbed his chin. "Makeda's healing could be using his energy to fight, which would explain the coma."

"So, he's not dying tonight?" Dad asked. When Mimi agreed, he went on. "It's been a long day. Let's all get some sleep. In the morning, we need to pack up the vans and make our way to Harker."

"Everything is packed and ready, Mr. Ranger," Mimi stammered out, clearly nervous.

Dad smiled at her. "Mimi, please call me Mike or Ranger. We are on the same team here." He caught Boulder's eye. "Same for you, Boulder."

Boulder nodded. "Thank you, Ranger. I'll do what I can."

"Welcome to the team, Boulder," Dad said with a grin. "Tommy, help Abby to her room. We'll show Boulder to a room where he can get cleaned up and get some rest. Oliver can stay here with Marcel and Mimi if you two are alright?"

WHAT? Pepper screamed in my brain. *I'm not leaving. I'm staying right here.*

Pepper, I need to sleep. I'm exhausted.

"I'm fine," Mimi said, glancing at Blaze. "I don't want to be away from Blaze."

If she's staying, we are staying! She dug in, trying to keep me from moving.

Fine. How much good will we do if I'm passed out on the floor?

Um. It doesn't matter. At least I'll be near him. I could feel her losing her momentum.

And when Mimi needs to sleep, I'm sure Mom or Abby can watch over him since we'll be out cold.

Oh, alright. Sleep, but we aren't going for long.

"I'll keep an eye on things, Ranger." Marcel moved to the control panel and pulled up a map. "Here to Harker should take about fourteen hours, given the bad roads we are going to have to use."

Dad frowned. "Longer than I'd like to be out in the open, but we need to try everything we can to save Blaze. We leave at five a.m."

He led Mom out with Boulder in tow. I helped Abby to her feet, well foot really, and we went down the hall a lot slower than the rest.

"What's it like having a woman in your head?"

I thought about it for a second. "It's strange having someone talking to you but comforting at the same time, like she's watching out for me."

Abby grinned at me. "Well, if anyone ever needed supervision, it's you."

I thought the same thing. Pepper chimed in.

Great. As if I didn't take enough grief without it bouncing around in my head as well.

38

I dropped a very tired Abby off in her room and headed to mine. All I could think about was sleep. I flipped on the lights, and everything I owned was in its place, including my backpack. I kicked off my shoes, went into the bathroom, and turned on the shower.

Um, what are you doin'?

I'm going to take a shower before I go to bed, why?

Because I can see through your eyes, and I have no desire to see you naked, especially while I'm stuck in your head.

What am I supposed to do, not shower? I also have to pee, but you didn't seem to have an issue with that when we stopped to go earlier.

You used a urinal. I couldn't see anything.

After the day I'd had, I needed this like a hole in the head. *Well, close your eyes.*

I don't have eyes. I'm a ghost in the gray matter, dope.

Uggg. I just about had my witty response ready when the alarms sounded. "Proximity alert. Armed hostiles," blared over and over throughout the base.

I slammed off the shower, grabbed my shoes, and ran for the control room. *Seriously?* I thought to myself and my passenger. *We just got away from those goons. This is bad.*

It may have been the understatement of the year. The one thing we had counted on was the safehouses being off the Protectorate's radar. We had injured people who couldn't make a run for it. This was a disaster of epic proportions.

Abby came out of her room right behind me. "What the hell is going on?" She yelled over the blaring of the early defense system's warning.

"Nothing good." I threw Abby's arm over my shoulders to help her walk with her injured leg. We hit the stairs; Mom, Dad, and Boulder were already on them. Boulder ran up to us, picking Abby up and carrying her like a bride down the stairs. We entered the control room in a group.

Marcel had the monitor's full of images of Reclaimers as they moved up the roads toward our location. Mimi sat on the floor next to Blaze, holding his hand. I heard a small growl from Pepper, but there were more important issues than jealousy. Waxenby mumbled something over and over in his restless sleep.

"How bad is it?" Dad asked as he got to Marcel's side. I'd never seen Marcel so haggard; his clothes had spilled food on them. His hair was matted in place from where he'd pushed his hands through it. It was easy to forget how hard Marcel worked to keep everything going when we were in the field.

"Bad." Marcel's fingers danced across the keyboard. "I've been able to jam their communications and seal the outer entries. Depending on their hardware, we could stay here for an extended period. Of course, they could just nuke us."

"Is there any way they don't know where we are?"

Marcel banged away at the keyboard. The map of Castle appeared on the wall monitor over the control panel. It spun in hi-def glory as Marcel oriented it correctly. "I don't think they know where the entrances are, but they got almost all the roads covered."

"Almost?" Dad moved to the Castle map Marcel had pulled up.

Marcel pointed to where we had driven in. "This is the main entry." His finger hovered over the screen, but putting your fingers on his monitors was sacrilege. "These two are access tunnels we don't use, but they had troops moving up the roads that lead to them." He jammed his finger against the screen, smearing it. My mouth fell open. "There. It's an escape hatch. I found the feed. There are a few vehicles there, but who knows if they work, and that's not the worst news."

My stomach sank. What could be worse than Reclaimers moving in on our sanctuary?

"I pulled up Castle's schematics. Whoever built it installed enough explosives to level the mountain, but they didn't automate it." Marcel gestured to the far wall. "The only way to trip it is to have someone push the button."

"Can you automate it?" I asked, my voice barely quavered. Either I had gotten used to being in these situations, or I was too damn tired to care. I knew the answer as soon as I saw his chin drop.

"Not without a week or two to build it out. Any mistake would set off the charges."

"We'll need time to get our injured to the escape area, that is if any of the vehicles are in working order. From the screen, it looks like they were set up for long-term storage. Let's hope they are readier than the self-destruct system." Dad rubbed his face. "I'll stay behind and set off the explosives so you can get Blaze to Harker."

"Dad, no!" I'd just gotten him back; I wasn't going to let the Reclaimers retake him. "I'll stay. I can survive the blast."

Dad shook his head. "That's worse. When the mountain blows, you won't be able to get out again."

"There has to be another way," Mom said firmly. "Marcel, can you rig something to push the button remotely from all this stuff?" She gestured to one of the tables strewn with tools and gadgets.

Marcel stroked his chin. My hopes soared. Marcel had hacked the Megadrome; he could make a simple machine to push a button. "I don't know if I have enough time. I could attach an actuator to the—"

I knew Marcel well enough to not let him get started down the rabbit hole. "Marcel, we need something simple."

"Oh, yeah, probably if I had a couple of hours."

"Like you said, we can hold for a long period. Get started." Dad turned to the rest of us. "Susan, we need working vehicles in the escape bay. Mimi will go with you. Boulder, we need Blaze and Oliver situated in whatever vehicles we can get working. Abby, go with Susan, we can't chance your leg."

Abby stiffened. "I can fight."

Dad looked annoyed at best. "I know you can fight, but you're injured, and if things go sideways, you can fight to get everyone away."

She frowned but didn't say any more.

"Tommy, you're with me. We are going to the armory and supply to load up. It's a long trip to Harker." Dad returned to Marcel. "Get something rigged up so we can blow this place from miles away, then get to the escape vehicles. Does everyone understand their job?"

Everyone broke up to get to where they were supposed to be. I followed Dad through the hallways and across to the training rooms where the armory was.

"Dad, why are we getting weapons? Won't Harker have the same setup?" I asked as we descended the stairs to the corridor leading to the training center.

"I've never heard of Harker, which, being they were secret bases, isn't unusual, but none of the big teams had places in the Adirondacks. I'd rather not find out after the fact that the base isn't stocked." He entered through the door and crossed through the gardens. "We can get food, but it's not like we can go buy guns. Not like in the old days."

"You could buy guns?" No one owned a gun other than the police and military now.

"You could," Dad paused to open the old command center door. "The Protectorate outlawed gun ownership once he took over. I'm sure there are still some out there, but they aren't legal."

The world had changed so much since the Dark Brigade attacks that I wondered whether I'd recognize anything if I went back in time. Dad punched in the code and the door hissed open. The walls and five rows of displays in the center of the room were lined with every gun imaginable from Colt revolvers to the Adaptive Combat Rifles with their own wall. Loaded magazines sat in bins under each weapon.

Why would Gifted need this kind of firepower? Confusion swirled around the question. *They could do anything; why use guns?*

I smiled. I'd asked the same question when Dad showed me the room for Blaze's training mandates. *According to Dad, the government would task the teams with covert missions against other countries. They didn't want to advertise Gifted were being used since it was against some convention's rules.*

Why not just send soldiers then?

Gifted are stronger and can heal wounds that would kill a normal man. They would go in, do the dirty work, and get out again. I grabbed a rucksack from under the first row of weapons and filled it with handguns and all the clips we had for each weapon. Dad did the same with the rifles. I went over to see if we wanted to take more. I stopped dead in my tracks.

"Is that a disruptor?"

Dad spun on his heel. "Sorry, you startled me, Tommy. Was lost in thought, I guess." He removed the black and gray weapon from the sack. It had a pump action on it like a shotgun but held a cylindrical canister at the back. On top, it had a handle with a computerized sighting mechanism on the front of the barrel. I'd never seen one up close. "It is. These are hard to come by, and with the Syndicate out there, we need all the advantages we can get. There are only six bands here, but I'll take what I can get."

He passed it over, and I examined it. The grip had a rubber coating that molded to my hand as I held it. The sights popped up, and a small LED screen showed the targeting grid. As cool as it was, I wanted to destroy it. With one shot, it could take away my Gift and leave me almost helpless. Blaze's training is why we could still fight, even with a band on. It had saved us in Dallas. I handed it back.

Dad took a second bag. "Your mother's preferred kit is at the end of the next row if you can get it. I've got rifles, grenade launchers, and the disruptor." He hoisted the first bag up to his shoulder. "With the handguns, we should be covered. Well, assuming we can get out."

I jogged down the aisle, seeing the long, black case and camo backpack that sat there. I propped the gun case on my knee and flipped the latches. The bag held Mom's HK G28 with the sniper package and a full complement of magazines, each labeled with the type of ammo they contained. I locked the case and threw the backpack containing a ghillie suit the snipers wore for camouflage. Gone were the days of briefcases and killer pumps for my mom.

I met Dad at the exit as he locked up and then fried the entry pad using a burst of electricity. He caught my eye. "If they get in, I don't want them having access to this stuff." We went around the floor frying all the pads, to be sure. Who said you can't share vandalism with your dad?

We had just gotten to the garden when Mom ran in. "Oh, I hoped you guys were coming this way." Sweat stood out on her forehead, and her breathing had a ragged edge to it.

"What's wrong?" Dad asked.

Mom took a deep breath. "None of the vehicles in the escape bay work. The engines had corroded to the point where they'll need to be rebuilt. We have the van and the jeep in the main garage. That's it."

Dad hit his leg. "Damn, if we hold out until dark, can we make it down the mountain from the escape bay?"

"You, Tommy, Boulder, Mimi, and maybe Marcel and Abby could." Mom let out a long breath of frustration. "Do we leave Oliver and Eugene to die?"

"No, we can take them with us." I bulled ahead with my idea. "We can carry them down until we find transportation."

"I don't think so, honey." Mom rubbed my arm. "Abby is hurt, and we can't carry them both."

"We need to go and get an update on the situation. Where are the others?"

"They are in the main garage, loaded in the van." Mom moved toward the stairwell, wistfully looking around the garden that had provided us with food and her a place to unwind. "It's the only way we are getting everyone out of here."

"Good thinking, babe."

We went up the stairwell. What a mess this had become.

You will try to save Blaze, won't you? I can't bear to think of him dying when there might be a way to help him at Harker.

I silently wondered if any of us would make it out alive, but Pepper had been through so much, I didn't want to crush the little hope she had left. *If anyone can get us out of here, it will be Dad. He's a great tactician, and Marcel will have some trick up his sleeve. You'll see. It's not as bad as it seems.*

You don't believe it. Don't lie to the person sharing headspace with you.

Sorry, this is as bad as we've faced, and Alyx won't be dropping in to save us. I have no way to contact the Council for help.

I know, but we'll give the Reclaimers a black eye before we go.

My parents both looked at me like I had three heads when I laughed. "Sorry, Pepper said something funny."

"Oh," was all I got from them. We finished the walk in silence.

Marcel had a mutant R2-D2 unit sitting in the middle of the floor. "So, I can control this with my tablet, and it will roll over and push the button." The case protecting the red button had been duct taped, so the button was exposed.

"Duct tape?" Dad asked in a sarcastic tone. "Couldn't you take the cover off?"

"Duct tape fixes everything. Besides, the cover is unbreakable, and I couldn't budge it." Marcel eyed the floor while he spoke. "It only needs to work once."

"True. What's the situation outside?" Dad scanned through the camera feeds, his face reflecting his diminishing hope. "They've got us surrounded."

Marcel sighed deeply. "Yeah, but the good news is they found the escape bay."

"What?" Mom sounded incredulous. "How is that a good thing?"

I reviewed the feeds, and Marcel had it right. Half of the Reclaimers had moved into position around the escape bay doors.

"When you told me we couldn't use the vehicles to escape, I opened the doors long enough for them to notice. They moved half their forces to cover the door, and more are headed down the mountain in case we had fled. That leaves only three squads guarding the main exit."

Dad clapped Marcel on the shoulder. "Brilliant, absolutely brilliant, Marcel. I wish I knew how they found us. We were so careful."

Marcel glanced at me. "Um, they hacked one of the helmet comm-links and traced the signal back to the source."

If Marcel had dropped me in acid, I couldn't have felt any rawer. It all made sense now: Turk wasn't trying to kill me, he had been after my helmet. I put my hands over my face trying to hide my anguish. "Turk took my helmet. This is all my fault."

Dad moved over and put his arm around my shoulder. Mom took my hand in hers. "Tommy," Dad said, his tone serious, "we don't know that."

But we did. Turk had run off with my helmet and cut a deal with the Protectorate. Tears welled up in my eyes. Everyone was going to die because of me.

"Honey, Abby lost her helmet, and your Dad's broke on the way to the translocator. Three helmets aren't accounted for."

My head came up. "Oh. I didn't know."

Marcel added. "Besides, with the way you break gear, I doubt it worked by the time he got it."

Leave it to Marcel to know just the right thing to say. I rolled my eyes at him even though it did help.

Marcel made a face at me. "It doesn't matter, because we don't have long before we have company."

The two outside cameras at the exits showed portable rocket launchers being set up. In a couple of minutes, the doors would be blown open, and no one in the garage beside Boulder could fight.

"Marcel, is this thing ready?" Dad pointed at the robot contraption.

"Yeah, and I rigged a camera to steer it by." It rolled so it was two feet from the button, a piece of steel aligned to push the button when it moved forward.

"Let's go; we need to get to the garage and fast."

Dad slung Mom over his shoulder as we ran for the door.

Do you think we can get out of here? Pepper asked.

If we don't, none of us will be alive to care.

U p the stairs we went, Mom squawking indignantly to be put down. The two vehicles were sitting just inside the entrance, poised to flee. Dad swung Mom off his shoulder; she punched him in the arm. "Don't do that again, at least not in front of the children."

Gross!!!

Aww, it's sweet.

They aren't your parents. Mom and Dad deserved to be happy after all the years they'd been separated, but I didn't want to know anything about it.

Boulder and Mimi joined us at the rear of the garage. They looked as tired as I felt, and we still had a long way to go.

"I pulled the cars back in case we need a running start to get out of here," Mom said as she adjusted her combat suit. "Eugene is in the van, and Oliver is in the jeep."

Dad nodded. "Makes sense. We'll put Tommy and Boulder in the jeep, and you and I will take the van and..." He stopped talking as Abby approached.

Her right hand had blood on it. She held it out and dropped a bright red slug that bounced off the floor. "I took care of my leg."

Mom paled. "You did what? You need a doctor."

"No, I don't. The wound is already healing. We've got to fight our way out, and I can't be limping around."

Man, she's got steel balls, Pepper said admiringly. *Doing your own surgery; that's bad-ass.*

"Glad to have you. We'll need all the help we can get." Dad didn't get to add anything else as a huge boom echoed through the cavernous garage.

The reinforced door shook but held. A second and third blast hit quickly after that. The rocket launcher had started its assault on the outer entry. Marcel checked his tablet. "They are breaching both doors. We don't have long."

The next volley broke part of the door away from the industrial hinges. I realized the vehicles were in the line of fire. I ran to the jeep and shook Waxenby. "Commander Gravity. You need to protect these two cars." No response.

A hand settled on my shoulder; it was Mimi. "Let me try." She sat in the seat next to Waxenby and held his hand. "Head back to the others, Sport. I'll see if I can get through to him." She winked at me.

"Thanks, Mimi." I returned to the group and heard a gasp of surprise from Mom. A translucent bubble appeared over the two cars, shielding them. Just in time, it turned out, as the last set of projectiles tore the door off the hinges, sending shrapnel flying everywhere. The shield lit up like a pinball machine, but it didn't break.

Dad launched into the air; the garage ceiling might have been twenty feet high, allowing him room to maneuver. Reclaimers shouted orders as their soldiers moved to the edge of the doorway and opened fire. I ran at them, inviting the bullets that would energize me. A piece of rock struck me from behind, knocking me to the ground as energy flooded through my depleted system. I looked back, angry that Boulder had hit me, but saw the blue of a disruptor band about ten feet from where I laid on the concrete floor. I gave a thumbs-up to Boulder, who lifted his chin in acknowledgment.

Abby grew as she charged, her injured leg barely noticeable. I laid down a fan blast of electricity to make the soldiers take cover and give Abby a chance to close the distance.

I heard Mom's sniper rifle firing and saw two soldiers drop in rapid succession. More stone flew, impacting against the walls and soldiers in equal measure.

"They've breached the inner doorways of Castle. We need to blow it soon," Marcel yelled over the clatter of machine gun fire.

I got to my feet and raced after Abby. She had dropped five or six soldiers, but they were flanking her, trying to take her out. Outside the entrance, a plateau of about fifty feet held the Reclaimer forces. They were in two groups, with the abandoned rocket launcher set up at the far edge. Off to the right, a gravel road ran through the ravine and held three trucks that had brought the Reclaimers up to fight.

"Abby, down!" She dropped to one knee. I sped up, stepped on her back, and jumped for all I was worth. As I landed, I directed my punch into the ground, adding all the force I could to the blow. The impact rocked the ground like an earthquake, knocking the soldiers off their feet in the process; it was the break we needed. Dad swooped in, striking at the Reclaimers as they tried to right themselves. Boulder emerged, using his rock encrusted arm like a bludgeon, knocking people out or off the side of the landing. The drop was steep; once you went off, you bounced all the way to the bottom.

I punched or threw Reclaimers out of the way. Within minutes, we were clear. Mom and Marcel joined us on the landing. Marcel poked at the tablet screen, cursing under his breath.

"What is it, Marcel?" Dad asked as he landed next to us.

The tapping became more frantic. "The case I taped up fell and the bot can't push the button."

"So much for duct tape fixing everything," Abby said sarcastically.

Marcel's face darkened. "Well, I'm sure you could have come with something better, Miss—"

"Stow it!" Dad said, raising his voice. "Marcel, can you get the robot to open it?"

"No, I built it to roll forward and push the button. The Reclaimers are almost to the center stairs. I've got to go back."

Dad shook his head. "No, I'll go. I'll open the case and return. You can set it off then."

"I'll go." Boulder had his hands up in front of him as if to stop any arguments. "I'll run back, put a rock pillar in place so the cover can't fall and return."

I caught his eye. "Boulder, you might not make it back. We need you."

"Tommy, I can block off the halls if need be. I'll be back." He turned and ran back through the garage.

Mom stared after him for a moment before clicking into family field-trip mode, or field general mode in this case. "Abby, get Eugene and Oliver into the last Reclaimers' truck. Tommy, you and your father load all the gear and the food into the back of the trucks. I'll take care of the other two trucks. Go. When those charges go off, we need to be away from here."

Marcel leaned against the wall as we loaded people and gear into the Reclaimers' troop transport. Each transport had eight huge tires and a metal shell over the rear of the bed, making it safer for the soldiers in the back. I pulled the latch that lowered the rear gate. Twelve white seats equipped with full body restraints stood ready to take us. My palms started to sweat, and I couldn't breathe right. It looked like the buses we were forced on for our monthly trip to the Block.

It's okay, Tommy. Nobody is taking you back. Pepper's voice soothed over my frayed nerves, lulling my panic attack as she spoke. *We are going to get out of here and save Blaze.*

I nodded. Slowly, the panic receded as Pepper talked me through it. Would my memories ever stop haunting me? I didn't know and wouldn't until they stopped. Fear and pain linger. I needed to get Waxenby moved and standing here wasn't doing it. I ran from the truck before it messed with me again.

Mom shot out the tires for the other two and cut the wires under the dashboard to stop anyone from following. I climbed into the Jeep to get Waxenby moved over. Mimi had her head leaning against the headrest of the back seat. I touched her hand, amazed at the complexity of the tattoos that covered her arms.

Her eyes snapped open with surprise. "Tiger, you scared me. Had a hell of a brain burn after the fight." She blinked a few times before she continued. "Are we moving Ollie?"

"Yeah, there is a military truck we are going to use to get down the mountain. We need to move him fast."

She did a seated bow. "Your wish and all that junk." Her brows furrowed a bit before Waxenby's eyes opened and he climbed out of the Jeep.

"That's..."

She waved me off as she went in Waxenby's wake, guiding him to the truck. Abby and Dad carried Blaze but stopped to watch the strange procession as Mimi took him up the ramp and into the seating. I could see Dad was freaked out. Once Waxenby settled in, she exhaled sharply, rubbing her temples with both hands. "Man, I feel like I've been kicked by a mule. I think it'd be easier to carry him."

"How are you doing that? It's wicked cool." I thought back to Wendi's mom, but she could erase memories or plant false ones.

Now that would be a handy talent to have.

No kidding, especially when I pissed off Mom.

Dad and Abby slid Blaze into a seat, hooking up the restraints so he wouldn't get hurt. Abby pulled the padding out of another seat and used it to protect Blaze.

I felt a sob from Pepper. *It's like he's cargo. He deserves better.*

Once we get him to Harker, the machine should be able to heal him. At least I hoped it would.

Mom joined us, her sabotage of the other trucks completed. "How much longer until Boulder is back? We need to leave before they realize we've taken out their rearguard."

As if summoned, Marcel ran over. "We've got a big problem." He held out the tablet, so that we could see. The camera in the control room was pulled up, showing Boulder standing by the button. A wall of stone had grown between him and a group of Reclaimers. He was trapped.

"We have to go get him." I looked around, but I didn't like what I saw. No one moved to go.

"Bruh, he did it on purpose. He led them to the control room. He never meant to come out."

Salvo. Boulder was convinced he'd killed his best friend, and he meant to die and take the Reclaimers with him. About fifty soldiers had entered through the escape hatch.

"Load up," Dad said softly.

I stood rooted to the spot, refusing to give up on him. "We can save him."

Mom gripped my elbow. "Honey, he is trying to atone for Salvo's death. We can't waste his sacrifice."

I glanced at the screen again. Boulder shouted "go!" over and over at the camera. Bullets struck him in the leg and shoulder as we watched.

273

"We need to go now!" Dad shouted. He ran to the driver's door and climbed in. Mom got in the cab with him. Abby and I pushed Marcel up the ramp as Mimi strapped into the seat across from Blaze.

The ramp closed with a dull thud. I dropped into a seat beside Marcel as the truck started up with a roar. I snatched the tablet; blood flowed from Boulder's multiple wounds.

"I'm sorry, Salvo!" he mouthed before reaching over and pushing the self-destruct button. Nothing happened. The soldiers closed on Boulder, firing non-stop, his body jerking like water dropped on a hot skillet.

We started moving. I pulled myself to the front of the troop section and pounded on the metal panel. It slid open. Mom's face popped into view. "The self-destruct didn't work. Boulder is gone."

"Damn," Dad said as he accelerated into the ravine. "Strap in; we've got company."

Ahead of us, I could see two trucks blocking the escape route. The engine roared as we tore over the gravel that stood between us and the trucks. I braced myself for impact. Bullets bounced off the front windshield as we crashed into the two vehicles. The one closest to the drop off spun around, sweeping the men behind it as it tumbled down the incline. The other hit the wall; a shower of rocks fell from the force of the impact. I slammed into the side of our truck before bouncing into the aisle. Abby grabbed my arm and threw me into a seat. I snapped the harness around me just in time. It probably saved all our lives; absorbing all the energy from being thrown around could have set me off like a bomb.

We slowed but kept moving forward. We had made it past the blockade. I felt more than heard the shockwave when the base exploded. I couldn't see what happened, but our transport arced sideways away from the base, tumbling down the mountainside with a deafening crash as we rolled over trees, rocks, and anything else that stood in its way. I don't know how many times we flipped and twisted as the truck fell.

We finally came to rest in a gully near the bottom of the mountain, well away from the Reclaimers. I unbuckled and fell to the roof since we landed upside down. It was just about pitch black; the electrical must have shorted out in the accident. I found the release, but the ramp didn't budge. I punched as hard as I could, wrapping energy around my arm to increase the impact. The door shuddered and buckled. Two more strikes and the door had bent enough to exit. Abby and I got each of the others from their seats and out the impromptu exit.

An outcropping of rock had stopped us and held the ramp closed. We sat at the bottom of a low gully; trees grew up on either side of us, except where the transport had knocked them down like bowling pins. Smoke and debris still fell from the explosion. The top of the mountain had been leveled. Nothing could have survived that.

A loud crack announced Dad had gotten out of the front though he didn't have to move a rock to do it. Mom's face had streaks of blood, and bruises were darkening around her eyes. Dad didn't look much better.

"Any landing you can walk away from," Dad said then spit out a mouthful of bloody saliva. "I've seen worse, but I hadn't been a passenger at the time."

Mom came over and checked each of us for wounds. Lots of bruises and a broken tablet. We'd survived, but for how long? The Reclaimers would search the surrounding area as soon as they could.

"Can everyone walk?" Dad asked. Slow nods answered. "Abby, can you carry Oliver?"

"Sure thing, Ranger." She hoisted our old teacher over her shoulder, fireman style. Dad did the same with Blaze. We headed down the mountain, away from our past lives and into a new future.

I hoped it would be better than what we'd just left.

4 0

A couple of hours later, we found a small town, which was a godsend. The North Carolina mountains were cold enough that we worried about Blaze and Waxenby being exposed for overlong. The nice part of small towns is how trusting they are, leaving cars unlocked. It turned out Mimi could hotwire a car in under a minute. We took advantage of their trust and her unusual skill and traveled to Harker with the heat going the whole way. We spent a full night and into the next day finding the Harker entrance since it had been built into an old oil silo in the Adirondacks.

Dad and Mimi took the car and drove back to where an old dirt road cut through the hills. About an hour later, they returned. Marcel's phone had survived, allowing him to access his remote backup server. It took a while since the signal in the mountains left a lot to be desired.

When the door hissed open, musty air escaped from the mildew-laden silo. I missed Castle. After a tour, we all missed Castle.

Harker consisted of an old kitchen, a main area with a table and chairs that belonged in a Western movie, eight small bedrooms, and one bathroom. At least the hot water still worked.

"There has to be more than this." Marcel stared at his phone screen as if it could magically produce a new hideout. "According to the records, there is a medical bay and the Cellular Regeneration Immersion Device."

Mom's bruised face had molted into a camouflage pattern. "Everyone pick a room and search. See if you can find anything out of the ordinary. Mimi and Marcel, stay with Oliver and Blaze. We don't want any surprises."

I took the far bedroom and started moving furniture around. It took two minutes since there was a bed, a nightstand with a lamp that had a moth-eaten shade, and an old chest at the foot of the bed. Opening the chest only made the smell worse. The dust had to be an inch thick and dotted with tracks of things I didn't want to think about.

Blaze is going to die. If Pepper could have shed tears, she would have. My eyes welled up for her. *After all we've gone through, he's going to die.*

I didn't know what to say. Without the machine, we had no chance of saving him. *I'm sorry.*

It's not freaking fair. After everything we've gone through, to end up in this dump is infuriating.

I left the room; no sense wasting time searching the same area twice. The bedroom across the way held the same awful furniture. There must have been a sale at Ugly-Mart. The same setup, the same results. Like Pepper had said, it was time to face the fact that Harker wasn't what we thought it would be.

I stepped into the kitchen where the rest of the team stood, eyes downcast. Blaze laid on the table and Waxneby sat in a chair, eyes blank.

Whatever Parasite had done to him had messed him up. I wondered if the soft-spoken teacher I knew would ever come back.

"Anything?" Dad asked, already knowing the answer.

"No."

Marcel scratched at his chin, the faintest wisps of hair starting to grow there. "How could the data be so wrong?"

Pepper's hopelessness washed over me. We had failed, through no fault of our own, to save Blaze. My teacher and friend. When he died, part of me would go with him. I kicked the refrigerator.

The door sprang open, and the smell of rot filled the air. Flashbacks of melting faces froze me in my tracks.

"Tommy, we checked in there; it's covered in mold. Close the door before I puke," Abby said as she pinched her nose to the smell.

I snapped out of the memory, grasping the door to shut it, but something wasn't right. The mold looked like plastic.

"Oh my God, do I need to do it for you?" Abby stomped toward me, intending to slam it shut.

I held up my hand to stop her. On the bottom shelf, where the growth thickened, I could make out a shape. I breathed deeply, just in case I was wrong, and I pushed my hand into the slime. Relief flooded me when it felt more like petroleum jelly than anything alive. My fingers found an indent in the metal. I pushed my fingers in deeper until I had a lever in my grip. I pulled. Nothing happened. I stepped back, examining the room, certain I would find a change.

Abby noticed it first. "The refrigerator moved." She pulled on the back, and the whole unit glided across the floor, revealing a small door with a keypad. She turned to me. "Even a broken clock is right twice a day."

I returned her smile as Marcel pushed past us. He stroked the phone screen a dozen different ways until he found whatever he had been searching for and opened the door. Dad entered first; I followed.

What the hell was that memory from? Biology experiment gone wrong?

Her mentioning it brought it back into my mind. I let the full scene play out for her, "hearing" her gasps of horror as the soldiers melted into the green slime.

That is all sorts of messed up!

A short hallway opened out into a sizable living space. The full-sized kitchen sat off to the right; there were couches and chairs to the left and a large dining table divided the room.

"Hello, may I help you?" A voice filled the room.

Dad glanced around, but there wasn't anyone visible. "Yes, we are looking for the Cellular Regeneration Immersion device. Our friend is very ill and needs medical attention."

"Please follow the blue pathway, and it will take you to the med bay." The female voice had a friendly tone to it.

Tommy, I could kiss you. Pepper's happiness burnt away the earlier despair. *We're going to beat this yet.*

I most certainly hope so.

Dad returned to the kitchen and carried Blaze in; everyone but Mimi and Waxenby, who waited outside the door, were on his heels. We followed the blue lighted strip embedded in the flooring. Down a short flight of stairs, we found the med bay. It had three curtained areas like in a hospital, and an array of equipment unlike anything I'd ever seen before.

The voice came on again. "Please take the patient to the machine at the far end of the room. The doctor will be right with you."

Marcel glanced around. "Doctor? Here?"

Dad found the machine and waited. A disk in the ceiling slid open, emitting a bright light. After a moment, an older man dressed in a lab coat stood next to Dad. He wore glasses and had long gray hair curling in interesting ways around his head. "Hello, I am Gideon. How may I be of assistance?"

"Our friend has cancer and is dying. We were told the Cellular Regeneration Immersion Device could save his life," Dad said to the hologram.

"Accessing." A soft whirring noise came from above us. "Accessing." Gideon froze in place; my palms started to sweat.

"Yes, it may, but there are side effects we should discuss before we choose this course of treatment. Our facility can provide a full range of chemotherapy and radiation treatments that have a relatively high rate of success. Can I detail these options for you?"

Dad shrugged; this wasn't his area of expertise. Mom stepped in. "Gideon, can you tell us if this device can remove the cancer from our friend?"

Gideon froze again, the noise picking up as he stood there immobilized. "Yes, it can eliminate cancer, but the side effects can be extreme, and I will need authorization before beginning."

Mom touched her face and winced. "Gideon, can you diagnose our friend?"

He didn't freeze this time. "Certainly, please place him..." The light winked off and Gideon reappeared by an examination table near the center of the room. "Here."

Dad set Blaze on the table. I could barely make out his chest rising as he breathed. A sweep of lights cascaded over his body as we looked on. When they turned off, Gideon faced Mom. "Your friend has a late-stage Carcinoma that has metastasized to most of his other organs. He is currently experiencing renal failure and has brain activity indicative of a coma."

"What is our best course of action?"

"Cellular Regeneration Immersion is the only option available to you at this stage, but we need to review the side effects."

Mom interrupted the hologram. "Gideon, I give consent to begin treatment and to take any measures you deem necessary to save this man's life. Understood?"

"Understood. Please return him..." Gideon reappeared at the device. "Here." An audible snap preceded the top of the chamber opening. The machine had an inner chamber, and Dad laid Blaze inside. The bottom had metal studs rising out of the white material of the lining. Once Blaze had been put in, the top swung closed. The lid held an array of monitors and switches.

"The machine will do its work. I will have Glenda inform you when the procedure has completed."

"Glenda?" I asked.

"The facility has an AI to control all non-medical functions. Ask for what you need, and she will provide it. Good day." Gideon blinked out of existence as the projector shut off.

Mom shrugged. "Glenda, a member of our team needs medical attention. The rest need showers, food, and a place to sleep."

"Yes, ma'am. Please place your wounded member in bay three for assistance. You can follow the blue lighted path to the commissary. Yellow to the living quarters." Glenda's voice was soft and soothing, like a mother reading a bedtime story.

Abby had to pull Marcel away from examining all the equipment in the med bay. We went back to get Waxenby. We located bay three easily. Mom and Dad helped us make Waxenby comfortable in the bed. Gideon appeared and began to work.

"A medical workup will take hours. Glenda will notify you when it is complete."

The four of us walked out of the bay. Marcel lingered by some machine that did something. "I think I've died and gone to geek heaven."

I don't think he meant to get an answer, but Glenda provided it. "Harker is a state-of-the-art medical facility created to ensure all members could receive healing in a secure location."

Marcel's mouth pursed. "Members? Members of what?"

"The Dark Brigade."

We all stopped. We were in the safehouse of the worst terrorist organization known to man. "Do they come back here?" Dad asked, shocked at this revelation.

"This facility did not come online when the Freedom Initiative began.

The members who oversaw the construction were eliminated during the mission."

I took a stab. "No one knows about Harker?"

Glenda didn't answer for a moment. "Beyond those already present, unknown."

I guess that was the best we would get. We continued back to the main area. "The yellow band will take you to the bedrooms. There is a food replicator in the kitchen, should you need anything to eat or drink."

We followed the yellow lit path to a hallway of doors. We each grabbed a room. Mine had a queen-sized bed, a dresser, two nightstands with lamps, and a full bathroom. I fell on the bed and was asleep before my head hit the pillow.

I don't know how long I slept, but it wasn't long enough for someone to be shaking me. I pried my eyes open to find Marcel's face floating before mine. "Bruh, you need to see this."

I pulled the pillow over my head. "Can't it wait?"

"No, you need to see this now."

I debated stunning him, but my reserves were low and, oh yeah, he's my best friend. I dragged myself out of bed and let him pull me down the hallway. We traced our steps back to the med bay, but instead of going to where Blaze was being healed, or Waxenby examined, he took me to what looked like the freezer door at the Secret Lair.

"Glenda, open the door." Marcel virtually vibrated with excitement. If this was a new video game console, I would be forced to kill him on principle.

The door swung open, revealing long tubes lying on gurneys. "What are these?"

"Come here." He led me to a container that he then moved to an open space near the front of the room. My heart stopped. The card on the side read "Raychel Downs."

That's me.

I peered through the glass window and saw shocking orange hair and a cute face. *How did you get here?*

I was dead. How the hell would I know?

Marcel rolled the capsule out into the med bay. "Gideon, can you revive the person in this stasis tube?"

The projector came to life, bringing Gideon back. "Unknown without examination, sir. Please move the capsule over…" He flickered into view on the far side of the freezer. "Here."

We pushed the capsule over to where he indicated. Divots in the floor held the gurney in place as a disk protruded from the wall, connecting to the stasis chamber. A click and the tub lit up, the readouts flashing vital signs. "The patient is in a brain-dead state. She will not function off life support."

"Understood," I said clearly. "Open the chamber, Gideon."

"Tommy, opening the cryogenic capsules is against standard protocol. She will die if you take her out of stasis."

I didn't hear Gideon. Something within me knew what I needed to do.

"Gideon, open it now." The lid popped slightly as the latches opened. I reached out and lifted the lid. Pepper Spray lay there perfectly preserved.

Stop looking at me. I'm naked!

I reached out and put my hand on her forehead. Her skin was soft and warm. When I absorbed energy, it swirled in me like a hurricane waiting to be unleashed. This felt different; a low hum of a song you know but can't remember. The touch of dew when you run your hand through the morning fog. A flowing of silk across your hand, cool and shimmering.

Nothing changed; I could still sense Pepper. I pushed further into the experience, making it part of me. I realized I could sense Pepper's body. The way the cold table felt against her back, the sensation of pressure from where I touched her. Sounds came to me as if echoed, produced from two separate sets of ears.

I focused on the melody of the energy that was Pepper. The music swelled as if an orchestra had joined in, each note a memory or a feeling. I could tell she danced as the song progressed. Then it stopped, and I was alone.

Pepper's eyes snapped open. "Tommy, you did it. I'm alive."

I stared at her, unable to speak. Pepper had no such limitations. "Well, stop staring at my boobs and get me something to cover up with."

It was the last thing I heard before I did what any sensible man would do in this situation. I passed out.

THE END

The Unbreakable Storm will continue...

To keep up with all the news about The Unbreakable Storm and other releases from Patrick Dugan, plus get a free Unbreakable Storm short story, please join his newsletter - https://mailchi.mp/cde71d8d5863/patrick-dugan-newsletter-sign-up

ACKNOWLEDGMENTS

Any published book takes countless hours of work once the story is written. Editing, proof reading, cover design, formatting and publication takes an inordinate amount of effort. I'm lucky to be surround by the amazing staff at Falstaff Books. John Hartness, the publisher, took a risk on Storm Forged and I hope I haven't let him down (too much). Erin Penn works amazingly hard to make the words and ideas flow together. Paul Barrett did the copy editing to ensure what I missed got caught. Alisha Bulkley did the proof reading so that the typos the rest of us missed don't end up in the final version. Melissa Gilbert does all my ads that you see them on Facebook or Twitter. Davey Beauchamp did another brilliant cover. I'm running out of wall space to hang his artwork. I am continuously amazed at the quality of the work that comes out of Falstaff's authors and am humbled to be counted among them.

A special thank you to my Gifted team of beta readers helped strengthen the story and offer lots of moral support. They are Chuck, Jon, Regis, Catherine, Cheri and Joe. If I've missed anyone it is completely unintentional.

My family deserves an award for putting up with my long nights of writing and traveling schedule. Emily and Nicholas are terrific kids and have inspired many of the virtues in the Darkest Storm characters. We've weathered a lot and they've always been by my side.

We lost Emerson last year and our family had been diminished without him. I miss having him lay under my desk while I worked and he always made sure I took breaks to get him treats. I'm sure he's happy to have the spotlight in Unbreakable Storm and he certainly deserves it. Our new puppy Blaze (yes, named after the character) hasn't learned to chill yet, but he will, I hope.

My wife, Hope, is the bedrock of our family. She is my first reader, edits my work so that Erin doesn't kill me and is always supportive. She picks up the slack when I'm buried in edits or burning the candle at both ends. I couldn't chase my dream of being an author without her love and support. I'm a very lucky guy to have such a family.

And a special thank you to the readers who bought, read, left reviews, read my newsletter and come see me at conventions. I appreciate you more than you'll ever know.

FALSTAFF BOOKS

**Want to know what's new
And coming soon from
Falstaff Books?**

Try This Free Ebook Sampler

https://www.instafreebie.com/free/bsZnl

**Follow the link.
Download the file.
Transfer to your e-reader, phone, tablet, watch, computer, whatever.
Enjoy.**

ABOUT THE AUTHOR

Patrick Dugan was born in the far north of New York, where the cold winds blow. This meant lots of time for reading over the long winters. His parents didn't care what he read as long as he did and thus Patrick started with a steady diet of comics and science fiction novels.

His debut novel, Storm Forged, Book One of the Darkest Storm series, was published by Falstaff Books in May of 2018. Unbreakable Storm followed in 2019.

When you start out as an author, nobody tells you about all of the other "jobs" that you take on in addition to writing novels. Being a full time technologist has led Patrick to start a blog on the uses of writing technologies and how to apply them to the writing process. He delves into software, hardware, social media, and all things web related.

Patrick resides in Charlotte, NC with his wife and two children. In his limited spare time, he's a gamer, homebrewer, and DIYer.

You can find out more at www.patrickdugan.net, https://www.facebook.com/patrick.dugan.3781, https://www.instagram.com/patrickduganauthor/

ALSO BY PATRICK DUGAN

Storm Forged

Made in the USA
Columbia, SC
21 February 2023